Tessa

Good Girls Book Eight

Christine Young

Published by Rogue Phoenix Press, LLP

ISBN: 978-1-62420-870-6

Editor: Amanda Armstrong
Cover Art: Designs by Ms G

Chapter One

Glasgow 1832

Rain pelted the windows. Eerie wind howled around the eaves of the two-story home while lightening slashed in blue-white streaks electrifying the night air. Thunder pounded, jarring the stillness. Rain fell from the sky in torrents. The horrific weather fit his turbulent mood, the conflicting emotions raging within his brain soured his gut. This was not where he should be. He couldn't find a way to tell this beautiful woman he wouldn't see her any longer. He needed to fix all that had gone wrong with his life. The woman he loved for a year now must be the focus of all his attentions.

Jason Kenworthy watched the lady's slight form in the bed he shared at their convenience. He'd been with her the last four years, ever since her husband passed. The woman lying naked in the bed gave him pleasure. She was sweet. Sincere. Loyal. Sarah was always ready to take him into his arms when he came around to see her. Jason understood he used her to assuage his sexual needs. She never complained. He took unholy advantage of her giving nature. Depended on her to right his sinking ship this last year. He found he was drowning in the depth of misery. The melancholy was of his own making. Problem was, he didn't know how to go about changing his situation. Sarah told him he needed to take the bull by the horns. His huff of air told him he didn't *ken* how to do that. Sarah suggested to him to make it clear how he felt toward the love of his life who danced around him, leading him on by the nose. He needed to make his feelings as well as his intentions obvious to the lady of his dreams.

Jason reached over to brush a slow caress on Sarah's arm. She shivered as if she was responding to his touch. Toward Sarah there existed a deep tenderness in his heart. His Sarah, was a woman he would always care about. If she ever needed him, rain or shine, he would be there for her.

He stepped back. Sarah was beautiful. Her dark brown hair glistened in the candlelight bathing her form, highlighting golden strands that had been bleached by the sun. She defied custom, seldom donning a hat to shade her features while she tended to her flower beds. Gardening was her one true joy. Her blue eyes were banded around the outside with silver. Her bottom lip a bit too full to be considered fashionable. She possessed a stubborn streak that got her into trouble from time to time.

Earlier this evening she told him he was no longer welcome to see her in the evenings or to entertain her in this big bed. Tonight was the last night they would share together. The lovemaking was bittersweet. In this, they were of a like mind. He was ready to cut the entanglement between them. Before he visited Sarah this evening, he knew he was leaving her. This dalliance with her was their last one together.

She told him he sulked. Well, he did. After spending his days at his home, he needed a bright spot in the evenings. Sarah proved to be that tiny bit of light that brought him out of the depression his life had become. Jason understood he couldn't hide behind Sarah's skirts any longer. He needed to face his future. Tessa MacRae was that future. He just didn't know how to go about convincing Tessa it was time for her to make a decision concerning their lives together. What he saw in Sarah's eyes, told him he might well be in for a lecture on his behavior. He didn't need anyone to expound on his misconduct.

Sarah pushed hair behind her ears while she brought in a deep breath of air. "It's been more than a year, Jason. You've done nothing to right the matter that has you befuddled. Are you going to allow another year to pass you by before you do something about the *wee tendre* you have for the lass? You cannot continue in this vein. I will no longer support what you are doing to yourself. You've become less of a person…less of a man. You do not belong in my bed when your heart is elsewhere."

"…and…" Jason pulled on his boots while he debated with himself over the necessity to tell her the truth. "What am I doing to myself?" The *tendre* he felt for Tessa was far from little. He was head-over-heels smitten with Tessa MacRae. Sometime in the last year, the little flirt withdrew into herself. She changed right in front of his nose. He didn't know how to reach her. After the first few weeks with her here in Glasgow, he thought he would be wed to her by the year's end.

"Sulking," she replied so quick the word stole his breath. She reached for a full glass of wine sitting on her nightstand. Before they made love, she'd not tasted the drink, seeming to understand this time would be the last one for them. She sipped now, closed her eyes as she let the red burgundy slide down her throat, savoring the slow glide. "You have been brooding for the last year. Take the pretty *lass* by the hand then explain your feelings. Lay down the law. She might well be thankful. Perhaps she is in as much a quandary as you. Might not understand how to turn around something that has gone so wrong."

Unable to help himself, he snorted his aversion. *Sulking?* No matter his thoughts to the contrary, what she said was true. He would have called his mood brooding. Sulking sounded like a description for a little boy. Brooding was more manly. No matter, the words presented the right picture as to his frame of mind. "If you must know, I asked Tessa to marry me." He found himself hoping for sympathy or empathy at the least. From Sarah, he wasn't likely to get any type of emotion. She always called the situation as she saw it.

As she smiled, the small dimple on the left side of her mouth deepened. While she tapped the crystal with the tip of her nail, she seemed to be thinking. Before Sarah spoke, she set her head to a slight angle, pursed her lips while she appeared to deliberate the right words, "Let me get this right. Tessa said no to your proposal. Was it romantic? I daresay, knowing you the request was anything but amorous. Blurted the words out, did you? Ah, I see by the glint in your eyes that's what happened. You gave up with one try. Correct me if I'm wrong. Over a year ago she fancied herself in love with you. How long ago was the question popped?"

Sarah sat up, pulling the sheet around her, tucking the fabric beneath her arms to cover her substantial breasts. He'd miss burying his face in her generous bosom. Over the years, he'd come to adore her breasts almost as much as he loved her agile mind. Ah, but there was always Tessa's mind if he could change her way of thinking.

For a tick of the clock on the mantle, Jason was surprised by Sarah's actions. In his presence, she never covered herself. He supposed that was another sign this relationship had seen its last days. "Six months give or take a week or two." He didn't understand why he told her. Four years of sharing confidences was most likely the reason behind his confession.

"That long? You are resigned to remaining a bachelor. Hmm… I would not have expected that after you returned from Ireland. Why haven't you asked her again? Seems that half a year ago, she was in the midst of her season. Of course she wouldn't agree. The poor girl needed new experiences. Wanted to feel alive as well as learn that other men might find her attractive." The rest of her wine disappeared down her throat. She set the glass on the table. Touched a small drop that was heading down the glass. Brought that bit of wine to her mouth.

"Suppose I am, at least for the time being. Tessa spends her free time alone. If I seek her out to talk with her, she tells me she's busy. I need to find some means to coax the Tessa that I know from her hidey-hole. She's pouting about something. God knows what it is. I don't. I'm just a man infatuated with the love of my life." He tied his cravat then tucked his shirt into his britches. "Tessa is so quiet. Reserved. Never fails to surprise me when she asserts herself. I'm of the opinion, all she wishes to do is curl up by the fire with a good book. From earlier experiences with her, I know she is vibrant. Alive with curiosity. I don't understand where that woman has disappeared to."

"Are you giving up on Tessa? Is the young lady not worth a bit more effort? As you just said, coax her from her hiding place. Find out the truth. Tell her how you feel. If you don't, I've a mind to pay her a visit. Someone or something needs to shake the two of you out of the deep pit that's been dug. I'm certain the girl loves you as much as you love her. Have you mentioned that tiny fact?" Sarah smoothed the big quilt that was covering her with her hands. Her nails were well-manicured. Buffed to shine. Without closing his eyes, he knew in detail what Sarah now hid from his view. The thought of her naked beneath the covering did nothing to arouse. With this new discovery, he turned a major hurdle in his life. Thinking of Tessa set him on fire. Scorched him. His body leapt to life.

While he looked for his frock coat, he turned to Sarah. He felt the need to defend himself. He waved his hand through the air, unable to understand the direction of his anger, "You don't understand anything."

Her hefty laugh caught him off guard. To Jason there was nothing humorous about his relationship with the disagreeing woman who bedeviled his life. Sarah's brows drew together as she spoke, all humor cast aside. She cleared her throat before continuing with her lecture, "On the contrary, I understand all you've told me. It's what you don't say that I can't comprehend. There is much you are keeping to yourself. Which is your right." She lowered her lashes before opening them. "You should..."

Sarah was going to tell him to leave. The discussion would go nowhere. "Yes...well..." He thought of the way he saw Tessa the other night. Past midnight she showed up in the library wearing her night clothing. He'd wanted to pull her into his arms. Kiss her until she moaned with feminine pleasure. Fighting for control at the time, he did nothing. "Some thoughts are private. Restricted to the two participants involved. You know more than you should."

"Have you kissed the *wee* lass?"

Jason choked on her question. Over the year, he'd thought of little else. A purpose, Sarah pushed his patience. "You are prying, madam. I would never kiss and tell." He'd kissed her, yes. Not enough times to suit him. It wasn't that she shied away. The reason was...hell if he kissed her again, he might not stop with a brush of the lips or even a deep taste of her. When he saw her, he ached for what he couldn't have until they wed. She refused him. When she was near, he felt the need to test the curve of her hip. Wished to hold her breasts in his hands. Feel the humid softness between her legs.

Sarah lifted her shoulders in a feminine gesture that used to make him hard. "Make love to her. Get her with child. That would set events in motion that could never be stopped." Sarah sent him a sly smile. "You are a nice man. You deserve some measure of happiness. For some unbeknownst reason, she is playing you for a fool. Find out what keeps her from committing. In that way, you'll be able to fight. Until you know the truth about what holds her back, you are at a disadvantage."

"I've considered your proposal. Getting her with child...

Considering then doing are far different scenarios. Good God, she is living beneath my roof. Doing so would ruin her reputation even more." Jason rubbed his hand on his chin, thinking. He could never impregnate the lass in order to get her to the alter. To force her was repulsive. He did want her in his bed. Damn tired of waiting for her to grow up. Now that she seemed to reach that state, she didn't want anything to do with him.

"You won't act on it though. Too much the gentleman. You should forget that fact about your nature. Your twin did…forget. Seems the bedding came before the wedding. They are in love. Aren't they?"

He sat to put his boots on. Yes, Maggie and Jasper were in love. The baby, conceived from their stay in Ireland. For Maggie, learning to sit on a chair then stand was comical. He was more determined to do right by Tessa. "I won't compromise Tessa for my own ends. Can't do that to her. Don't wish to force her hand. If she walks down the aisle to me, she must be willing."

Jason bent over to brush a gentle kiss across her lips. "Goodbye, Sarah. I'd send you a parting gift if you wouldn't yell at me." Jason found himself grinning at her. He understood how she'd reply to his outrageous suggestion. Over the four years he'd been seeing her, she'd accepted gifts only on her birthday along with Christmas.

Her stiffening shoulders coupled with the tightening of her brows told him she was not agreeable to a goodbye present. "I'm not under your protection. Not your mistress. Never have been. I make my own way. You *ken* that."

The long whisper of air that leapt from his lungs didn't make him feel any better. Her scowl left him winded then wishing for something that could never be. Perhaps he would send her something anyway. A gift might put a smile on her face. If nothing else, the small present could serve to remind her of him. Jason settled on that idea as being perfect. Tomorrow afternoon, he would search for the perfect gift. She didn't need jewelry. Something to remember him by. Something she couldn't send back to him. He would figure it out. She mentioned several times how much she loved animals, dogs to be exact. He could buy her a puppy. She would never send a puppy back to him.

"Will you be at the Laughton's ball?" He needed a change of

subject after speaking of presents. Though he wasn't looking to a future with Sarah, he would miss her company. A dance might ease his mind. If he saw her with another man, he might not feel such a cad for his desertion from her bed.

"Of course, I would not miss the event. That ball was a favorite of my late husband. Lady Laughton is a dear friend of mine." This time she sounded indignant. Sarah was drawing into herself as they finished the conversation. The time had come for him to let himself out the door.

"I'll find the door for myself. No need to get up," Jason told her as he bowed in the open doorway before leaving the room. "Take care of yourself, Sarah. If you ever need anything… Well, you realize, I will never stop caring for you."

A few seconds later, Jason stepped into the cold night air. The weather was not so cold, just stormy. The rain that pelted the windows earlier died to a thin mist. The storm appeared to have moved on to different territory. During his conversation with Sarah, a weight seemed to be lifted off his shoulders. He felt lighter. Figuring out Tessa's change of heart would be his sole purpose until the knowledge came to him. Maybe he should kidnap her. Take her to Ireland. The cottage was still there. The ploy worked for his brother.

Jason motioned for his driver to follow him. He needed to walk for a time while he cleared his thoughts. Wasn't about to walk the miles to his home. He had to think about Tessa. A plan of action might be nice. Jasper, his twin, talked about moving to the country for the summer months. A respite in the clear air away from the city would be welcome. A change of scenery might distance Tessa from whatever was troubling her. The travel would take the girls away from their summer entertainments, the soirees they disliked. None of the girls enjoyed the crush of the season. During the summer months the number of entertainments diminished. Jason didn't think any of them would be devastated by that. Though they did have their friends they enjoyed doing things with.

If Jasper moved, Maggie and the baby would follow. Since Maggie's sisters were under the guardianship of Jasper, they would have no choice but to tag behind. Though Nellie along with Fannie were old enough to not need a guardian, the protection was the necessary catalyst that would force their hand. Even in the country, there would be activities to contend with. The nice thing was that most of the actions would be during the early morning hours when the weather was not too hot. They could visit with the Murrays. Play some lawn tennis. He wondered if any of the girls ever played before. He enjoyed the game. The Murray men took the game to a different level.

Tessa would come along. Yes, a move to the country would be nice, very nice indeed. He would find the time to get to know her better. Jason felt less out of sorts now that he plotted a course of action. There would be extra moments where he could walk with Tessa. If she enjoyed riding, there were numerous trails to explore. Perhaps steal a kiss or two away from the curious eyes of her sisters.

During their strolls, she would open up to him about whatever it was that was troubling her. Something was bothering her. He had no doubts about that. Getting to the bottom of her difficulties would be his mission this summer. He didn't appreciate feeling as if he was on tenterhooks. While he wasn't the serious twin by far, he did possess a smidgeon of that singular attribute that seemed to run in the family. Knowing why Tessa was acting the way she was, took up a major portion of his thoughts during the day as well as the nights. An end to this scenario was a necessity. He was ready for a wife. He wished for Tessa to assume that role. He waited with as much patience as he could derive.

Knowing he needed to get home, he signaled for his driver to stop so he could climb into the carriage. He did so just as the wind changed and a gust of rain showered down on them. Perfect timing if he did say so himself. For the rest of the journey home, Jason set his head on the back of the seat then closed his eyes. He meant to relax. The hour was not too late. He could settle in the library with a snifter of brandy. If he got lucky, Tessa might join him. The plan could begin tonight. He gave a silent thanks to Sarah for setting him on the right path.

During the next ten minutes, Jason listened to the sounds surrounding him. Heard the steady beat of the rain on the roof. The clip clop of the horses' hooves on the cobblestone street. Waited for the carriage to turn into the drive leading to the townhouse.

After he entered the house, he made his way to the library, half hoping Tessa would be curled up on the big, overstuffed chair she favored. Half hoping she would be sound asleep in her bed so he could wait for the inevitable encounter. Safe inside her room she wouldn't serve as a temptation for his lust. If he didn't see her, he wouldn't want her in the most elemental ways.

That was part and parcel of the problem. Jason needed to know if what he felt for Tessa went deeper than lust. Had to know if Tess had a *tendre* for him. A year ago, he thought she did. She'd been curious about kissing. About him. Believed by the end of the year they would be engaged. A wedding would be planned. In the present, he was farther away from her in spirit than he'd been on their first meeting.

In the library, he splashed two fingers of brandy into a snifter. Sipped. Swallowed. Felt the heat of the drink rush down his throat. Sipped again before walking to Tessa's favorite chair. She was not sitting in it, waiting for him. Looking up toward her room, he thought perhaps she'd retired for the night. Didn't know if that should please or upset him.

Just as well. It would never do for the two of them to be together, alone at this time of night. He still needed to figure out his plans. Stay in the city or go to the country? What a conundrum? Going to the country seemed to be his preference. What if she refused? He couldn't leave her here to fend for herself. She still needed protection from Lord Nelson Abernathy as well as her mother.

He heard the rustle of footsteps outside the door. Reached for the knife he kept tucked into his boot. With silent footsteps he made his way to the door. Whoever was out there was not wasting time on trying to hide the fact they were intruding. The door creaked open. When he recognized the wealth of light blond hair, he sucked in his air. *Tessa.*

"What are you doing?" Under the circumstance, his voice sounded harsher than he wished. With as much aplomb as possible he placed the knife back into his boot. He didn't want to see fear in her eyes.

When she looked up at him her blue eyes were clouded over. He saw no sparkle in the depth. Hadn't seen that sly semi-mischievous look that Tessa used to toss his way for a very long time. Who stole her vivacity? These last month's, Tessa became a shadow of herself. Did he do this to her?

“I could ask you the same. It’s late.” Tessa took the crystal glass from him then drank. She closed her eyes as the liquid slid down her throat. When she opened them again, he was certain she wished to tell him something of importance. Instead, she turned away shuttering her expression, hiding from him.

“You went out without a chaperone?” The accusation was there. His gut clenched at his question at the realization she was alone. Abernathy was still a threat. She needed to take care every time she ventured from her home. Tessa was not a prisoner. She could still come and go as she pleased. Both he and his twin warned her of the dangers awaiting her with one slip up, one poorly made decision.

She seemed to take umbrage with his question. Sent him a fierce little scowl, her brows tight together. Tessa would do the same with his thoughts if he spoke them. “I used your driver. I was safe. Mother sent me a message. I needed to know what she wanted.” She unfastened her cloak then shook it out sending a pattern of tiny raindrops on the floor. After that she walked to the sideboard, filled his glass then poured one for herself. Turning, she leaned against the wood, watching him. Seeming to wait for more words to sputter from his lips. That wasn’t going to happen. She had every right to her opinion, even though he understood it to be wrong.

Strands of Tessa’s thick blond hair loosened from the chignon and tumbled down her back to reach her waist. She was slim, not coltish as she was a year ago. Her body filled out over the past months. Curved in all the right places for a man’s hands to enjoy. What Jason liked best about her was the vibrancy in her eyes. Now, when he looked at her, hunted for what he’d come to admire, the vitality of life was gone. Vanished. He needed to discover the reason. Needed to know how the spark was stolen.

Several questions about her whereabouts this evening rambled through his head. The first one being why did she venture out in this storm to see a woman she disliked? None of the girls held good feelings for their mother. The second being, why the devil did she believe herself to be safe with her mother? That was the farthest notion from the truth he could think of. Lord Abernathy made it clear he was no longer interested in any of the MacRae girls as a wife. That didn’t mean he lost interest in them as a conquest.

Not about to argue with her this evening or any other one, "If you say." Jason wasn't agreeing with her. He was giving her the right to a different opinion than his own. "However, next time, I would suggest you tell either Jasper or myself when you intend to leave as well as your destination. Even if it's seeing your mother. Don't believe for one heartbeat you are safe with your mother." He paused as he watched the change of expressions across her face. "Especially if it's to see Anice. We both understand the woman cannot be trusted." His gut clenched at the thought of Tessa falling victim to the woman.

"You don't trust my mother." Her small voice held an accusing edge to the tone. She rubbed the back of her neck as if tension knots settled there.

If he could, he'd ease those muscles. Jason felt side-swiped by her statement. After all that had gone on over the last year, Tessa should never put her faith in that woman. Tessa should realize that without being reminded how dangerous Anice was to her. Again, no reason to raise his voice or put forth his sentiments on the ghastly topic. Confronting her with her feelings for the woman seemed important.

"Do you? You know as well as I that she is a pariah." Anice was a man eater. At one time, did seem to hold a tender spot in her heart for her daughters. A very tiny tender spot. Now the lady was willing to hand them over to any man for her personal gain. That fact was repellent. A great distance from what could be termed motherly love. Anice had no redeeming qualities as far as he was concerned.

A small breathy sigh waffled from Tessa's lips. Her shoulders slumped as if in defeat. "I don't either. Trust her." Tessa took a moment to drink more of the brandy she poured. "She is my mother. If she asks to see me, I can't refuse. There are times I miss her. She can be nice. Last year, Christmas morning, after she figured out none of us knew where Maggie ran off to, she relented. She let us eat more than bread and water. We opened the presents under the tree."

At that never previously divulged bit of information the air he sucked into his lungs served to choke him. Anice punished the girls by not allowing them food, a basic need. "If she is getting what she wants…" Jason sat down again. Studied the woman who bedeviled him for more than a year now. "Let me get this straight, just to clarify. If Anice is getting what she wants, then the woman is nice."

"Mother almost always gets what she wants. That doesn't ever make her nice. Makes her arrogant. Mean. Malicious. What are you doing here?" Tessa looked on her hands resting in her lap then through the flutter of her lashes peered his way. "Thought you would be with your friend, Sarah. Did something happen?"

Little minx, she was flirting with him. Even heard what might be a smidgeon of jealousy in her tone. For the beat of his racing heart, he was taken aback by her question. She shouldn't know anything about his lady friend or her name. Jasper never would have mentioned Sarah. He sure as hell didn't. "What do you know about my…friend?" The fact Tessa asked questions about Sarah terrified him. He never mentioned her. What she was doing was plying him for more information.

Tessa lifted her lily-white shoulders in an indifferent gesture. With quiet confidence, she sipped her brandy. "Nothing much. Is she pretty? Nice? Can she talk to you? You know?" The questions were stated once more beneath the flutter of her dark lashes.

Jason wasn't certain if he was about to dig his grave where Tessa's feelings for him were concerned. Treading with light footsteps would be his best advice to himself. He wasn't about to lie to her. Neither was he going to tell her anything she didn't ask. He supposed she did deserve answers. If she agreed to marriage, he wouldn't hold anything back. Now, his relationship with her was tentative at best. Nonexistent at its worst. At times they spoke of feelings. In the present, that was all there was between them. To get to the depth of his relationship with Sarah, she would need to ask him things she would not feel comfortable asking. He hoped she would confide in him also.

"Very lovely."

Her lashes jerked up, telling him his answer surprised her. She must have expected a different response. The widening of her eyes confirmed his conjecture. On the way to her mouth to sip a portion of her drink, her hand trembled. Beneath those fluttering lashes there were more questions.

"You are seeing a woman?" With her hands, she pressed the fabric of her gown tight across her bosom. “Never mind, I don’t…”

True, she might not want to know the answer. In this case, she might. If she cared anything for him, she would appreciate what he was about to say. “No.” He wouldn’t offer her the information that this was the last night he intended to visit Sarah. She would have to be more explicit in her questions.

She appeared stunned by his answer. “Do you lie?” The crease lines in the middle of her forehead deepened.

Jason thought it would be nice to pass his finger along them, soften them until she had no more concerns. “No.” He found himself shaking his head at the statement a small smile forming. “No, Tessa, I do not lie.”

“You were seeing a woman. A lovely woman.” Her voice was a whisper thin exhale of air quivering on the last words.

For a blink his heart stopped. This was a question he didn’t wish to answer. He could ignore. Discounting would be too close to a lie to suit. “Yes.”

Tessa face turned ashen. Her eyes narrowed. She sent her tongue across her lips, moistening them before she sipped more of the potent brandy. The pause was long, tiresome. “Like…like that…way?”

Jason kept the amused chuckle stuck in his throat. Tessa wanted to know if they had sex. Didn’t quite know how to ask the imposing question. She probably wanted to know more. She was innocent. He wasn’t going to change that fact this evening. He fiddled with his glass, rolled the crystal between his hands while he watched the amber liquid play with the light from the fire. When he felt in control of his emotions as well as his thoughts, he spoke his heart. “Ask me what you wish to know. Be specific. Don’t hedge when you have the words. Cannot guarantee you’ll appreciate the answer. While we are discussing my past, don’t forget I asked you to marry me. If you had agreed all would be different now. I’ll be honest with you. Promise.” His voice was gruffer than he wished. She was delving into his personal life. One that just this evening he put an end to. Sarah was a fond memory. Nothing more. Tessa was his future if she would allow that to happen.

One more time she whetted her mouth while she tried to drum up courage, lips glistening with the moisture her tongue left behind. Her eyes wide, "Did you fornicate with her?" Tessa did blurt the words that shocked him to the tips of his toes.

Brandy flew from his mouth. Drops splattered on his white silk shirt. He tried to wipe them away with the palms of his hands. Had never expected such a question. To his surprise Tessa stood behind him, pounding him on the back with her tiny hands. She thumped him a couple of times before he stopped wheezing. Jason grabbed her hand. She was stronger than expected. Her little fist packed a wallop. "I'm fine."

"You don't look fine."

"Trust me. I'm just dandy." *Did he fornicate with Sarah?* Well, that was one way to put what they did. The words seemed crude. What they did together never reached the level of fornication. Between them there was tenderness along with caring. He cared for Sarah. Would never hurt her even though he did admit he took advantage of her. They both had physical needs. Maybe she also took advantage of him.

Tessa seemed to be over her concern for his wellbeing. She faced him, her chin tilted upward while she demanded the answer. "Well? Did you?" She persisted with this line of questioning. "Fornicate?"

"Can you not come up with a different way of putting the act of making love? I would not wish to put what two people who care for each other do together in that obscene vein." Sexual games were many and varied. Sarah was a sensual passionate woman. There intimate relationship shouldn't be brought down to that level.

"Well?" Tessa persisted, her voice taking on an edge he didn't recognize. She continued to stare at him waiting for an answer. "Did you?"

If he didn't misunderstand the emotion, Tessa was angry. He cleared his throat more than one time before he could speak. "We were intimate, yes." Jason held up his hands either in surrender or in hopes she wouldn't ask for details. Good God, the word she used for something very special was leud. Who gave her that word? The only person who came to mind was her mother, Anice. It would be just like Anice to call the intimate act of making love fornicating. Was that the reason Anice summoned Tessa this evening? To put vile thoughts into her head?

Her face turned a mottled shade of red. That was good. A true innocent could never use that word without becoming flushed. Maybe she had nothing else in her arsenal she could substitute. What the devil was he going to say if she asked him anything else?

"So…so you did do it…fornicate." Tessa was studying her hands which were wrapped together in such a tight clasp her knuckles were turning white before his eyes. Now, it didn't seem she would look up. He wanted to step closer to her. Put his fingers beneath her chin to tilt her head higher. Wished he could see into her eyes.

Needing to clarify, he began, "We are done with each other. I won't bed her again. Tonight, we both decided we would no longer see each other. We don't suit. The decision was mutual. This is more than I should tell you. More than you should know. If you agreed to my proposal six months ago, I would have ceased my nightly visits at that time."

To his surprise, Jason felt his own flush of embarrassment at the revelation. His face heated. Something unusual for him. Couldn't recall the last time he blushed. He never considered what he did in bed with a woman as fornicating. With women, he had a slow hand. Never left his lover unsatisfied. His touch was easy, gentle. He always saw to their pleasure before his own. Never exploded inside her until she reached that magical pinnacle. Thought of himself as a considerate lover.

This woman, the one standing in front of him, drinking his brandy, was the woman he wanted in his bed as well as for the rest of his life. Just as he could have done a year ago, he could take her into his arms. Kiss her until she wanted what he wished for with all his heart. Make love to her. He pushed the promiscuous lock of hair from his eyes instead of ridding himself of wayward thoughts.

"Why?" Tessa downed what was left of the brandy. She sat down in a plop as if she didn't have the energy to remain standing.

The question was blunt as well as to the point. Why? Why did he call off the relationship or why did he make love to her? Because Sarah wasn't the woman he needed in his bed. Sarah served her purpose. Earlier, he admitted to the fact he used her. Sarah used him also. She needed him to warm her bed in the lonely nights that stretched in front of her after her husband's death.

"She was willing."

"Is that all that is needed? A woman to be willing?" Tessa

questioned while she continued to direct her frown his way.

Not wishing to continue in that vein, he didn't answer with a direct word of yes or no. "Sarah is a sweet woman. I cared a great deal for her. She is still important to me. We filled a need for each other that was left vacant." More than most would ever know. Only his brother understood what Sarah meant to him. Tessa would never understand what he was saying. There was a time he wished he loved Sarah enough to marry her. The fact he thought of marrying her never mattered. Sarah was adamant in her denials of marriage. She'd told him she was independent now, a free woman. Needed her life to remain that way. All the wealth from her deceased husband was hers. Even though he had more at his disposal than she, Sarah didn't want marriage even to increase her wealth. One husband, for her, was enough. One too many, she once told him. Didn't need or want anything she didn't have.

"I'm willing." Tessa stepped forward. Her finger wrestled with the buttons on her blouse. One popped free then another. "I want you to fornicate with me." She continued unfastening her blouse until a creamy expanse of white skin was revealed. Her silk chemise did little to cover her breasts. He saw the rose-colored nipples he longed to taste. Felt the slow burn of arousal. The urgency the sight of her created was impossible to ignore.

Struck wordless by her actions, he coughed. Clutched at his mind for something to say he wouldn't come to regret in the morning. He wasn't about to do her bidding. She wasn't ready for sex. Someone put her up to this. Anice came to mind. He didn't understand what bug got into her head. Good God, did she understand what she was asking? No, Tessa wasn't asking. She was showing.

The stubborn glint he'd come to know over the course of the year he'd been with her was shining crystal clear in her sky-blue eyes that were no longer vacant. More buttons were becoming unfastened. This wasn't the time for her to disrobe. He had no intention of carrying out Sarah's wicked thoughts of getting Tessa with child so she would have to marry him. A forced marriage was not in his plans. He wanted her willing compliance, yes. Nothing less would do. This evening, he didn't understand her intent.

Stepping forward, he clasped her hands in his. Held them away from her, behind her back. That was a mistake. Her breasts pushed forward. The softness against his chest beckoned to a starving man. "No, not tonight. Not like this."

The soft sheen of moisture growing in her eyes, terrified. Something else was at play here. He wondered again if it had anything to do with her visit to her mother. "No, Tessa. I'm not going to let you hurt yourself. Won't use you like this. Despite your actions, I know you don't want to have sex without benefit of marriage. You've always maintained that you would hold your innocence close to your heart. You need a real wedding night. Not a sordid dalliance in the library." He caught another glimpse of tender white flesh. Through her silk chemise he again saw the rosy tips of her nipples. Her breasts were round, firm. Bigger than he thought they would be. She was so slender.

A tear slipped down her cheek. With his thumb he whisked the silver droplet away. "I've been…" The words that she didn't finish caught in her throat.

"Why the sudden need to…?" He couldn't say the word she used. After he let go of her hands they moved to the buttons. This time he fastened them.

"Believe I'll go to my room." Her voice was harsh. He saw her deep mortification. The emotion was etched in her expression.

Jason wasn't ready to let her run from him. Answers were needed. "What did your mother say to you?" He reached out to stop her. Caught her elbow. Turned her so she faced him again. The need to know why all this was happening threatened his calm exterior. Anice must have said something that had Tessa reeling. The facts pointed to something unnerving her. She would have never started to disrobe in front of him if not provoked. Never spoke of intimate acts between a man and a woman.

"N-nothing."

Under the circumstances and with the softest voice he could manage, he spoke to her, "Little liar. Anice told you to do this. I know. What is she holding over your head? Whatever she wants, together we will fight your mother." He held his breath while he waited for an answer that wasn't going to appease him. Anice didn't deserve such beautiful daughters.

"N-nothing."

"That's not an answer I can accept. Why don't you sit. Drink another brandy. Think about telling me what happened with your mother that has you acting so out of character." With each unsteady breath Tessa inhaled, his determination to remain calm faltered.

"No, I don't want another drink. Don't wish to sit. I'm leaving." She whirled. Stumbled on legs that appeared to wobble. She grasped for the back of a chair. Managed to right herself.

Jason wasn't all that certain Tessa would make it to her room. He could keep her here. What possible good would that do? He couldn't make her talk. Despite his misgivings, he watched her walk out the door.

Not only did he hurt her feelings this evening, he humiliated her when he stopped her from giving herself to him. She reached out to him. In the process, he felt as if he slapped her in the face by denying her what she tried to gift him with. If he believed this was her idea, he might have given the notion more consideration.

Frustrated, desperate to learn why, he threw the glass at the fireplace. The delicate crystal shattered into tiny shards, clattering to the hearth then the floor. He set his forearm on the brick mantel before burying his head on his arm. Long rasps of air filled his lungs while he searched his head for some way he could have proceeded in a different manner.

~ * ~

For Tessa, her evening went from good to bad then moved on to very, very bad. Sitting on her bed after her mortification at Jason's behalf, she allowed her mind to travel over the events of the day. No, Jason wasn't at fault. She gambled on one last fleeting hope then lost. If given a chance, there was so much she would do different. First and foremost, she would never have gone to see her mother if she'd known Anice's plans for her. People always spoke of hindsight. She made the worst decision of her life. Now, she would pay. Her mother would wring her dry. She could never fall into her mother's plans. How to avoid doing that Tessa was unable to grasp. She needed Jason's help, but after this last confrontation, was afraid to ask. She'd stuck her foot in her mouth.

Back to the good part of the last ten hours. The beginning of her day brought light to her eyes, coupled with joy to her heart. She laughed. Felt carefree. For now, she didn't intend to do any more thinking about her mother along with all she told her. Recalling the good parts was her intention.

Her sisters were in her bedroom with her, chatting nonstop about whatever popped into their heads. To some extent, they all enjoyed the debutant scene. The dancing. The men all decked out in their best finery. They loved flirting with the line of men seeking a wife. No one planned on making a choice any day soon. As the days progressed, they all became a bit jaded as well as bored. The time was nearing the dinner hour. They each had a small glass of sherry in hand. Tessa added a log to the cheery fire.

Standing back, hands clasped in front of her, her thoughts were on Jason. The red-gold flames danced in the hearth. She was in love with the man. Had been since the moment she saw him. True, she told him no to the proposal. True, doing so was more difficult than she expected. She wanted what their oldest sister had…love. Jason didn't seem ready or willing to give his love to her, only his protection. She couldn't live her life with no love in it. In Tessa's mind, a marriage would never last without love. She could site her mother and father's marriage as an example. There was no love between the two, only bitter hatred. There were other couples she knew who felt the same about each other.

"The Laughton's ball is coming up next week. Do you think we'll be going?" Nellie asked as she concentrated her attention on Tessa then her sherry. "I've a new gown being made for the occasion. The green silk brings out the color of my eyes. That's what Maggie told me. I for one am excited to see if there is anyone out there for me. Hope we don't move to the country before then."

Move to the country? She hadn't heard about a departure from the city. Tessa felt a dreamy wave pass through her at the prospect of the ball. "I'd like to dance with Jason. Don't care about dancing with anyone else," Tessa said as she wove unreal dreams in her head. Wanted to feel his arms around her. Sway to the music with him. Needed to feel the warmth of his body while he twirled her around the dance floor. Didn't intend going down the marriage path unless the man loved her. From what little Maggie told her when she wasn't busy with her husband and now her baby, love was something to hold out for. Maggie told them all, she'd loved Jasper almost from the first time she buried her nose against his shoulder then felt the heat of his body, knew his protection would be strong. Would last a lifetime. Protection was nice. She needed love to sustain her.

"Jason this…Jason that," Fannie said, laughing as she spoke. "One would think you didn't have a coherent thought in your brain unless it revolved around Jason Kenworthy. He's all you ever talk about." Fannie was putting finishing touches on her needlework. There was a myriad of mistakes. She let her work rest in her lap, unable to stare at the piece any longer. "I would that I had that problem."

"True. I do think about him most every second of every day." Tessa would go only so far in her thoughts about the man who stole her heart over a year ago. She was so ignorant of what went on between a man and a woman. Maggie told her she was innocent and that wasn't a bad way to be. In time, Jason would teach her what she needed to learn. She was eager. Impatient. Urgency flooded her when she recalled his kisses. Before she committed, she needed everything to be perfect.

"True?" Nellie laughed again. "Is that all you can say?" She leaned forward, her glass resting in a precarious manner between her fingers. "What I don't understand is why that besotted man…he is besotted with you… has not asked you to marry him. Thought he would have done so by now. We all know he's wanted you for more than a year. The way he looks at you, as if he wants to devour you, tells the entire story. Still, he goes to see his lover in the evenings, leaving you here."

Lover? Goes to see her in the evenings?

"He has. Twice. Asked me to marry him. What's that about a lover he is seeing?" Tessa cringed at the reaction of her sisters. Before this afternoon, she'd never told her favorite people in the whole world that truth. Now, they told her Jason went to see a woman in the evenings. Said that was where he was off to when she couldn't find him.

When she began recounting her day, she never intended to dwell on anything that made her unhappy. That was the unfortunate part about today. Bad news thrived.

Fannie rose, took the glass from her hand. “Then why aren’t we planning a wedding? If he’s asked, we should be picking out gowns, planning the wedding ceremony as well as the celebration after deciding on the colors and everything else that needs to be done beforehand. The two of you are not running off to Gretna Green… Are you?” She refilled the glass. Handed it back to her. “Would like to understand the truth here.”

“Jason doesn’t love me. What did you say about a lover?” Her voice cracked with the seeds of humiliation. That couldn’t be true. He would never ask her to marry him then keep a mistress on the side. Would he? She was far too uncertain of the ways of men. Her mother always was off seeing people…men…different men. Was he seeing another woman? Now, the fact seemed obvious to her.

“Of course, he loves you. We shouldn’t have said anything.” This from Nellie who sounded indignant. She was waving her hand in the air. “That man dotes on you. When the two of you are in the same room, he never takes his gaze away from you. If that’s not love, I don’t know what is. As to his lover, a man has needs. I’ve heard talk about that at some of the galas we’ve been to.”

Needs?

She huffed out a breath of stolen air. “Staring at a person does not translate to love. What do you know about this lover of his?” Tessa said, her voice soft. The hurt she felt was tangible. Jason treated her with care along with consideration as to her feelings. When he asked for her hand in marriage, he never got down on one knee. She didn’t understand why that was important to her. What she did comprehend was that love was the single most important factor in deciding to marry. So far, the words were not said. Now her sisters spouted about a lover. She didn’t intend to let this go. She wasn’t going to have a life such as the one her mother had.

“True. Lord Abernathy stares at all of us when we are in the same room. He makes my skin crawl. Never fails to raise goose bumps on my arms. Jasper says we still need to take care that we don’t put ourselves in a precarious position where that man is concerned,” Fannie said, while she shot a look at her. Sipped her drink. “Might as well tell you what you want to know. We heard Jasper arguing with Jason about the woman, Sarah is her name. Jasper told him he needed to let her go. Said she wouldn't mind. Would understand why."

"Yes, Jasper told his twin he should end the affair," Nellie continued the conversation. "He should end it if he truly wants you. Can't have a lover along with a wife at the same time. Not right. Not right a'tall. Is what Jasper said."

"I wouldn't stand for it," Fannie spoke up with a small giggle. "Not that a wife ever has much of a say in matters of the heart where the husband is concerned. We all *ken* mother wasn't faithful. Father never appeared to care. He seemed happy to be well rid of mother. She is difficult to get along with."

With those words, Tessa found herself rubbing her arms where goose bumps appeared out of nowhere. Both conversations sent shivers down her spine. She didn't wish to think of Jason with another woman. Couldn't stand to think of Lord Abernathy at all. "Me too. My skin does react when I'm around Lord Abernathy. The small hairs at the nape of my neck stand on end. No matter how hard I try, I cannot forget how close Maggie came to being wed to that man. If not for Jasper…" Her voice trailed off. Abernathy wanted her a year ago. Now, from what she heard, he no longer wished to marry her. He wanted her as a mistress. That would never happen. Jason wouldn't allow something so dreadful even if he didn't love her.

"Neither can any of us…forget. Jasper saved Maggie's life by stepping into a situation fraught with danger. When he reached out to help Maggie, he didn't know who she was. Believed her to be homeless. That night changed all our lives," Tessa relived those terrifying days when they didn't know if Maggie was alive or dead. Didn't know if Lord Abernathy found her then hid her away somewhere. Jasper spirited her out of the country to keep her away from Lord Abernathy along with his disgusting plans to marry her. During that crazy journey the couple fell in love.

"Let's get back to something more enjoyable," Nellie said, interrupting the next wave of nostalgia. "Thoughts of Lord Abernathy leave my stomach churning. Don't need that to ruin my dinner. You danced with the viscount more than once." She looked to Fannie grinning at her sister's look of discomfiture. Tilting her head a bit, she asked "Do you have a *tendre* for the man? What's his name? Leo?"

"Heavens no, no *tendre* for me. This man didn't step on me feet, that's why I danced with him more than once. Yes, his name is Leonard. His friends called him, Leo. All the other hopefuls bruised my toes. Left me with the feeling they wanted just one thing from me, my body," Fannie laughed while she stuck her bare feet in the air to wiggle her toes. "The man is too old for…" she stopped, seeming to realize the huge differences in ages between Tessa and Jason.

Tessa waved her arm in the air to silence any further comments before she could say anything. "Age doesn't matter if the two involved in the relationship love each other. Like Maggie and Jasper," she finished then, needing reassurance from her sisters as well as her best friends. "Do you think age makes that much difference? I don't feel the difference so much with Jason." The question erupted on a weak thread. If Jason was seeing another woman, he didn't love her. She understood that for a fact.

In unison the two sisters blurted. "Of course not!"

"Love is the important factor, you're right," Nellie added in agreement, then finished her sherry. She set the glass down with an emphatic bang. "I'm not going to settle for anything less than love. Neither should the rest of you."

"Love is all important," Fannie granted in compliance with her two sisters.

"Love…" Tessa sighed, wishing for something that wasn't going to happen. Her hands were clasped beneath her chin. Jason was never going to fall in love with her though it was obvious even to her, the man wanted her. His eyes blazed, changed colors when he looked at her. The way he gazed on her warmed her until she burned. Her blood rushed through her at blinding speed. Tessa, in her unworldliness didn't understand what that entailed. She was willing to learn, even though she'd been taught from the cradle a woman shouldn't give her body to a man before she wed.

The missive requiring her presence at her mother's home came ten minutes after her sisters left to dress for dinner. What she should have done was tossed the letter into the fire without reading the contents. Instead, she wrote a quick note to her sisters telling them she was fine. Afraid of a lecture when she returned, she didn't tell them where she was going. Told them she would be home as soon as possible. They would guess though. Where else would she go? If confronted, she would never be able to lie.

The ride in the carriage seemed to take an eternity, her mind racing with the potential reasons for her summons. Tessa was aware of the sounds flitting along the streets. Saw the fires from the homeless who milled around the flames attempting to warm themselves. Couldn't help but think back on the night Maggie met Jasper. Hacks driven recklessly passed by them. Young men out for a good time walked the streets in search of whatever free female entertainment they could find. The shivering response to her thoughts set her nerves blazing. She understood from gossip, more than one woman found herself enceinte after these young men found their amusement from some unlucky girl.

After the carriage stopped in front of the MacRae townhouse, she swallowed several gulps of air. The lump in her throat didn't vanish. She told herself the breaths of air were for courage. They didn't help. True, she needed to pull whatever bravery she could find from herself to tackle this issue with her mother. She didn't wish to be anywhere near her mother. Had to find out what Anice wanted. For several minutes she sat, frozen. This was…

For the benefit of your sisters.

That's what the note said. Tessa didn't have any idea how this meeting would benefit any of them. For over a year they had no correspondence with Anice. Now, she wanted to see the youngest. The one she believed to be the most vulnerable. Their mother tended to bring chaos into their lives whenever she entered into it. She almost told the footman to take her back after he opened the door then placed the steps for her.

With a disapproving look, he held out his hand to help her down. Cleared his throat. "You shouldn't be here without Lord Kenworthy's permission. Without him along for the visit, I'm not liking this a'tall. Can you reconsider going inside?"

Weak was not going to be the way people described her character. *I'm not weak. I've a mind of my own. Opinions that don't need to be changed.*

"No, nothing to change my plans."

She found herself shaking her head. Lord Abernathy wanted her because he believed he could mold her into a proper wife. Thought she was someone who would jump to do his bidding. Whatever that might be. Weak willed. Spineless. She was not that person. Jason understood her true nature. Letting Jason mold her to what he wished her to be was also not part of the plan for herself. He would need to come to understand her way of thinking. Tessa stiffened her spine before tilting her chin higher. She could do this. Confront her mother. Find out what she wanted with her youngest daughter.

"Are you certain you want to be here?" her driver asked again while he escorted her to the steps. "I should insist on taking you home."

No. I'm not certain. "I'll be fine. Wait for me, please. Don't intend to spend a moment longer than necessary with my mother. Need to find out what she is after. Need to be certain I've a way home." The man was right to worry. Tessa knew she had no business walking into her mother's domain without protection.

He cleared his throat before he gave her one more reason to hesitate. Her hand was at the knocker. "Can't say Lord Kenworthy will be pleased when he discovers where I've taken you. He might…"

Startled by his words, she was quick to reassure. She'd not thought beyond her needs. "Don't fret. I'll make certain Jason understands I pleaded with you to bring me here. Perhaps I'll tell him mother sent a carriage. No, on second thought, I can't lie. Understand you will stay here. I'm safe with my mother. No harm will come from this visit. You'll see." Tessa didn't believe anything she told the driver was true. Her mother could turn on her with a blink of an eye. She was crazy to answer the note. Foolish to arrive on her doorstep without Jason or her sisters. A damn fool for not telling Nellie where she was going. Should have tossed the hated message into the fire. Should be sitting down to dinner with her sisters.

"Could lose my job," he grumbled.

"You know that won't happen. How long have you been working for the Kenworthys?" Tessa asked, feeling more than a little responsible for this man's fears. "I'm sorry if I've made your life difficult."

"Longer than you've been alive. Longer than Lord Kenworthy too."

After she made up her mind a second time to stay, she patted his hand. "I promise nothing will happen to your job." The promise was made with sheer bravado. Tessa understood she had no clout with the Kenworthy twins when it came to hiring and firing employees. She did think perhaps this time her reasoning might prevail if the situation came to the possible termination of his job.

"I'll be here waiting for you, Miss MacRae. Don't think I won't. Not going anywhere without you inside that carriage. Not without you tucked safe and sound into the vehicle. Won't let you down. Nothing is going to happen to you on my watch. That's a promise."

Standing on the tips of her toes, she kissed the elderly man on the cheek before she opened the door. The foyer was empty when she took off her cape to hang her garment on the coat stand. The scent of fresh picked roses clung to the air. Tessa expected someone to appear soon even though she didn't knock. She wiped her sweating hands on the fabric of her dress. Wished she wasn't so nervous.

"Mother, I'm here." Tessa called out then smoothed the cloth of her gown, shaking out a few creases from her stint in the carriage. She walked the length of the foyer, peering into several rooms before she satisfied herself that her mother was nowhere to be found. Anice wouldn't appear until she could make an orchestrated entrance. Her mother would play a waiting game with her, stretching her nerves with the insecurities Anice would know she was feeling.

"Mother?" A few thoughts of disgust fluttered through her head. She came all this way to be welcomed to an empty house. Did her mother think she wouldn't come? Perhaps. With no purpose in her head as to what she was going to do, she wandered into the drawing room. Noted the fire burning in the hearth. A somber glow illuminated the room, bathing the furniture. Lights had been lit in preparation for her visit. Her mother was expecting her.

She always loved this room. As she looked around, she imagined her sisters sitting around the fire chatting. Her mother rarely disturbed them in the evenings. The times together, here, were fond memories.

A tray was set out with refreshments. A teapot with two dainty cups. Small plates at the ready. The sugar bowl along with several slices of lemon. A pitcher with milk. Napkins.

So, mother did expect her most obedient daughter to do her bidding. Obvious Anice was confident that she would comply to the command. She would give her credit for reading her mind. Had to since she fell into her hands by following her directives. Tessa realized her acquiesce in this matter wasn't caused by obedience. It was due to curiosity. For all her sisters, Tessa wanted to learn what it was that their mother expected of them even though she put herself in a precarious situation.

Tessa poured herself a cup of tea. Bit into a spice cake. Savored the taste. Anice did employ the best cook. She closed her eyes, enjoying the intoxicating flavors.

"Ah, the little mouse has come home." The grating voice of her mother startled her out of her contemplations.

Choked by the sound behind her, Tessa dropped the cake on the small bone China plate. She coughed, trying to clear her throat of the tiny obstacle that was lodged halfway down her throat.

"Drink some tea, dear," Anice encouraged while she fixed herself a cup. "Wasn't certain you would show up. Was your handsome protector not at home to end your venture into the evening by yourself? I would have expected your protector, Lord Kenworthy, to put a stop to this excursion or to insist he accompany you."

She cleared her throat. The last remnants of spice cake slipping downward. "What do you want, Mother? I'd like to hear you out then leave. Don't wish to stay here a moment longer than necessary." Tessa didn't want to remain here a second more. She wanted to leave this moment. Seeing her mother again brought back memories she'd rather forget. To dwell on whether or not she should be in this home was a moot point. She shouldn't have responded to the summons.

"So brusque. I would have thought your manners would be better. A year ago, you would never cut to the point of a requested visit in such a curt manner. You are becoming more like your sisters every day." Anice sat back, one hand holding the saucer, the other the cup. Her eyes narrowed while she studied her youngest daughter.

"Why don't you have another cake, dear. Had the cook bake your favorite." Anice nodded her head toward the plate of delicacies.

"You were so certain I would come?" Of course Anice was certain. She never defied her mother. Anice would never believe she would start now.

"Once a mouse, always a mouse. I suppose Lord Kenworthy appreciates the fact you fail to have an opinion. Such an easy girl to shape to his way of thinking. Have you slept with the man? Of course you have. When I last saw the two of you together, you were smitten with that man."

Tessa had enough. Anice was rude beyond anything she expected. What she did or didn't do with Jason Kenworthy was none of her mother's business. "I should go."

Anice motioned to the now empty chair. "Oh, do sit down. A snit will not get us anywhere. I've important information for you. Don't wish for you to leave until you understand."

"My driver is waiting for me. Get to the point, Mother." Her anger rose not so much at her mother but at herself. Anice was acting true to form. She expected as much. If she still thought to harbor a few soft sentiments for Anice they vanished the moment she asked if she'd slept with Jason.

"Sit. Not speaking with you if you're standing in front of me with that horrid glare on your delicate features. You will get wrinkles sooner than later. Can't imagine how you came to be so fragile considering who your father is." Anice took a cake from the tray. Bit with delicate precision.

Anice wasn't going to get to the point of the visit any time soon. With a heavy sigh, Tessa sat. She'd come this far. Why not stay until she knew what her mother wanted? Waited for her mother to get through playing with her prey. Anice spoke about her father without mentioning a name. She'd always been certain her father was not the same as her siblings. Her sire was a different man. She wondered what it would have been like to grow up in a different home. If she had, she would not have come to care so much for her sisters. On the other hand, she might have been loved by her father.

Would the man who is her father be nice? Would he have cared about her? Too many questions to count. What she needed now was to stick this out. She was here for a reason. The intent of her mother would not bode well for her.

"What do you want, Mother?" Tessa found she was exhausted as well as frustrated with the cat and mouse game Anice played. "Tell me now so I can leave. As I said before, don't wish to be here a moment longer than necessary."

By the time Anice finished explaining her plans for the two of them, Tessa was sick to her stomach. She couldn't ignore what her mother wanted. Had to find some way to play the game long enough so she might find the means to win. Enlisting Jason's help was out of the question. His lover would stand in the way. She'd tossed out several names of possible fathers. Left her guessing just who she intended to blackmail with the information they had a bastard daughter.

Heart-sick, Tessa welcomed the friendly presence of her driver after she left her mother's home. He gave her a fatherly pat on her hand as if he sensed her disillusionment. Tessa understood whether she came to visit tonight or tomorrow or even the next week, Anice would have found a way to put her disgusting threat in front of her.

When she walked into the library of the Kenworthy home, she felt dirty, cheap. Was that the way a whore felt? Couldn't imagine. She needed to wash the filth from herself. No amount of scrubbing would make her clean again. Her mother used her. Did that surprise her? No! Anice used everyone who was pathetic. All she needed was to find a weakness. As she discovered while visiting with her mother, she had more than one weakness.

So unlike her, she grabbed Jason's glass of brandy and downed the contents. Almost laughed at his stunned look of surprise. The fiery liquid sliding down her throat did nothing for her disposition. Her confusion must have shown through her bravado. She splashed more brandy into Jason's glass then poured herself another drink.

She was confused as well as frightened. Proceeding with the plan was difficult. She didn't wish to be part of her mother's plots. Didn't know what to do or how to escape. She could never explain any of this to Jason.

As she began to fiddle with her buttons, she understood she exploded into dangerous territory. Having Jason make love to her wouldn't solve her problems. No, doing this would create more than she had any idea how to deal with.

When he rejected her ill-thought-out advances, her cheeks flamed. Heated. Mortified to the tips of her toes, she wished there was some hole she could climb into then hide from him forever. He learned she visited her mother. He was angry. Told her Anice was not safe for her to see.

Jason demanded answers. She had nothing to give him that would subdue his burgeoning anger with her. When they spoke of the woman he was seeing, she wished she dared slap him. He couldn't ask her to marry him in one breath then run off to warm himself in the bed of his mistress. The woman wasn't his mistress. He told her as much. After the brief meeting, she raced to her room. To seek solace by herself was her motivation.

Still feeling the filth from her mother, coupled with the humiliation from Jason, she pulled the bell cord for a bath. Not much later the heated water arrived. Tessa poured scented oil into the steaming liquid before she stripped then settled into the hot, comforting liquid.

To cease thinking about this day would be her dream. To have had the day never happen would be a miracle that would never happen. She soaked until the water turned tepid. Washed. Finally, stepping from the water, she wrapped a towel around her hair then one around herself.

She placed another log on the fire. Watched the flames leap into the air. Tears slid from her eyes. She pushed them away with the backs of her hands. Tessa didn't know how she was going to face Jason tomorrow morning. If she got lucky, he wouldn't be around. Sometimes he left early to ride. She could hope.

The knock on her door startled her. The person on the other side could be one of her sisters. Who else would it be at this time of night? She didn't want to see them. They would take one look at her then ask a wealth of questions she didn't dare respond to.

"Tessa!"

The devil, no! This was worse than her sisters.

"I don't wish to see you!" The panic she heard in her voice would also be heard by Jason. He would insist on entry. He'd not given up on finding out why she set out to see her mother or what her mother wanted from her. She wouldn't be able to withstand his gentle persuasion. He had that way about him.

"You've no choice," Jason spoke with a calming voice. His words though, did nothing to soothe her. "One way or the other I'm coming into your room. Must speak with you about tonight. You ran off before I could get answers from you. Need to get a few things understood before I sleep tonight."

"No!"

"As I just said, you've no choice." Jason persisted on this theme. His voice was gentle. While he wasn't giving her a choice, he was using tactics that would subdue someone with greater strength than she possessed. "I'd like you to open the door for me. Now."

"I'm not decent." She groped for one excuse after another. "I've…"

"Put a robe on," he said as he turned the handle. "I'll give you to the count of ten." Jason began to count. "One…two…"

Tessa didn't have time to find the lock to the door. She would look for the key afterward. This wasn't going to happen again. She raced to the armoire. Dropped both towels before opening the doors. Where was her nightgown? Her robe? She was such a bundle of nerves. Her fingers fumbled while she searched in desperation. She didn't recall where she saw them last.

"Ten…"

"Oh, no…no…!"

Wide eyed, she turned to see Jason open the door then step into the room. With haste, she reached for the first thing she could find. Air was what she found. Saw one of the towels lying a few feet from her. Dashed for it. In a moment, she had the towel wrapped around her, her blood rushing through her at an alarming pace.

"Jason…" she breathed out his name. "You shouldn't be here. I…" He saw her naked, without a stitch.

With his hands behind his back, he rocked on his heels. With deep husky words, he spoke. "I see that. Go on. Find your nightgown and robe. I'll turn my back while you look. Need for you to calm down."

"Calm down?" she parroted. Panicked. "How can I calm down when you're in my room and I'm na…naked?"

The throaty chuckle following her statement did nothing to relax her. "If I recall a little while ago, you were undressing yourself in front of me. What am I supposed to think? Seems you're running a bit hot and cold. You don't seem to know your own mind."

"I…can't we talk in the morning?" Even while she uttered the question, Tessa comprehended what his answer would be.

"No."

That was what she thought. She gulped down a smidgeon of air. Wasn't enough. She choked. "I'm not going to be telling you anything about my visit to my mother. I won't. If that's why you are here, then you're wasting your time."

"Find the robe, Tessa. If you don't, I will. My patience is running thin."

By the sound of his voice, what he told her held the ring of truth. "Oh!" She dropped the towel. Searched. Found a gown that would never do. The fabric was gossamer, silky, meant to… She didn't know what it was meant for. Not warmth that was for certain. Nonetheless, this piece of silken fabric her mother gave her before the sisters had a falling out with her was better than nothing. She slipped the gown over her head just as he was turning around again.

His eyes darkened. He stepped toward her. His hand outstretched. "Your hair is all a tangle. Still wet. Go sit by the fire. I'll comb it for you."

"That's not why you're here. What do you want?" Frantic, she searched her mind for some tidbit she could tell him. Something that might ease his mind. "Why are you here where you've no business?"

"We will be married. Don't know when. However, you need to get used to me seeing you with little to nothing on."

"I said no." She backed up a step for each one he took toward her.

"Yes. A man needs to know where his woman is as well as why she put her life at risk. Don't you think? Give me a reason I can't refute."

"Not your woman." She wished she was his. Needed him to love her the way his twin loved her sister.

"You are. I've waited far too long for you to figure it out. Tonight put a period to the waiting. If you won't say yes…well there are other ways to get a reluctant woman to the alter."

"What are you talking about?"

"Sit on the hearth. I'll comb your hair.

Dazed, Tessa obeyed without further argument.

I am a mouse.

~ * ~

"You know Tessa went to see mother. What do you suppose she wanted?" Nellie asked, her voice growing paper thin with the question. They were all afraid Anice would find some means to make the youngest sibling do her dirty work. They both understood Anice would blackmail her if she got the chance. She'd always been underhanded in her dealings. Nothing would have changed in the year since Maggie's wedding.

"What information does she have to hold over Tessa's head? There is nothing that I can think of." Fannie asked while she watched the door for movement. "I'd like to learn what it is. We need to speak with our sister so she can tell us what Anice wants. Do you think she would be forthcoming with us?"

"No, not if the threat included us. In that case she would tell us nothing. Tessa was out late with mother. I would suspect Jason saw her before she went to bed. She won't be down yet. It's far too early. We need to be patient with our little sister. There is a lot of pressure on her. I'm certain Jason has been applying thumb screws to get her to talk to him. We need to make certain she understands she can count on us to protect her best interests."

"Do you think our talk about his mistress shook her so much she gave into whatever mother wanted?" Fannie was drumming her fingers on the armrest of her chair. It was a nervous habit that drove Nellie half crazy. "If mother summoned her, Anice would be confident that Tessa would have no choice in the matter."

"There is no mistress…no other woman in my life. I'd appreciate it if the rumors along with the gossip to stop." The gruff voice brought both girls to attention. They both groaned. Both felt heat flush their faces. "What goes on between Tessa and myself needs to be between the two of us. I've explained to Tessa what she needs to know. She understands the woman is in my past not our future. A man cannot be expected to be celibate. Tessa is the only woman I want. Still, she refuses my proposal of marriage."

"It can't be just between the two of you," Nellie said, quite frankly finding the need to lecture this man surfacing with rapid speed. "We all share everything. We are as close as sisters can be. That's not going to change. Not ever!"

"No longer. What goes on between Tessa and myself is private, between the two of us, no one else." He poured himself a cup of tea then set about dishing up a plate of food. He sat down before speaking again, "Tessa won't be down for another hour or more. She's exhausted from the evening. There was a great deal that happened that was out of her control."

"What about your mistress…Sarah?" Fannie blurted with angry words while she persevered on the topic Jason just told them was not their business. Fannie folded her hands together. "If Tessa is going to shed tears over your lovers, past or present, she needs to be able to confide in us."

Jason didn't seem to understand how best to deal with Tessa's siblings. He pinched the bridge of his nose before clearing his throat to move on to a new topic. "As I just mentioned, I have no mistress or lover. There is nothing to share. Tessa doesn't need to confide in her sisters. She has me to unburden her thoughts now." Without giving them more attention, he thumped the egg he was about to eat then carefully peeled the shell away.

"Jason is right." Tessa made her way into the room. Beneath her eyes were dark shadows giving testimony to a sleepless night. Jason was correct in his assumption. She was exhausted. "I will…entrust in Jason. No one else. He's made himself clear on that matter to the two of you this morning as well as to me last evening. There will be no arguments or persuasive lectures. What is between Jason and myself stays between us."

"You should still be in bed," Jason said as he stared pointedly at Tessa. "Last night was too much for you. You need your rest."

Nellie and Fanny shared the direction of their gazes. Both were concerned for their little sister. She looked as if she'd been run over, trampled by a speeding carriage.

"I couldn't sleep. Under the circumstances, there's no point in staying in bed," Tessa murmured as she sat down at the breakfast table.

"Eat…" He waved his arm to the sideboard where platters of food abounded. "We are traveling to the country today. There you will find some rest. You can sleep as long as you wish. Anice will not be allowed to bother you. The butler has been given the order that whatever missives come to you they must go through me first." He turned his attention to the sisters. "You will follow after the Laughton ball if you would like to join us. As you all can see, Tessa needs a change of scenery. I'm worried about her. We are all concerned for her health."

What he wasn't saying was that she needed to be away from Anice. Nellie closed her eyes, obvious that she understood Tessa was their mother's latest victim. Jason would do all in his power to protect her. He loved her even though Tessa didn't realize that yet.

Nellie wanted to be loved. The rakes she met so far were not ready to find a wife. She realized she needed to look for an older man. At twenty something, young pups, as Jasper called the men who were eager to find wives at the debutant balls, wouldn't do unless they were closer to the thirty mark. Younger men seemed to need to figure things out. They were not seasoned enough. Nellie wasn't at all certain what needed to be figured out. The only logical explanation she could think of was the need to bed as many different women as possible before turning that ripe old age of thirty.

Jason turned thirty a couple of years ago. He must have everything all figured out. Tessa was lucky his roving eye landed on her.

Chapter Two

The sleepless night Jason spent set his frayed nerves further on edge. He surprised her. Had not meant to. Walked in on her while she was dressing after her bath. Naked, Tessa was more beautiful than he could have ever imagined. Her rose tipped breasts beckoned to be tasted, savored by him. A tiny waist flared to curved hips then long slender legs. The soft covering of hair on her woman's mound was a slight shade darker than the blond hair curling down her body, playing peekaboo with the tips of her breasts.

It took all his restraint to keep from pulling her into his arms then teaching her about the physical side of loving between a man and a woman. After seeing her wearing nothing at all, Jason understood he needed to convince Tessa that marriage to him should be sooner not later. Imagining Tessa in his arms burned him to the core. His passion rose swift and hot.

Now, sitting in the carriage on the way to the country estate, she turned from him, keeping her gaze riveted on the passing country side. Tessa should have been turning toward him, confiding in him. He needed to clear the air between them. The only way that could happen would be for her to reveal her secret meeting with Anice. She was silent to all his questions. Mute. The more he asked, the stonier her face became. This was a side of her he'd never encountered. Stubborn little darling. He needed to tread with tender care around her. If he ceased with the questions, she might, if he were lucky, let down her guard. Any small piece of information would be welcomed by him. Treasured. Stored in his head until he knew all the pertinent facts. He did need to protect her.

What the devil was her mother blackmailing her with?

It had to be some form of threat that was keeping her thoughts inside her head. A piece of information that would devastate her. Good

God, she didn't confide in her sisters. Maybe he should have let the siblings have at each other. The girls might have wrested some piece of intelligence from Tessa. It certainly would have made sense to try that ploy. Too late now, the girls wouldn't be together for more than a week, if at all.

Jasper and Maggie weren't going to leave for another three weeks. Jasper had business to settle before he could vacate the city. He would be alone with Tessa. Privacy would be nice. Might lead to the intimacy he needed to convince her marriage to him was what she wanted. He would have her all to himself. Maybe the sisters would opt to remain in the city too. They didn't need to leave on Tessa's account. He meant to protect her. With forethought, he took the endless possibilities into account. Neither Anice nor any of her retainers would be allowed through the gates to the Kenworthy estate. If a message got through, he would be the first to read the missive. The first to decipher any hidden meanings.

"How much longer?" Tessa asked, breaking the silence. "I'm tired. Hungry. Couldn't eat at breakfast." She sounded petulant. A child who wished to have her way. She looked at him through shuttered dark lashes, her eyes still shadowed by blue smudges indicating a sleepless night. At least she was talking to him. Her stoney silence was annoying.

He wished he could read her thoughts. Could see into her mind to learn what trouble was brewing for her. All he could do now was wait with patience for her to come to him. Ask him for help. Jason reached beside him for the basket of traveling snacks their cook packed for the trip this afternoon.

"Probably an hour, give or take, on either side. We've snacks for your pallet. Believe cook baked a spice cake…"

Tessa choked when he mentioned her favorite cake, her eyes wide when she spoke. "No…anything else? Sorry. Didn't mean to be rude. It's just the sound of a spice cake is not appealing."

"Thought spice cake was your favorite," Jason mused as he tried to understand the prevailing atmosphere. Who got upset over the type of dessert offered? What could have brought on the distress? Moving on with the conversation seemed to be in Tessa's best interest. "There are thick chocolate cakes. A bit heavier than the norm. Personally, those are my preferred dessert. Do love my chocolate."

"I'll have one of those, thank you." She graced him with a beautiful smile. One that would get her anything she asked for. Tessa touched her finger to her lip. That was something he'd like to pursue. Not now, though. She wasn't ready for an afternoon dalliance in the carriage. "Is there anything to drink?"

"Just water…" He rummaged into the basket to bring out a pitcher along with two cups. "Would have liked something a bit stronger. Need to explain to the cook that we'd rather have…" Jason mumbled, thinking he needed a big glass of ale to wash all the dust from the ride away. When he looked to her with an expectant smile she responded.

"Wine would have been nice." She bit into the cake. Swept her tongue around her mouth to capture a few errant crumbs that didn't want to go into her mouth.

Jason found he couldn't remove his gaze from the ripeness of her mouth. Her sweet kissable lips, the bottom one plump as a pillow. "Wine…no not this time around. Next trip we take, I'll need to put in a request for something heftier than water. Even tea might have gone well with the cakes." She seemed to be coming out of the pique she was in for the last few miles. With his words she slanted him what appeared to be a hesitant smile.

"I'll miss my sisters while they stay in Glasgow," her voice sounded distant, vague. Her smile vanished with her thoughts.

"You'll have me. There is much to do in the country. We can take walks in the garden. Have midafternoon snacks at the gazebo. We can pursue our relationship. The weather is warm but not hot in June. Cool breezes blow down from the craigs." He stretched out his legs. Brushed her skirts with one. Noted the changing color of her eyes. He tried for nonchalance. Didn't want her to know what he was doing. Touching her even once was his intention. Needed for her to want him as she once did. "Do you like to ride?"

"I could learn." She lifted her chin, tilted it a bit to the right. Moved her skirts away from his leg. He shifted again, following her. He heard a soft broken noise of annoyance come from the back of her throat. "You would teach me?" Now she sounded enthusiastic. "I've never ridden anything before."

Choking with her statement, he would teach her a lot of things. Riding could be taught many different ways. "Would enjoy teaching you to ride." His grin felt good as his spirits lightened. Perhaps he was right about leaving the subject of Anice's threats to tread on lighter topics. If he dared, he was tempted to pull her onto his thighs for a lazy midmorning kiss. One that would last for a long time perhaps all the way to the country estate. So much time she would burn him to cinders. Her kisses could do that.

"I miss you too. You've been distant the last months. For a time, I thought I'd done something wrong." She was playing with the fabric of her skirt while she watched his leg next to her, her fingers weaving through the material as she tried to appear as if he wasn't seducing her. He was trying with as much subtlety as he could drum up the patience for. Subtlety was never his strong suit.

Distant? Hell, yes! "You told me no. That's all. I had a hard time with the rejection you delivered in my direction. Hope to God, you don't do it again the next time I ask you to marry me. There will be a next time. A man can only take so much rebuff." Jason meant to be blunt with his honesty. "Didn't expect that to happen. Not after the few kisses we shared. Believed you like them…the kisses. Thought you had strong feelings for me." Recalling how she appeared last night he meant to test their relationship a bit farther. Needed to share another kiss, then more, if she would allow more intimacy. He didn't forget for a moment the sisters were taught not to share a bed with a man who wasn't their husband. Maggie gave in to Jasper. If he had his way, Tessa would give herself to him before the marriage unless she agreed to marry him soon. He didn't know if he could wait for the reading of the banns. In Scotland, no one needed the reading. Hying off to a village church seemed more what would work for him.

"No one has ever told you no?" Her light laughter surprised him. The soft smile on her lips enticed every hard male part of him. He felt himself swelling with need for her. She could harden him to his bones with that simmer in her dark blue eyes. Looking at her excited him until he ached with his urgency to possess. "Don't know what I expected. You seem to have everything the way you like."

"No one," he chuckled, watching her eyes shimmer with what appeared to be amusement. "Don't appreciate being told no, when I know the person denying me means yes." He needed to understand her refusal. If he understood her at all, he knew she wanted to say yes. Why the devil didn't she? Thinking about her refusal baffled him.

"So, I'm the first? Believe I like that." She watched her foot make lazy circles on the floor of the carriage. "A man should never have everything the way he wishes. Builds character if he has to work at what he wants."

Her message surprised, baffled again. "I don't appreciate anything about the fact you told me no," he muttered, as he realized this wasn't going to be a topic that he would like to recall. "Tell me what you and your sisters did to spend your time. Do any of your sister's ride?" He meant to begin with getting to know Tessa better. Learning about her would delight him. Though they lived in the same home for months, he never just sat and chatted with her. Soon after they arrived, she began to distance herself from him. He allowed the separation because he thought to give her space. Tessa told him she wished for a season. He intended to give her what she asked for.

After his question, she lifted slim shoulders, her mouth set in a fine line while she drew her brows together in concentration. "We did needlework. Mother insisted we play the piano even though none of us enjoyed the instrument. Maggie was the best at needlepoint. Fannie the most proficient on the piano. Not to say she was any good. She wasn't. She was just better than the rest of us. Mother cringed every time she heard us play. Sometimes to make a point, she put her hands on her ears."

"I couldn't sit still long enough to play well or push a needle through fabric," Jason said with a laugh.

Jason chuckled at the expression on Tessa face when he mentioned him doing needlepoint. "Pushing a needle through fabric?" One eyebrow lifted. "What is so funny? Men are known to be skilled with needle and thread."

"I cannot see you plying a needle. Goes against all that you are," she pointed out. "Your fingers are too large for finesse."

He lifted an eyebrow speculating at her thoughts which paralleled his own. Physical activity was what he enjoyed. The wind in his face when he raced a horse over the next hill. Water sluicing along his torso while he swam. "Always enjoyed riding as well as swimming. Jasper and I would go to the boxing ring twice a week. It was good exercise. Still go. Unless Jasper is with me, no one will get in the ring and spar with me."

"You enjoy fighting?" The impish grin on her face surprised him. "I would never have thought that about you. You're such a sweet man."

He beamed, even though he never considered a description of his character as being sweet. He was hard. Sometimes ruthless. When she told him she thought he was sweet, that pleased him. "Why do you ask?" Jason leaned forward. His forearms rested on his thighs. He needed to know what was behind her questions.

"Seems you like to play games with me. I don't know. Curious, I guess. That's why I went to see mother. I was curious about what she wanted. She understood the vagueness in what she wrote would draw me to her. The missive was curt but gave no explanation of what she was going to tell me." Her expression changed. She waved her hand in the air. "Never mind. Don't wish to speak about that night or what was said." She cleared her throat, the lines of her mouth turning down, "The night in question. The one that has you fuming."

"Whatever you wish," he told her, a bland note to his voice as he sat back, stretching his arms across the back seat. What she said was more than he knew this morning when they began this trip. "Wonder if any of the Murrays will be in residence. The four brothers live close to the estate."

"Murray brothers?" The sparkle in her eyes was back. She was showing her inquisitiveness to him. "Why? Who are they to you? Important people?"

There were a multitude of answers to this question. His very removed cousin was married to one of the brothers. Actually, she wasn't related in any way. He planned to skirt the issue, keep her curious. Seemed Tessa thrived on curiosity. "Do you know how to play lawn tennis?" he asked but didn't wait for a response. He continued recalling how competitive the four brothers were. "The brothers take the game more seriously than anyone I know. They play to see who has to go to London on business. However, Gordan, the youngest, always wins. His wife is the best player of all of them. Once the men learned, Gordan along with Dawn are unbeatable, they quit challenging the pair."

She was shaking her head. "I don't know how to play." Pushing a flyaway strand of hair behind her ear, she looked puzzled then a bit down in the mouth. Her smile turned upside down. "Don't know how to do much of anything. Mother insisted we take painting lessons. Nellie is the artist among us." She lifted her slim shoulders as if thinking about something long ago.

He picked up her hand, held it for a moment, rubbing his thumb across the top. She was soft. Small. Exquisite. When she didn't look up, he lifted her chin. Saw the confusion in her beautiful blue eyes. "What is Tessa the best at? Hmm…"

"Not getting in anyone's way," she blurted without thinking. Tried to move away from his touch. "I…I don't speak up. I'm the most biddable. Mother calls me a mouse. That is what everyone tells me. It's why you rushed to protect me from Lord Abernathy while we were still in Ireland. Also, the reason you asked me to marry you." With a gentle stroke, he caressed her cheek. "Don't want that. Pity from you is not something to be coveted."

"I would never ask you to marry me if that was all I intended to do. Protect. I don't pity you. You fought for your sister. Told me in no uncertain terms how you felt about my brother's intentions toward Maggie. You are a force to be reckoned with."

"It's what you did. Don't deny. You don't wish to marry because you've tender feelings for me. Protect me from the big bad lord of the realm, that's all you want to do."

"No, love, you are quiet, that's all. No, to all your other statements. I've learned you're stubborn. Beautiful. Opinionated." He searched for other adjectives that might describe her to greater perfection. Adjectives she would never take issue with. "As to the reasons I wish to marry you, very little has to do with the big bad lord as you describe Abernathy. That man is out of your life. He is no longer a threat to your person or your sisters."

Her cheeks turned the color of a sunset. She put her hands there as if to cool herself. He enjoyed watching her stumble through her words. Didn't like how she put herself down. That was Anice's doing. The mother made the daughter feel small, less than herself. That wasn't right. Not right a'tall. He supposed he needed to continue to boost her feelings about herself. Doing so would never be difficult.

"You think so?" her voice turned to a breathy little whisper.

Jason wondered if that was how she would sound when they were intimate. "I know that you are not as you've been made to believe. You can't be walked on or over. Many times, I've heard you express your opinion when it was different from the others. You said no to me. Can you say the same to your mother?" The pointed question won him a scowl from Tessa. He kept the crack of laughter to himself.

"Yes!" she spoke up then seemed to shy away from herself. "Yes, sometimes. Not about this situation. There is nothing I can do except what she wishes. She has me where she wants me…under her thumb. While that's unfortunate. It's also true."

"You have said no to Anice. I wonder when." Beneath his chin, he tapped his fingers together as he thought over what Tessa told him. "Was it last night? Did you refuse something your mother wished?" He prayed from this point forward, she would always refuse that woman. She had a good mind. One that was agile. She was able to sift through any number of facts to derive an opinion. The only reason she might cave to her mother was blackmail.

Tessa withdrew into herself. When she looked up again, moisture clouded her beautiful blue eyes. Last night she didn't say no to her mother. Jason already assumed as much. She just said her mother held the reigns. Tessa agreed to do whatever Anice wished. He needed to find out why as well as what that request was. He still searched for the thread Anice bound Tessa to her with. Knowledge of some sort she held over her head. Thought if she told him, she would start a dominoes affect that she didn't think would be good for him. She is trying to protect someone. He didn't believe her silence was meant to keep him from harm. That was the true nature of blackmail. So, who was it she was attempting to protect?

"Does this have something to do with me?" he questioned, hoping she would give something else away. Seemed the slow chipping away of her secret was torture to both of them. If she would trust in him, this would go so much easier. He wouldn't feel as if he was pulling teeth from a baby.

She was shaking her head, her shoulders trembling. A small shudder swept through her before she stiffened. "No…" She gulped a long drink of water then another. "That's all I'm going to say. You can't know…if you…"

"Then…" He paused as he continued to study her expressions. "This threat affects only you." He didn't see how that could be right. She wouldn't play into her mother's hands like that if she was going to be the only person hurt by what her mother threatened. Tessa would stiffen her spine then ignore the intimidation. There had to be another person involved in the extortion. "Your sisters?" He felt as if he grasped at straws. They were the only people she cared about. In some fashion only Tessa knew about, the intimidation must include the girls.

Tessa turned to stare out the window. One more time he pressed too hard, too far. She withdrew into herself again. He let out a long slow breath of air realizing that was all the information he was going to get for now. So far, he played every card he held including everyone she tossed out. She gave him very little intelligence to make assumptions about. What was clear, however, was the threat involved someone she might care about. Another relation of some sort? Did she have any? An aunt or uncle? Cousins?

"The countryside is beautiful." A long breath of air shifted from her lungs. "Except for the time I spent in Ireland, I've only been out of the city once. That was when I was about five. Don't remember much," she spoke to him again. Looked at him. That was a good sign. The topic turned too mundane to suit her purpose. He would carry on in the vein she directed.

"Except for the time in Ireland, you never left the city since you were five?" Jason needed clarification. Seemed strange that in an affluent household there would be so many restrictions. "Your mother never went on a vacation of any sort?"

"No, we didn't. Mother left every summer to play in the country. Anyway, that's what she told us. She would leave us alone at the house with a nanny while she travelled outside Glasgow. Think she went to

Edinburgh several times, Inverness too. Didn't want the girls along. Said she had better things to do than babysit us." The wistful tone of her voice shook him. Growing up Tessa had neither a mother she could count on or a father. "I'm happy that you're taking me outside the city. I do wish to learn to ride. The walk to the gazebo sounded nice, too. If there is a stream close by, wading would be fun. Don't you think?"

"Wading?" One eyebrow shot upward. When she grinned at him, he thought the look must be a *wee* bit comical. "Do I get to teach you to swim also?" Thinking of all the private time he would have with Tessa, lit up his spirits.

A heavy sigh followed from her. "As you've guessed, I also don't know how to swim. I thought wading barefoot in a creek would be nice." The look she sent his way was puzzling. "What does one wear when swimming?"

This time his bark of laughter echoed in the small confines of the carriage. He bent forward, capturing her small hands in his larger ones. His thumb traveled across tender soft flesh. Heard her tiny intake of breath which he hoped was pleasure. "As little as possible." Watched crimson paint her cheeks.

Trying to imagine what it would be like to grow up in a home such as the one she did was next to impossible. No wonder the girls were so attached to each other. All they had were their siblings. The need for each one to protect each other would be astronomical. His parents had been loving, doted on them. While he was very close to his twin, they did share a birthday, Jasper wasn't the only friend he had. Sometimes Jason felt certain he understood his twin's thoughts, they were so very close to each other.

"Did you have friends?" he asked, afraid of hearing the answer.

"Just each other," Tessa murmured, her voice soft sounding hesitant even wistful. "That's all we needed…each other. When Maggie ran from the ball that night, she had no friends to turn to. Just as I have no one now."

"I'm your friend," he said, his voice gruff. "You can turn to me any time, for support, for advice." *For love.* "As far as I'm concerned, you will always have me. Forever."

"Thank you. I would if I could. I would turn to you for help."

He needed to return to the topic of her mother. Under his watch, she would make some friends. First thing, he would send a message to Gracie's husband. See if he could finagle an invitation for them to meet. Gracie, his niece of sorts, would make a wonderful friend for Tessa. The four of them could play lawn tennis for entertainment. "What did your mother do on these trips where she wouldn't take her daughters?" Jason was afraid he knew the answer. Felt positive the woman was seeing men on the ventures out of the city. She did seem to have a penchant for adultery. None of the daughters were sired by her husband. Who then? He put that thought into a place where he could recall the sentiment with ease. He meant to employ someone to discover the truth of their parentage. Maybe the father knew. Since the man was in prison in Ireland, that venture would need to wait for a better opportunity.

"Rumor or fact?" Tessa questioned with a small lift of her shoulders. "Nothing I can tell you can be guaranteed as absolute truth. Some of what I'll tell you, I've overheard. Mother was never careful when she talked with the men who came calling."

Jason cringed when he realized his answer didn't make much of a difference. "Either will do."

"Men. Anice went to see men. All sorts of men. They would even be so bold as to pick her up at the front door, not even the back one, before they left. None of her men stayed the night at our house. Nonetheless, there were numerous times she didn't come home until the *wee* hours of the morning."

"Men? There was more than one man?" He'd heard the rumors surrounding the woman. Was also certain her husband preferred men to her. Jason supposed if he was caught in a marriage such as that one, he would also be unfaithful. How did one get caught not understanding their partner's peculiarities? What other option would there be? He didn't feel sorry for the bargain she made. What they all knew after Maggie's wedding was that the man who had lived in their home was not their father. What they also guessed was that Tessa had a different father from the other three.

"Rarely the same man. She would be gone for a week, sometimes more. She would come back flushed with happiness. Giddy. There were times Anice would bring us each a gift. Other times, she would regal us with tales of the places she saw. Some of the things she did. There were plays along with the opera. She traveled to London as well as Paris. Once they spent a few weeks in Madrid."

"Seems as if she could have spared a few outings for her daughters. Anice wasn't maternal at all. Was she?"

"She uses us. As to being maternal, sometimes she was. We've known for years her intent was to form the best alliances possible when we married. She did make sure we never lacked for anything material. Loving us was her problem. I'm shocked she gave in so easily to Jasper's and your wish to be our guardians. She's a stubborn lady. Never gave up easily or quickly as was the case with our guardianship."

"After the shenanigans in Ireland, Anice didn't have much of a choice. No right-minded judge would give her girls back to her. After she realized what she was up against, she gave up without a fight because there was no other choice for her."

"Yes, you're right. I imagine she didn't. Mother always calculates all the possibilities. Weighs the pros against the cons. She did what was best for herself at the time."

"We both understand after last night, she hasn't given up on using the three of you. Maggie is out of her reach. You and your sisters are not so lucky. If you were to marry me, you too, would be beyond her power. There would be nothing more she could do that would hurt you," Jason added, hoping Tessa was listening to him.

"Yes and no. She has information that would hurt someone. She threatened me with the information. I won't be the catalyst for that to happen. Even though Jasper is my guardian, she still uses me to get what she wants." Tessa fisted her hands beneath her chin. Looking at him she blinked a few times.

"Do you know that person?" After he asked, she turned to gaze out the window withdrawing from him again. She would ignore the question while she thought of something to say which would reveal nothing important.

No matter his opinions on the woman, she still had control of one of her daughters if not all of them. Anice saw after herself. Would always take care of herself first. Damn anyone who got in her way. Her daughters were only important to her as pawns to use to improve her life. He wondered what her plans for Tessa were. He needed to marry her before her mother could set anything into motion. He felt certain Lord Abernathy moved on to another possible woman for his wife. The rumor had it that he was seeing a young debutante. Not to be surprised, he'd been told the young lady had much the same look as Maggie. Same color of hair and eyes. She was of slender build. Smaller than Maggie. He'd caught a glimpse of her dancing with Abernathy at one of the balls he attended with Tessa. From first appearances, the young woman complied with all Abernathy's wishes.

Jason was stunned when Tessa turned back to him, her face void of color, so pale. The sparkle vanished from her eyes.

"No, I don't know him." Her breath seemed to break as she spoke.

Him...?

Jason had not begun to hope Tessa would answer the questions he put forth. All he needed was a wealth of staying power and he would learn what he needed then he would proceed onto the best part. One small slip of knowledge at a time. So, Tessa didn't know this man who Anice was blackmailing her with.

Then why did she remain mute? What difference would it make if she told him?

He pointed out the window. "Look, we are here. The ride was not that long. I will show you around the house. The driver will see to our luggage. You can rest or eat, perhaps take a walk to the gazebo with me. Do whatever you wish. Take a bath or venture into the gardens for a brief stroll. Your time is yours. If you wish for me to join you in whatever venture you choose, I'd be pleased with an invitation." Jason opened the door then jumped from the carriage. He set the steps. What Tessa didn't know was he included her bath in his request to spend time with her.

"We are here." She stood up straight, seeming to take stock of her surroundings. Hesitated for a few seconds before holding out her hand.

Changed his mind about the steps. Foregoing the hand, he lifted her, his fingers circling her waist, then whirled to set her on her feet in front of the steps. She caught her breath with a little gasp when she landed on the ground. He offered her his arm to escort her up the pathway to his home. Placing his hand over hers, he felt the fine trembling where his palm rested. He hoped for so much from this beautiful woman. Convincing her she should say yes to his proposal was his mission. The next few weeks before the others followed were important.

"Don't be nervous," he told her, his voice tender, enjoying the soft texture of her skin against the tips of his fingers. "I'm not going to let anything happen to you. You should understand that fact by now. Enjoy the time in the country. Anice cannot reach you here in my home. If you receive a message from her, don't act on it until I've read the request."

"I understand. There are some things beyond your control. I will trust you. Though I've no other choice in the matter." She leaned into him. The softness of her womanly curves pressing against him, stirring him to life and reminding how much he burned for her. He waited far too long to initiate his plans. Should have asked her to marry him every week instead of backing off in order to give her time to adjust.

Tempted to wrap his arm around her then draw her as close as possible, he refrained. Escorted her to the home as a proper gentleman would. He and his brother were always proper. Always, until Jasper met Maggie. Jason understood to get what they both wanted he might need to change the tenor of his thoughts. Clancy stood at the open door waiting for them, a smile on his face, seeming pleased to see both of them.

Jason nodded. "You remember Clancy?" He bent low to whisper close to her ear. Soft strands of her golden hair floated across his face, caught in the stubble of day-old growth. Tickled. He grasped the scent of lavender. The flower had become his favorite. She seemed to favor lavender.

"Yes." She smiled at the butler. "I remember Clancy. He was quite nice to us while we were living in Ireland."

The sight of her lips curved upward in pleasure melted him. He hoped to see her smile more often. He would give her things to make her happy. Whatever she asked for. "Clancy, I'm going to show Miss Tessa around the house. We are tired from the trip. Tessa, would you like a bath? If so, I'll have one prepared for you."

"That would be nice. After that, I'd love a small glass of sherry. If that isn't too much trouble." She released his arm and was looking up the long winding stairway to the rooms above. "You will show me to my room?"

"Of course, I can give you a guided tour later. Seems you've made your first choice for the afternoon. You didn't sleep well last night then you rose earlier than necessary. I should have been more observant. We could have made the trip tomorrow. Though I was impatient to escape the city for the peaceful countryside." The ride here must have been taxing for Tessa. Her nerves would be spread thin with all his questions. "I'll show you to your room. Let me know if all is fine. We have servants who will attend to your needs."

They walked the rest of the distance in a comfortable silence. One of the things he enjoyed about Tessa was that they didn't need to talk all the time. He was waiting for the small explosion of anger when she discovered her room adjoined to his. This would be something she would never have anticipated. He wanted her close even though she might not appreciate his decision.

Opening the door, he stepped inside. "Here we are." Jason walked to the windows to open the light blue curtains where she could look out to see the rose garden then on to the gazebo. The room was cheery. Decorated in the same colors as his. The blue of her eyes being his favorite color of blue. When the rooms were draped in his chosen colors, he'd yet to meet Tessa. "Do you like it?"

She smiled at him again. Walked around the chamber then into the dressing area. When she saw the door between his and her room, she stopped. Turned to face him while he awaited her reaction. Her brows were drawn together tight when she looked at him. A few small crease lines formed in the middle of her forehead. "What is this?" Not waiting for an answer, she turned the knob. The door swung open into his room. He heard the startled gasp of air. Tessa looked back to him with accusing eyes.

Jason wasn't certain what she accused him of yet. She would need to speak her mind, blast her cannons at him. He understood the most obvious accusation. Before she could ask, he volunteered the information. "My room. What did you think? I would not place you next to just anyone.

If I'm to keep you safe, I need to also keep you close."

"Why? What you just said makes no sense!" Her fisted hands settled on her hips. The full lips he wished to taste more thoroughly were thinned in a downward fashion that didn't invite a kiss.

He rubbed the back of his neck, hesitant to give her the full reason for the placement of her room. "Want you close to me. Not taking any chances." After his brief words, he held up his hands as if surrendering. "I don't intend to take advantage of the placement. Not going to sneak into your room in the middle of the night then help myself to your sweet charms. I've had ample opportunity to do just that back in Glasgow." He paused seeing he held her attention. "Though…wouldn't mind a'tall if you snuck into my room."

"Jason!"

~ * ~

If she wasn't so taxed, Tessa might have laughed at his outrageous response along with the reddening of his cheeks. Embarrassment was not something she associated with Jason Kenworthy or his brother. He looked as if he'd been chastised by his mother. He understood what he did was suspicious. She didn't need to say a word. Though, from past experience with this man, he wasn't going to change his mind. Tessa was certain she didn't wish to sleep anywhere else except maybe in his bed. If he did come to her, she would need to say no. Still…the idea had merit. Lord Abernathy wouldn't want her if she wasn't a virgin. Who better to see to her deflowering than Jason, the man she loved?

"I've no intention of sneaking into your room tonight or any other," Tessa told him, even though she just had a few wayward thoughts about doing so.

"Darn." The red flush to his cheeks disappeared quicker than it arrived. His smile sent a heatwave of pleasure through her. "Hoped you would have been more obliging. A fellow can always dream of all the possibilities. Do you comprehend how much I want you? No, you can't know. I've been burning for you since that first kiss back in Ireland."

Tessa felt as if some of her options were being ripped from her.

She needed this man. Loved him with all her heart then more. Wanted to give him whatever he wished. The one good idea that Anice put into her and her sisters' heads was that a woman should never give herself to a man unless she was married to that man. The more time she spent with Jason the more difficult it became to stay away. If he kissed her again, held her in his arms, savored her as if he needed to devour her mouth, she would give in to his ploy. She would never be able to fight her raging hunger for him, the urgency he created. His eyes following her sent fire blazing from head to toe.

I told him no.

Maggie didn't heed her mother's dictates. Maggie was happily married with a baby. This was something she wanted with all her heart. Green with envy, she wished for what Maggie had. Was it so bad to let the man you love take you to his bed before you were married? While she used to agree with the words, she was no longer certain. Jason wanted her for his wife. He'd asked her twice. She told him no twice. What would she do the third time he asked? Would there even be a third time? He told her he was tired of rejection. Implied she might have to meet him half way. Tessa suspected he hoped she would give into him. Show him in some small way she wanted him. Sleeping with him might do that.

Unable to think with a clear head, she began, "I…" Tessa ran her tongue across her parched lips. She wasn't certain what to say to this charming man who all but put her in his bed when he gave her the adjoining room to his. This room was meant to be the wife's chamber. The husband would wish for easy access to his lady wife. Would believe it was his right to seek her out whenever he wished.

Turning away for a moment, he cleared his throat. When she encountered his face again, his brow was raised. "You want the bath, not the tour. I understand. Clancy is having the water heated as we speak. If I'm wrong, we can stroll through the house then the lawns outside." He walked to the sideboard in the room, pulled out a full bottle of sherry then a small crystal glass. He opened the bottle before splashing the sherry into the glass until the liquid reached the brim. After handing the glass to her, he set the bottle on a nearby table. "Enjoy. I'll bathe in the other room. Meet you for dinner. If you are amenable, we can take a walk through the gardens before you retire for the night."

Tessa nodded, hoping he would kiss her again. He seemed to have put anything but creature comforts for both of them from his head. She wanted to feel his lips on hers, the touch of his mouth against hers. The thought that for so many months he hadn't acted, was maddening. Without thought she brought a finger to her lips, saw the all-knowing masculine smile of satisfaction curve his mouth.

"Oh!"

"I would also enjoy a kiss after we've seen to our other needs. Is there anything else I can get you? Ring the bell cord if you wish for a servant. If you would like me, come into my room. I'll give you whatever you wish."

Dear God, he read my mind.

They were interrupted when Clancy directed the footmen into her room with her trunks. A maid followed. Tessa assumed she would unpack as well as help her from her gown. When she dressed this morning, she never thought about undressing without help. If not for the maid, Jason would have to unfasten all the little jet buttons that went down her spine. The thought caused a small shudder to ruffle through her. She imagined his knuckles sliding along the narrow expanse of her back.

Seemed the man was still reading her mind when he stated. "If you ask, I would unfasten every last one of those tiny, black buttons." His voice was husky as he murmured his intent, his eyes a dark brown shimmer of warmth.

Startled from her reverie, she jerked. *Dear God, he knows what I am thinking*. Discomfited by the thought, she started to speak. Licked her lips instead. Then, "I don't think…that wouldn't be appropriate." That was all she could think of as a rejection of his intent. Having him unfasten her gown was wicked. She was wrong-headed to even think something of that nature.

"Nothing about our relationship is going to be appropriate. We both understand that fact. Your sleeping in the adjoining chamber is far from suitable to two couples who are courting. However…as I said before, I want you close to me. Need to comprehend where you are if you are not with me." He watched her as she shifted from one foot to the other then played with her skirt. Never to admit to the fact, she couldn't help wishing for what he wanted. Her mother would be upset if she gave in to him.

To hell with mother!

What her sisters thought of her made a difference. Maggie gave into Jasper. She slept with him before the marriage. There were complaints at first. After the initial shock, they all accepted the fact. Understood there was a wealth of love between the couple. She loved Jason. He didn't feel the same about her.

Love is what counts. My love for the infuriating man will need to be enough.

On the other hand, Maggie thought she was married when she let him make love to her. I know we are not married. Therein lies the difference. He asked you. You refused. If you'd said yes, you would no longer debate with yourself. You would most likely be expecting yours and Jason's first child.

Tessa didn't believe she could take much more. She wanted her bath. Needed to close her eyes while she soaked up the soothing warmth. The hot bath would make her feel better. Might give her clarity where her thoughts wobbled between right versus wrong, the devil on her shoulder against the angel. Between nineteen years of believing one thing, then a few months of believing something else. Tessa needed space to make her thoughts coherent. When Jason was close, she couldn't think.

"I would like it if you left my room. I understand you are implacable so I won't argue the sleeping quarters. Will trust in your word as a gentleman that you won't take advantage of this situation." Tessa didn't know what else to say to the man who bedeviled her at every turn. If she were to be honest with herself, she would welcome Jason if he took advantage. She still warred with her feelings.

"As you wish," he spoke with a soft chuckle that served to stretch her nerves further. Seemed to understand her indecision. "I'll be bathing in the other room. Feel free to join me at any time. I would welcome the company."

At his words, Tessa felt prickling heat slide down her spine. Her hands trembled. She tried to imagine him naked. Couldn't. She'd never seen a man wearing nothing at all. His eyes twinkling with amusement, he sent his gaze to her eyes. What he saw, she didn't know. He might have been able to see how much she wanted him.

With a quick bow, he left the room. Closed the door with infinite slowness. Stretched her nerves to a point of snapping. She didn't know how she was going to combat the whims of her mother. Anice wanted her to find information that would harm either of the Kenworthy twins in exchange for her silence. She would never do that. She also gave mention to candidates for her father. The names were unfamiliar.

If she knew these two men better, she would tell Jason Anice's plans. On the other hand, the third man she was meant to harm wasn't known to her at all. He was a well-known judge in the city of Glasgow. This all happened over nineteen years ago. Would this judge be damaged by the information Anice held over her head? Did he even know he had a daughter by Anice? Would he care? Lots of men had bastards. Tessa didn't like thinking about herself as a bastard. Until it was pointed out at Maggie's wedding, none of them knew they were nameless…fatherless. Anice kept that secret carefully guarded.

She didn't know the answer to a single one of her questions. She needed to see Jason again. Wanted that walk in the garden. The idea of going to the gazebo sounded romantic to her. The place would be a chance for a kiss then maybe one after that.

Tessa hurried with her bath as best she could when the heat of the water surrounded her. For a few seconds she luxuriated in the steaming liquid. The maid who hung up all her clothing poured some of her scented oil into the water. Cupping water in her hands she allowed the liquid to glide over her shoulders then across the tops of her breasts.

She thought of Jason's lips touching hers. The last kiss was nicer than the first. Each time he took her into his arms then pressed his mouth on hers, the caress was longer, more arousing, more insistent. Richer. He touched her deep in her soul. Maggie told her once that Jasper slipped his tongue inside her mouth. Just the thought of Jason doing that sent a wave of hot fire from her head to her toes. Sent her heart bursting. How to tempt him was what eluded her.

She recalled the way she fit against his big body when he held her. How he felt. He was so hard. Hard everywhere except his mouth. His lips were the softest brush against hers when he caressed hers from one corner to the next. Nibbled. Her hand rose to touch her lips. At the memories, she felt as if tiny golden butterflies flitted within, warming all of her.

Shaking her head, perplexed by all her imaginings, she picked out a gown the maid didn't need to help her with. The heat of the day gave her reason to select something lightweight. The rounded scoop of the corsage would show off a modest portion of the tops of her breasts along with most of her shoulders. She finished with her hair along with a small dusting of makeup. Looked into the mirror to make certain all was the way she wished. With a deep breath, she set off.

In a hurry to see Jason, he told her he would meet her in the drawing room, she rushed out the door. Ran into the object of all her wayward thoughts. He caught her in his arms almost the instant she raced from her door. Warmth from his embrace flooded her. His light chuckle close to her ear stole some of the shock at finding herself held by him. Crushed against his hardness. His hands were placed at the small of her back holding her close.

"Oh…!" Surprise made her stiffen while she wanted to relax into him. When she tilted her head up, she gazed into the softness of his heated dark brown eyes. "I didn't know you were there. You…you surprised me. I'm sorry." For a second, she closed her eyes. "I should have paid closer attention as to where I was heading."

"Don't be sorry. I'm not. Glad to see you are in a hurry to meet me. Love holding you. Believed you would have taken longer to get yourself ready." Even though his hands remained on her, he gave her room to move away from him. "You look fetching. Love your gown. The color suits." His gaze slid to the tops of her breasts.

She felt the flush of embarrassment at the direction of his eyes. Where his focus settled, Jason didn't seem all that interested in the reddened tint. The thought he was staring at the tops of her breasts unnerved her. She tried to fight the fire that built the longer he looked. "I was…I am. N-need to see, well." Tessa brought her hand to rest against her chest. "W-where I'm going to be," she couldn't breathe. "L-living this summer. What…what about you?" She felt as if the gods stole her breath from her lungs. To top it all off, she babbled. "Did any of that make sense?

I'm sorry. It's just you surprised me." With considerable effort she calmed herself.

Breathe in breathe out. Breathe in...

"Shocking, yes," Smiling, appearing well-pleased, he offered his arm. "I planned to have a brandy while I waited for you. Unless you would like a drink, I'll begin the tour of the house. After that we can take a stroll outside. It's cooler now than an hour ago. The weather will be quite comfortable for a walk. The garden is shaded." He stopped midstride, "Would you be wanting to take along a shawl? Would not want you to get cold if we stay out later than the sun."

She wrapped her fingers around his elbow. "Tour first please. A shawl...I don't believe I'll be needing one." Her breathing was still erratic though growing more comfortable. With thanks to whomever, she was pleased the air was reaching her lungs. When she looked at his long slender fingers, the nails were clipped short. His face was clean shaven. Her strong-willed fingers wanted to caress the outline of his jaw. She looked down, hoping he didn't see the desire in her hungry eyes. Didn't wish to see his amusement when he figured out what she must be thinking but didn't know how to ask.

By the time he finished showing off the house, she found herself relaxing into his body. She leaned on him. Felt the warmth slide from him into her. Found she loved the texture of his husky laugh. How his lips twitched when he seemed amused at a reaction to words that were said. The way he moved with supple fluid grace. Nothing seemed to be an effort for him. His stride was long yet he tempered it to accommodate her needs. Jason kept the conversation light. Not once did he return to his curiosity about what her mother asked her to do for her.

Outside, the perfect temperature made the stroll comfortable. Since the time was nearing six o'clock, the sun's rays were not so intense as they would have been earlier. The heat from an overwarm day was tempered by a slight breeze shifting through the trees then shading the walk. The pathway they strolled on was lined with stones, flowering moss grew between the rocks. Delicate flowers were planted on either side. All the garden was well-tended. Soon the horizon would become ablaze with the colors of a sunset. Tessa loved to stare at the setting sun as the color finally faded into a velvet dark sky.

They stopped at a small pond with a fountain where water cascaded in silver braids to land on the rocks around the pool. Droplets from the spray rose within the vibrant sunlight to catch the dying rays of the sun. Tessa wanted to hold out her hands. Touch the silver liquid. Let the coolness caress her fingertips. Startled by their approach, a frog hopped into the water when they walked too close. Where the tiny animal landed, liquid spread across the pond in pulsating rings. Little animals skimmed across the surface as if they walked on water. High above in the trees, a bird called out its song. Bees buzzed around the flowers near the pond. She caught the perfume of jasmine in the late afternoon sun. Soaked in the pleasant aroma.

Content, Tessa leaned her head against Jason's arm. They stopped to enjoy the scenery. She didn't ever want to leave this idyllic scene. Breathing in she turned to him, "It's so beautiful, peaceful as well, wish we could have come to the country sooner. How can you ever leave this paradise?"

Jason set his hand on her shoulder then ran his finger across the expanse of her collarbone. His smile was one she would never forget. It seemed to light up his face. "I never grow tired of being here. All that keeps me in the city is business. If not for that, I would make my home here at the country estate. This is where my heart lies. While Jasper holds most of the responsibilities along with the major title, I must keep up my part. My twin must also enjoy some relaxing time with his wife." He pointed ahead. His breath hitched. "Look, we aren't at the gardens yet. We should keep going." He smoothed a strand of hair behind her ear. Gazed at her. She caught the hungry look of desire in the way his eyes smoldered, changed color while she tried to see into his mind. His voice was husky when he spoke. "I hope you will be pleased. I had Clancy leave a treat at the gazebo. Concerning this evening, I've a few plans of my own. Had all the cushions arranged for our enjoyment."

"What?" She tilted her head up to see him better. Wished she was taller. "What do you have planned? Tell me." Tessa didn't understand why she had to learn of his plans this instant. She would know soon enough.

His mischievous little boy smile spread across his face. At that instant, she understood he wasn't about to tell her. He meant to keep his secrets. He was playing with her emotions. Teasing her. Stubborn man. She could be surprised now as easily as in five minutes when they arrived. He didn't need to keep this secret.

"You must wait to find out what I've planned. You will need to be having a *wee* bit of patience." He held her hand close to his heart. "Can you do that?" He tapped her on the nose with his fingertip. It was enough for her to want more.

A kiss…a kiss is what I be needing.

Blast. Why was a kiss from him all she could think about, in her dreams as well as when she was awake? There were more things that should be on her mind. Such as just how she was going to go about getting out from beneath her mother's thumb. Defiance this time wouldn't work. "Why, when you could tell me now?" She decided not to pout but to allow him to have his way. He appeared as if he was enjoying himself, teasing her with some piece of information he held while she did not. Without experience to tell her how to proceed, she wondered if this was what all men did or just Jason.

"Want it to be a surprise. Though," he paused for a short breath of air, "I would be willing to guess you have figured out my *wee* surprise." He continued to walk as he wound his fingers through hers. He brought her hand to his mouth. Touched each knuckle with his lips then his tongue. He slid his teeth with a light caress across each one. The hot stroke glided from her fingers to the tips of her toes then back. Her breath caught with each tiny contact.

She shivered from the inside out. The golden butterflies within her danced a jig deep inside while the rest of her burned. He charmed. Seduced with ease. Knew what he was about. The act seemed to be natural to him. Tessa decided she was not about to guess what awaited them at the gazebo. She would have the patience he wished upon her.

"Alright then…if that's what you want. I won't ask again or beg."

"Good," was all he murmured.

The path they followed wound into the rose gardens where one could find all different colors of roses. She stopped to smell a few. The scent was warm and soft to her senses. The petals held droplets of water from a recent watering. She touched her cheek with a petal. Rubbed the velvet flower on her skin. Was surprised at the fragmented noise Jason made. Found that she also made a tiny broken sound of pleasure with the caress.

Jason touched her cheek with the back of one hand while he squeezed her other. Ran his fingers between hers. Before this, she never knew how sensitive her fingers were to the gentle slide of a man's caress while he held her hand. As if he couldn't resist or didn't wish to resist again, he brought her fingers to his mouth one more time. The tender skating of his tongue on her flesh surprised her with a soft gasp of shock. Still holding her hand within his, he focused on her over their merged hands.

"Do you like that?" he asked in the throaty voice that emanated from him every time he touched her. "I know I do. You're full of surprises, little one. What's the next surprise you have in store for me?"

"I don't know… Thought the surprise was yours." She licked her lips. The were so dry. Parched as was her throat. "I don't know what you mean?" Her voice was reduced to a thin whisper as he continued his assault on her fingers. He turned her hand over. Touched his mouth to her palm. Swept his tongue across her there. Slid his teeth over sensitive skin. She jerked then shuddered. The golden butterflies flitted as if they needed something more.

"You don't. Of course you have no idea. Should I teach you? We should get to the gazebo. The couch there will be comfortable. Are you still tired?" He wound his fingers through hers again before he started walking.

The sun descended farther, resting now just above the horizon, the heat of the day cooling even more than when they started from the house. They walked through a row of aspens, the leaves shimmering with silver on the underside as they caught what remained of the sun's light. The sunset tonight would host a myriad of colors. Birds flitted from branch to branch. A squirrel scurried up the trunk of one of the trees. A curious rabbit poked its head below a bush to see who invaded his space.

He pointed ahead. "Over there. That's where we are headed. We'll stay until you say you'd like to go back or it starts to get too dark. There are lanterns along the path that will be lit if we stay longer. Clancy has the order to light them if we've not returned before dusk. We could remain here until the moon rises and the stars shimmer in the night sky. Would you like to stay with me in this private heaven until then?"

"Y-yes…maybe." She didn't know how to answer. Truly didn't know what she wanted except to spend more time with him.

"Yes, and maybe?" He cast her a puzzled look. "Imagine that's better than maybe or no, even a resounding no."

Her breath caught when she saw the gazebo shaded by massive oak trees. Jasmine as well as honeysuckle wound around lattices. The scent was heavenly. During a few shattering seconds, she held her breath deep while absorbing the ambiance of the scene in front of her. Their branches hung over and across the top of the white structure. The lattice work held up the roof. Inside was a couch along with a couple of chairs. Colorful pillows had been placed on the pieces of furniture. On a small table a bottle of wine sat along with a tray with various food.

Tessa turned to look at him, her eyes dazzled by the sight of the small structure. "It's beautiful. You went to a lot of trouble for me. Why?" Tessa wanted to clap her hands together with delight but didn't want to remove her hand from the warmth of his. She needed an answer to her question.

"Why?" he asked with a bit of amusement laced in his tone. "I would like to please you. Thought this small gesture might do that."

"It does please me. I…" She set her hand on his chest. Felt the solid thump of his heart against her palm. The same one he kissed only a moment ago with tenderness.

"Are you thirsty? Hungry? Clancy left the food for us. Shall we see what there is? I would pour you a glass of wine. Feed you if you like. You can bite my fingers." He stepped forward, tugging on her hand. In his eagerness to reach his goal, his steps were too fast for her shorter legs. With both hands she clung to him as she tried to keep up with his pace. When she stumbled, he caught her. Brought her up against him.

"I…" When she once more looked into his warm brown eyes, all Tessa could think about was the possibility of a stolen kiss in the sultry heat of this night then another one after that. Just thoughts of his kisses caused heat to coil then spiral some more. Her breath hitched in the back of her throat. “I would like that…” She wished for whatever he hoped to give by setting up this private retreat in the garden.

Jason brushed his mouth on one corner of hers before travelling across her mouth, one tiny caress at a time. He entwined his fingers between hers. Brought them around behind her. She found herself pressed against him as his mouth tasted her lips. Savored the bottom then the top. Nibbled with fevered intent. Explored back and forth with tenderness with what felt like longing. His tongue ventured across the full bottom lip rubbing again then another time. As she received the first taste of him in such a long time, her body shivered with the flames of desire. The velvet glide of his investigation heated her. A shattered sound escaped the back of her throat. Needing something more, she pressed closer to him. Heard the rasping of his breath. Captured the spicey scent of Jason mingled with what seemed special to Jason. This was the only way he’d ever kissed her. Just his lips on hers. Sometimes the sweep of his moist tongue wetted her lips, creating a hungry desire that pulsed deep within her body. From what Maggie told her there would be more intimacy between them if that was what Jason wanted. Intimacy was what she wished for. The increased familiarity was also a question she didn’t know how to ask for.

“Wine?” he asked as he lifted his head, touched her mouth with the tip of his finger. The hungry flames from his eyes met hers. Devoured her senses from the top of her head to the tips of her toes.

Dazed from the slow reverence he paid her mouth, she wasn’t certain what to say. “D-dizzy…” What he did made her head stumble. She found herself wrapped within his steadying arms. Held tight.

“Dizzy? I won’t let you fall, little one,” he murmured, while he whispered the words next to her ear, touched the lobe with the tip of his tongue swirled within. Bit with gentle precision. “I’ve got you…now and always if that’s what you want.” Jason brought her hands around then up to circle his neck. Her breasts molded against the hard frame of his chest. His hands pressed against the curves of her hips. Then around to mold her bottom so her belly settled between his legs. A hard ridge touched her softness.

She whimpered.

He kissed her again, touched her mouth with his, traced her lips with the humid heat of his tongue, gliding, sliding, torturing increasing the enchantment he created within. One more time, his tongue travelled across her mouth again then again while she thought if he let her go, she would end up in a heap at his feet. With his teeth he tugged on her lip. Pulled again until they parted for him to taste in a more familiar and deeper way. Stretched the bottom until she felt the velvet glide of his tongue on the inside of her mouth then across her tongue. A small whimper flamed from her core to escape into his mouth. Swallowing the evocative sound, he delved inside, deeper then deeper still. Touched with confidence into the sultry dark part of her that he'd never known before. She tasted sweet mint.

The rumble of his masculine groan startled her. Shook her to wonder if somehow, she hurt him. He moved his tongue in then out then slid inside again and again. His hands tightened on her bottom. Once more, she felt a hard ridge of male flesh against her belly, solid and long. Wondered. Questioned what the firmness meant.

The continued assault on her mouth brought another broken sound of feminine pleasure from the back of her throat. She ached. Burned for him, for something. She was unaware of what that was. Just understood she needed more of what he was doing. More soft caresses. More touches that would enflame her. The tips of her breasts ached where they settled against his chest. Despite his size and strength, he was gentle. His caresses upon her were evocative as well as sensual. What he was doing left her weak in the knees, trembling.

Tessa's fingers skated through the length of his dark hair. Nails scraped across flesh. The silken texture surprised her, brought pleasure to her. When the humid touch of his mouth descended lower, she tilted her head back, somehow understanding that was what he wanted. His mouth journeyed down her neck. Laved with his tongue at the base where she knew her blood pounded hard and fast. With unconscious need she gave him more of herself.

"That's right, little one. Open yourself to me. Let your head fall back so I can learn more about you. Promise, I won't hurt you." He paused; his voice thick and deep as he set his forehead against hers. "Perhaps we should slow this dance of ours down. Do you want some of that wine now?

Believe we should…" he didn't finish.

His throaty question shocked her. She didn't wish to stop or slow down anything. Not even a fraction. The voice she heard didn't sound like his. Jason's eyes simmered, shot starving, hungry waves in her direction. Burned her from the inside out. She recognized the mercuric hunger. The desperate need to give as well as receive. She needed more of him not less. Didn't want him to stop the sweet kisses that weakened all of her.

"Alright…" Tessa didn't know any other way to answer. She would be too embarrassed to tell him what she wanted was for him to keep kissing her. Too shy to say what she wished, she agreed with him. "Wine would be nice." She swallowed, realizing she might need some liquid relief. "My throat is parched."

Not as nice as the kisses we were sharing. Want to understand why you stopped.

Jason touched his lips to her forehead. Then held her away from him. Tense lines radiated around his eyes as well as his mouth. "We…should have some wine. Don't want Clancy to feel as if his efforts were for naught. Take pleasure in the food he delivered to us." Jason pulled away from the sensual clarity of their kiss. He retreated from her, handing her no reason why.

Tessa touched her lips. They were swollen. She ran her tongue between them, wishing his lips were there instead. He did that to her by putting his mouth on hers. "Wine?" she asked her voice weak, dazed as well as disoriented from the sweet sampling of his kisses. Still clinging to him because she felt certain her legs would give way if she let go, she responded again. "Wine…yes…I suppose so." Tessa wanted to taste Jason again not the sweet Bordeaux. His taste was more potent than the wine, more addictive. "If that's what you want."

He unwrapped her hands from behind his neck "It's necessary."

"I don't know why."

Jason held her hands once more behind her back. "After we drink a bit of wine then indulge our palates in whatever delights Clancy has brought for us, we can…" Jason left the last part dangling as if he wished for her to guess at his intentions. He walked her to the long couch that would fit three people comfortably.

How did she tell him this wasn't what she wanted? "Jason?" she questioned. "What's wrong? Did I do something I shouldn't have?"

His smile failed to reach his eyes as he pinched the bridge of his nose. "Tessa, sit, please. I'll serve you. Relax. there is plenty of time…for other things. No, you did nothing wrong." He turned from her as if they hadn't just been sharing something so very intimate between them.

With the crystal wine glasses filled, he brought her one then joined her on the sofa. He sat close. His leg touched hers. The movement made her skirts rustle. She felt his heat through the layers of fabric. Heard the ragged breath of air she sucked into her lungs. Even with the smallest of contact, blood surged with violent speed. When she lifted the glass of wine her hands trembled.

"Let's see what we have to eat. Shall we?" His voice, rough around the edges, he cleared his throat. Jason uncovered the first tray to reveal an assortment of meats and cheeses. There were several types of bread that were cut into small squares. Another tray held an assortment of seasonal fruit as well as a few vegetables.

He picked up a bright red strawberry. "Hungry?" he questioned as he ran the fruit across her mouth just as he'd let his tongue roam before he stopped without a reason.

She looked at him with wide questioning eyes but found nothing to say.

"Bite."

"Hmm…" The beat of her heart stopped for an instant before pounding again.

Jason ate the part she left behind. "Good." He filled her plate with the collection of the food Clancy set out. She sipped the wine while she watched and tried to think of something witty to say. She could think of nothing humorous or otherwise. The taste of the wine was sweet. She didn't care about the food. She needed Jason. His taste was sweeter than the strawberry or the wine he would insist they eat and drink.

Her plate overflowed when he set it in front of her. Her eyes widened as she looked from the plate to him in silent question.

"I'm sharing with you. Do you mind?"

"No. I don't mind." Tessa was shaking her head. They ate in silence that was far from comfortable.

The wine in her glass vanished. The food on the plate did the same. He poured more wine before he sat back, the stem of his glass resting on the hardened plane of his stomach. Between the two, silence thickened. Seemed to go on forever. She didn't like the sensations emanating from Jason. His light smile of a few moments before vanished. His lips thinned in a way that seemed this upcoming conversation was meant to be serious. She didn't want to be confronted with her mother again. Didn't want to feel the tug of disloyalty. When she thought about all she didn't tell him, she cringed.

"Tessa, I want you to marry me." He stopped her reply with a finger to her lips. Touched with gentleness. "I don't want an answer right now. Need for you to listen. Hear me out. Can you do that? Listen and nothing more? I'll give you all the time you need to figure this out. I understand you are young. Maybe you want to know more men before you commit to me. I have given you a year to sort out your life along with what you want from it. If need be, I'll wait longer though I won't be pleased." Jason sounded hesitant, unsure as to whether she would agree or not. He removed his finger from her mouth. She slipped her tongue across the spot where she felt the pressure.

With a nod to her head, she spoke, "I can listen. That's a characteristic of mine I've always exceeded at. I listen very well. Form my opinions from facts." If he asked, got down on one knee, she might be receptive to his proposition. If she agreed, would marriage truly take her out from under her mother's thumb as he told her earlier? Tessa didn't think it would. Her mother had a tight hold on her.

"Good." He cupped her face with his hands. They were warm hands. Strong hands. Potent in their ability to draw forth pleasure. Tessa didn't believe he was a man who could inflict pain. Though he was capable. "I need for you to listen. Understand I just mentioned that fact. Hearing all that I tell you is important."

Every gesture reassured her strained nerves. She needed to give him what he asked for. If she said yes, he would make love to her. While she didn't know with exactness what that entailed, she did understand she wanted the familiarity she knew could only be found with Jason. No other man would do. She should tell him she didn't need time to see if she wanted someone else. She didn't. She loved Jason. Would always love the man. To Tessa, now that she felt the deep intimacy of his kisses along with the tender caring, she would share whatever he asked, whenever he asked. In her mind, there was no reason to wait until the vows would be said. She would go the same route as Maggie.

"We are meant for each other." The sound of his deep rich voice vibrated in the stillness of the night.

She nodded again. "Maybe." While she agreed with all he said, she decided he might need to work harder to convince her his way was right.

He cleared his throat with an arched eyebrow following. "Maybe? While I never expected to marry for a few more years, my gut tells me it's time. All my instincts are yelling at me that you are the right woman for me. I've never been attracted so fast and so hard to a woman. When I see you, I burn for you. On fire to have you in every way possible. Want everything a man and woman can share together." Still holding her head between his hands, he brushed a soft kiss on her mouth. "The sight of your lips moist from my mouth, distracts me. Have trouble thinking. Need to have a clear head when I set forth the details of this proposal." He let go of her only to turn her so her back was against a pillow behind her. He was above her, his hands holding hers on either side of her head.

"I don't know…" She felt breathless. He was so close. Touchable. He held her hands, stopping her.

"Hush, you are the woman I want to spend the rest of my life with. No other. Just as Jasper understood Maggie was the woman for him when she entered into his life, I also knew I would have no need of looking farther. I want you." Jason's breathing turned ragged. "Need you more than my next breath. Don't want to wait another year or even another month. We need to settle this before I take something from you that you're not ready to give."

Tessa watched him swallow. Felt the weight of his body settle on top of hers. "I want you too," she murmured, turning her head to the side so he wouldn't see the gathering of moisture in her eyes. Tessa didn't know if she could tell him yes to the marriage. Now that she decided she wanted him, Tessa could tell him yes to anything else he asked of her.

"…then…" the pause, after that a sigh that sounded a bit like exasperation, echoed from his mouth to wrap itself around all her insecurities. "Say yes, Tessa. Tell me you will marry me. Give us what we both want. We can plan the wedding any way you like. We can wait the three weeks for the reading of the banns or go to the small church that is not too far from here. It's where Gracie got married. Everything will be the way you want it to be. Don't believe I can wait longer than the necessary three weeks. Would rather wed you tomorrow."

When she spoke, her voice wobbled with uncertainty. She had not expected this tonight. Expected more questions pertaining to her mother's quest. "I need to think." Just because he wanted her didn't mean he loved her. Tessa didn't know if she could settle for something that was so one sided. Knew she'd never marry another man. Never allow another man to kiss her the way Jason did. With that affection she gave him all her heart as well as her soul. Who could love more than one man in one's lifetime?

"Very well. If time is what you need, I can give you some. Not a lot, mind you. Nonetheless, tonight I plan on doing a bit of convincing. I've waited long enough for more than a kiss or two. Perhaps I should proceed in the manner of my twin. If you are with child, would you give me a different answer?"

With child? Panic then longing swept through her with blinding speed. She felt as if she was hit by a bolt of lightning.

"With child?" she questioned back at him, felt her body vibrating with subjects she had no answer to. "I don't understand what you mean." She did comprehend. That was what Jasper did with Maggie even though she believed herself to be married to him when it happened. If getting with child involved kissing, Tessa didn't believe she would mind too much. She knew they would need to share a bed for a child to be put in her womb. Understood, Anice protected…sheltered all her girls. Told them as little as possible about what was expected in a marriage. While she should understand how it was done, she did not.

"If you say no again, I'm going to make love to you until you change your answer to the response I'm hoping to hear. If you say yes, we'll proceed the way you wish. I won't touch you until the wedding night just as I *ken* you wish." He was still on top of her, holding his body apart just the tiniest bit with his forearms. Stroking her cheek, he had the look of a man well pleased with his endeavors.

She hissed in air, angry with his words. “You won’t kiss me again until the wedding night if I say yes?” She did need to know the answer. Hoped to learn if anything came after the kisses. Felt certain at this point he would teach her. Her patience was running thin. “If I reject your proposal, you’ll kiss me more?” She brightened at the idea. Didn’t want to give up kissing. “I’d like that.”

The soft curse he muttered under his breath surprised her. “I don’t like the way your mind travels. You are not going to bend me. Yes or no, Tessa, tell me. After that we’ll proceed in the manner best for both of us.”

More confused than ever, she brushed the tips of her fingers across the hard plane of his jaw. “I offended you? Sorry. Didn’t mean to. I don’t wish for you to ever stop kissing me.” She paused while she thought. Ran her finger down the thick column of his throat. Saw the hard pounding of his pulse at the base. Caressed him there. Understood he was affected by her touch. “I’m confused.”

“Tell me yes.”

“If I do, according to what you just said you won’t kiss me again. Won’t kiss until I comply with whatever you ask. That’s not what I want. So…if I tell you no, you will continue kissing me?” She beamed at him, satisfied now with her answer.

He groaned low and deep in the back of his throat. His mouth framed hers. Took as much of her as he could within the shelter of his lips.

~ * ~

Anice paced the large bedchamber in her townhouse. Stopped at a window to stare out to the streets below. There was little traffic in this part of town. One loan carriage rumbled past. A dog trotted across her yard into the neighbors. Lights from the lanterns along the street were lit, giving an eerie glow to the evening. There were no people about though the weather was nice for a stroll with a lover.

Tonight, so far, she was alone with her thoughts. She missed the lively chatter of her daughters. It had been a year since they left her to live with the Kenworthys. Even though it was a rare event for her to find herself included, she would sometimes listen to them. The other night Tessa's face had been as pale as a ghost when she left her childhood home. She'd been afraid. Anice didn't trust Tessa to do her bidding. She needed to think of a means to threaten her sisters. The girls always came together when either of them was at risk. The sisters were the reason Maggie had been able to escape the ball where Lord Abernathy announced his intentions.

Blackmailing her with threats that would reveal the name of her father might not work. Her father was above gossip and rumors. The man would most likely be pleased to discover he had a daughter. Not if he told Jason Kenworthy any of the details of their long-ago relationship. She'd not planned on another pregnancy. The babe in her womb came as a complete surprise. She'd been told she would be unable to conceive a fourth time so she took no precautions. Trust the man to go to the source if he discovered what she told Tessa. The man was a wildcard in her endeavor. Afraid she'd lost the battle before the war could begin. If all was lost with Tessa, she had two more daughters. There must be a way to bring the girls to heel.

From their reputation for honesty, Anice understood both Kenworthy men dealt with truths not gossip. They were straightforward men. Doubt if they could be blackmailed. If Jason learned what she held over Tessa's head, he would never be swayed to comply to her wishes. Would never give her a dime. Neither would the judge or his twin. She needed to look to a new father for Tessa. Anice felt certain, she made her wants clear to Tessa. Told her what would happen if she didn't follow her directives. Complete silence on Tessa's part was necessary in order for her strategy to proceed the way she planned.

Tessa had always been weak…weak until a year ago. The youngest of her daughters found her backbone. Despite the fact Tessa's new found courage played havoc with her plans, there was part of her that was proud of her daughter.

"I should never have played those cards," Anice murmured to herself. For the last year with no one in the home to talk to, she fell back on talking to herself. "I should have waited for something better to come along. I won't ever win this hand. The people involved are too confident, too above themselves to cower to blackmail, too honest. Tessa doesn't know that. Therein lies my power. All I need to do now is to figure out who to accuse." She felt doom settling around her. Just as she had when she learned of Maggie's escape from the ball. Just as she had felt when Maggie wrote her to tell her she was marrying the man who helped her when all should have been lost.

Neither the judge or his twin will ever be blackmailed. When confronted, he would laugh in her face. *If I were to send a note to his house telling him about his daughter, he would be in the blue drawing room demanding answers. He would be furious with me for never telling him about Tessa.* The man she was accusing wasn't a judge when Tessa was conceived or when she was born. He was a well-established lawyer. A lonely man. Anice filled one of his needs after his wife died and before he remarried. She might have been the second wife except she made a grave mistake in marrying a man who liked men better than women. At the time, she'd also been lonely. The man who sired her first three daughters passed on. Died at sea when his vessel went down in a hurricane.

Tessa's father is now one of the most powerful men in Glasgow. No, in all of Scotland. He would never understand the lie. She never lied to him. She just withheld essential facts. The information she kept from him. Didn't wish for any of her daughters to be labeled bastards though all four were exactly that…bastards. When he asked through a missive if she was pregnant a few months after their yearlong affair, she never responded to his question. He would remember that. He came to her after he heard she conceived. She denied him. Told him he wasn't the father. He accepted her word.

Foolish, naïve man.

"Damn…I've got to go through with this. Need to see what I've started to the very end. I've too much at stake if this fails. I lost out when Maggie married Jasper. If this doesn't pan out for me, I will…"

It has to work. She fisted her hands, determined to follow through with this ill-conceived plan of hers. Desperate, she needed the money.

The knock on her bedroom door surprised her. "What?" she opened the door. "What do you want?"

"You've someone downstairs waiting to see you. A couple of someones. Told them you didn't wish to see anyone tonight. They wouldn't take no for an answer."

"I do?" She smoothed her skirts before looking in the mirror at her appearance. "Who?"

"Your oldest daughter along with her husband."

~ * ~

"Don't think we should go see your mother," Jasper told Maggie while he lay back on the big bed they shared, his hands behind his head. "Seeing her will only serve to stir up a hornet's nest of trouble. You've been stung too many times by your backstabbing mother."

Maggie set her hands on Jasper's chest while she placed her chin on top. Stared into the flecked golden-brown eyes she adored. "Tessa's in trouble. We need to discover what has happened. I saw her before she left with Jason for the country estate. She looked awful but wouldn't say a word as to the why of it."

"What type of trouble? Believe Jason is capable of handling any difficulties that might arise between Tessa and Anice. You…we don't need to interfere."

"I don't know. Yes." She rolled over onto her back, staring at the ceiling. "Yes, Jason is capable. It's just that mother is full of tricks along with lies. Tessa is too trusting."

Jasper sat up. Touched the hardened crown of her breast. Ran his palm across the crest. Smiled when he saw her shuddering reaction. "You wish to go see your mother. It's too late tonight. Got other things planned for the rest of the evening." His tongue curled around a nipple. He tested the tip with the rake of his teeth.

Despite the surge of pleasure he orchestrated, Maggie wasn't about to give up on this quest. She had to talk to her mother. Look in her eyes when they questioned her. She had a good idea blackmail was involved. Needed Jasper to be with her. "We have to, if only to appease my curiosity. Mother might let something…a piece of the puzzle…slip."

Bending closer to Maggie, he pulled the crest into his mouth, sucked until she arched beneath him. The hot wet suck of his mouth sidetracked her. She whimpered. "Not fair to distract me this way. Yes…we need to visit her. You have to come with me. Can't go alone."

He lifted his head, "Whatever you want. You're right. I will never allow you to visit your mother by yourself," he spoke with a soft voice before turning more attention to the other breast. Wrapped his tongue around the hardened crown. "I'm not excited about seeing your mother again. It's been more than a year since we saw her at the church. That episode left much to be desired. Tomorrow, when I'm through with the few business meetings I've scheduled, we'll arrive unannounced. Won't give her time to plot strategy. Who do you think she's blackmailing?"

"Thank you. Besides Tessa? I don't know." Maggie too had fears about seeing her mother. She understood she was safe with Jasper beside her. Was certain at this point Lord Abernathy would want nothing to do with her. Couldn't be positive. She was no longer wife material. There were other ways to use a woman. Lord Nelson Abernathy knew all of them.

What she didn't know was how Anice was able to persuade Tessa to visit. The note must have been compelling. Tessa's curiosity often got the best of her. Of all the sisters, Tessa liked their mother the least. Anice always treated Tessa with more disdain than the other sisters.

The next day, Maggie waited expectantly for Jasper to get home. He was later than usual which annoyed her. While she waited, she spent time staring out the front windows to the driveway then beyond. She'd hoped her husband would make certain they were able to visit at a reasonable hour. As it turned out, the time was after eight o'clock before they could leave. It was likely her mother would be out.

When he arrived home, he pulled her into his arms for a deep hard kiss then, "Sorry I am late. Are you ready? Let's get this over with. When we're finished with your mother, I'll take you out to dinner. Wherever you would like to go."

Now, they sat in the drawing room of her childhood home waiting for the butler to deliver his message to Anice. They were told she didn't want to see anyone. Anice would see them. They wouldn't leave until she waltzed down the stairs to make an appearance. For the third time in the last half hour, Maggie had misgivings about being in her mother's home. As Jasper told her, they should have left well enough alone. Should have waited until they could speak with Tessa. That might have been a few weeks from now. Jasper told her he wouldn't be able to get away from his duties anytime soon. Maggie heard the click of her mother's heels before she entered.

"Are you here for a particular reason? Last time we parted, the two of you weren't fond of me. I'd know if you have some nefarious plan that concerns my well-being."

Maggie let out an unladylike snort. Jasper grinned at her. She shot a quick scowl his way. Knew he'd almost let go with a crack of laughter. Anice would have been displeased with the noise if she'd heard.

"Mother, you are the one who hatches reprehensible plans. I recall what you tried to do to me. Marry me off to a man who I despised. What are your plans for Tessa? You are scheming. We all understand what you are about. She is with Jason. Soon to be wed." Maggie didn't know if that was true or not. It was worth the shot to see her mother blanche.

"Well, get to the point. What is it that you want from me?" She motioned for her butler to come into the room with the tray he held. She poured them each a glass of wine. Offered little lavender cakes which they both refused.

"Why did you bring Tessa here?" Maggie asked. She wasn't certain she should drink the wine, afraid it was tainted in some way. After Anice poured all the glasses from the same bottle then sipped hers, Maggie figured she was safe.

"I invited her to come see me. Tessa came here of her own volition. She could have refused the request to visit. Chose not to do so. We had a nice time. Talked about the past. She never mentioned anything about marriage." Anice inspected the red burgundy in her glass, sniffed.

"That statement didn't answer my question."

"Why I asked her here is between my youngest and myself. The reason is not your concern. Now…if that's all you came for, I suggest you leave. It's late. I'm tired. Don't wish for company. If you'd been anyone else, I would not have made an appearance."

"You're expecting someone. A lover?" Maggie asked with a snide emphasis Jasper didn't ignore.

Another hoot of laughter from her husband told her that gesture might not have been prudent even though it could be true.

"Again…none of your business. I've divorced your father. So, I'm free to see anyone I choose. Could have obtained an annulment but after all these years I chose to forego anything that would take too long. A divorce was quicker."

"That man was not my father in any way. We both know that for the truth. You might have given birth to me but you were no more a mother to me than he was a father." Her indignation was obvious. Maggie stood, smoothing her skirts. "If you have nothing further to say…"

"We can leave anytime. Whenever you're ready," Jasper muttered while he also stood, waiting for what Maggie might choose to offer. "Just as I suspected."

"You told me this would be a waste of time."

"Yes…should I accept your apology?"

"No, just all my gratitude that you allowed me to see for myself. You could have refused to accompany me."

"Not on your life."

Chapter Three

Good God, Tessa used his words against him. He would need to emphasize what he meant by his ultimatum. Did she have any idea what he intended? She was too naïve, too innocent by far to understand, he meant to make love to her. Keep her in his bed until she either said yes or she conceived and was forced to agree to his proposal. She didn't blanch at his words. Instead, she embraced them.

Tessa wanted his kisses. The admission sent his body into flames. She was a hot fire burning in his soul, scorching him without even knowing. He didn't know how to combat the raging passion along with the urgency she created by her hesitation each time he did something different or more outrageous. Without knowing she was doing it, Tessa was managing to wrap him around her little finger. He needed to focus on his plans. The thought of letting her have her way both aroused and confounded him.

He needed to see her wearing nothing at all. Suck the crowns of her breast deep inside his mouth. Savor the sweetness that was Tessa. Make her so wet the moisture would soak her pantalets. The small whimper of pleasure would send heat waves burning him from the top of his head to the tips of his toes, searing every part of him that lay in between. The hunger she created with a soft sigh or the touch of her lips against his was more than he'd ever encountered. She'd become a raging fire in his soul. Never before this woman had he been aroused so fast and so hard.

Being straightforward was the only way to deal with this bit of rebelliousness, not to mention her convoluted thinking. "You want to be in my bed before we are married?" he asked while he tried to decipher what she knew from what she didn't. The feeling she understood nothing was the most prevalent of all his thoughts. He would see just how far she would let him go before she put a stop to this amorous adventure.

"Yes, if you'll keep kissing me. Your kisses leave me breathless. They make me ache in places I've never thought about before. While I don't understand them, I love the sensations. Teach me more."

Ache…yes that happened to him too. Burning, throbbing ache rushed through all of him until all he wanted was to bury his swollen member in the sultry heat of her body. "Oh, I intend to do just that. You need to know that if you are in my bed we'll be doing far more than kissing. Though there are many places I'd like to kiss you that I haven't sampled yet."

"What?" Her eyes were deep, dark pools of puzzled blue. She bit down on her lower lip, seeming to concentrate.

"I'll show you." He closed his lips over hers. Swept his tongue across the small space between top and bottom. Pushed inside trailing his tongue across her teeth then deeper into the humid recess of her mouth, exploring the satin interior. He touched tender sensual places inside. Thrust deeper then withdrew to do the act time and again. He nibbled on her bottom lip. Sucked the tender flesh.

He held her hands in his, not trusting himself if she touched him. After she mimicked him, caressed his tongue with hers, he let her hands go to cup her face between his. He sucked, danced, played with her while he fought the inferno rising within. With his teeth he made gentle bites along her neck, stopping where her blood pounded in a heated rush against his mouth.

With veiled thoughts, he ran his hands along her shoulders. The soft flesh responded with a warm shiver of appreciation. His hunger for the small delicate girl who didn't understand what she asked for raged hotter than anything he'd encountered. Lightning struck. Sent bolts of pure pleasure into him. Jason knew he was in too deep to claw his way out. She wanted his kisses. He needed a hell of a lot more than mouth against mouth. Tongue rubbing against tongue. She didn't understand what she did to him. He needed to temper the seduction so he wouldn't frighten her. Didn't stand a chance in hell. With nibbles meant to entice further, he made his way across her collarbone to the silken shoulders that were creamy. Unable to resist her sensual lure, needing to see more of her, he pushed on the fragile sleeves holding her dress and hiding her feminine secrets.

He licked, touched upon her sensitive skin. She arched against him. He placed wet heated kisses across the tops of her breasts. Nibbled on sensitive flesh he'd never touched before. With her freed hands, she wove her fingers into his hair then lower to press against his chest. As her sleeves moved down her arms, he rose above her. With wide sapphire blue eyes, she looked at him. Her mouth was damp from the kiss she wanted so badly she was willing to give up a belief that must have been engrained into her thoughts since birth.

Jason didn't object to seducing her before the marriage. What he did object to was the fact she might regret his actions. He would get all he wanted. In this he was ruthless, not caring if the child arrived early. Tessa played with his emotions far too long. For more than a year, he'd been a patient man. Soon she would need to make a decision. He would see to that tonight. Tessa might make the choice for him. He could live with that.

"Little one, you can say no anytime." Jason understood he was close to that point where it would be a devil of a hard time stopping if she asked it of him.

Her answer was to arch against him, thrusting her hips to meet his. Against the hard line of his sex, he felt the softness push against him. The second answer was the tiny whimper when his teeth raked with delicate precision along her bared shoulder. With slowness he needed to savor, her sleeves moved downward to her elbows. Each patch of bared skin that was revealed, he tasted.

Jason waited with baited breath for the unveiling of Tessa. Soon her breasts would be for him to see. He'd teach her kisses on the hard crowns were more delightful than the caress of his mouth with hers. They would thrust upward with rose colored tips begging for his undivided attention. His blood raced, pounding in his ears with a desperate need to take all she was willing to give. Tension ripped through his body while he held back. Forced himself to be slow.

"Do you want me to look at you, Tessa. In a moment, your breasts will be mine to see. Yes, I'll keep kissing you. There are many places to kiss. We've explored one or two. If you tell me yes, I plan on giving your breasts their fair share of consideration. I will draw you into my mouth.

Bite with gentleness. Nibble then lave with my tongue. The velvet-texture of your nipples will give me great pleasure. You too. I promise. Is that what you would like?"

"I do… I want…" her hungry moan of concession both pleased as well as worried. "Jason… I don't want you to stop."

He didn't want her to regret anything they did here in the gazebo beneath the moonlight. Ah hell… "No regrets." Giving her more opportunities to tell him no was on his mind.

"Please…" she murmured, her voice a ragged line of passion in the wavering shadows.

One more nudge to the sleeves. Her freed breasts were bathed in soft light from the moon. He passed his palm across one hard bud then the other. With his touch, the pair moved with delicacy. The twin globes were fragile. They would need to be seen to with gentleness. The taste would be evocative, redolent of woman. Seeing all of her would be heaven to the hard pulsing of his sex pressed tight against his pants. One taste of her mouth brought him to the edge. Looking at her might send him past the turning point. He didn't wish to frighten her by spilling his seed too soon.

Tessa clung to his shoulders. Her fingers tightened as if he just became her lifeline. Passion within her small frame flared to life with each new sensation. All this was new to her. When his mouth captured one taught nipple, she jerked. Cried out. Her hands tightened more. Her hips lurched up to meet his enflamed member. Tessa didn't know what she was doing. Her body understood what she wanted, all she needed.

"Easy honey. I'm not going to hurt you. I know you don't understand. Relax. Let me give you pleasure." He moistened the hard crest with the hot, wet suck of his mouth. Her body arched against him. She pressed her hips against his sex. If he didn't focus, she could have him spending himself before she was ready. If she insisted on this course, he would bury himself deep inside the sultry heat of her passage.

When he rose one more time to study her, Tessa's eyes were closed, her lips parted. He watched the uneven breaths she was trying to inhale. Knew she was feeling the rise of her first passion. Hunger within her flared to life, hot and fast. While he understood from the past, she thought this should be left for the wedding night. Maybe he was taking his actions too far. He was still in control of himself. While his body longed for her in too many different ways to count, he wasn't an untried youth with his first female.

"Jason…" she moaned softly as his teeth raked across each nipple again then again. Her hands rose to his nape, fingers wound into his hair. She pressed her breast against his mouth, unconsciously begging for more.

With a heavy sigh of frustration, he pulled the sleeves of her dress back to her shoulders. He made his decision. One he knew all along could never be changed. He would wait. How long, he wasn't certain. For this evening though, Tessa would remain a virgin. "Not tonight, honey. Not tonight. If we went further, I would have regrets as would you. Between us, I don't wish for misgivings." After her look of confusion, he went on to say, "This isn't easy for me either."

Wishing she wasn't a virgin wanting to have a real wedding night, Jason stood. Tried to tamp down the fierce heat enveloping his body. Requit the fire she orchestrated with such ease. A few deep breaths of air helped control his urge to start this again. To kiss her again. Slide into the warmth of her willing body. He spilled wine into their glasses. When he handed her the drink, the look she presented him was one of bewilderment. Disillusionment. She looked as if he hurt her.

I did hurt her. Beast that I am. I could not control my raging feelings.

"Why? I didn't say no. I told you yes." Her unsteady voice tore at his heart. She raised her trembling hand before letting it drop back to her lap.

This was what he wanted. To give her pleasure, to watch her eyes glaze over with the melting of her body over his. To feel all her beautiful curves pressed against him would be heaven. Tessa would never tell him no. What was going to happen between them was his to compose. He understood waiting would be the most judicial thing to do. Hard when her eyes begged him to make love to her.

He let out a half-sigh then shot her a tender half-smile. The answer was formed before he could give thought to more words that would wound her pride. "You're not ready for more. You're not… Hell! To me, you're more than a quick romp on the couch in the gazebo. You mean more to me than that." Jason understood he was brusque. His voice sounded abrasive to his ears. His fingers tightened around the stem of his glass threatening the fragility. Stopping was up to him. Under the circumstances, ceasing was the only thing he could do. To disappoint her would be to disappoint himself.

"When?" she asked, her voice wavering on the single word as she came out of the silken fog of raw hunger that swirled around her. "When will you make love to me? You say I'm not ready. How do you *ken* something like that?" She was interrogating him, asking questions he could deal with.

"You'll be ready after we are married. Not a moment before." His words came out of his mouth with a pompous air that he didn't like. He wasn't pretentious. If he didn't believe having her now without benefit of vows was all wrong for her, he'd take her without a complaint. She meant more to him. His life…that was what she meant to him. Her lips thinned while her brows drew together. Obvious she didn't appreciate his mandate. Didn't matter. This evening, he wasn't going to allow her to distract him further.

In addition to the scowl, she sat up straight, pointing her chin into the air. Beneath the silken gown the tips of her breasts pushed out. She tugged in a deep breath of air which gave more attention to her breasts. "I am ready now. Told you there would be no regrets on my part. Are you afraid? I would understand if you are afraid of making love. I am…a little." Her face turned a rose shade to match any sunset. "I realize you've done it before but…"

A hoot of laughter filled the tiny space where they sat. He decided the best he could do was to take a short walk. He needed a *wee* bit of time as well as distance from this beguiling woman who meant so very much to him. Getting his thoughts under control would be prudent. For a few seconds he stared down the walkway toward the estate home. Several long deep breaths helped him decide what to tell her.

Jason walked back to the gazebo and to Tessa. Sitting on the couch bathed in the moonlight she was beautiful. Her hair flowed around her shoulders as if the silken strands held a life all their own. The urge to run his fingers through her hair flashed through him. While his body burned for Tessa, telling her no was more difficult than he ever thought possible.

A small sip of wine helped him clear his throat. Swallowing the liquid gave him another second of thought. How Tessa would take his comment wasn't clear in his head. He spoke with a slow measured voice, gauging her expression. "The moment I break through virgin territory you will have regrets. In Ireland you took a patch out of Jasper's hide when you discovered he made love to Maggie before the vows were said. I know you wouldn't want anything different for yourself. Would you?"

"I haven't said I would marry you." The pique in her voice didn't surprise him. Neither did the underlying anger resonating from each carefully placed word. He aroused a passionate woman who was left without her pleasure.

"True, but you will. The only question is when." Jason held every confidence she would say yes some time. When was the only salient factor. "I would hope sooner than later. I'm eager to start our lives together."

"You are rushing to conclusions. You've no idea what I do or do not want." Her breath caught on the words she was hurrying to say to him.

"By letting me touch you like I just did, that yes was enough for me. You're a passionate woman, Tessa MacRae, soon to be Tessa Kenworthy. I would give you the pleasure you seek but only in the marriage bed. If you want me the way you just showed me, you will say yes to my proposal. We can plan the wedding now, while we finish our wine along with food Clancy delivered here." Inside he smiled. Her look of chagrin followed. She mulled over his words. Didn't intend to show this lovely young woman that he knew he won this game she played with him.

"Pleasure?" she questioned. "What you did was nice. Better than nice. Is there more? Would you keep that from me just because I *dinna* say no to you? You're not acting as a gentleman should act."

His chuckle stopped her speech. He found she was grasping at whatever floated through her lovely head. Tessa was used to getting her way. In this scenario, she wouldn't. "I'll have the banns read this Sunday at church unless you wish to marry me tomorrow. Personally, tomorrow would be my preference."

"Why would I want to do that?" Her voice tight, she turned her stiff back to him. The line of her shoulders was rigid.

When she turned away from him, he didn't appreciate the gesture. Jason couldn't help wondering what she was thinking. By the tiny little cries of pleasure she made when he caressed her, the wispy feminine sounds told him she was aroused. The crowns of her breasts hardened with his first touch, peaked, grew as he tested their velvet crests with his mouth. He'd never tasted a woman more passionate than Tessa. Never savored one so sweet. She was fire in his blood. Waiting for three weeks would be difficult.

"Because you want to know what comes next." He swirled the burgundy in the glass. The colors played against the light bathing them. "You will have all the truths you seek on your wedding night. Not one moment before. Say yes and you might learn the truths you search for as soon as tomorrow."

"I don't know anything." She stiffened further while she made her denial. "What I do understand is that something was missing. Want you to show me." She paused. "Well, if you won't show me, I'll…"

"Do what?" he asked, his voice far too harsh under these circumstances. Wondering what new plot was hatching in her fertile little mind. "Do what, Tessa?"

"I don't need you. Don't need anything you wish…don't want your kisses…" She drew in another long drink of air.

"Little liar. You know you do want more. You are still hot. Hungry for more pleasure. There is moisture on your mouth left there from my kisses. Do your breasts tingle? Do you want me to suck them into my mouth again? Did you like those kisses as much as the ones on your mouth? If I chose, I could give you a woman's pleasure right now. I'm not choosing to do so."

"I didn't tell you to stop." Her indignation was another small pleasure for him. "Didn't like it when you did…woman's pleasure? Is that what this is all about? Are you telling me there is more pleasure? Not certain that's possible."

"Good thing I have a bit of restraint."

A man needs control when he's faced with a woman who burns for his touch. Tessa did burn. She flowed over him with liquid heat flamed higher by each caress. He wanted to touch the softest part of her. Needed to see if her honey rained down on him from her secret depths and darkest mysteries. Everything about this woman enchanted him. She created a burning fire in his blood.

The look in her eyes told him she once more mulled over his words. She sipped her wine. Tilted her head a bit sideways. She blurted. "Did you make love to me? Is that what this is all about? You think that if you tell me we've already done…I don't regret anything. If you wish, you can do so again."

Her curiosity seemed to grow more with each passing second. How to answer was the problem. "Yes and no." Jason figured that would get a rise from her. He needed to keep her on edge, keep her guessing as to the culmination of what they were doing on the couch.

"What is that supposed to mean?" She tossed out the question looking as if she would rather toss her wine at him. "Yes and no. Either you were or you weren't."

"It's not that simple," he told her with a bland voice.

"Of course it is."

"I was preparing you for my entry. That was easy. You were on fire, passionate, responsive to all that I did. When I set my hand on the hardened crown of your breast, thought you would tell me, no. Slap my face. There was no protest, just the sweet sound of a woman's surrender. You arched into me seeking me along with all I can provide for you." Finding out what she did as well as what she didn't know about making love seemed to be appropriate. He guessed she knew next to nothing. Understood even less.

"For what?" That was asked with more hesitation, more wobble to her voice until she picked up speed. "What were you getting me ready to do? I would know the truth."

"I do believe the conversation has gone as far as it should for now, for a virgin's ears. Tomorrow, I would like us to take a journey to that small white church we passed on our way here. I'm certain Clancy would be a witness for us. We could wed at that time; only then will I elaborate on making love. Believe you've learned enough for this evening. We should—" He was interrupted before he could finish his thoughts.

"You think so!" Tessa downed the contents of her glass then stuck her arm out asking for another glass. Her anger was palpable. There wasn't one thing he could do to help her tamp that fury down.

Except make love to her.

"Are you hoping that if you are tipsy, you won't still…" After she pushed back the hair that had come undone while he was kissing her, Jason lost the direction of his thoughts. Her breasts danced with the motion. The jiggle was adorable. Her lips begged for him when she swept her tongue across them.

"I do want you. Need another glass of wine, after that another one. The wine will help me relax. Won't get married without my sisters as witnesses. Since none of them are here, we will not go to the church tomorrow."

"So…that's a yes to marriage." The statement wasn't a question. Even though she answered in the negative to his wish for the wedding to happen in less that twenty-four hours, she did say yes to his less than romantic proposal. He would need to go to the village to buy her a ring. They could do that together sometime next week.

I'm an engaged man. Maybe I'm jumping to the wrong conclusion.

He wasn't quite certain why he was so thrilled by the prospect of tying the knot. He'd not expected to marry for a few more years. Tessa changed that notion.

The look on her face told Jason he rushed to his conclusion. "It's a no to tomorrow. Haven't said yes to anytime in the future. Don't know if I will." Tessa rearranged her skirts, lifting then smoothing the fabric. Every time the skirt rose, he caught glimpses of well-turned ankle.

"Yes…Tessa…say yes. You know you want to marry me. You might want your sisters at our wedding, then again you might not. Do you remember Maggie's wedding. Your father, who is not your father, tried to kill Jasper. Your mother was also a thorn to deal with. Do you want to go through with that again? A private ceremony is all we need." Jason lobbied for a small church wedding. Just the two of them, then Clancy as a third person. There would be no threats of personal harm as with Maggie's ceremony. She held out to get her family to Ireland. Both Maggie along with Jasper wished they'd done it different.

"Not until you're more convincing that marriage is something I would wish for." She paused for a while, looking out into the growing darkness. With a jerk she turned back to ask Jason, "Did I conceive? You said you would make love to me until I was pregnant. Did that happen just now? Is that why you stopped? There was no need to go farther?" The seriousness to her tone was a shock.

Wine spewed from Jason's mouth at her demands. *Oh my God.* The question was nothing he could have ever anticipated. Tessa was far more naïve than he thought. Anice withheld far more information about sex from her daughters than any mother should. No wonder Jasper found it so easy to take Maggie to bed. The girl had no idea what was happening to her. Just as Tessa melted in his arms, Maggie must have done the same with Jasper.

The answer 'no' was on his lips along with his thoughts. He should tell her the truth. Give her a *wee* bit of education about sexual pleasures this evening. Something she could understand. After that first thought, he let all the good intentions slide through his head. He answered the only way he could. Deadpan, he told her, "You might be. One can't tell right away."

Even in the shadowed night he saw the flush of color come to life on her cheeks as well as the tops of her breasts. Tender breasts that he wanted to savor again. He regretted his answer as soon as it passed from his lips. Couldn't call the words back.

"How will…when will I know? I don't want to be pregnant. Not yet, not until I'm married. I haven't decided…" Her wide sapphires eyes told him how confused as well as torn she was. He was stupid, an idiot. A man should never tell the woman he loved such nonsense when he knew it to be untrue.

Here was another topic her mother should have enlightened her daughters about. If he answered truthfully, she would turn a deeper, darker shade of red. Embarrassing Tessa further was not his intention. This wasn't his place to inform her about her sexuality though sooner or later he would need to do so. Jason opted for later. Trying for nonchalance he didn't feel, he lifted his shoulders. "You will know when you will know." He berated himself for his shallowness. Held within him no intention of distressing her more this evening.

He needed to tell her he lied.

Her eyes flared. Her voice challenged. She was no longer mortified. “What the hell does that mean?” Anger from her pointed words slashed him to the bone. Ripped into him. She repeated his response. “You will know when you will know. That answer doesn’t tell me anything.” She pointed a long slender finger at him. Shaking, “Since you would be the father, don’t you think you should be more exact in the explaining?”

Combining indifference with his inborn need to protect himself, he once more lifted his shoulders in a shrug that would serve to infuriate her further. “How should I know? I’m a man. Can’t get pregnant. Isn’t that a woman’s job to know all the necessary details? Your mother should have explained things like that to you.” He could kick himself. God above, he didn’t believe for a moment it was his job to teach her about things she should know. He’d tell her to ask Maggie but she wasn’t here. Might not be for several weeks. Also, he needed for her to continue to believe they’d made love. If she didn’t say yes soon, making love would happen. Getting pregnant would follow. How did he get himself into this position? He wasn’t at most times a dunderhead.

The time had come to retreat then lick his battle wounds. The conversation was going way beyond his meager abilities to control. He needed to find some topic that would not embarrass both of them. “Come, we should go back to the house.” He held out his hand, hoping she would take it. She folded both hands in her lap then peered at him beneath dark lashes.

“No, we haven’t finished our wine or the conversation. You need to answer my questions. When will I know if I’m pregnant?” she asked again. Her mouth set in that firm thin line that told Jason she wasn’t going to give up on this topic.

“We have finished. There is nothing left to tell or explain. We are going.” He wished he could send for her mother to do the explaining. That wasn’t possible. Nor was doing so prudent. He didn’t wish Tessa’s mother anywhere near her. Raked his brain for someone else who could answer what she wished to know. Thought for a moment he could send for Gracie. She would be a good woman to sit down with Tessa to explain the facts she’d never been told about love as well as how a woman could become pregnant.

"No!" Seemed she was holding firm on her stubbornness. "No, Jason, I'm not going anywhere until we settle this to my satisfaction."

"What do you want? What is going to result in your satisfaction?" Rubbing the back of his neck he searched for the right words. He had no idea what those words might be.

"Answers. Don't you think I deserve a few answers. You did make love to me. You said I might have conceived. You…said it was possible. I'm not certain how. Don't feel any different." The firm stubborn voice that started with that last 'no,' faded. "I don't have anyone else to turn to. Can't you…"

"Yes. You deserve a response. Yes, you're right on all counts." He wasn't the person to explain. Heat climbed his cheeks. He needed to tell her the truth. Didn't wish to backpedal too far. Appeared he put his foot in his mouth when he blurted a response that was far from accurate. At first, his intention was to tease. Joking with her about something serious concerning both of them backfired. Failed because she understood nothing about what went on between a man and a woman.

"Then…" She tapped her fingers on the pillow she was holding in front of her as if it was a shield. "What are you waiting for? An engraved invitation?" she asked with too much sarcasm for Jason.

He stripped his fingers through his hair, all the while wondering how the devil asking her to marry him turned into this fiasco. If he hadn't lied to her in the beginning, they would not be having this conversation. Going back on what he told her at this point was not an option he could consider.

"I'm tired. Don't wish to talk tonight. How about tomorrow morning after we've both slept on your questions as well as mine?" That was the truth. Talking to Tessa exhausted him. They should be planning their wedding. He would find the village priest or minister, whichever ruled over the church nearby. Tessa deserved a wedding…a real wedding just as Maggie had, despite his concerns. While he didn't wish to wait three more damn weeks for Tessa's happiness, he would. Knew the mother would show up if she got wind of the event. He didn't want to see her mother. For Tessa's sake, he would survive Anice.

"Well, I wouldn't be able to sleep. Too much on my mind." The back of her hand rose to brush moisture from her cheek. Silver streaks slid downward from her eyes. This wasn't tolerable. All over the fact she couldn't be teased about something she had no knowledge of.

"You're not crying. Don't tell me you're…" Damn, he made her cry. In all his life, he couldn't think of another time where he made a woman cry. This was the woman he loved. With his callous disregard for her well-being, he was the catalyst that hurt her. Hell, he should have made love to her!

I made her cry. I should kick myself. Unfeeling bastard!

"I'm not crying."

Jason sat down beside her. When he tried to pull her into his arms for comfort, Tessa scooted away from him. Setting his hand on her back, he told himself he deserved the rejection. If he explained anything now, he would dig a hole so deep he might not be able to climb out. His impulsiveness got him into trouble. Jasper, the solid, competent twin would have never blurted something so untrue to the woman he loved.

While Jasper wasn't perfect, his twin wasn't stupid either. He was both stupid as well as imperfect.

"Little one, don't cry. I'll talk to you. Tell you all you ask. Though I'm not comfortable with the words you need to hear. This was something your mother should have spoken of to you. I'll do my best but I'm just a man. Imperfect. Flawed." Decided he shouldn't go on berating himself.

She brushed more tears from her eyes. "You don't have to say anything. I understand you're uncomfortable. That's okay. I'll ask Maggie next time I see her."

That was a relief. He didn't know where to start except with the truth which would be his undoing. He wanted to be married before she discovered his lie. The marriage had to be consummated too. Didn't want to leave anything concerning their future to chance.

"Are you certain? You might not be pregnant." He now compounded his lie with reinforcement of the same damn words that got him into trouble the first time. His mind so rattled, he didn't know how to proceed. Thought maybe he could make this a bit better. "Just kissing…" yes. "…just kissing doesn't always make a girl enceinte." He was on a roll. Perhaps this new avenue of thought would be a success. Reassuring her the situation might not be quite so dire as she might think. "Just kissing sometimes is just that…kissing. Nothing more. You might not have conceived. There are lots of different kinds of kissing," he finished, believing that was a good way to end.

She turned to face him. Her beautiful sapphire eyes filled with moisture. "I don't understand. What do you mean?"

Neither did he. The hole deepened. Grew darker as well as thicker. Saving himself was out of sight. "What part? What did I say that is confusing? Would you like another glass of wine? I'll pour." Maybe if she finished the bottle, she would forget the questions plaguing him.

Tessa turned to face him. He pulled her into his arms. She buried her face against his chest. He heard the short, ragged breaths, a sniff here and there. He stroked the silken length of her hair falling through the sensitive insides of his fingers.

When she pushed away from him then turned her face up, the silver glide of tears stained her face. "I'm sorry. Tell me what you don't understand."

"Everything. How does kissing get a person pregnant? I wouldn't think… I don't know. Mother told us the stork brought us. That's not true. I learned that when Maggie was pregnant. I think they did more than kiss. So…" She lifted her tiny shoulders as if giving up on the idea he might tell her what she asked.

That was a legitimate question. Yes, they did more than kiss. For this evening, he needed to skirt the edges of her questions. "Sometimes that's all it takes. One kiss leads to another then another… then more…so many kisses…so many places that can be kissed in different ways." He didn't know what to say after that part which was true. So much kissing could lead to more serious lovemaking. The type that could get a man in trouble if he didn't want to sire a bastard.

"Oh, are you certain?"

"Yes," he told her. "Now, did that help? We can finish the wine. Clancy will send servants to retrieve whatever we've left behind."

"No, not much. I don't want to be pregnant before…"

A lurch took hold of his stomach. Maybe she didn't like kids.

Blurting the words, afraid of her answer, "Do you want children?" While unlike Jasper, he didn't need an heir, he did want children. He loved children. Babies were adorable. He didn't even mind changing their diapers. Would adore a little girl who looked just like Tessa. If they had a little girl, she wouldn't be so inexperienced and fact starved about men and women she didn't know anything about anything. He would make certain this imagined daughter of his was well-informed. His daughter would know everything about sex as well as sexual encounters with the male species. She would hold the upper hand.

"Oh, yes, of course I do want to have a few children. It's just that…"

"It's just that…what?"

"I don't want to have a baby before I'm married. Don't wish to have conceived this evening," she murmured, as if she was thinking over all the facts that were brought up tonight.

"Neither do I," he told her while he ran his hand up then down her back. "Neither do I. We should do something about that if you want to kiss some more. Maybe tomorrow night. What do you think?"

"Yes… I'm saying yes to your proposal. I want to kiss. Want to conceive. All of those things." Her words were swift. Breathless. Even a bit erratic.

Thank God.

Capturing her mouth in his, he kissed her hard and deep. Backed away. Smiled. He was pleased. They were getting married. He could withhold more sexual information until it was necessary to explain things with more exactness. Once they were intimate, explanations might not be so difficult for him. By doing things, she would understand more.

"Do you want a wedding in three weeks or tomorrow?" He imagined he might be pushing too far and way too fast. Needed an answer so he could see to the details. The sooner they were wed, the sooner he would be able to tell her about his lie.

"Don't wish for my mother to attend. If we wait, she will learn the truth. Who knows what she will do at the wedding. Something to embarrass us both. Tomorrow. If that's too soon, the next day would work. Don't you wish for your brother to attend?"

"We'll have a huge celebration. Whatever you wish for. He and Maggie will come to the event. Your other sisters too. We'll have the cake along with flowers and… And what else does one have at weddings?" Perplexed was how he felt. "We can invite the nearby village. Tomorrow. Want the wedding to be tomorrow. Before we go to the church, we'll stop at the jewelry store. I'll buy you a ring. Sapphire, I think, to match the color of your eyes. What do you say?"

"You've quite stolen my breath."

~ * ~

"Mine too." He laughed then pulled her close for another kiss; one that lasted longer than the last one. Was deeper and more intense as well.

"Jason…?" Tessa felt as if her world tilted in the right direction. On his shoulders, her fingers tightened. Moved higher until they sifted through his dark hair. She pressed herself closer to him. Felt the hardness of his chest. She'd wanted him for over a year now. He told her they made love. From all that Maggie said which was, she was certain, abbreviated in some way, Tessa didn't think what they did was the same as what Maggie and Jasper did. They were in a bed. Did a bed make a difference?

"What? Are you half as pleased as I am?" he asked, grinning as if he was the happiest man alive. "For me, tomorrow won't come soon enough."

Tessa understood Jason brought her out here for this purpose. Brought her to a private setting to seduce. To get her to agree to a wedding. She didn't think she would have said yes when all this started.

"I don't know." There were still no words of love exchanged. Amorous words would make this so much better. She'd always thought to marry for love. "Yes, I'm pleased…" Understood she was far too hesitant.

"You will be. I promise." Jason wrapped his arm around her. "We should return before Clancy comes looking for us."

Appalled at the thought of what the stately butler would do, she turned to Jason. "He would come out here to look for us? What if he did and he…he saw me with my…" Tessa swallowed hard at the thought of what might have been seen.

"Clancy wasn't here. If he came for some reason, he would have made so much racquet we would have heard him from the moment he left the house. No worries that he saw you half-naked. I was the only one." Jason laughed outright at her concerns. Pulled her close to his big hard body.

Tessa wished she could have seen Jason bared to the waist. He was so big, so much man. "Doesn't seem fair you saw me almost naked. I… You… Want to see you…"

"I'm pleased if what I'm thinking is true. You wish to see me naked? That can be arranged soon as we are man and wife." His smile was broad. In the dim light of the lanterns along the walkway his teeth showed very white.

"Yes…" Mortified at her brazen words, she looked down at the stones. Murmuring, "Is that bad of me?"

"No…you should want to see your husband without clothes. Just as I wish to see you, all of you, wearing nothing a'tall. If we can wed tomorrow, so be it." His fingers played with loose tendrils of her hair.

When she looked into his eyes, they were almost black in the darkness of the night. "What are you thinking?"

"That you should get to bed. You need to be rested for tomorrow evening. Plan to keep you up all night."

After they reached the house, Jason left her at the door to her bedroom with a long, deep kiss that left her breathless, hungry for what she knew was missing. There was more to this than kisses. After he lifted his lips from her, she asked. "What are you doing tomorrow? What if the minister is busy? What will we do?"

With a gentle tap on her nose, he smiled. "If not tomorrow, then the next day. We will set up an appointment with the man. Will that suffice?"

"On such short notice, he might not want to perform a ceremony. Now that we've come to an agreement, I want you to become my husband." Tessa found herself thinking about the night. His kisses. The different ways he told her she would be kissed. How he would look wearing nothing at all. She wanted to see him…all of him. To see the differences between them. He would be hot, hard.

"I will. Soon. This man is looking forward to tomorrow. Now, it's time you got to bed. It's going to be a long day for us. I'll see the minister first thing in the morning. You can stay in bed until you wish to rise. Figure out what you'd like to wear. Something…your best ball gown might be appropriate for a wedding. I don't know."

"I'll think about it. Maybe what I wore at Maggie's wedding." She thought that one would be nice. It was special.

"No!" Jason didn't hesitate. "You need to wear something that will tell all of your innocence. Do you have anything white?"

At her look of chagrin, he shook his head.

"I'll think about it. White isn't a popular color for a ballgown. Maybe a light blue."

"Would enhance the color of your eyes."

After she stepped inside then heard the tread of his steps down the long hall to his room, she leaned against the door. Her eyes fluttered. She tried to calm her racing heart. Attempted long slow breaths of air into then out of her lungs. Her body hummed with life. Excitement leapt. Tomorrow, Jason would be hers. He was everything she ever wished for in a husband, a lover. He said he made love to her.

Thinking about the evening to come, I don't know how I'm ever going to find sleep.

Tessa's sleep was broken, sporadic. Most of the evening she stared out the window. The brilliant light from the moon cast dancing beams into her room. She woke with the first rays of the sun slanting through the open curtains of her window. Dust motes floated where they caught the light. Fascinated, she watched the ever-changing patterns. Closed her eyes again. Understood it was far too early for her to rise. She should try to sleep some more. Jason did tell her it would be a long day. An even longer night.

Another hour or two must have passed. The gentle knock on the door brought her dreaming back to reality. This was her wedding day. She had no idea what gown to choose. Told Jason she would think on the subject. He wished for white. This was special. Imagining why Maggie had the devil's own time when it came to the wedding. The gown was important. She wouldn't have a wedding gown. Changing her mind now…no, she didn't dare tell Jason she would like to have a real gown for this special day. She remembered what happened to Maggie's wedding.

"Yes?" Tessa answered the second round of knocking. Was it the third? She was in such a dream world she couldn't tell.

"Can I come in?"

"Megan?"

Her maid opened the door. "Yes, it's me. He believed you'd be awake. Lord Kenworthy thought you might like some hot chocolate along with a croissant for breakfast. I also added strawberries in a puddle of cream."

"Yes, thank you. After that I'd like a hot bath. You can help me choose a gown. With luck, seems I'm getting married today." Her stomach was all a jitter. Was turning somersaults. "Is it normal to be nervous?" Tessa held out her shaking hand. "I don't know why. It's what I want. Jason is the most perfect man."

"Oh, yes, Miss Tessa. All brides are nervous on their wedding day. It's such a big day and all. Why does no one know? Shouldn't everyone be here? His brother? Your sisters? I don't understand," she asked as she began to sort through Tessa's wardrobe. "Do you have a best dress. Something like a ballgown? Do you have white? A bride needs to wear white on her wedding day."

She had several ballgowns. Didn't wish to wear the gown the one she wore at Maggie's wedding. Jason was negative about color. Some of what kept her awake last night was thinking about her wardrobe. Tried to decide what might be appropriate. "Find the ivory silk. It's simple but beautiful." She wore that one at the last ball she and Jason attended. He might remember the gown. Maggie always told her men didn't pay attention to that sort of thing.

Jason didn't dance with her that night. He stood with his hands clasped behind his back rocking on his heels, staring at her dance partners. Scowling would be a better description. Now that she recalled the look in his eyes, she couldn't help giggling. He didn't like her dancing with anyone but him. Nonetheless, he never asked for a dance. She would have given him all her dances if he appeared the least bit interested.

"What is it?"

"Nothing, truly. I was recalling the last time I wore that particular gown." Tessa stopped talking for a moment while she thought about the day he spoke of last night. "Jason wants to go into the village before we go to the church. Could you wrap the ivory, silk gown in tissue for me. I'll wear something else while we…he's going to buy me a ring. Imagine that's important to do before a wedding."

"Why yes, Miss Tessa. A ring is essential for a marriage." The maid went about wrapping the gown then searched for another dress for her to wear to the village then on to the church. "Neither of you have family here. Who's going to stand up for you?" Megan asked as she went about her duties.

"Believe Clancy will do the honors. Would you like to come with us? I would be pleased if you would be a witness. Be my maid of honor." Tessa liked her little adorable maid. The girl wasn't very old. Maybe eighteen or so. That wasn't much younger than she was. She was eighteen when she met Jason. "Do you have a beau?" That wasn't her business. She was curious. Megan could always tell her she overstepped with the question.

Megan clapped her hands together. The smile on her face lit up the room. "I was hoping you would ask me to be there. Clancy and I can come together. Just let me know what time. Should I look for another gown for you to wear into the village? I've got just one in mind that will be beautiful."

Tessa's nerves seemed to disappear as Megan flitted from one thing to another. Seemed to ignore her question, "Which one was that? I've also one in mind."

"Oh, I wouldn't wish to pick out the wrong gown," Megan told her as she stopped flitting through her gowns. She looked up. "No, I don't have a beau. However…" she paused for a few seconds, "there is a boy who works for the village blacksmith. He's ever so handsome. So big. The muscles…his arms…" Megan lifted her shoulder with a disappointed shrug. "Doesn't notice me."

"Smile at him. You have the most beautiful smile; he'll have to notice you."

"You think so?"

"Yes. Tell me," Tessa smiled at the girl, "which one do you think would be best?"

"The blue one, here," Megan held it up. Shook it so the fabric fell in delicate folds. "It matches the color of your eyes. Lord Kenworthy will see how beautiful you are. He won't be able to stop looking at you. What do you think?"

Tessa stole a deep breath of air. "I hope so. It's also one of the ones I had in mind."

"Oh, he must already think you are the most beautiful woman around. Why else would he wish to marry with you?" Tessa hung the gown up.

The next few minutes were taken over with an entourage of servants bringing hot water into the bathing chamber for her bath. Megan directed the servants. Lavender oil was poured into the bath. Tessa knotted her hair above her head then slid into the heated water.

"I'll wash your hair for you if you like?"

"I don't know. It takes so long to dry. Don't know if I've enough time." Tessa drank the chocolate Megan set out for her before taking a bite of the croissant. They both were delicious. "Yes…" she made the decision. "This is my wedding day. Unconventional wedding, though I wish everything to be perfect. Jason said we can have a big party after my sisters all get here. My hair should smell like lavender."

"None of my business but I was wondering why you didn't wait for them. Plan a big wedding with your family. That's what I would want. I've three brothers along with two sisters. None would be happy with me if they weren't there on my special day."

"No, you're right. It isn't your business." Tessa stopped for a few seconds seeing the look of distress on Megan's small face. She continued over the ensuing apology by her maid. She put her hands in the air to stop the words. "Why, is no secret to my family. Maggie's wedding was a disaster from the beginning to the end. Jason and I decided we didn't want a duplicate. Everyone will understand. Jasper wanted the same as Jason. A quick wedding. In the end, he gave into Maggie's wishes. They needed to wait the three weeks necessary to have everyone there." Tessa found herself shaking her head. "I'm not going to risk a repeat of Maggie's wedding. Jason is in agreement."

"I'm so sorry. I never knew. Certain the two of you are doing what works for you. If not, I wouldn't have the chance to stand up for you."

By the time she was bathed and dressed, Tessa was feeling more stable. Her nerves weren't stretched so thin. Megan had a way of dissolving her fears into nothing. When she held out her hand her fingers were no longer shaking so bad.

Megan stood back; her hands clasped beneath her chin in silent approval. "You are beautiful. Should I go find Lord Kenworthy? Tell him you are ready for him?"

"No, I'll go down myself. He is probably in his office or the library. Imagine he is just waiting for me." Tessa found herself eager to see her groom. Tradition said she shouldn't see him the day of the wedding until she walked down the aisle to him. Balderdash. That was just a bunch of superstitious nonsense.

"Alright then. If that's what you wish. I'll find Clancy. He'll know when we are to leave so we can meet you at the church."

"Yes. Clancy will know. Thank you, Megan. Wear your best dress." Tessa found herself humming as she skipped down the stairs looking for Jason. She poked her head into the drawing room then the library. After that she headed for his office. Seemed he always had work to finish.

He works too much.

Maybe once we're married, he'll play more. Have more fun.

The door was open. She stood framed by it while she watched his dark head bowed over pages which he appeared to study. When he looked up, her heart stopped for a few seconds. His smile made his dark brown eyes shimmer. He was so handsome dressed in a frock coat and white silk shirt. His cravat was tied in intricate folds. His shoulders were so broad. Hips narrow. Legs long as well as muscled. Heat flooded her face when she thought of seeing him naked.

Tonight.

"You're beautiful, Tessa. Are you ready? I am. Just been waiting for you to appear." Jason moved around the desk to meet her. A large smile on his face, he held out his hands. She placed hers on top of his. Felt the warmth seep into her. Saw the male hunger in his eyes as the dark brown color deepened.

Jason must be thinking about tonight too. He told me he was hungry for me. Just thinking about his kisses makes my heart run hot.

"Not as beautiful as you," Tessa murmured, her voice didn't sound the way it should. Deep, husky, she thought she would jump from her skin as his thumbs brushed the undersides of her wrists. "I…" she stopped wondering at Jason's laughing expression.

Jason hooted, his lips twitching with amusement. "Appreciate the sentiment. Men aren't beautiful. You do understand. We're big and hairy all over." Now, he ran his thumbs along the tops of her hands. "You are though. I've missed you this morning. I take it you slept well last night? I wanted to look in on you."

With his words, Tessa felt the rush of heat to her cheeks. With vivid clarity she recalled last night, the way he held her in his arms. The weight of his big body pressed against her while he kissed her. "Handsome then," she amended, while she brought her lips tight. "The sight of you makes my breath catch in the back of my throat. As to sleep, it was elusive. I kept thinking about today then tonight. I worried about not pleasing you."

"Not much sleep for me either. Thought about you for most of the hours I lay abed. I should be saying those very things to you. Looking at you does the same to me. Fire races in me. Hungry for your heat. Urgent to learn about all of you. Don't worry about pleasing this man. You always make me happy." He coughed. "Shall we go? Clancy will meet us at the church in two hours. That should give us enough time to find a suitable ring for you."

"I," nervous, she moistened her lips. "I asked Megan if she would stand up for me. Is that alright with you? She was ever so eager. I wanted someone I knew to be with me at the church. She is not a sister but she is sweet and a girl. Megan will help me dress at the church."

"Megan?" A dark eyebrow rose. "Who is Megan?"

Her laughter bubbled up in a fanciful rush. She didn't understand why. His perplexed expression delighted her. "My maid. Don't you remember? You hired her. She is very young. Sweet though. She was excited about the wedding. Thought it would be nice to have two people there for us instead of one."

"Of course, whatever makes you happy. You can ask anyone you wish. Don't need my permission. If you wish, we could include all the servants." He brought her hand to his elbow to usher from the room then into the waiting carriage.

"Don't want all the servants. Clancy along with Megan are enough."

They reached the village then strolled through the shops. People greeted them, seeming pleased to see Lord Kenworthy though most didn't know if he was the older or the younger twin. Didn't seem to matter. Tessa didn't know what he had in mind. Jason didn't seem to be in a hurry. If they had two hours before they were expected at the church, she assumed there was a great deal of time to waste.

"It's supposed to be bad luck for the groom to see the bride before the wedding. What do you think?" He'd stopped, pulled her so close she felt the heat from his body. She realized his hand was just below her breast. A sip of air caught in her throat. The moment vanished when his hand slid to curl around her waist. Tessa wanted to yell at him to behave himself. Everyone in town would be watching them.

The day of their marriage they could be seen by the entire village strolling arm in arm. He sounded so worried, she had to laugh. "I imagine it's nonsense. Two people make their own luck. Don't you think? Besides, you're not seeing me in my dress. That will be a surprise." She stopped, struck by something that hit her hard. "I don't have anyone to give me away. Who will do the honors? Even if he could be here, I wouldn't want the man who brought me up thinking he was my father to stand by my side at my wedding. He tried to kill Jasper. Might try the same with you."

"If he were here, we would never ask him." Jason tapped his chin for a moment as he appeared to be thinking. "Maybe Clancy can do both jobs. Seems he's more family than not. Though he is no father figure." Jason patted her hand as if to reassure. "We'll think of someone. I'm certain of that."

"No, it's fine. I'll walk down the aisle by myself. Clancy doesn't feel like a father to me. Though he is a nice man. I'd rather be by myself than pretend something that isn't true." She wondered what a father would feel like. She didn't have one. Never had. What was a real father like? How did he act?

With an unexpected motion, Jason stopped to face her. He set a finger beneath her chin, lifting. "I will be a good father to our children. On that front, you have nothing to worry about. I promise. I will always be faithful. Loyal beyond your wildest imagination."

Seemed he read her mind. How did he know she needed that kind of reassurance? Tessa moistened her dry lips all the while looking into the deep brown of his sincere eyes. She nodded. "I *ken* that. Never doubted your abilities. Just don't know what that would be. Do you?"

"I've a very good idea how to be a good father. My father was the best of men. He was a good role model for my brother and me. A father…well…is a man who loves his children to begin with. A man who will take care of them above his needs as a second. There is so much, Tessa. I promise you that you will have a good life with me. I understand your concerns." He traced the line of her jaw with the tip of his finger. "I know you're worried. Don't be."

"Will hold you to that promise." Felt the smile of longing form on her lips. She wished he'd kiss her right here in front of everyone in the village. He wouldn't do that knowing, despite her longing, she would be embarrassed.

He cleared his throat. Tapped her chin. "Shall we pick out that ring now? We've a wedding to attend." Jason looked at his pocket watch, before he spoke, "In about one hour." He led her to the jewelry store.

After they stepped inside, the proprietor nodded. "Welcome. I see you brought your lovely young bride. I set aside a sampling of sapphire rings for your inspection. We've the best here." He brought out a tray holding an assortment of rings. The primary stone in each one was a sapphire. Most were surrounded in some pattern by diamonds.

Jason brought her to the counter where she could see the rings. At the sight in front of her, she gasped with awe. She looked at him. Knew her eyes were wide. While she and her sisters never lacked for anything, they also never spent money on things that cost so much as any one of these rings. "They are so beautiful. Expensive. Are you sure? Do you…" That was stupid. She'd always known Jason was rich. Tessa knew from

Anice's drilling lectures one didn't speak of money when one had more than they could spend in a lifetime. She'd always told them they would end up marrying that type of man. That was a promise Anice couldn't keep. The sisters would do what they wished. They would all follow their heart, marry for love.

"Pick out one," Jason encouraged her. "One of these will be your engagement ring. There is a matching wedding band for each ring. You can see them in combination if you like." Jason nodded to the jeweler who brought out a second tray of rings. The man stood back; arms crossed in front of him.

Looking at Jason, she spoke, her voice soft. "I don't know if I can pick one out. They are all so gorgeous. Is there one you like best? I would like that one." Tessa turned to look at him. "Before I decide, I would know your opinion."

Jason rubbed his chin, looking at the display. "I do have a preference. Nonetheless don't wish to sway you."

A wave of disappointment swamped her. She found she needed his opinion. "I'll never be able to decide on my own. There are too many here. They are all so beautiful." She bent closer to look at them. Didn't know how to figure this out. They only had so much time before the ceremony.

After giving a small cough to catch their attention, the proprietor asked. "May I make a suggestion?"

"What? Oh! Of course," Tessa said looking up from her perusal of the rings. "What is that?"

"If you're wanting help, why don't you allow your soon to be husband to pick out a few of his favorites. You can choose from the ones he sets out for you to consider. Then…" he paused for a few seconds appearing to study them, "You can make your choice from among his favorites. Well…there is always the off chance you don't choose one of your favorites…"

"That would be fine," Jason cut in. "Doing so might point out a favorite to Tessa even if the ring is not among the ones I set aside." He turned to her. "Do you wish to try that method?" he asked with a mischievous glint in his eyes.

"It has worked for other couples," the proprietor said.

"Believe so. Yes. Let's do it." Instead of feeling overwhelmed, she was now eager to move forward. Narrowing down the choices was just what she needed.

"I'll choose three," Jason said as he bent low to peruse the rings.

"Four," she said with a soft voice. "Four would be perfect. Truly, I don't know how to choose. This would have been much simpler if you picked one out for me." She touched his arm. "Pick four."

"Whatever the lady wishes. Four it is." Jason went through the tray of rings methodically studying each one. After several minutes he set aside four engagement rings with their matching bands. They were set upon a white velvet piece of fabric. Because of the dark stone the rings stood out.

"You can try them on."

She gasped. Then jerked in surprise. "I can?" Tessa did wish to see what they would look like on her finger.

"Not worried about Jason Kenworthy running off with the rings without paying," he said with a bland tone to his voice, coupled with a slight twitching of his lips. "Besides, I know where he lives."

"No, of course you're not," Tessa said as she once more looked over the rings. She still couldn't decide.

"Put this one on," Jason told her as he picked up one of the rings. He slid the ring on her delicate finger. "This one is beautiful. Simple. You can have one more ornate if that would be your wish."

She was surprised when the ring wasn't too big or too small. She looked at him puzzled. "It fits," she knew she sounded amazed.

"I borrowed one of your rings from your jewelry box. This nice man sized all my favorites. We expected you would want the number to choose from narrowed down. What do you think of this one?"

There was one large sapphire with two smaller diamonds on either side. The matching band alternated small sapphires and diamonds. The ring was simple. The other ones were nice though more ornate but this one…yes. She didn't need to try any of the other rings. Somehow, she knew without him speaking the words, this one was his favorite.

"This one…" she repeated lowering her lashes before she looked back to Jason. "This is the one. I don't need to try on any others. It's your favorite. Mine too."

"Yes, now…" Jason slipped the ring from her finger. Holding her hand, he touched the ground with his knee. "Will you do me the honor of marrying me?"

Her heart skipped a beat. This wasn't something she expected. "You know I will. Yes…" She could barely breathe. Intoxicated with happiness was how she felt. Blinded by love. "Yes," she breathed the word.

"Gracie? Lord Kenworthy?"

Tessa swiveled when she saw Jason staring at the man who entered the room. "Who is that man? Why did he call me Gracie?" Tessa whispered, her voice a single thread. She was brought back to her mother's words, the blackmail she had in mind. Terrible cold swept through her as she wondered about this man.

"Judge Seymore? Hello. This isn't Gracie, though now that I think on it, Tessa does have a similar look about her. I'm certain you realized the fact by now. This is Tessa MacRae. She's agreed to marry me. The rings are picked out. We are on our way to the church."

"You must be Jason." Miles extended his hand. "I'm never certain unless the two of you are standing together. Congratulations on the pending marriage. I take it…" Miles stopped abruptly as if he realized what he was about to say wasn't appropriate.

Tessa gasped when she realized who she stood in front of. Her head spun. Her gaze flew from Jason to Judge Seymore. While Jason rose to his feet, she found herself sliding to the ground. The world seemed clouded. Fog swirled around in her head. His hands closed around her waist in an effort to keep her on her feet. Lifted her. She heard all the voices as if they were distant. All seemed to echo in her ears.

Judge Seymore? How can that be?

"What's wrong?" the judge asked. "She looks too pale. Only a moment ago, I heard her say yes to your proposal. What made her faint?"

I can't tell anyone the horrible truth. Mustn't let it be known.

To the jeweler, "Do you have a place I can set her down. Put the rings on my tab." Jason took the tiny box the man gave him that held the wedding band. Tessa wore the engagement ring.

"Is she alright?" The judge hovered over her.

"I hope so." Jason pulled out his pocket watch. "We're getting married in less than an hour. What the devil made her faint?"

"Wedding jitters can cause a lady to swoon. I've heard that from more than one source," Seymore suggested. "You say, less than an hour."

"Yes." Jason cradled her in his arms.

Tessa worked hard to come around. To get rid of the horrible gray fog in her head. She could never tell him what made her faint. With an effort, her lashes fluttered open. "What happened? I…" She swept her tongue across her mouth. "I don't know why I fainted. Can we still get married? I'm fine. Everything, well, it's all so overwhelming."

"Yes. Yes, of course we can. Wouldn't want to put this off another day. How do you feel?" He touched his hand to her forehead.

"Embarrassed. Mortified. I've never fainted. You were on one knee asking me to marry you. Yes. Yes, as I said last night. This is what is best." He didn't say anything about love. She would need to have enough love for both of them.

The jeweler handed her a glass of water. Tessa sipped while two men hovered over her waiting to see…what? If she would faint again? She wasn't about to do something so stupid. She wanted to get married. Hoped nothing would stand in their way.

"Should we go to the church now?" Jason asked with a small chuckle as if to minimize what happened. "Imagine Clancy and Megan will be there waiting for us. Assume you need to change into your wedding finery."

"I do have a gown to change into. Megan will help."

Jason brushed a soft kiss across her forehead. "I like those words 'I do.' I do too. Just remember to say them in front of the minister."

A small ripple of laughter that sounded more broken than anything else leapt from the back of her throat. "I won't forget."

"Say, I've nothing to do for the next few hours. Do you mind if I join you? Do love weddings. My Gracie's wedding wasn't what she expected. Nonetheless, we got the deed done before anything bad happened to her. What do you say? The two of you seem to be in a big hurry."

"Tessa?"

"Why not? It couldn't hurt to have one more witness." This man would do quite well if Anice ever questioned the validity of their marriage.

~ * ~

Miles along with Jason stood inside the rectory still talking about Tessa fainting, as well as her uncanny resemblance to Gracie. They both puzzled over the fact the two women could have been sisters. Their eyes were a different color. Tessa's hair was a lighter shade of blond with no hints of red. That wasn't where the resemblance ended.

"When Tessa saw you, she looked as if she saw a ghost. Have you met Tessa before?" Jason asked, puzzled by both Tessa's reaction to Judge Seymore as well as her similarity to his daughter. Before Miles could answer, Jason spoke again. "No, it was when your name was mentioned. How would she know your name? Tessa has been sheltered her entire life."

"No, never met your bride though I wish…nothing. Never mind. What I'm thinking isn't important. Not on your wedding day. Would never wish to set any ideas in motion that are all wrong." Miles was having trouble processing two things that disturbed him more than he wished to admit. The first was that Tessa looked much like Gracie. Too much like his beloved daughter. The second was that the moment his name was mentioned, she fainted. Why would hearing his name cause her to faint? None of this made sense.

Miles could write both happenings off as coincidence. Did something like coincidence come in pairs? He didn't know. What he did understand was that he wanted to be part of this wedding. What he didn't know was why. The Kenworthy twins were upstanding young men. Men who should be emulated as pillars of society. Jason Kenworthy would make a wonderful husband to this young lady. She was quite a bit younger. Miles supposed that didn't make much of a difference if they loved each other. As long as the young lady was of age, the difference between them shouldn't matter.

Hesitant to ask the question knowing he would anyway, Miles spoke up, "Would you mind if I tagged along to the church? Love weddings." That part was true. He did love a good wedding. Had officiated at too many to count on both hands. "Would do whatever you need done. Is her father here?" Miles thought about Tessa's father. He'd heard the man was in jail somewhere in Ireland. He attempted to kill Jasper Kenworthy.

Damn shame.

He watched Jason think about what he told him. When he looked at him with a small grin, "Would you walk Tessa down the aisle at our wedding? She doesn't have a father to do that small thing. Tessa will need to agree."

"Of course. Would love to escort your lovely young bride to you. Be privileged indeed." Miles let his mind wander to the wedding of his daughter to Fletcher Murray. Fletcher had to drug her to get her to say her vows. Even though she loved him, she was afraid. Petrified to be exact. He stood behind his soon to be son in law as the only way they could proceed.

"You would? It's not an imposition? I'm assuming you're in this village on your way to see your daughter along with her husband. Do you have the time?" Jason asked as he waited for Tessa to appear. "I'll ask her."

"No, allow me. You're wrong about the scenario only because it's the opposite. I'm on my way home. Fletcher and Gracie are headed back to Glasgow tonight. Business. Believe they are then on to London. Seems they lost the last tennis match to see who had to do the family business in London." Miles laughed to himself about that. The Murray brothers were competitive. "Appears since Dawn arrived on the scene the bouts got more intense. No one beats Dawn and Gordan. No one. The only time those two travel to London for business is when they volunteer."

"Tessa needs to agree. She told me no to Clancy our butler doing the honors. I'll send Clancy to ask her about…no, I'll go myself. Can talk to her with the door closed," Jason murmured while heat flooded his face.

"You should be embarrassed. A butler should not be doing something meant for…" Hell he wasn't a bigot. He didn't care about all the title garbage of the aristocrats. Yet he also understood common sense. "Go see if she'll allow me to escort her. I'll be very pleased if she says yes." With his hand on Jason's arm as he took off, stopped him. "Make certain the door remains closed, young man. Don't want any bad luck to come your way."

Jason hooted his laughter on both accounts. “Clancy is a good friend as well as an employee. Tessa said no. I don’t know why. She told me she could walk herself down the aisle. Believe she’s mourning the loss of never knowing her father. Anice would never tell her who that man was.”

Miles grinned at the young man’s evaluation of Anice MacRae. “Yes, all that is true.” The brief run in he had with the woman was not worth talking about. Seemed a lifetime ago. He’d rather forget the encounter. After his wife passed on, he was lonely. Anice was there panting for sex. He needed companionship more. Nothing came of the brief affair he had with the woman. One night in bed with her was more than enough to last a lifetime.

Nothing good.

All these years he waited for the possible blackmail. What he feared never came about. He’d thought that after his appointment as a judge, he’d hear from her. He wasn’t about to meet any demands that woman made. He didn’t care overmuch about the judgeship. Though he enjoyed his position, he’d never let anyone use secrets to make him less than the honest man that he was. Never knew if Anice understood who the man she bedded that night was. Didn’t make a bit of difference. What happened twenty years ago didn’t transform the way he conducted his life then. It wouldn’t now.

“You hurry up and ask her. I’ll either walk your beautiful young bride down the aisle or I’ll watch. Would love to participate.”

Chapter Four

Jason waited at the altar, Clancy at his side. Music played. He shifted from one foot to the other. The minister's wife was at the organ. The music drifting from her nimble fingers was beautiful. He felt both nervousness coupled with excitement as time passed at a snail's pace. He was pleased when Tessa accepted Miles Seymore as her escort. Though her agreement was unexpected. Miles did have a convincing way about him. Though his request might have had something to do with her acquiesce.

Clancy stood beside him watching, beaming as if this was the most wonderful moment of his life. First, Megan walked down the aisle. Somehow before the wedding, Clancy bought flowers for the two ladies along with a bottle of champagne. The bouquets contained miniature pink roses. He kicked himself for not thinking about bouquets. Because he'd seen the minister early this morning, his wife baked a cake. People stepped forward to make the wedding the best possible success.

The ceremony was a simple affair. The minister agreed to say only what was necessary. Jason had thought to write vows to Tessa. There was no time for her to prepare anything. He decided to say them to her tonight in the privacy of their bedchamber. He hoped she would reciprocate with some spontaneous words.

By the time they finished the cake as well as the glass of celebratory champagne, Jason said a silent prayer of relief that Anice didn't somehow get wind of the unexpected wedding. She would have shown up here if she had heard. By not planning a big wedding they were able to sidestep the disaster that could have waited for them if she arrived unannounced. Jason could let himself forget that where her youngest daughter was concerned, she had an agenda.

Now, what they looked forward to was the wedding night. There would be so much to teach his innocent bride. Jason pulled her close. Kissed the top of her head with such a slight caress she didn't know quite what he'd done. Felt the shuddering rush of pleasure sweeping through his bride. Against him, her heat emanated.

Miles stepped up to give Tessa a hug. "Good luck, young lady. You've married a fine man. My Gracie thinks the world of both the twins. They are related…a great distance…not certain exactly. Believe they just want to call each other cousins. Otherwise, there is nothing more. You know. Never say a bad word about either man."

"Thank you." Red shaded her face at the mention of Gracie. "It was nice to meet you. Maybe I'll see your daughter while we are here. Jason mentioned we might join them in a game of lawn tennis. Though we won't be much competition. I've never played."

There was nothing said that should have caused her to blush with such intensity. Since Tessa met Miles, she seemed distracted by his presence. Preoccupied whenever they spoke. Tessa told Jason she'd never met or seen Miles before today. For that matter, Miles claimed the same. It was beginning to annoy that he couldn't give himself a reason for the tension he sensed in Tessa coupled with the strange way Miles looked at his wife.

"Yes, she and Fletcher spend most of their time away from the city. The two enjoy the peace they find here in the country. The city can be noisy as well as dirty. If you don't run into them at the main house, they spend time in the small nearby cottage. Brings back fond memories for the two of them."

Jason walked Miles to his carriage. He leaned on the door, still focused on the judge. "Hope to be seeing more of you now that you've a vested interest in our marriage. The acting father of the bride must have a few responsibilities." Jason chuckled even while he felt there was something wrong in the changing of Miles' expression. He needed to get to the bottom of what was troubling him but he didn't have any ideas on how to do that. He could ask Tessa. She would never say anything even if she knew.

"I'll swing by next time I'm visiting Gracie. Maybe you will have learned something as to why Tessa had such a strange reaction to me. Said she never faints. My, my, if that was the first…" Miles' voice trailed off as if he wasn't certain what else to say. He looked away for a moment then back to Jason. "Keep me posted."

Once the good judge's carriage was on its way, Jason turned to retrieve Tessa who was having trouble getting away from the minister's wife. The poor woman almost seemed starved for company. She was chatting nonstop. Tessa looked as if she needed rescuing from the good woman. A smile caught on his lips. A rush of heat whipped through him as she brushed a strand of hair behind her ear. Saw the blush of color on her face after she glanced his way.

What the devil was she thinking? She couldn't be reading his mind. If she did, she would know how the gentle sway of her body heated him until he burned for her. He didn't need to close his eyes to imagine her naked. Last night he tasted her delicate flavor, touched his lips on the hardened crowns that beckoned him. "Tessa," Jason stepped up beside her. His throaty words exclaimed how much he wanted her. Waiting was an integral part of his plans. "Are you ready? Time to go home." His blood ran hot for her. Rushed through him, pounding in his ears. While he didn't intend to seduce her on the ride home, he did feel a few kisses would be in order. Prepared and begging for him by the time he carried her into the bedchamber was how he wanted her.

"Oh, yes!" She looked away from him, seeming to search for someone. Scanning the area her gaze rested on her maid. "Megan!" she called out. "Megan! Catch!" Tessa tossed her bouquet at the young maid who reached high to snag the flowers with a giggle. "You're the next to marry. Maybe that handsome young blacksmith's apprentice you told me about will pop the question soon." From what Megan told her about her young man, Megan would need to make certain he noticed her first. This might give her the needed incentive. If she could, she would give her advice. She had no idea how to make a man sit up and take notice.

"I'd remove your garter then toss it at Clancy. What do you say? Will you let me?" Jason asked as he watched the flush on his wife's face grow more brilliant. He had no intention of stopping. Though he knew what she must be thinking. He would need to reach beneath her dress. Thought that was a bloody great idea. Trail his finger along the silken flesh of her calf then higher to her thigh. One step closer to the preparations for the evening.

"You can't." More color rushed to her face. She was a wonderous shade of red. "You…not here. I *ken* it's done. It's just that…" she was blabbering faster as the words of denial tumbled from her lips.

The panic in her eyes shot a tenderness into his heart. Still, Jason had no intention of stopping. This was part of tradition. He didn't intend to leave out anything that might create any type of havoc in his life. "Do not want bad luck. Said so yourself."

"Bad luck?"

"I'd learn why. As you say all grooms are privileged to retrieve the garter. *Dinna* deny me," Jason caught Tessa's fingers to bring her to him. His hand captured her ankle then brought her foot to his bended knee. "Hush…" he told her when she started to protest again. "This will only happen once, only one wedding. Don't you think we should make certain all the traditions are seen to? This is one we will not overlook. Megan received the bouquet. Who do you think will catch the garter? Hmm…"

"I'm not wearing…"

"You must have a pretty ribbon or two holding up your stockings. If there is nothing to hold the silk up after the garter is removed, I'll take it off." He slid his hand along her calf then higher to the spot above her knee where the garter should be. The shuddering response to his caress set him on fire. He felt the hot rush of Tessa's passion. Wished he dared roam higher. Touching intimate skin was meant for the bedroom. "Here it is." With deft fingers he undid the bow. Jason hollered his butler's name. "Clancy!"

Jason wadded the ribbon into a ball then sent the ribbon flying toward the older man who caught it. He let the blue ribbon unfurl. Waving it around in the air, he searched the small clearing in front of the church. Clancy grinned. His smile broad. He yowled with his laughter. "I'm too old to be tying the knot with anyone. Who'd want an old codger like me. You should have tossed it when the good judge was still here. Seems he's in need of a beautiful wife."

"Maybe our cook. She's about your age. Single, last time I heard." Jason thought that might be a fine idea. The lady was round from all her cooking. Jovial too. Her hair was starting to turn gray around the edges. She would make a man a fine wife. He'd have to look into that. Put the two in question together from time to time. He didn't think she would mind a bit of attention. Clancy did love his food, though he was rail thin. The two were a perfect match.

"Go on with you. That sweet *lass* is too young for the likes of me," Clancy shot back his protest, still grinning. "You two go on now. Be off with you. Megan and I will be right behind your carriage. If there's anything you be needin' when we get back just ring the bell cord. The servants will all be ready to bring anything the two of you need."

"Don't wish for company." Jason had other plans for the rest of the evening. Those plans didn't include any other people. "Want to see to my wife myself." Every sweet part of her. "Though some food upstairs would be appreciated along with wine to last the night. Have Megan set out the lingerie I bought Tessa for this evening. She *kens* what I want." He meant to see to all his wife's needs. At the present time, she looked as if she didn't know quite what to do with herself. The blossoming embarrassment vanished. The stocking he'd removed earlier was in his pocket, her shoe in his hand. Turning, he winked at his wife. She turned her attention to her feet. Her little toes delighted him. He would have to see if they tasted as good as they looked.

Jason turned more of his attention to Tessa. Before she could protest, he swept her into his arms. set her in the carriage then climbed in to sit beside her. After he tapped on the roof, they began to move. He heard the rumbling of the wheels along the drive. Knew when they turned onto the main road leading to the village then further to the Kenworthy estate. Ten minutes from his bedroom. Fifteen minutes from intimate privacy with his new wife.

"It won't be long before we are home. Are you happy? Pleased to be Mrs. Kenworthy?" he asked, his voice deep, throbbing with unfulfilled desire. Sunlight danced in the strands of golden hair that slipped from her chignon.

"Jason?" She queried, watching him from a sideways slant. Her eyes sparkled. "Of course, I'm pleased. It's what I've wanted for over a year now. You are everything to me. All that I've ever dreamed of."

He wondered why it took so long to convince her she should agree to the proposal. For now, it didn't make much difference to him. He did get what he wanted. "Did I tell you how beautiful you are? When I watched you walking down the aisle, I couldn't breathe for a few seconds. I wanted you then and there. Didn't wish to wait one second to have you. Would you like a few kisses on our way home? To keep us occupied?"

"Occupied?"

"Yes. Need to keep my hands busy. Explore. Seduce with kisses." Jason held his hands on her cheeks while he studied her mouth. Let the warmth of her skin spread through him in a glittering urgency that was hotter as well as sweeter each time he felt her heat. She would taste of woman coupled with warm honey. He needed to feel her nectar rain down on him. Soon. Soon he would satisfy himself with her intimate moist sultry heat. After he watched her moisten her lips preparing herself for the kisses that were sure to follow, he slid his gaze down the length of her neck to the fast-beating pulse at the base.

"I like your kisses. Told you that I've no objection."

"Occupied. Engaged in kissing," his husky murmur coupled with the stroking heat of his eyes gave rise to the rosy blush on her cheeks he loved.

He continued to caress her with his gaze. Followed the line of her corsage where lace touched the tops of her flushed breasts. Inviting him to push the delicate lining aside to see what was below. She was his. He could do whatever he wanted. Whatever she wished. He could give her choices. This or that? Here or there?

"I think I'd like that, kissing. To stay occupied. Are you going to kiss me? May I stroke you? Kiss the softness of your lips." she asked with a puffy breath of air that was scented with peppermint. When he kissed her, she would taste of the mint along with the champagne she drank after the ceremony.

"If you ask, I'll do most anything you wish. Where do you want the first kisses?" With the back of his hand, he traced the line of lace decorating her gown. "Here? There?" He wanted to push the fabric aside then see if the rose-colored tips of her breasts hardened with anticipation. She adjusted herself on the seat. Moved closer to him. The soft curves of her pressed against his hard planes. He needed to taste now. His body hardened more with each seductive motion of her small body. Wasn't certain he could wait until they reached the house.

Her answer was a fragmented cry and a shiver of pleasure as his teeth scored slightly over her neck. Touched with the tip of his tongue. Tasted salt along with lavender then aroused woman. Delighted when she made a soft noise deep in the back of her throat. Needed to hear more throaty sounds ripple into the sultry air. He saw the shadows between her breasts. The curves of the soft mounds he needed to suck deep into his mouth.

The passionate cry his caress brought forth was a blade unravelling the cords of Jason's control. Telling him she enjoyed the small nip. The touch of his teeth against sensitive flesh. His Tessa was so much an innocent yet so responsive. He needed to move with tender care. Must wait to take her until he could settle her on his big bed. Needed the first mating to be perfect for her. Until her sweet honey rained down upon his hand. Had to keep from stripping Tessa's gown from her then burying himself in the sultry softness he knew waited for him within the intimate sweetness of her body. All those visions had to wait. He wasn't going to let her first time be in a moving carriage with her legs straddled across his hips. Jason bit back the hungry groan of need that escalated every time he caught her scent or savored her silken flesh.

In these confines, he could kiss her though. Kiss her as he taught her the night before when she would have granted him more intimacy. Given him the darkest most secret parts of her. She thought he'd made love to her. He wondered how she would feel later after they did learn about each other in every possible way. Looking at her sent an aching need so deep. A demand so painful he couldn't ignore. Jason pulled her onto his lap. Cradled her on top of his thighs. She was fluid, pliant in his arms. Tessa would allow him to do whatever he wished. He wished to kiss her as she'd never been kissed before. Kiss her so long and so hard it would be difficult to come up for air.

"You liked kissing. Ask me for more of the same if that's what you want." His voice turned husky with the burning desire she inflicted in every part of him. "Tell me what you need. What you want. Where it is you would like my lips."

"Kiss me," Tessa whispered, her voice soft yet thick with her passion. "I do want you to touch your mouth to mine. Will you use your tongue? Can I rub mine over yours? It's velvet softness makes me ache in places..." she didn't finish. "I remember last night."

At her question then her innocent, unrestrained statement, he hissed in a swift rush of woman scented air. Jason understood where she ached, as well as why. He also knew how to ease her. He had to steady himself to give her an answer. Needed to pull in a deep breath of air before he could form a reply. "If you open for me first, I'll give you everything you ask for. You have to part that pretty little mouth of yours before I can give you the pleasure you might be remembering. If you don't, I'll assume you don't want to taste me as much as I need to savor you."

"I do want to realize the flavor of you. I love the way it feels when you're deep inside me. When can I taste you. Today, will you taste of champagne? Last night the wine was what I recognized."

Her innocent replies, then the statement, caused another groan of craving to rumble up from the pit of his stomach. In the back of his throat, he growled his pleasure. His enjoyment was hot, molten. With slow precision Jason didn't feel, he put his mouth over hers. She made a gentle sound of revelation along with remembrance from the previous night. The warm hungry searching of his tongue along her lips caused her to shiver with the pleasure he evoked. For long sweet seconds he understood she relearned the velvet patterns of his penetration and retreat, absorbed once more the textures of his deep kiss, felt again the heat of him spreading through her in wave after wave of pleasure. Ecstasy so hot they would set the night on fire, flames rising to challenge the sun. Against him she maneuvered herself as if she tried to get closer then closer still. The sensual torment of her body was no longer enough.

"Tessa," he murmured her name on his lips, his voice husky with unfulfilled desire. He needed to feel more of her. Hold the silken weight of her breasts within the palms of his hands. Savor the hardened crowns. "You burn me alive." Jason wasn't at all certain he could wait until they reached the mansion. He pulled back a moment to look into the sapphire depths of her eyes. Saw the shimmer of her unleashed passion. Witnessed the shiver of hunger showing itself in the increased tempo of her breathing as the semi-revealed mounds of her breasts taught him how much she enjoyed the kissing.

If I'm not careful, Tessa will burn me alive. She'll capture all that I am. Need to have her hold me forever in her heart as I will hold her within mine.

"You do the same to me. You make me burn from the inside out. How does one quench the flames? How does one ever find surcease from the ache?" She wound her hands around his neck before she searched higher, slipping her fingers through the length of his hair, setting her nails against his scalp. The sharp nails raking along his flesh sent lightning bolts of desire straight to his aroused flesh. "You set me on fire as well as make me shiver at the same time. When you're kissing me, I can't think. All I understand is that there is something I'm missing. What is that missing piece? I want to learn."

"That's the way it's supposed to be, little one. No thinking allowed. Just feeling…all the sensations that cause you to shiver and burn at the same time. Later, I'll gift you with that piece you believe is missing." The scent of her, lavender and sunshine, filled him. He couldn't breathe for a few seconds while he tamped down his rushing need for her.

Tessa tried to draw his mouth to hers once more, but he was stronger. He waited, holding his lips just above hers. Felt her ragged breath coupled with the scent of champagne he'd tasted before with the first kiss between them. He teased her with the kiss he withheld just as he was holding himself apart from her. Nibbled on her mouth. Passed his thumb across the moistness of her lips. If he allowed himself to give in while they were still in the carriage, her skirts would be tossed before either one could think. He would claim her innocence in a rumbling carriage with no thought to comfort or romance. He couldn't do that to her on the night of their wedding. Holding himself back was taking all his strength.

"What do you want?" he whispered.

"For you to kiss me. Need to feel…"

Again, he teased, brushing her mouth with his lips. Nibbled across her mouth. Waited for her reaction. He heard a tiny mewl but nothing else. "Like that?"

"No. Yes. Not like that, different. That too."

"No? Yes? Different?" he questioned, while he attempted to keep the humor from his voice along with the grin that was close to showing itself. Hooting his laughter at her innocence would never serve the purpose he sought. She was too damn inexperienced to understand what she needed to say.

The tip of Jason's tongue teased Tessa's lips apart while she struggled to pull herself closer. She arched, rubbing her breasts across him. She responded with abandon that would have brought him to his knees if he'd been standing.

"That's it," she told him, shivering at the touch of his tongue sliding along her mouth. "Something like that. More…"

He withdrew.

"Not yet!" she cried out sounding both frustrated as well as aching.

"Make up your mind. A man needs to understand what his woman wants from him. No or yes. That's all I need to understand. More or less?"

"Jason," Tessa said with what sounded to Jason as urgent need. Her voice was a thin wail. "I want more. More of what I don't know. I can't tell you what I don't understand. All that you haven't taught me. Please…" she whispered. "Please, Jason, don't keep teasing me."

His breath rushed in as if she flicked him with a whip. All he could do at the present was tease her so damn much she would beg when they were in the privacy of the suite of rooms they would soon share. When they made it to the bedchamber, her sweetness would rain upon him. She would be soft, ready to accept him.

"Part your lips for me," Jason said in a deep voice. "Kiss me that way. Let me see that you want this as much as I do. Put your tongue on mine. Rub its velvet softness against mine. I'll understand. I'll give back to you everything you give me. We need this to culminate in the bedroom, not the carriage."

Sunlight slanting in through the open carriage window glistened on Tessa's lips as well as on the tip of her tongue. Moisture clung to her mouth. Jason made a low guttural sound before tightening his arms, with the back of his hand, lifting her face up to his.

"More," he said, brushing his parted lips over hers. "More…Tessa.

Wider. Let me explore deep inside your heat. I need to taste the sultry dark secret that is you. Give that part of you to me. Trust me."

Tessa quivered then did what he asked. She opened to him. A rose bud opening at the first rays of the sun could never be as exquisite as this unflowering. Tessa was made for him. She was his. Only his.

Jason's mouth closed over hers. His tongue slipped into the warmth that opened to welcome his advance. Heat greeted and hot moisture received his deep penetration. He took her mouth as he meant to take her body, completely; a seamless melding of flesh coupled with the honeyed passion that was Tessa. Her breath came in disjointed. The heated glide of his tongue over her mouth scattered his thoughts. He forgot all but the hungry, sensual pleasure flaming to life within his hands. All his attention was focused on her lips. They were vividly alive, hot where his tongue was touching and cool where it had passed. Her arms tightened around him until she was pressed hard against his body. He helped by arching her back then rubbing his chest against her clothed breasts, bringing her even closer. His tongue dipped beneath her upper lip, gliding, probing, circling. His teeth caught her lower lip. He tugged with gentleness. Touched the sensitive inside of her lip.

She didn't seem to know that she made a broken sound then opened her lips wider. His tongue was hot inside her mouth. The taste of her was sweet beyond bearing. To his delight, she gave him back the kiss, sliding her tongue over his, probing the sultry, dark corners of his mouth before catching his tongue with delicate precision between her teeth. She bit.

At her bold contact, his breath came out with a hoarse sound before fracturing.

In that instant, she released him.

I'm sorry," she told him in the next moment. "I don't know anything about this. You're the only one I've ever kissed besides blood family, a kiss on the cheek. We both understand that's not the same."

She was bloody right. It wasn't anything the same. Kissing Tessa wasn't like kissing any other woman he'd known.

Tessa stroked her finger across his lip where she bit. Her woebegone expression tore at his heart. "Are you alright?" she asked with a strange sadness in her voice. "I didn't mean to hurt you."

"You could never hurt me. You delight me. The little nip you gave me was perfect."

His voice was husky when he looked at the smoldering blue of Tessa's eyes. She pressed her lips together as if she didn't believe what he told her. Perhaps she didn't. Her naivete shown clear with each new revelation. While he always expected she was a virgin, the stark knowledge she knew nothing overwhelmed him.

"You groaned," she countered as if she still didn't believe him.

"So did you, only a few moments ago."

"I didn't realize."

"You won't be mistaken next time."

"Hush," Jason said, lowering his mouth over hers again. "It's just kissing. You understand what that is all about. I know you do. All we're going to do in this carriage is kiss."

"Mmph."

The softening of her body told him she was no longer anxious about what might happen in the bedroom. Instead, she was returning the intimate kiss with a shy, hesitant, yet passionate thoroughness that made his head spin. He forgot he didn't want to kiss her so senseless in the carriage that he'd have her skirts tossed before they were in the privacy of his big bed. Forgot about everything except the hot secrets of Tessa's mouth.

At the back of his mind Jason knew he should stop before he got in over his head. He'd been a long time without a woman. Sarah had been gone from his life for months now. This woman, his wife, appealed to him far too much. It would not take much more of her innocent exploration for him to lose command of his body.

He merged his mouth with hers the same way he wished to meld his body with hers. Slow. Gentle.

Completely.

Tessa matched him breath for breath, touch for touch, hunger for hunger, until Jason felt all restraint sliding away, leaving only Tessa in all her beauty. He didn't know he'd pushed the corsage lower, so low the hardened crowns of her breasts were freed from the ivory lace gown she chose for her wedding dress though not free of the chemise.

Didn't think of anything until the coach slowed. Until he realized the feeble control he held on his body didn't help conceal his need. She might not understand what she saw or felt against her. He was hard, aching for the woman he just married in a quick ceremony before three witnesses. If the journey had taken another ten minutes, all his plans would be wasted. He would have taken his wife in the carriage. Would have pushed into the velvet soft heat of her aroused flesh that ached with her need.

Her wide sapphire eyes were dazed with pleasure. She moaned. With a soft sigh breathed his name. Beneath his breath, he cursed himself as well as his hungry desire for this woman who beguiled all his senses the first time he saw her. That first kiss had been the beginning. The kiss stolen on the banks of a small stream in Ireland. Unlike the first one, this kiss would seal their future. With both regret as well as relief, he pulled away from her. Her swollen lips were dewy with the moisture left behind from the heat of his mouth capturing hers. He smoothed his thumb over the sensitive flesh.

"We're here. Home," he told her, his voice a soft caress against her as he pulled her up to a sitting position. Ran his knuckles atop her breasts that he'd inadvertently revealed. Awkwardly pulled the gown up to cover her. "Would you like me to adjust your gown. The top. I…" He saw the bodice was askew. Jason didn't remember touching her breasts.

He must have.

Tessa looked down then back up to meet the potency of his gaze. She gasped. "Oh! I…what…"

"Let me help. The driver will open the door at any moment. We don't want him to guess what we've been doing or see you in such a state of déshabille." He grinned at the changing expressions on her lovely face, his wife. Jason didn't understand how he found this passionate endearing woman when he wasn't looking.

He was discovering she came with secrets as well as a past that wasn't known. Anice was part of her past. She held something over Tessa's head. Together they would discover that past seeming to threaten their future. He hoped it wouldn't hurt her. Sometimes what one didn't know would never harm. Her mother was not a woman to ignore.

With Tessa's nod of acceptance, he helped her straighten her corsage along with her hair, tucking in strands that he managed to loosen. There was nothing he could do about her kiss enflamed lips. He moved back, pleased with his endeavors. The driver set the steps by the door. He leapt from the vehicle then turned to help his wife down. He saw that Clancy and Megan arrived minutes before them.

Clancy stood at the open door waiting. Megan behind him with her hands clasped in front of her. Both were grinning. They would wish to be part of the night. He expected privacy. Didn't wish to have interruptions. Megan should go see the young man she was enamored with. Tessa told him about the young blacksmith's apprentice who had yet to notice her maid.

"You both have the night off," Jason told them as he walked up the steps. "Don't want to see either of you until tomorrow morning. Have a good evening."

"Who will help…?"

"I will," Jason was quick to interject his opinion. "Though my wife enjoys your company, it's not needed tonight. We want privacy this evening. Have the night planned. No interruptions appreciated. Thank you for standing up for us." He didn't want to think about servants hovering at their door. Didn't wish for anyone to hear them in the throes of their ecstasy.

Clancy bowed smiling as if he understood why Jason wished to be alone. Megan appeared puzzled. "Before we left, I told your cook to have food along with enough wine for the night sent to your bed chamber. All should be in order for the wedding night. The two of you shouldn't be needing anything."

"Thank you." Jason swept Tessa into his arms before he entered the house. Her arms clamped around him to hold on. Her lovely curves pressed against his chest. He bent to whisper close to her, "I will see to your pleasure. If there is anything your heart desires, let me know. When you do, whatever you've asked for will be yours."

Tessa's answer was to bury her face in his chest. His long legs carried her up the stairway to the second floor then to their room. After he closed the door, he let her slide down his body. Felt the press of her generous curves against him. His kiss was tender, filled with sensual pleasure. He didn't want to frighten her with all the pent-up yearning that built inside since last night. The ride in the carriage brought out hungry desire. The evening before had been good for them. She learned that he wouldn't hurt her. He couldn't make that promise tonight. He would do everything he could to ease her way.

Holding her close, he fitted his mouth to hers. With seamless ease, he ran his hands along her back while she melted all over him with pure enjoyment. He backed her away from the door. Needing the bed more than anything even though he understood he rushed her. As if he was her lifeline, she clung to him. Held tight.

"The bed…" His head rose from her. Once again, he captured Tessa in his arms.

The last dying rays of the sun glistened on Tessa's lips. Tasting the sunlight then the sweet inside depth of her with his tongue would be the death of him. Jason made a low sound as he tightened his arms, lifting her closer. She rubbed against him. Knives of pure pleasure sliced through him.

"Again," he told her brushing his parted lips over hers. "Another kiss then another one after that. I'm not going to stop kissing you."

Tessa shuddered then did as he asked. She opened for him. Slid her tongue inside his. They danced. She withdrew as if she needed air.

His tongue slid into the warmth that parted with sweet promise for him. Explored deeper. Seduced another small whimper of pleasure followed as she clung to him.

~ * ~

"The bed…?" Her whisper flitted across his cheek. "So soon?"

His hunger too intense, "I can't wait," he murmured. Jason settled her on the bed. Came down on top of her, blanketing her with his huge body. His weight on top of her felt wonderful. She clung to him, so small and fragile. She arched against him hoping to get closer to Jason. Wishing for fulfilment. The ache was painful as well as filled with bliss.

Again, his mouth touched upon hers. Nibbled. She arched giving him more access to those parts of her she understood he wanted to kiss.

His lips teased down her neck then across her collarbones then the tops of her breasts, the sensations so intense she whimpered. Her fingers slid into the silken strands of his hair. While he nibbled on the heated pulse at the base of her neck, a broken sound left her. She heard his deep groan. Knew now she didn't hurt him. She fumbled with his cravat wondering how to get it off. All she understood was that she needed to feel more of him. Caress the masculine lines of his jaw, the stubble of his beard. As he did with her, she wanted to run a tip of her finger along the softness of his mouth.

She didn't realize he'd pushed the sleeves of her gown down her arms until his mouth closed over one hardened crown. She gasped. A startled sound brought his head up. The heat of their eyes met, shimmered with passion as well as promise. He grinned as he looked at the damp tip he uncovered then suckled.

"Beautiful…such a soft rose…so hard…glistening with the dampness of my mouth on you," he murmured, then passed his cheek across the crest that came to life with the suck of his mouth.

"I…I thought we were just kissing. Do you need to do more?" While all that he brought her was more sensual awareness than she could ever imagine, Tessa wasn't certain this was something they should be doing. Before Jason, she never imagined the glide of a man's tongue on the tips of her breasts. Never apprehended the awakening would be so sweet.

"It's difficult to kiss through silk and lace," Jason rose above her staring down at her then her breasts. "What would you have me do? I must remove the barriers if we are to continue to kiss."

When she understood what he was saying, her eyes closed then opened. Her flushed lips along with her cheeks heated her until she burned anew. "I'm not wearing silk and lace over my mouth. You can kiss me there."

While she sent moisture across her lips, she stared at him. His eyes were dark brown, circled with golden flecks that warmed the heightened color of his skin. Every time he moved his head the faint light left in the room shimmered over the dark day-old stubble of his beard. His lips were wet from the pressure of their shared kisses.

"I want you to kiss me," Tessa murmured, wondering if she wanted his mouth on her breasts again. Needed to feel the sultry heat caress the tips.

His thumb touched her mouth then ran the length of her neck to circle the tip of her breast he'd been kissing. "Do you? Why the protest? I'm not understanding. Do you not want to kiss? I would kiss you everywhere I hope to touch. Kiss all of you," the husky sound of his voice sent more heat through her.

"You do?" Tessa didn't understand though she was pretty certain she wanted that too.

"Yes, as I said…kiss all of you," he told her. "I want to keep on kissing you and kissing you until the nectar courses and you are as soft as I am hard and we…" With a sharp breath Jason stopped. He inhaled a ragged breath. For a moment looked to the window as if he needed help.

Tessa waited for the rest of the sentence he left hanging. *He wants to kiss every part of me. Dear God...* Passion overpowered her thoughts until her innate wariness came into play. She watched his mouth rather than his eyes. His lips were stretched into a thin line.

"You've got the right notion now. Keep staring at my mouth," he told her with that husky voice he got whenever they kissed. "Watch me. Watch us kissing. See how good it feels."

His lips and hair were silky against her ear, her neck, the pulse beating just beneath her skin. When his tongue probed the hollow at the base of her throat, her breath stopped. Disintegrated into a thousand different pieces. He sucked on the sensitive flesh he found. Bit her with the tenderness she was beginning to associate with Jason. Shared with him the rippling response that swept through her.

By the time the sleeves of her gown were pushed from her arms, she had no idea how or when he bared her to his heavy-lidded gaze. All she knew was that her nipples were firm, rosy crowns standing up against the thin silk of her chemise, seeming to beg for more of Jason. She'd never seen them so large, elongated. His kissing them made them different.

He bent close. His lips parted over one veiled nipple. Swirled then suckled. Bit with gentleness that brought her hips so high she pushed against him. Felt his hardness against the softness of her belly.

"Jason?" she asked, uncertain as to this kind of kissing. A wave of panic washed over her.

"Easy. Only kissing. Nothing to worry about or get anxious over. We're going to do a lot of kissing tonight. All in different places. Promise you'll love everything. If you don't, tell me. I can always find some other place to kiss."

"I'm not kissing you. Is that right? I like the feel of your mouth on mine, on my nipples." Found she needed to explore more of him. She ran her hands along his neck. Loosened his cravat. As Jason was doing, kiss him other places on his hard, lean body.

"There is more than one way to kiss each other. Take a look. Watch my mouth on you." He bent to sip on the opposite breast.

The vision of him nibbling on her breast made an odd, breathless feeling twist through Tessa. She pushed herself to get closer. Needed him to take more of her into his mouth. The stark contrast of dark masculine stubble coupled with fragile silk somehow heightened the intensity of the caress. The ache his mouth created grew.

Seeming to stroke with deliberate slowness, he licked the thin cloth that separated his tongue from her taut nipple. Licked again then another time. With each caress of his tongue, he stopped to look at her.

Sensations glittered through her like hidden lightning strikes in secret parts of her. Embarrassed, fascinated by the building sensations, held in a delicious net of pleasure, she watched the silk darken beneath his tongue. The circle of wetness spread wider with each touch.

Before she knew what he was doing, the tip of her breast disappeared into his mouth. As he had once seduced her lips, now he enchanted her breast, fondling the soft mound with tongue as well as teeth. Sucking on the hardened crown. Retreating only to pay more attention to the other tip.

Her back arched instinctively, rubbing her nipple even more firmly over his tongue. He responded by increasing the sucking pressure until she whimpered and held him to her breast. Her hands glided through the length of his hair, encouraging him.

When Jason stopped and lifted his head, her chemise looked as though the silk had dissolved, leaving her breast naked to his questing tongue. Tessa understood she should be mortified to see herself so clear that all of her was revealed. To know that Jason was seeing her in the same light. She reminded herself Jason was her husband. He had every right to see her wearing nothing at all. He'd seen her before. She wasn't naked yet. Almost. Told herself this was normal. Maggie said as much. Even though she told herself all those things her cheeks still flushed from passion coupled with raw hunger rather than shame.

She loved watching him stroke her.

With delicate precision, repeating over then over again, he sipped at the tight pink crown. When his teeth closed with tenderness around the nipple, she cried out from the pleasure ripping with intimate exactness into those places that ached. The sound sharp in the silence of the evening. She shivered, hunger radiating more heat with each caress.

Jason lifted his head with question in his eyes.

"Did I hurt you?"

"No," she shook her head. Fumbled with the buttons on his shirt. She wanted to feel his flesh along with the warmth.

"Your eyes are as big and as deep a blue as the *loch* up north," he whispered. "More kissing is what you need. Wish to kiss you everywhere."

Tessa looked down at her breast. Once more puzzled by the long-hardened tip the hot wet suck of his mouth created.

"What did you do? I'm not… I've never looked like that even when snow covers the ground and the frigid air finds its way inside my room."

"Here?" he asked.

Jason touched her nipple with the tip of his tongue.

"Yes," she whispered, hoping he would continue the sweet seduction.

"It's your bodies way of telling me it likes what I'm doing. The tight crown is kissing me back."

"Just…kissing?" she murmured, dazed by the sensations, confused by her body's reaction to the intimate caresses of Jason's tongue.

He made a rumbling sound that must have been agreement. Tessa wasn't certain. As if Jason understood what she needed, he slipped from his shirt. The palms of her hands touched his bare chest. The dark crisp hair fascinated. His small nipples intrigued. She passed her hands across his chest enjoying the width of him, feeling the warmth. She was caught in the grip of pleasure.

"Indeed," he said, his voice deep, husky with vibrations. "If you wouldn't mind, I would love to pet those lovely breasts while I'm kissing them. You can continue to explore me more thoroughly if you wish. Pet me anyway you like."

Tessa shuddered at the shimmering look in his dark brown eyes that seemed darker than the norm. Half open, heavy-lidded, he watched her breasts the way a starving man looked at a banquet.

"Just petting? What if I want more?" Tessa asked in a small voice that didn't sound anything like she thought her voice should sound. She let her palms slide down his sides then to rub across the front of his chest. To touch upon his hard male body.

"Only petting," Jason told her looking pleased. "Unless there is more you'd like to do. I'll let you decide. You need to tell me what you want. Don't like to guess."

She hesitated then let out a ragged puff of air.

"All right," Tessa told him in a breathless rush. She wasn't sure of herself. "You can do what you just said. Pet. I'm not certain what that means. I trust you. Don't know what to ask for."

"I'll show you, honey,"

"This will feel better if you're not wearing your chemise," he paused for a few seconds as if watching her for a reaction. "For both of us," Jason finished. "I need to take it off. Undo the laces. Feel your softness."

"N-naked. Nothing covering me?" she stammered while she thought about what he told her. Last night he uncovered her as he did in the carriage. This wasn't anything new. He was naked from the waist up. She wished she could see that part of him she understood would also be very different from her.

He lifted his shoulders, the shrug nonchalant. He looked relaxed. Jason wasn't new to this scenario. "My mouth. My hands. Everywhere. Kissing." Again, he waited, seeming to sense her fears along with her insecurities. He also realized from the way she stared, she wished to know more…to see more of him.

She shuddered at the thought of wearing him as intimately as her own underclothing.

"All right," she whispered again. "You can do that. You are the teacher. I am the student." Her mouth was too parched to speak any other way.

He took off her gown, shifting her until the gown slid beneath her hips and was lying on the floor. His big hands slid along her ribs beneath her chemise. He lifted his thumbs to ease the silk and lace over her taut aroused breasts then over her head.

When there was nothing covering her breasts, all he did was look at her. His smile grew. He stared with so much intensity, she lifted her hands to cover herself. He caught them pressed them down to the mattress.

"The devil, woman," he breathed the words in seeming awe. "You put the sun and moon to shame. Never cover yourself when we are alone together in the privacy our bedroom."

Tessa heated from the tops of her breasts to her forehead then everywhere. Heat flamed at his soft-spoken words. She felt certain her toes were also flushed with red.

He bent and smoothed his face against her, from her collarbone down over each breast then back again, kissing then stroking every bit of the way. He shuddered then redoubled his caresses devouring her with tenderness. He seduced her with a sensual spell of ecstasy.

To Tessa this was like her dreams all over again with the man she loved worshipping her naked skin. She'd heard as well as seen her sister with Jasper enough times to understand enough of what happened to realize the emotions she was feeling now were very real. The rough stubble of his day-old growth brought her breasts to aching peaks that were soothed by his tongue then at alternate times caressed by his fingertips along with his palms. Her breasts were flushed as well as taut, fully alive for the first time in her life.

She made a hoarse sound then jerked when his mouth closed over a nipple. Hunger danced along her body, within as well as without.

"I've never done this with a woman," Jason whispered lifting his head to watch her again. "You'll need to tell me if I do something you don't like."

At first, she didn't truly comprehend his words, for she was too caught up in the pleasure that rippled and shimmered through her to understand anything else. When she finally understood what he said, his words made no sense.

"Never done this?" she questioned in a gasp of air as his teeth bit down on one hardened crown.

"Not like this," he murmured. "You're so passionate."

"How is it different? It's not like this is your first time with a woman."

"I want to take all the fears about your past then what might wait in the future and leave sweetness in its place. Never made love to an innocent. Before now, all I wanted was…"

His voice vanished as he kissed the inner curve of Tessa's breasts then raked his teeth with exquisite care over each tight hard crest. The jerk of her response and her fingers clenching suddenly in his hair made him look into her eyes as if needing to read her expression as well as feel her response.

"The devil," he said his voice husky. "I can't even remember how it was before. All I know is that it wasn't like this. Never like this."

He lowered his head then, with a delicacy Tessa didn't believe a man could possess. He consumed her breasts, lingering over each hard pink tip. Twisted with aching pleasure as well as tender finesse.

"There is a whole lot more of you I want to pet…to pleasure…to kiss. You are so very special," he told her. "Do you want that too? Will you let me discover more of what makes you so delicious?"

The only answer she could manage was a dazed sound while her fingers urged his head back to the hungry breasts he was bent on ravishing. She arched against him, delighting in the feel of his crisp dark hair against her.

"You'll like what I've in mind even more than what I've done so far," he said. "Let me touch all of you, little one. Let me. You won't regret anything. Give me permission." He brushed the stubble of his beard across the tenderness of her breasts.

"Just kisses…will it hurt?" she asked on ragged sigh. "Don't know…"

"Have you ever felt something so good it almost hurt? Pain and pleasure all at the same time?" he whispered the questions while he settled his chin between her breasts then gazed at her.

"Yes, Christmas when all my sisters are laughing and the tree is decorated. Mother has the maid bring us hot chocolate… We don't get sweets often. Mother never wanted us…oh…to eat…sugar," she finished.

"Yes… I remember when my parents were still alive. We all decorated the tree. Drank eggnog not hot chocolate but it must be much the same. Until this moment, I forgot about those times. It's like something wonderful piercing through to your soul. That's not really a hurt. Is it? I won't hurt you. Not ever."

"Maggie said the first time hurt. You didn't hurt me the other night when we made love." She paused. Her fingers wound tight within his hair. "That wasn't making love. Was it? Tonight, you're going to do something else." She thought he lied to her. "Why?"

Jason kissed her with gentle care as if he tried to keep any pain from ever reaching her. Trailed his lips over her collarbone then each hard tip of her breasts. "You are so innocent. I teased you about our making love before I realized you truly knew nothing. Suppose that was not well done of me. Can't take it back."

"I'm not pregnant," she said with a bland voice, beginning to realize the depths of her stupidity. "Anice kept us in the dark about everything."

"I'd give my soul to take back what your wicked mother and that father who isn't a father has done to you. It isn't just the fact they didn't…hell. Your mother is not a good person," he whispered so close to her ear, warmth touched her. Felt the heat of his anger.

Tears came with sudden surprise to her eyes. She touched his mouth. The caress as gentle as she could make it.

I love you. You make my world better. Teach me that life can be wonderful and not filled with surprises that hurt.

"You can't take the past away. It's part of what makes us who we are. All you can do is look to the future. Try to bring happiness to those around you."

With a rasping sound, he put his forehead against her heart. With slowness that startled her his mouth slid downward until he reached her navel. He probed the sensitive hollow with his tongue. This was more kissing. He told her he wanted to kiss every part of her.

She gasped in sudden surprise at the sensations radiating through her with each movement of his tongue. Her muscles constricted where his tongue laved. His hands circled her breasts then plucked the aching peaks. At the same time, he repeated his velvet probing of her navel. Her back came off the softness of the bed as she reached for more of the mercuric ecstasy he was orchestrating. Her cries of pleasure rippled through the air. He repeated the caresses again then again.

With tenderness.

With recklessness.

The sultry heat of his mouth against trembling flesh.

She felt the tremors of his hands when he pulled on the silken strings to her pantalettes. He eased them down her legs, exposing all of her to the flame of his dark gaze.

"You smell like lavender along with sunshine all coupled with the scent of feminine arousal. You're a heady perfume to this man."

"Jason?" she asked, her voice uncertain quivering with indecision. "I've never…"

"The sun, the moon, the stars, nothing is more beautiful than you." He ignored her statement.

The dark fire of his eyes devoured her. His hands along with his mouth on her body were as gentle as the golden shadows of the flame dancing in the hearth.

Torn between embarrassment and the raging heat that couldn't, wouldn't be doused, she watched him caressing her. She didn't object when he slid her pantalets off her legs then tossed them to the floor. She didn't tell him no when he laid his cheek on her body then stroked her belly as he once stroked her breasts, teeth, tongue as well as hands all combined.

After that he began smoothing his forehead along with his stubbled cheeks over the top of her thighs. His silky mouth and sensuously hard hands followed the path his lips travelled. The sweet conflicting textures were heightened by the tender raking of his teeth. With each intimate caress, she arched.

With gentleness he seduced her legs just as he'd seduced the rest of her body. She forgot that she was vulnerable to his much greater strength. Tessa forgot the fact she knew nothing of what was yet to come. She savored the pleasure gathering deep inside her with each kiss he gave her, each caress, each husky whisper telling her how much he cherished her body.

The stiffness of her legs melted away before his tender assault. In a dazed state, she realized he was kissing and working his way along the insides of her knees, her thighs, her…

"Jason!" She clung to his shoulders. Didn't know if she tried to push him away or bring him closer.

He made a hungry questioning, oddly soothing sound while his tongue made gentle forays on tender, sensitive skin.

"You're inside me," her voice quivered on a high thin wail.

"God, yes. You're pure sweetness, honey and nectar so pure…innocent. I touched your maidenhead."

He moved his hand again. A slow stroke. Deeper. Still so gentle. Her breath caught in a fragmented sound in the back of her throat.

"I…"

"Don't worry. Your sweet nectar along with flames high enough to set the summer sun on fire greeted my first exploration," he whispered, touching her with the sweet caress of his tongue. "I'm going to make you so ready; nothing will hurt."

Tessa tried to speak. She couldn't form a single word. A wave of intense pleasure burst through her as she arched her back like a drawn bow.

With heavy lidded eyes, Jason watched the shock coupled with surprise then her innate sensuality as he overwhelmed his little innocent. She no longer protested the intimacy of his finger while he moved it with familiarity within her. Instead, she gave herself over to his caresses with trust.

"You humble this man. I'm wanting you more than I can say."

With slow steady precision he doubled his presence inside her body, testing then stretching her in the same sensuous motions.

She made a ragged hoarse sound.

"Does this hurt?" he asked.

She couldn't answer in any way except to shake her head to tell him no. He shifted until he was kneeling between her legs. He watched then repeated the caress. So slow. So deep. So very perfect. She gasped with the pleasure. She didn't care that her legs were spread. That he could see all of her. Nothing concerned her except the ecstasy that increased with each caress of his mouth along with his hands.

In that instant, Tessa realized she was open, vulnerable to him. She started to protest her helplessness, but words became a husky cry of pleasure as his fingers moved again. When he was deep inside her once more, his thumb rubbed over a sensitive place that sent more penetrating waves of hungry urgency rocking her.

Intense shocking pleasure burst inside her in a gentle overwhelming wave, drenching her with heat.

He shifted again, moving over her. He was everywhere, hot and powerful, tender then caressing, surrounding her.

"Tell me if I hurt you." He said with his deep husky voice.

She heard the words. They didn't resonate. She knew only a sense of heat between her legs then a stretching that went on and on and on, delicious, frightening, endless, sensuous beyond belief.

Jason made a throttled sound that jerked her back to a moment of reality. She felt the resistance of her body both pushing against him then at the same time inviting him to penetrate deeper.

"Tessa?" he asked. "Does this hurt?

"I…Jason…I feel strange…don't know what's happening to me."

She shuddered.

"It doesn't hurt," she told him. "I don't know…" Words seemed to fail her.

She would have cried out at the sensual pleasure of her body nestled against his. The only cries the mating of their mouths allowed were small noises from the back of her throat. He drank the passionate whimpers into him then demanded more teasing and kneading of her sensitive breasts. Long fingers stroked and shaped and tugged until she twisted with wild abandon beneath him.

Only then did Jason shift again, flowing over Tessa, giving her what she needed without knowing that her passion flooded into him. His hips pressed against hers, sinking into her until she moved her legs apart in an instinctive effort to match the aching softness between her thighs with the rigid proof of Jason's hunger.

Tessa didn't know who made the hoarse sound of discovery when Jason fitted himself against her. She knew only that fire spiraled, burning hotter, brighter. Her nails dug into the flexed muscles of his back as she gasped in the grip of pleasure that singed.

Jason never objected to her nails. He groaned his response then dragged his hips over her.

Shock froze Tessa until Jason's hips moved again sending wildfire racing through her body in a burst of heat, she could neither deny nor conceal. When he repeated the movement, his tongue shot into her mouth in a possession that was total yet so tantalizing in its lack of completion that Tessa wept.

One of Jason's hands moved between their bodies. The sound of his britches coming undone was lost in the passionate protest that came from Tessa when he lifted his weight from her hips. She needed him with an elemental primitive fire. Didn't want him to stop. She clung to him, pulling him toward her.

He sensed her silent plea. "It's all right, little one. I'm not going anywhere. Not leaving you." Jason said, his voice thick as he eased himself from the confinement of clothing.

Tessa heard the words. So dazed with the hunger he orchestrated, they didn't mean anything. She knew only that Jason's weight was settling back on top her, blanketing her as if he never left. Just missing the part of her that ached for the pressure of his body. She twisted against him, needing more than he was giving her. No matter how she moved, he managed to evade her.

"Jason," she said with a ragged breath, "you're teasing me…"

"What?" he asked when she said no more. "Just getting you ready. Don't want to hurt you."

As he spoke, he raked his teeth over her neck, sucked on a tender spot.

Tessa had no words to answer him. She had never felt as she did now, wild for something she couldn't define but knew existed.

"What is it?" he asked again. "Tell me what you need."

Instead of answering, Tessa's voice splintered as his teeth closed with more force on her smooth skin.

"I can't…I don't…" she gasped unable to take a solid breath, "…know."

He caught her nipples in his fingers once more then twisted with enough force to generate more frenzied need. Her breath came out in a throaty whisper as she curled against him. The motion made him settle deeper onto her legs, spreading them wider. Still not where she wanted him. Her hands clenched in unbearable frustration. She twisted up against him in unknowing demand.

"Wider," he whispered. "Part your legs more. Give me room…"

As Jason spoke, he moved his hips just enough to brush against Tessa's fire. The caress drew a raged cry along with a rush of heat from her. She shifted, wanting more of the sweet ferocity he teased from her.

"More," he said through gritted teeth. "Let me see that you want me."

She moved again. Did as he asked. Moaned with the fierce need she couldn't deny.

"More, little innocent. Draw your knees up on either side of me. Let me see you, the cream of your desire."

She did as Jason asked, opening her legs until he lay easily between her thighs. The breadth of his shoulder pressed her thighs to open wider. With slow control he continued teasing her nipples, watching her as he plucked the sensitive rosy peaks with his fingers.

"Yes, that's it," Jason said when Tessa lifted her hips toward him. "Just like that. Tell me you want me."

The sensual torment of his hands on her breasts was no longer enough. Tessa's head moved with restless need just as her hips were shifting, seeking release from the vise of need that was closing around her. She arched then coiled with every caress.

"Jason, I…" Tessa bit down on her lip, shivering as more sensations ripped over her through her until the inferno rose higher.

"I know. I can see it."

His fingertip flicked over her in secret intimate places.

"I can feel it too."

Tessa gasped in a combination of fear coupled with raw hunger as she realized she lay open and vulnerable before him. The intimacy he saw was something he created.

He plucked then circled a spot that sent her body vibrating then arching with need so intense she cried out.

"Again," Jason said, rubbing his thumb all around her, teasing her with what he was once again withholding.

A fragmented noise broke from the back of her throat. A moan followed then a soft whimper.

"Let me feel your pleasure rain down on my hand. Need to feel your nectar," he whispered. "Now."

Again, he touched her and it seemed she must have given him what he demanded. The hoarse sound of satisfaction was another light caress, another delicate flick of passion's lash across her delicate, sensitive flesh.

"Your nectar is running hot with your sultry desire," Jason said in a low voice. "Hunger for me, sweet one."

His fingertip caressed again, drawing forth another rush of pleasure.

"I like that, my little innocent. I like what your body is telling me the way I like to breathe." His fingers traveled, brushing her slick, hot flesh with the smallest touch.

Tessa writhed with the honeyed teasing that sent fierce streamers of fire through her. She didn't know when Jason's fingertips were replaced by blunt, satin flesh. She knew only that he wasn't touching her the one place she must be touched. Her nails raked down his back in a demand she couldn't help making.

Jason smiled then teased Tessa some more, circling the sensitive spot without quite touching it. Her hands raked again. He laughed deep in his throat seeming to delight in the aching pulse he created within her. Tessa knew she needed more of something. Inside her body clenched, pulsed with throbbing passion.

The twisting motion of Tessa's hips beneath Jason caused a fine sweat to break out all over her body. "Your entire body is crying your need. The slightest brush of my fingers sends your response spilling over me."

No matter how hard she twisted, fought to make him touch the hungry spot he had drawn from her softness, he eluded her.

"Why?" she moaned her voice trembling with the need.

"I need to hear you ask for more. Must make certain there will be no pain when I finally come inside you."

She made a frustrated sound then shifted again, then again Jason left her barely touched, wholly aching.

"More," Tessa said quivering. "Please. I want more."

Jason brushed his fingers against her swollen, sultry flesh again then again.

"Harder," she told him on a ragged breath.

Her fist struck his shoulder as she strained toward the unattainable fire that withdrew just as she reached it.

"That's not enough," she said. "Please…you're torturing me."

"What if I tell you that's all there is?" His voice held the makings of amusement.

"No! there has to be something else. Tease me no longer. I know there is more. You would never leave me like this."

Jason touched her again, drawing his nail with exquisite care over the swollen bud. She gasped. Jerked with the flames igniting then reared again.

"Jason," she breathed against his hot chest.

Her voice broke as she twisted then bucked against him.

"This?" he asked. "You're right there is more. You're ready for me. No more teasing."

Flesh that was both smooth as well as hard pressed sensually against her, parting her even as she moaned with the pleasure.

"Yes," she said as her breath broke. "Yes." She felt him sliding inside her, stretching her.

Jason moved with exquisite slowness as he entered her. She clung to him. Her nails dug into his skin. She brought herself as close as she could, biting into his shoulder as his penetration deepened. He filled her. His heat sent more vibrations pulsing inside.

"Now," he whispered. "This is going to sting a *wee* bit."

Jason drove into her, breached that small barrier that shouted out her innocence.

Tessa's eyes flew open as pain rather that pleasure stabbed through her body. "Jason!" she cried out his name.

"I'm sorry." Jason held still. Waited until Tessa stopped writhing and bucking beneath him trying to rid herself of him. "Hush, my little innocent. I'm not going anywhere. The pain will go away. This will be as if there was none at all. After that I'll give you the pleasure you deserve."

"You hurt me…" her voice trailed away.

"I'm sorry. There was no other way."

He rose over her. Braced himself on his forearms as he rubbed his fingers with gentle caresses on the silver glide of her tears. He kissed the teardrops away. Brushed his tongue along the separation of her lips. As she parted for him, he sent his tongue inside, penetrating then withdrawing as her muscles began to relax.

"That's it, little one. Relax. I feel the pulses sweeping along me. It won't be long before you feel the same urgency." He framed her lips with his. Dipped more thoroughly into the honeyed depth of her mouth. Penetrate. Withdraw. His fingers played with the tips of her breasts, teasing them again.

The pain inside vanished. He circled the place that sent her climbing the walls with her frenzied passion. "Jason…"

As he drew forth more desire, she arched against him. Her body seemed to hum to life again responding to the sweet torment. He began to move inside her. Enter. Retreat. Move deeper.

"Am I hurting you?"

"No…I!" The sweetness of his penetration stole her breath. Hunger rose swift, with more intensity. She felt herself going over a precipice of sensation. Her body shattered as she lost all sense of control. She cried out his name as the fractured pieces of her soul sent shivers of heat into her.

He moved inside her deeper then faster. His loud groan came while she seemed to be descending from the aftermath of reaching the sun.

~ * ~

"To what do I owe this visit?" Armstrong asked his twin brother Miles. They were identical just as the Kenworthy twins were. They had the same penetrating blue eyes, only Miles were rimmed with a hint of silver. Armstrong's were pure sapphire blue. The very unusual vibrant color was one reason why Miles decided to pay his twin a visit today. What he witnessed today gave him good reasons for a discussion. He'd never seen Anice's youngest daughter before this. Her startling similarity to Gracie unnerved him.

"Checking out the lay of the land," was Miles' reply while he swirled the amber liquid around in the crystal glass watching the play of light with the ever-changing colors. He still considered what needed to be said against what didn't. In any case, his brother needed forewarning. The past might come back to haunt him. He would need to get a feel for his brother's thoughts.

"Believed we were due for a visit. Some interesting things have been happening that you might wish to be aware of before they sneak up on you then bite you in the butt." His brother's ordinary expression told him little except that he wasn't easy to startle. Something he knew beforehand.

"Talk like that from an esteemed judge? My, my, my, what's this world coming too, little brother?" Armstrong asked with a bland voice then a lift of his eyebrow. "You might wish to clarify. What is going to bite me in the butt?"

"Anice MacRae?"

The brandy Armstrong just sipped sputtered from his mouth. He took out his embroidered handkerchief then mopped the brandy from his waistcoat then his lips. There was nothing wishy-washy about that reaction. Armstrong put his hand over his mouth before he coughed several times.

"Haven't heard that name in years. Wish I didn't hear the name today. If she's the reason you're here, I'm sure I don't know why. Has she done something illegal? Not that her crimes would have anything to do with me." He sat down then tossed the remaining brandy down his throat.

"Nothing illegal she can be convicted of." Miles found himself tapping his nails on the brandy snifter. He didn't know how much to tell his brother or ask. Perhaps he was premature with the visit. This might not have anything to do with either of them. Armstrong did see the woman for almost a year a long time ago. How many years? Twenty years ago. That would make him the perfect reason for the blackmail.

No, Armstrong needed to be warned. He needed to understand as much as he did. Not many facts but a lot of suppositions. Surprise was never something either of them dealt with, with reasonable finesse. He recalled when he was shot just before his daughter, Gracie's, wedding. He'd been impulsive then. Believed he could deal with everything as well as anything by himself. Found out the hard way he could not. Might have died that day. Got lucky. This time might not be the case. Though he didn't think Anice had shooting in mind. Her usual instrument was misery.

Miles cleared his throat thinking just how he could put this delicate subject. Needed to point out everything in the obvious order. There was no easy way except to be blunt. Blunt wasn't his style. He skirted the edges before he blurted the issue. His brother might jump to conclusions. Wondered if he hedged a bit, traveled around the borders of the problem if Armstrong would catch on to the issue at hand.

"Tessa MacRae was married today. She is nineteen. A young bride I would say. Not very long out of the classroom. Married an older man." He watched for another reaction. No brandy sputtered from his mouth though his eyes widened with what Miles thought might be curiosity on his brother's part.

"Her youngest? Anice has four daughters, am I right? Why mention the youngest? Didn't Jasper Kenworthy wed the oldest?" Armstrong questioned, a note of curiosity in his voice. "What does that have to do with me? I don't know the *lass*. Who did she marry?"

"Jason Kenworthy." Miles' tone was soft, waiting for his brother to come to some type of logical conclusion. Armstrong couldn't be that dense. He wasn't about to set thoughts into his brother's head that might lead him astray.

"Gracie's cousin?" Armstrong asked. "Interesting."

"You understand that's an honorary title. She is no more his cousin than I am," Miles was quick to point out. "Remember how close our families were? Cousin was a title, no more."

He and Armstrong were close neighbors as well as friends with the Kenworthys. Their parents were rare individuals. It was too bad they passed on so soon. They weren't very old at the time. She passed on giving birth to a baby she was too old to carry to term. He died from a broken heart. Once, he'd been that in love, though he didn't die from a broken heart after his wife passed away from a terminal illness. Still, he missed her. He had Gracie to give him reasons to smile. Their babies as well to dote on. He was glad he'd not been so foolish.

"So…why are you here if you don't wish to…" Armstrong stroked his chin, a look of unease cantered through him. "Yes, why are you here? Are you implying something? I can assure you there is no connection between Tessa MacRae and myself."

Miles understood his brain was twisting then turning, shifting in different directions, denying the possibilities. He would be thinking back twenty years. Trying to figure out dates of birth as well as the months of his affair.

"Just thought you might like to know about Tessa's marriage to a good friend." Miles fished for something he could sink his hook into. Seemed his brother wasn't giving anything away this evening even though he managed to set his mind twirling in a different direction.

"Why? You were always closer with the twins than I was. Had more interest in common." Armstrong paced the perimeter of the room. Stopped to stare out the window. With his hands behind his back, he rocked on his heels.

"I don't know who was closer. Doesn't matter much. I played the role of her father. Walked her down the aisle to her groom. They make a rather attractive couple. His dark good looks coupled with the sunshine brightness of Tessa. You realize Tessa doesn't look anything like her sisters."

"Again, what does that matter?" Armstrong asked, appearing a bit peeved.

Miles continued without answering. "The wedding was small. There were only three people to witness the vows; the butler, the maid and yours truly. I did enjoy the short but sweet ceremony. If I'd known ahead of time, could have performed it for them. Didn't seem the lovely coupled wanted anything elaborate."

"That makes no sense. Was Jason not Anice's first pick? She's the type of woman who needs total control. Always assumed her daughters would do her bidding. Understand Jasper wasn't her pick for the oldest daughter Maggie. Is that true?"

Whatever was going on here, his brother wasn't taking the bait. Time to be a *wee* bit less subtle. In the next sentence, he meant to cut to the chase.

He cleared his throat. "You had an affair with the mother. What was it? About twenty years ago? The lass is nineteen," Miles pointed out.

"So did you."

"Yours lasted longer. Almost a year. I had a one-night stand after you left her. Took precautions. How did you stomach that woman for a year?"

"What are you getting at?"

"Blackmail."

Chapter Five

Tessa was his now. There was no turning back even if she wished. Even though he'd told her he would not, he'd hurt her. As he drew her into his arms, he knew there would be her virgin's blood on her thighs as well as the sheets. Tessa would be embarrassed when she saw the blatant evidence that she'd been innocent. He didn't know how to handle the situation. His experience with virgins was limited to Tessa. Before they wed, she knew nothing of the wedding night. What went on between husband and wife. Though he caused her some pain, he also gave her a great deal of pleasure.

He should take charge.

Tessa would be embarrassed.

Somehow the lie he began last night managed to come to life when she started to realize that his mouth on hers would never result in a pregnancy. She'd heard enough to understand that much. A small chuckle of pleasure left his lips. She was an intelligent woman. Tessa would adapt to their lovemaking.

"What?" Tessa asked while she was cuddled next to him. Her face pressed against his chest while she petted the hair on his chest then wound her fingers into the dark thatch. If she kept this up, he wouldn't stand a chance of leaving her alone. "What do you find amusing?" She looked up, her chin resting on his breastbone, a wicked smile across her kiss-swollen mouth. She blinked a few times waiting for an answer. When she put her head back down, he figured she must have given up waiting for an answer.

Now, her head rested in the hollow of his shoulder. While her fingers danced along his chest, he stroked the silken strands of her hair then down her back. Reveled in the satin feel of her flesh. The first time, before he penetrated her, she'd been so ready for him. Felt her arch then writhe with need beneath his hardened body. Touching Tessa was like touching the sun. Hot as hell when he entered her dark, sultry core. He'd felt the fragile barrier that pronounced her innocence. After he tested it a few times, he realized the thin film of flesh would never give way without hurting her. Decided the only way through would be to do it fast. Get the deed over with as soon as possible. Afterward they would move on to the enjoyable side of lovemaking.

The cry of pain he heard was his undoing. His body lurched with the sound. His stomach cramped. Knew it was inevitable. There wasn't anything he could have done to change what happened. The tears sliding down her cheeks were worse. She'd been so ready for his entry. Her sweet nectar rained down on him. Later, she reached her climax. That was the best part. She learned how beautiful loving her could be.

"For real?" he asked lifting an eyebrow.

"Yes, for real. What's so amusing?"

He stroked her hair, adoring the silken texture that wound between his sensitive fingers. Stroked again. He could get caught up in the sensual feel of her hair sifting through his hands, gliding along naked flesh. What to tell her about his amusement? Subtlety might be his best bet or the worst option open to him.

"Now, after what just happened, you could be with child. What we did this time is for real. No turning back. We are married in every way possible. The marriage was consummated. Tell me you understand the difference." He was watching her with great care for the reactions. Wondered what form it would take.

Her exploring hand stilled. With seeming caution, she shifted her head. One more time turned to look at him. "What? Oh!" She blinked a few times as if she allowed the truth to sink into her head. With her small fist she hit him on the chest once then again as if for good measure. "Are you teasing me again?"

"Yes and no…what happened was my fault. I will take all the blame. I got caught up in something I believed to be a joke then discovered you didn't understand the joke. Didn't know what to do." He placed his hand over hers. Felt the slight tremble beneath his hand. He should remember how quiet as well as reserved Tessa was. She took everything with too much seriousness.

“I was so ignorant. Most likely I still am. Though, now I do understand a woman can’t become pregnant by kissing alone. You must have laughed your head off,” she said sounding defeated.

No, he didn’t laugh at her. He adored her with all her innocence. “It’s good that you’ve learned something. I didn’t laugh. What I did at the time was berate myself for not coming right out and telling you the truth. Bottom line, I was a coward.” His chuckle deepened, realizing he would be the man to teach her everything.

“I could be pregnant now? Can it happen the first time?” Seemed she returned to the subject that launched him into trouble in the first place.

He wound his fingers between hers. A gentle smile filling him as he watched the perfection of her small body. He wanted children. The sooner the better. “Would that be so bad?” he asked. She’d told him before she wanted children.

“No. You lied to me though. How can it happen with only one time? Is that something else mother should have told me about?” Tessa questioned.

Her curiosity was a delight to his senses. He meant to answer everything with pure truth. “Yes, I did tell an untruth. As I spelled it out to you, I meant only to tease. Never thought…ah hell…never would have believed anyone could be so innocent they thought my tongue in her mouth could create a child. Sorry.” He felt contrite. Needed to make amends to her. Would have never brought this up if she didn’t. If she hadn’t realized the truth, would she still be thinking kissing could cause her to conceive?

“How? After only once. Isn’t it something we need to do more than one time? Do you want to do it more than once?”

The devil, he didn’t *ken* how to answer that. All he could do to keep his laughter from spilling out. Was she teasing him now? Telling him she’d like him inside her again. “What are you trying to tell me, Tessa? Do you want me inside you again?” Listening to her words, his body was rock hard. She ignited flames the only way to douse would be to become one with her again. He needed to be careful with her. Taking her more than once might cause more pain. This was something he didn’t know about virgins. He made a hell of a lot of guesses where she was concerned.

Thinking about the hot hungry channel he possessed such a short time ago, his body flamed to life. Heat surged straight to his loins. Jason didn't know how she could do that to him with two innocent questions. Decided answering her questions might be prudent.

Tessa beat his chest with her tiny fist, asking him once more about the possibility. "Yes, can we? I want…" She left the rest of her sentence unfinished. "You're laughing at me again."

"No…well… I'm not laughing at you. I'm finding your curiosity…er…stimulating. Yes, first I'm going to answer your other question. A baby can be conceived with one time. It has to be the right time of the month for the woman. There are…" He stopped, looking at her questioning face then as realization hit, the rosy hue of her face changed her smile to a thin line.

"What time is that?" This time she sounded belligerent.

Jason understood he needed to face the consequences of his statement. He didn't need to tell her anything. Should have left everything up to Gracie. Wasn't that talk for women? In for a penny, "When you are not bleeding."

Her cheeks turned red. "Don't think I want to know any more."

"Do you still want me?" his blunt question brought more color to her face.

"Yes…and I don't want to talk about the other anymore. Next time I see Maggie I'm going to ask her. Don't want you telling me. Don't wish to feel the embarrassment that comes with your answers."

"All right, you wait for Maggie. I'll pet you wherever you like to be petted. You do need to tell me where." With another chuckle of bemusement, Jason stroked her back allowing his fingers to glide down the vertebrae one at a time. Her silken flesh responded with a silent quiver. She snuggled against him. Rubbed her cheek along his chest.

A broken sound of pure bliss fragmented from the back of her throat. Again, Tessa shifted her face across his chest. The cool slide of her hair whispered across his arms. Her hand explored. His soft groan of sensual pleasure rose from his belly. He waited what seemed a lifetime for this. Allowing Anice MacRae to orchestrate their future was not going to be allowed. As soon as he could put out feelers, he would. If he had to travel back to the city for a visit, he would do that too.

"Are you sure? Tell me…" Nothing he was going to do would hurt her. He would be gentle with her. He could orchestrate her climax without penetrating her tight passage. She was so small. He was too big.

"Yes. You won't' hurt me. I know you won't." One more time her fingers found intimate places to discover.

Tessa placed kisses along his chest. Moist lips pressed. Sharp little teeth enticed. Her fingers wound into the hair on his chest as she experimented with different parts of his masculine body. With her innocence, Tessa had no idea what she was doing to him. He hardened more. Grew. Swelled with mercuric desire. It was too soon to make love to her again. That was what he wanted. Didn't know if he had the focus to keep from taking her another time if she continued in this vein. She was such a hot, passionate piece of woman.

"I know that now," Tessa said as if she needed to convince herself. "The pain was because I was a virgin. Is there anything else you need to tell me?"

"You said…" he groaned, his voice hoarse with the need he felt. Understood she would never appreciate him telling her about her virgin's blood. Decided against his first thought to get the speaking of it over with.

Her hands explored. Shifted lower as she followed the dark hair of his chest farther south. The light touch of her fingers tickled as well as aroused. Heated and cooled where her hand followed a parallel path. He thought to catch her hand, bring the long searching fingers back to his chest. Decided to let her sightsee all she wished.

"Are you still angry about the lie?" He tried to divert his mind from her searching fingers along with the heat from each caress that scorched him alive. No other woman ever brought him to attention this fast. All he needed to do was look at her. When she started exploring him, he thought he might explode.

"Furious." She tasted one of his nipples. Circled the nub with her tongue. Tested him with her sharp little teeth. Her hand dipped lower. Bit. Sucked. Wound the hair on his chest through her fingers.

Gritting his teeth, trying to ignore the fact that one of her hands rested on his belly just above his hard member, he cupped her breasts in his hand, testing the weight. "Be careful what you play with my curious, little kitten. You could be dancing with fire while you don't even know the outcome," he whispered close to her ear. Touched the lobe with the tip of his tongue. Swirled. Felt the shudder of desire pass through her into him.

"Good. If playing with fire means exploring you then that's what I want. Want to touch every part of you, especially the places that are different from me."

Tessa shifted again then bent. Repeated all she'd done before he spoke. Circled his nipple with her tongue. Laved with her teeth. Smoothed her soft hand on his belly. He caught her lavender scent, smelled sunshine when her golden hair glided across his lips. He smoothed his hands along her arms allowing her free access.

The devil, he taught her too well. What was a man to do when his wife wanted to learn everything about him? This was heaven. Pure torture as he allowed her the leisure to explore with inquisitive little hands. Seemed she took him up on his offer with eager cunning, coupled with avid curiosity.

"Can I?" Tessa asked, her imagination seeming to outdistance her shyness.

"Can you do what?" he asked deadpan, wondering if she was about to move her hand even lower than where her fingers rested now.

He wondered what words she would use. When she looked at him the pink on her face along with the tops of her breasts stole his breath. Even though her inquisitiveness was the leading force in this endeavor, she was still shy. He wondered what she was asking about now.

"Touch you? You know," she asked, her voice so soft, he needed to bend lower to hear the words. Her gaze drifted to that part of him that had been hard as steel since she began her gentle quest. "Can I? Do you mind?"

His curious kitten could do whatever she wanted to this man's body. "Where? Where is it you wish to touch?"

She left off her explorations. Brows drawn together, both hands were placed on his chest while she pushed up to look at him. Her sweet, pink tongue floated across her soft mouth leaving a shine of wetness that was damn hard to ignore. For a second, she lowered her lashes in a flirtatious way he thought all girls were born knowing how the look affected a man.

"You know." Again, Tessa swished her tongue along her mouth.

When she twisted to look toward his feet, the tips of her breasts sashayed across his chest while the cool silk of her hair slid along his arms. Jason didn't think he could burn more than he had two seconds ago. He did.

"You'll need to tell me, Kitten. If you don't, I can't answer." He teased her, needed her to learn she could say anything around him. While he acknowledged, she'd never be brave, he hoped she'd be comfortable around him. This was the most audacious he'd ever seen his new wife.

"Never mind," she muttered under her breath.

Unable to stop himself, he barked his laughter. Then…attempting to soothe whatever emotions were hurt by his amusement, he finished, "You can touch me anywhere you like. Be forewarned, you might be surprised with the outcome. You might learn something you've no…something new." Hoping to encourage, Jason placed his hand over hers. This was all part of living together, of loving. She should learn all the ways she pleased him.

Her palm lay flat against his belly. He squeezed her fingers, trusting she would continue her inquisitiveness. "I'm guessing you don't know what it's called. That part of me that was deep inside you not too long ago."

That lovely face of hers grew redder if that were possible. When she shook her head to tell him no, long golden hair sifted across him reminding him of sunshine coupled with raw sensual pleasure. Its heat. His temperature soared.

"I don't. Something else mother never told us. Should she have told us? I feel inadequate in this. Need to be everything to you," she paused staring down, the liquid silver of her hair covering her face.

"Look at me." The command came out harsher as well as deeper than he intended. His body throbbed with sexual need while he hung on to his patience with a slender thread. When her gaze shifted to his face, he couldn't stop the grin. "Not my face. That part of me you wish to explore. Look down."

"Oh!" Her lips formed a perfect oval.

"Tilt your pretty head so you can see what was deep inside you." He watched her hesitate. Spoke to encourage her. "Go on. It won't bite." Though he might bite certain strategic places if she continued on this path. He hoped she would.

She moved. Twisted then tilted. Looked down. He felt the deep, stiff breath of air she drew into her lungs. Knew the movement of her breasts as they sent more hot blood pulsing into his groin. With her gaze focused on him, he stood tall, eager. Her hand slid along his belly until she reached him. Her fingers circled his hard sex.

Jason gasped in a deep breath of air, startled by the fire she lit with the simple caress. Such a light stroke of her fingers, he barely felt the touch. He couldn't imagine burning hotter. The trace of Tessa's fingers was cool on his heat. She looked back to meet his gaze. Her eyes wide pools of astonishment.

At his gasp, she let go. Dropped his member as if she touched a red-hot poker. A low groan swept through him at his thought's, blatant thoughts. There were things he wished she'd do. Things he would never ask.

"Did I hurt you?" Her wide-eyed look of concern told him she'd no idea what was happening to him.

"No. you gave this poor man so much pleasure I might have exploded in another second. I'm hard so I can fill your softness. Your touch sends blood pulsing through me to ready me for you." Good Lord, this was too much information. Pertinent things he should never need to tell her.

Her bewildered look endeared her more to him. He needed to give her *carte blanch*. "Go on. Touch me again. Feel me. Promise I'll love what you do. Anywhere you like." He hoped she would continue the exploration of his male endowments. She was so shy. Her boldness now confounded him. He never expected her to touch him so soon into their sexual relationship.

One more time, she wound her long, slender fingers around him. Circled him. Touched him from the tip to the base. "You're so hard," she murmured her voice soft, like the rest of her. "So sleek, you feel like satin to my fingers. No wonder you…" She bit her lip, worried it. The lines in her forehead creased together.

"No wonder?"

"No wonder you went inside me with such ease. Until you hurt me…until…well anyway. You didn't mean to hurt me. The pain didn't last long. It was over then everything you did was amazing." She ran her hand up then down his swollen shaft. Repeated. Repeated again as if she was a child playing with her favorite toy.

He kept the groan inside unwilling to have her stop. Liking the notion he might be her favorite toy. "You inflame me all the way to my soul. Don't stop." Her wide-eyed amazement gratified his heart. Tessa didn't even notice that the blanket slipped to her waist. Her breasts shifted with each breath she inhaled with every stroke of her hand. Needed to hold her beautiful globes in his hands. Didn't wish to distract her.

She touched the tip of his member. Felt the tiny drop of fluid there. Looked at him with surprise in her eyes. "What is this?"

"Just my excitement showing through, telling you how much I want you again. If you weren't a virgin, we would make love right now."

"I want you too. Need to feel you fill me. I liked having you be part of me. You said it won't hurt anymore. Why not?" her question made it double hard to remain chaste.

Her passion matched his own. He'd never met a woman who burned him so hot and fast as she did. She explored again. Moved her hand on him. After that she shifted lower until she cupped him in her hands. He tried not to groan.

Didn't succeed.

She was relentless.

Tender.

Inquisitive.

Tessa must understand now his groan was one of pleasure not pain. He had a lifetime of this to look forward to with this lovely lady.

"Can I kiss you here?" She touched the tip of her finger to the top of his sex. Her slight smile sent a shaft of pleasure straight to the most awakened part of him.

Good God yes!

"Told you anywhere. Even there. Please there," he said with the huskiness of his voice grinding out his need for her. This night could never get better. What remained would be sweet torture.

Bending, she touched the tip of his shaft with her tongue. Slid the velvet softness along the side of his sex then the top. He closed his eyes reveling in the sweet, moist contact that he wished could go on forever. If she kept this up, he would climax. Would spill his seed on his belly. Given her innocence, Tessa would be shocked to the tips of her pretty little toes. Toes he wanted to taste. Hadn't gotten around to that the first time they made love. The second time he meant to kiss her everywhere he missed the first time.

They had all night.

She sipped on him. Swept her tongue around the rim of his sex. When she took him into her mouth, he jerked. Put his hand on her head. She stopped.

"It's okay, Kitten. You just surprised me. That's all. Never thought you would be such an intrepid little warrior. Do whatever you want." Two quick breaths into his lungs helped him stabilize the mounting hunger. Her smooth little teeth raked over him while she moved her mouth as she had shifted her hand earlier. "Love what you are doing."

None of Jason's relationships…hell…no one he'd ever been with took him into her mouth. If she didn't stop now, he would send his seed into her. If he did, she'd be shocked. Perhaps disgusted. Didn't wish for that to happen. Right now, she sucked on him as if he was her favorite candy. God, he could be her favorite bonbon anytime she wanted.

Now, though, he needed a moment's reprieve. Didn't think he had that long before he exploded. He drew her up to him, took her mouth with his just as his seed spewed across his belly. She accepted his growl of ecstasy within her mouth.

That never happened with a woman before either. His tongue penetrated then retreated made gentle forays deep into her mouth while he tried to calm himself. She was an enchantress, his sorceress. The magic she created with her curiosity along with the hungry desire that came with it meant everything.

"Did I do something wrong?" She asked while she pushed away as if she needed to look into his eyes. The Lord knew, he needed to look into hers.

Wrong? Never.

"No, my curious little kitten, you did everything right. Perfect." He panted and gasped for air. Air that didn't seem to want to come to him. She would see the evidence of his climax. Would wonder. If he wasn't second guessing himself, Tessa would have more questions, he needed to explain.

She touched his belly where his seed lay wet upon him. Tilted her head when she looked at him. Lowered her lashes then opened them again. Interest shone in the deep sapphire blue of her big eyes. She moistened her lips. Repeated. The long seconds that ticked by unnerved him at first. He was never quite certain what she would say or do. Waiting for her first question seemed to be prudent.

"Did…" she licked her lips again.

He wished to follow that little, pink tongue with his. "Yes?" He lifted one eyebrow still anticipating the question she would pose.

With a tiny sigh, she slanted him a hesitant smile. Touched him again with the tip of her finger. "Is this what you put inside me when we made love?"

"Believe so." This time, he couldn't keep the amusement behind his teeth. She wasn't going to appreciate the humor. It would be lost on her. He might need to do some quick backpedaling.

There were tiny crease lines on her forehead telling him she was overthinking. "You don't know?" Tessa asked as if she also saw a bit of absurdity here. "I would think a man of your worldliness would understand this." The ensuing pause seemed significant. "If you don't know, who is going to answer my question? Not mother. Never wish to see her again."

"Of course, I know." He was too quick off the mark. Didn't want her to think he was teasing her again, though he was.

"Well then, is this what makes a baby?" Tessa ran her finger on his belly, touching the wetness there. Looking at the milky fluid with fascination.

"Part of what makes a baby. Half of what makes a baby." He never expected to be his wife's educator about sex. Always thought he'd marry a virgin but not a total innocent. With each passing tick of the clock, he was changing her.

At least not all the worldly information from the very beginning. Her mother should have told her something. Anice had her own agenda. Still does.

One can't dwell on the past. Must look to the future. As Tessa's husband, it's your job to make certain she is not ignorant. Not just about sex but about everything necessary for her survival. The world could be a harsh master.

"What's the other part? The other half?"

Figured that would be her next query. "You. You're the other part. The other half of what makes a baby. When my seed…" Oh Jesus, he was about to tell her more than he wanted.

Tessa needed to learn.

"When your seed?" Again, she stared at the milky white liquid on his belly. "This is your seed. I don't see any. Seeds."

Unable to stop the deep rumbling groan, he let it rush out. His knuckles grazed her cheek. "The…er…seed is too small to see."

"Oh." He saw his words rattling around in her head. Understood it would take her a moment to figure out what to ask next.

After seconds ticked by on the clock. "I get that. Where does it go? How does it make a baby?"

Jason explained as much as he dared. He wanted to give her a second climax tonight. Needed to see her reach that pinnacle of desire. Wasn't going to hurt her so he thought the best way would be to give her the same startling pleasure she gifted him with. She would ignite beneath his fingers just as the first time. His plan was to feel her melt all over him.

By the time he kissed her from her eyes south to her navel he lay between her legs, pushing them farther apart. Loved looking at the softest part of her. Saw the sweet cream of her passion pour from inside her. His mouth swept a titillating path from the insides of her thighs to her toes. He tasted each delicate toe before he moved higher again. Now, her legs were over his shoulders. He saw all the sweet nectar he hoped to feel, to taste as well as savor all the magic.

He slanted his gaze her way. Took his fill of her breasts, the rosy tips that tasted so sweet, that made him burn so hot. Her hands rested on his shoulders. Nails scraped across his shoulders.

"Jason?"

"I'm going to give you the same kind of ecstasy you just gave me."

"Oh!" The dark blue sapphire of her eyes looked almost black in the dim light of the bedroom.

His tongue slid along the soft folds that welcomed him earlier. He touched upon her while she twisted then arched. He found the tight bud that would send her to the sun then hotter and higher than ever before. Nibbled. Sucked on the small pearl while she writhed. Bit with gentle precision. Sent one then two fingers into her sheathe.

"What?"

Her hips jerked. Just as he wanted her, she was on fire. Her honey rained. He tasted the sweetness that was Tessa. The scent of lavender coupled with aroused feminine pleasure filled him. He burned just as she did. When she cried out then fragmented, bucking against his mouth seeking more pleasure, he gave her all she needed.

After she calmed, he pulled her into his arms. Settled her face against his chest while he stroked her hair then her back. Thought to touch each small bone down the middle of her back. This was all for tonight. Perhaps in the morning, he could ease himself into her. Give them both more pleasure.

"Are you sleepy?"

She laughed. The soft sound whispered across him. "You can ask that after what you just did to me?"

"Apparently."

"No, but I'm famished for food. My throat is parched. Dry. I could use something to drink then eat. You did say Clancy brought food. A bottle of wine?"

"Can do that for you. Clancy left enough food along with wine to feed an army. Do you want some?"

"Both." Tessa sat up. Pulled the sheet beneath her arms to cover her breasts.

His grin brought a scowl to her face. Jason marveled at the thought she could be shy after all they shared the last few hours. Tessa was at times bold. Audacious. Curious. There wasn't anything he wouldn't allow her to be or do. If she needed to cover herself, he wouldn't stop her. If she wished to walk around the room naked, he would applaud.

He rose. Walked to the table where Clancy put the tray of food. Turning he stared at her. Her gaze was riveted to him. To his lower half. He needed to hide his amusement. After that bold perusal of his body, he was certain she would turn from him. He enjoyed the fact she wanted to look at him. The light in her eyes told him she liked what she saw. Unable to help himself, blood pulsed to his groin. Pounded in his ears…in his sex. She would see firsthand what she did to him.

Tessa continued to watch him flourish, to harden right in front of her. Her eyes widened, darkened as if she too was aroused by watching him. She had this way of doing that to him. All she did was look with appreciation. After all they'd done, he should be sated. With any woman other than Tessa, he would be.

She had this way about her.

"Jason?" she questioned. "Are you?"

Seemed his Tessa was getting the idea. "Yes. I'm aroused. I could make love to you again. I'm not though."

"I want you." The tip of her pretty tongue showed between her teeth. "Make love to me."

"No."

"Please…"

"Shouldn't."

She begged him. Would continue her pursuit. He'd learned enough about his woman to understand she wasn't going to stop.

"You won't hurt me."

With conflicting emotions, he tugged her into his arms. His mouth slanted over hers is a long drugging kiss.

He shouldn't.

She pleaded.

How could he tell her no?

They made love. He treated her with hot evocative kisses to every part of her body. Her fingers curled into his hair. With each loving caress, she arched, her head thrown back as her body begged and her wet hot channel invited him to explore.

After she climaxed, together they lay sated. His body was slick with sweat from the heated mating. Hers was damp, the scent of lavender coupled with sunshine permeating the air. She curled against him. Brushed her cheek across his chest.

"Love the scent of you. All man coupled with spice."

~ * ~

His fragrance would never fail to remind her of her wedding night. He was an enigma to her. So confident in his skin. He found amusement in her innocence. Told her she should shoot her mother. His was a startling but good idea. Perhaps she would do that sometime.

What she needed now was to concentrate on avoiding the blackmail her mother had in mind for her biological father. Tessa looked at the bowl of smooth river pebbles sitting on her bedside table. She liked to hold them. Used them to ease her disquiet when her mother berated her. Over the last two weeks since her marriage, she never felt the need to hold them, feel their satin finish beneath her fingers. Jason had a way of comforting her fears, easing her mind. every day that passed she was more in love with him.

Her mother amplified all her doubts about herself. She must have truly despised her father. So many times, Anice made her think she was unworthy of love, unworthy of anything. Jason did the opposite. His patience answering all her questions amazed as well as delighted. Before she met Jason, she never voiced an opinion. She'd never been assertive. Her entire outlook on life changed the moment he walked into her life.

She'd been afraid Jason felt obligated to marry her in order to protect her from Anice MacRae along with Lord Abernathy who decided she was the most malleable of Anice MacRae's children. He never told her he loved her. She never wished for protection. He never wished for an unwanted marriage to a woman he could never love. Even if he desired, there could never be an annulment. She prayed he would never ask for a divorce.

Nevertheless, they were. Married. Tessa understood she would need to love him enough for both of them. For her, the marriage must work. He enjoyed sex with her. She learned more than enough to write a book about the topic the last two weeks. Thinking of all they'd done together drew heat to her face.

The wedding night met all her wildest fantasies. Yet all she could continue to think was that Jason didn't love her. If he felt forced to marry her, he would come to detest her. That emotion was as inevitable as the passage of ticks on the clock. She could bear most anything except his hatred.

His infectious smile bore down on her. "You said you were thirsty." Jason held out a full glass of wine to her. "Drink up."

"Oh! What? I…yes thank you. I'm both."

Naked, he was standing in front of her. Unable to help herself, she stared. The man was too beautiful for words. Hard. Lean. Masculine. He stole her breath.

Seemed the last two weeks the two of them spent more time in bed together than anywhere else. During that interim, Jason explained more about conception. After several embarrassing conversations, she understood she might very well have conceived. Tessa's hand rested on her belly wondering if a life was nestled somewhere beneath her fingers. She congratulated herself on the fact she no longer thought it might be possible that storks did bring the babies to their mothers.

A letter from Jasper telling them he and her sister would arrive in a week reached them this morning. Her sisters would also be with them. She had a great deal to talk about with her sisters. Wished to hear about the balls they attended, the young men they danced with. If either of them might have fallen in love. The wine Jason handed her remained untouched on the bedside table while she considered the last weeks.

They were supposed to be planning their wedding celebration. So far, they'd made no plans. They'd been too busy to do that. Most of that busy time was spent in this very bed. Jason told her to make up a list of friends to invite. She told him she had no friends except her sisters. Her mother would not be invited. If Anice got wind of the celebration she would show up without an invitation. Her mother would cause mischief in some form or another. The woman couldn't help herself. Tessa supposed that was for the best. Sooner or later, she would need to see her mother.

Would need to explain to her, she no longer held power over her.

"Hungry and thirsty?" Jason asked, his smile wicked.

Tessa understood he would have something else on his mind. Truth be told, so did she. "Yes, still not sleepy. You can't imagine how I feel." The words came out with lack of thought. Jason had multiple lovers. Most likely knew her feelings. None of what she was experiencing with her husband was new to him.

"Drink the wine. After that you can regale me with all the details of what I can't imagine," Jason told her. "I'll be happy to listen. Do you have anything in mind for our celebration? Did you want to invite Judge Seymore? Suppose we should since he did play the role of father of the bride at the ceremony."

A tiny half-smile twisted his mouth. He sipped his wine then filled a plate with all kinds of wonderful foods. Fresh picked tomatoes. Sliced cucumbers. Snow peas that were so late in the picking that the tiny peas inside were full grown, sweet and so very delicious. Blueberries along with raspberries. There were tasty little cakes no more than bite size.

She recalled their wedding night. After the last time they made love, she washed the blood from herself. Jason said nothing. Saw the stained sheets. He explained to her the reason for the blood. Each night before they made love, she wore one of the silken transparent nightgowns he bought her for that evening as well as future nights. She knew he didn't want her wearing anything at all. Tessa wasn't quite ready for nothing at all to cover her body. Nonetheless, Tessa felt certain Jason loved to disrobe her. After that they would wear nothing at all until they dressed in the morning.

The range of emotions she experienced the first night with every evening after, would have sent her running to her room in another time. All she understood now was that she wanted Jason to love her. Her life would feel complete if he ever said those words. She didn't yet understand how he felt about her.

"I don't know if I can put anything into words," Tessa murmured as she pushed through her muddied brain. The wine swirled around in the glass picking up lights from the moon. "The party will be fun though. Do you have a lot of friends who might want to come? I'd like to meet them."

"Try. If you don't feel like it, don't. While I would appreciate knowing this is up to you. As to my friends, we will settle for inviting the village. They will enjoy this as much as anyone. I'd like Fletcher along with Gracie to attend. For that matter all the Murrays with their wives should receive an invitation."

The food was delicious. A long breath of air twisted into her lungs. She stared at her hands that were folded in her lap. Jason was a man she could trust. He needed to learn about Anice's plans for her, for Jason. She kept the secret far too long. He'd been more than patient with her. Not once during the last two weeks did he ask her. Her mother would be furious to learn of their marriage. She had other plans for her daughter's life. Just as she had plans for Maggie that the Kenworthy's stuffed into a tight, sealed bag. After Maggie eluded him, Lord Abernathy was supposed to be her husband.

"This doesn't have anything to do with the last two weeks," Tessa told him, reaching for the smooth river stone. She held the pebble in her hand. Rubbed her fingers along the satin finish that always calmed her.

"What then?"

She grimaced, furrowing her brows while she tried to form the words he needed to hear. "You wanted to know about Mother. What she was about the night before we left for the country. Needed to know what she…" Tessa paused, massaging the stone more thoroughly. With renewed confidence, she held up her free hand to stop Jason's next question. "Blackmail. She is all about blackmail. She is a woman who must have her way in everything. Twice now the Kenworthys have put an end to her plans. She wants all of you to feel her pain."

"What could that woman have to hold over your head that she isn't also a part of?" Jason's voice was harsh when he spoke the words. The tone shimmered with tension. It was not difficult to understand he was furious with Anice MacRae.

"Yes, you're right. The blackmail concerns her too. I don't understand why she would subject herself to the sting of gossip. There has already been so much that concerns her, reflects horribly on her person." She looked to the bowl of stones then back to Jason.

Jason picked up her hand. Seemed to understand the use of the stones. With slowness, he uncurled her fingers. With his thumb he massaged the palm of her hand. Touched between her fingers. “This makes you feel better?” The strokes of his fingers were more soothing than when she used the stones for that purpose.

The connection she felt to this man, her husband, her best friend was something she’d never known before. “Yes. I found them,” she turned to look at the small bowl of river stones that kept her sane at times, that helped her keep her thoughts to herself. “It was an outing. One of the few my sisters and I had with our mother along with the father who was not our father. I found these on the banks of the river. They were worn smooth from the currents flowing over them. For some reason the satin finish of them fascinated me. They are my pets. Always kept me company when my sisters were busy with their lives. Though that wasn’t too often. Anice kept us confined to the house unless she had use for us somewhere else.”

“Pet rocks?” A bemused smile crept across Jason’s face. The golden glitter in his dark brown eyes spoke of something more than amusement. “You have need of your pets? I would hope by now you would lean on me. Though I *dinna* wish to be thought of as a pet. I do, however, like to be stroked by your tiny fingers.”

“I’ve had my rocks since that day. Believe it has been about five years.” With reluctance, Tessa set the rock into the bowl.

She allowed Jason to hold her hand. With his thumb he continued to caress her palm. Heat flared wherever he touched. Even though they should both be sated form their lovemaking, she felt intense desire generated from his tenderness. He was by far the kindest person she knew.

“You have me now to lean on, to take care of your needs. I won’t allow anything bad to happen to you. With me as your husband you are safe from your mother.” His hands drifted along her arms then over her shoulders.

The ensuing shiver surprised her. Hot then cold, she found the two incongruent. Hot when his hands passed over her flesh, cold when they left.

“Safe,” she murmured, as his hands continued their path of seduction along her body. “I want to feel safe.”

If he kept this up, they would make love before she ever told him about the blackmail. Though she didn't know her mother's final plans. Whatever they were, her intentions were meant to harm the man who sired her as well herself. Would never leave Jason or Jasper alone. Everyone she cared about would feel the wrath of her mother's hatred.

"No, never safe." The truth would never go away.

The malady that was her mother hovered around her. Sucked air from her lungs. Drank the life out of her. Tessa didn't believe she would ever free herself from the bonds her mother tied her with. Even though Jason thought he could keep her safe, he couldn't. No one would ever understand the innate strength coupled with determination Anice possessed. She was evil.

With gentle fingers, he brushed long strands of her hair from her face. With his knuckles, Jason skirted the line of her jaw then down the column of her neck. His tenderness never ceased to amaze.

"Tell me if you can. Who does Anice blackmail? Besides you? What threat does she hold over your head? If you tell me, I can help." The back of his hand skimmed her breast. For the briefest moment, floated across the tip repeated before settling on her waist.

Her shuddering response to his subtle seduction didn't surprise her. With a tender kiss or a gentle caress, Jason created magic in her soul. He enchanted her. Her body absorbed everything, memorized until she could no longer think for the mesmerizing beauty of what he did.

The shivering of her body sent golden tremors gliding through her, filling her. Jason should never expect her to answer when his seduction stole words from her mind. He must know what he was about. Must understand they would make love again before she could answer. The touches were light yet redolent.

Holding her head between his hands, he kissed her eyes closed then placed a tender kiss on her forehead. His hands drifted lower to settle on top of her shoulders. She felt the brush of his lips across her mouth. The slide of his tongue along her bottom lip.

Tender.

Evocative.

Her breath shattered from her in a golden shimmer of air. Her hands rose so she could spread her fingers across his chest, to feel the burning heat of his naked flesh. Her sigh whispered across his cheek. "If you wish to have a discussion or an answer to your question, you need to stop seducing."

"Can't help myself." He shifted away from her to watch her unveiling.

The mercuric glitter of his eyes focused on the path of her sheet until the fabric settled around her waist. Cool air touched the hardening crowns of her breasts where there had once been warmth. When she reached for the sheet, Jason stopped her.

"No, not yet. I understand. In truth, I cannot stop needing you." Crossing his arms over the width of his naked chest, he sat back. His eye remained focused on her, unsettling her even while she warmed with passion.

With the slight distance, she found she could almost think, almost breathe. "Make love to me. Need for you to fill me. Make me complete," The soft tremor of her voice sent a visible shudder through Jason. "We can talk later. I need you now."

"I'm afraid we will always put off the discussion. If it makes you more comfortable, cover yourself." His words came out hoarse.

Tessa understood the meaning of the husky tone. Without his help, she pulled the sheet back so the fabric covered her then inhaled a stiff breath of hungry air, hungry for the scent of Jason, for the taste of the man she loved. Didn't seem he meant to make this easy for her. He was the one who wished to know what her mother was up to. Too bad she didn't have the answers he needed.

"Very well, if that's what you want. Seems you asked me who was being blackmailed besides me."

"Yes."

"The answer is that I don't know." She watched for the reaction to the statement. His eyes would tell the tale. They told her nothing.

"Thought she would have told you." To her ears Jason's voice was bland as if he understood she truly didn't know. Even though she had ideas, she couldn't tell him.

"What she told me was that she was blackmailing my real father. Nothing more about the name. You have as good a notion as to who the man is as I do. He could be anyone of her paramours. She has had many." Tessa disliked lying to him. Anice tossed out some possible names to frighten her. Should tell him how Anice wanted her to dig up information on the Kenworthy's so she could use the facts against the twins.

"Your real father," Jason repeated sounding stunned. "She knows the man will give her what she wants to keep the secret."

"I would gather so or she wouldn't have threatened me." Tessa reached for her stones in need of the reassurance they could give.

"No," Jason was shaking his head. Though he didn't stop her. "I'd appreciate it if you leaned on me when we are together."

He would be disappointed in her if she refused his request. "Lean on you…?" Tessa questioned.

Yes, the idea was good. She wasn't used to leaning on anyone except her sisters. In this instance, they were powerless to help. Jason asked her to do something she'd never done before.

"What can you do? We don't know who the man is. We can't give him warning of my mother's threats."

Jason held both her hands in his. "You are cold. Shivering. I'll put more wood on the fire."

True, once Jason quit seducing her to ask more questions, her hands took on the feel of an ice storm. "Freezing, in fact."

"How did Anice threaten you?" His eyes darkened to near black before he left the bed to give his attention to the fire.

A shudder swept through her. His eyes looked so cold, heartless. Cruel. To Tessa, he never looked at her that way before. While she understood the cold anger was not directed her way, this new side of Jason bothered her. Ruthless could be the only way to describe him.

"Our marriage." With her truthful words his eyes grew colder, darker. A moment ago, Tessa would not have believed it possible. It was so.

"How does she threaten our marriage? It is legal. Binding in every way." His harsh tone sent a shiver of ice down her spine.

"Just that I would regret marrying you. That was before we were married. Now…I don't know what she will do. My mother terrifies me." She sipped in air tainted by the situation. "She told me she would reveal to all of Glasgow who I'm the bastard daughter of. When that was common knowledge, you would despise me. Would seek a divorce. She doesn't wish for me to be your wife." The fear of telling Jason shifted.

"Bloody, bloody hell!" Jason speared his fingers through his hair.

"Jason, please…" Jason appeared to recognize her need. He pulled her into his arms to give comfort. Stroked her back. Her hair. Her arms. While the touch was both tender as well as gentle the caress stood only to comfort not seduce as he had earlier.

"Would this man care if the world learned of his daughter?"

"I don't know. How can we comprehend that if we don't know who he is?" She breathed in Jason scented air. Found she was content to snuggle as close as she could to his warmth. She felt so damn cold.

"Of course you don't know. You've no idea who he is? Why I asked…?" he seemed to berate himself.

"Mother told me the man is well respected in Scotland. He does have a title. She never elaborated as to what the title was. He does live in Glasgow but prefers to spend most of his time in the country."

"So, your father would care if he sired a bastard. Some aristocrats see to their bastard's welfare. Some do not. Did your mother mention anything about helping out with you?"

"No, she never mentioned anything. Mother might extort a fortune from him to keep his name as my father a secret. It is rare that a man with a title would accept a bastard as his offspring." Tessa paused then to give more thought to the situation.

"This man, whoever he might be, could deny any knowledge of your mother or you. Could claim she lied. Would be his word against hers. With your mother's reputation, who would believe Anice never slept with this man?"

"He can't deny me."

"Of course, he can."

"There are people who would delight in collaborating her story. That was her promise to me." Tessa's heart grew as cold as the sleek ice in Jason's eyes. She didn't want to learn the identity of this man whether he denied her or not.

"So, this wouldn't be her word against his." His blunt statement sent another chilled wave of emotions though her. "Who would they believe? I wonder. Imagine a lot would depend on his reputation."

Her body shook with fears roaring within. Seeming to sense her uncertainties, Jason pulled her closer in an effort to warm her. Tessa didn't think she would ever be warm again. Not even the feel of this man she loved could stem the cold. Moisture filled her eyes. Tears slid down her cheeks. Jason caught the tears with the tips of his fingers.

"He must have known when she carried me. How could he not? Even then the man didn't want anything to do with me." Bitter feelings toward both her mother as well as her father swamped her. She was glad she had her sisters and now her husband. While he didn't love her, he cared about her, about what would happen to her. He would make certain she survived this mess her mother orchestrated with her hate.

"That the babe was his? Maybe not. She was with your father then. If he saw her with child, he would think the babe was legitimate. They might have taken precautions against the birth of an illegitimate child."

"True to both. Angus renounced us at Maggie's wedding not before. We were all born bastards. The difference between my sisters and me is that they all have the same father. There was unity in that. I think they sensed from the beginning my father was a different man." Tessa paused in thought, "Even though they too have no idea who their father might be. Anice cheated with the same man for several years before she tired of him then moved on to someone else. He must have known about my sisters."

"Why didn't she use the same ploy with Maggie to bring her to heel?" The question from Jason startled Tessa.

"She might have. That could be another reason why Maggie ran that night at the Christmas Eve party. The infamous party meant to announce her engagement to Lord Abernathy. Maggie would no more wish to find herself blackmailed than the rest of us. Anice will try the ploy with Nellie and Fannie if she gets the opportunity."

"How are we going to figure out who these people are? The fathers? If Anice is successful with your father, she might try the tact with the other man. Both men need to be informed before Anice sinks her talons into them."

"It's all just speculation. Until you came into my life no one cared about me, no one except my sisters. Anice wants something from all her daughters. The man who sired me abandoned me. He doesn't care. As you said, he would disavow whatever Anice says. There is no proof of paternity."

"Cannot be certain of that. Must not take anything for granted."

~ * ~

"We are due in the country in one week," Maggie announced day old news to her husband. "We've made no preparations to leave. My sisters don't know of the plans. We should have sat down with them yesterday. I for one put it off, because I know what they will say. They do have the right of refusal. Both of them are of age."

"You don't say?" Jasper lifted a dark eyebrow; a gesture Maggie thought was unnecessary. Her husband's inflicted tone of voice made his meaning clear. "You would allow them to stay here alone, unchaperoned?"

"Of course not!"

They were sitting in the drawing room, expecting Fannie along with Nellie at any moment. The news would not be to her sisters liking even though all missed Tessa. Jasper reached out. Captured her despite protests then swept her onto his lap. Maggie couldn't help the giggle that erupted when he grinned at her.

"You are incorrigible."

"Hmm…" With a gentle finger he set loosened strands of hair behind her ears.

She understood what he wanted. Not right now. Maggie wasn't going to allow him to seduce her to his way when they were about to welcome company. She didn't want to be caught naked or half-naked sitting on his lap in the drawing room. He would tease her until she was embarrassed. Jasper told her more than once how much he liked to see her cheeks flushed a beautiful shade of pink.

"You cannot do what I see in your eyes." She pressed on him, an unmovable wall. "My sisters will be here any minute now. Don't embarrass me." To no avail, again she pushed on his hands. Squirmed.

Against her bottom felt the hard evidence of his need.

"I can." Jasper stroked up her back.

One large hand came up behind her head to hold her in place. With no hesitation she parted her mouth for his seeking exploration. She did want this kiss then one after that one. With firm gentleness, he framed his mouth around hers. The glorious feeling of his mouth on hers sent shimmering heated tremors through her. With the velvet texture of his tongue rubbing against hers, all thought of her sisters vanished. The ache he created within her grew. She could make no protest that he wouldn't counter with a gentle touch. Without a thought to the contrary, she slid her fingers through his hair.

His large hand cupped one breast with his thumb passing against the veiled crown. The potent caress gave rise to a shudder of passion. Beneath her gown she wore nothing except her chemise. Jason knew what was lacking. Arching, giving him greater access, her little whimper of pleasure brought his head up so he could see her glazed over eyes.

His audacious grin was coupled with another slow pass of his thumb across the throbbing tip. "More of that as soon as we discuss our plans with your sisters," he baited her. Knew how to arouse her. If he could, he would keep her body inflamed until they could seek out privacy if not in the bedchamber perhaps his office or the library. Once he made love to her on the dining room table.

Maggie was under the spell of enchantment he cast over her. "More…" she parroted with a slight nod. "More, Jasper."

Jasper focused his gaze on her damp lips. She passed her tongue across them knowing she tempted. "You always want me…"

"Yes…" Her sigh of pleasure kissed by the rays of the sun floated into the room.

The laughter along with voices could be heard coming from the entryway. Kier, their butler, was there taking the sisters' wraps. Talking with them as they chatted about the day. They'd been in the park with several others of their group. Each of her sisters thought they were in love. That love tended to change from one week to the next.

"Where is my sister? In the drawing room?" Nellie asked, her voice loud as if she expected an answer from her. "She's certain to be with

Jasper. Don't want to guess what we might walk into."

"She called us home. We were having fun," Fannie said, a disgusted tone to her voice. "Didn't wish to leave. It was early."

"I hope she has good reason," this from Nellie. "As you said, it's early. The sun hasn't set. We were going to watch the sun go down before we returned home. Hoped to get a kiss from my new beau." After saying the surprising words, her hand flew to her mouth while her skin turned a perfect shade of pink.

Maggie tried to bound off Jasper's thighs. Seemed her sisters were always catching them in a compromising position. Jasper hung onto her. His hands held her shoulders. His eyes were alight with the promise of more sensual fulfillment. With the promise, her body shuddered. She understood he felt the response.

Chuckling, he spoke with a soft voice close to her ear. Touched the lobe with his tongue. She felt his breath across the sensitive flesh of her cheek. "Not letting you go so fast, sweetheart. Going to keep you right where I can enjoy you." Jasper's laughing eyes smoothed her tense nerves. "Your sisters will think nothing of this. They have seen you sitting on my lap many times. Kissing."

Maggie understood where Jasper was concerned, he would do all this his way. While he considered her opinions, if he didn't agree, then…well, it was only these situations that he remained steadfast. Jasper told her the girls needed educating about male and female relationships. He knew exactly how naïve she was when they wed. Didn't believe her sisters should find themselves in the same position. Unless she wished to sit down then explain it all to them, they would be left vulnerable. A man wishing to take advantage would not have any trouble whatsoever. He would seduce. The girls would succumb if they believed they loved the man. Just as she succumbed to Jasper.

At first, Maggie denied the idea. To tell her sisters about what they shared in the privacy of their bedroom would mortify her. Jasper told her she didn't need to go into details. There were only a few things she should explain. He'd gone over a short list which Maggie agreed to. She meant to sit down with them tomorrow morning before they left for the country. They could have hot chocolate along with scones. She'd written down what Jasper considered the most relevant facts so she wouldn't forget everything. She didn't trust herself to remember.

"Oh!"

"Oof, what are you doing?" When Nellie stopped with no warning, Fannie bumped into Nellie on their way into the drawing room. "You two are cuddling again." The sound wasn't one of disgust. It was the "again" Maggie heard along with the distinct accusation. "Is that all you two ever do?"

Sometimes it seemed that was all they ever did. She couldn't very well admit it to her sisters. Maggie made a second attempt to remove herself from Jasper, pushing on his arms. His big hands on her waist thwarted her meager attempt.

"Jasper." Maggie knew the small pleading noise she made in the back of her throat would never cause her husband to relent. Letting her go was not in his plans.

"Why did the two of you call us home?" Fannie was doing the asking as she plopped down on one of the chairs. "Seems it's early. Better be important," she muttered under her breath. Maggie heard.

The look on her face told Maggie she wasn't pleased with the situation. Her two sisters would be less pleased when they learned that tomorrow afternoon they would be leaving the city for the rest of the summer. Maggie understood her sisters made friends. They both had numerous callers for chaperoned outings. Buggy rides as well as strolls in the park were among their favorite activities. There was also a group of friends who met for activities such as scavenger hunts. That's where they were today when they received the missive that brought them home before they planned. Maggie understood their reluctance to leave the city. Nonetheless, she was eager to leave Glasgow behind for the summer.

She chaperoned at times as did Jasper though he was reluctant to do so. Because of their situation, he understood the necessity of being the third wheel. The girls needed to be protected from more than advances from the young men who called on them but also from Anice who would have plans for her two remaining daughters.

Clearing her throat, Maggie began. "Your sister, our youngest, married Jason two weeks ago. We are…"

"What?" they cried out together, bright smiles lighting up their faces after that concern.

One smile vanished. "Tessa married your brother?" Nellie asked, sounding as if she didn't believe the news. "Didn't think that would happen anytime soon. They were at odds for at least a year. Never could agree on anything."

A second smile withered. "Why? She didn't want to marry him until he told her he loved her," Fannie pointed out while she stared unbelieving at her. "He must have done so. Told her he loved her. Without those words he could never have put a ring on her finger."

"Isn't that so romantic," Nellie said, her hands clasped beneath her chin seeming to change her tune a second time. "Oh…" she sighed her eyes closed as if she wished for the same. "I want to find that special love also."

"That fact is not our business. Believe the reason has more to do with what our mother said to Tessa the night she visited Anice," Maggie pointed out to her sisters while she continued to try to shift off Jasper's lap. The dratted man rubbed lazy circles along her ribcage. Enticing simmering feelings. The top of his hand shifted so it was below her breast, pushed against the weight of it, enticing her all the more. He was making this difficult. She could barely breathe let alone speak. "It was why the two of them left the next morning." She waved her hand, "That is neither here nor there." When he slipped the palm of his hand over the crest of her breast she choked. After he did the same a second time Maggie held on to his wrist. He slanted her a crooked half-smile. Oh, he knew precisely what he did.

"They never invited us to the wedding," Nellie said, the disappointment clear in her voice was also how Maggie felt when she discovered the truth of the situation.

"Believe it was the spur of the moment," Maggie informed them. "Clancy along with her maid attended the wedding. Jason wrote that Miles Seymore walked her down the aisle. Played the father's role since Tessa has no idea who her father is."

"So…why are we going now…after the fact? Now that they are wed?" That from Fannie who seemed to be making plans to go out again.

"I would like to stay in the city." She turned to look at Nellie. "That's also what you want. Right?"

"Yes. We are of age."

"For the celebration of their nuptials," Maggie tried to explain with patience. "You have no choice but to come along. Despite the fact the two of you are of an age, there is still the small fact that you are both unwed. You cannot stay here by yourselves. You should be with your sister when they celebrate their marriage."

"We leave tomorrow afternoon as soon as the two of you can get packed," Jasper filled in what Maggie was loath to say.

"No!"

Chapter Six

"You say Anice is blackmailing Tessa?" Jasper asked as the two men enjoyed a pre-dinner brandy. "How? Are you paying that woman money to keep some deep, dark secret from being revealed? I would call her on it. Make her tell you what she has over Tessa's head. I am assuming Tessa has not been helpful with the needed information."

"No, to paying her money. Yes, to the blackmail, though so far, she is not extorting money from me. Anice never told Tessa who the man who sired her is. Tessa, I believe has been forthcoming to me. Don't think she's held any pertinent information back. As to the father, I've a few guesses." Jason held his thoughts in his head. It wouldn't do to accuse a man before there was some proof other than a hunch. What Jason knew about his brother is that his twin would keep the information to himself. He could trust him.

"Care to enlighten me?" Jasper stretched out his long legs, resting the crystal snifter on his hard belly. "You can give me as much information as you feel comfortable confiding. I'm a good listener. Perhaps together we can sort this out. Find a way to combat the woman. What does she want from Tessa?"

That's what Jason wished. To put an end to Anice's reign of terror would make his day. "Anice wants her fear above all." He paused, tilting his head as if to listen. "Do you *ken* where the girls are?" Jason asked, unwilling to take a chance that Tessa might overhear the conversation he was about to have with Jasper. He didn't want her to hear his guesses as to the identity of her father before he knew for certain. If he wasn't afraid of damaging her tender ego more, he might be courageous in discussing this with her.

"You remembering another private conversation between the two of us?" Jasper asked, one dark eyebrow lifted toward the ceiling. "One of the girls overheard. Learned I wasn't married to Maggie. The sisters were outraged. It was all I could do to keep them from scratching my eyes out. You served as a calming influence. Believe that was when you set your sights on Tessa. Am I right?"

"Can't ever forget that moment. Yes, that was when Tessa caught my eye. As I recall she was a little spitfire. Was baffled when I was told she never spoke her mind." Jason rose then strode to the door of his office. He stepped outside to look around before he returned. With a sigh of relief, he spoke again, "Tessa understands if the door is closed, I'm not to be disturbed." He closed the door. Just to be more prudent, he turned the key in the lock. "There, we will have forewarning if any of the girls decide to pay us a visit. They will need to knock. One can't just burst into a locked office." He felt pleased he and his twin would not be compromised.

"Hope so for your sake. Though," Jasper paused, tapping the glass with the pad of his finger, "have to point out, it would not be all that bad if Tessa learns who Anice is blackmailing in her name. Would it? Anice will be accused of the crime if discovered. Perhaps prosecuted."

Jason lifted his shoulders in a broad shrug, hoping for the indifference he couldn't feel. He wished for everything surrounding Tessa to be easy. His family along with hers invading their private hideaway in the country affected their spontaneity. Thoughts that her only consolation all these years was rubbing the smooth river rock, disturbed him more than he ever thought possible. Anice would never be able to convince anyone of Tessa's guilt in this.

"That's a question that cannot be answered without proof. There were few ways of proving paternity." Jason rose to pace the room. Stopped in front of the window. "The sisters seem to be headed for the gazebo. We are in the clear for the time being. No one will disturb our conversation." He turned to confront his brother. "As you might have guessed I've conflicting thoughts on how to proceed."

"Good. As to the sisters, to your conflicted ideas, we will deal with those. You will have to make a stab at naming the man. Proceeding without some direction is not a good tactic. If we have an idea, we can assimilate the facts then try to eliminate the possibilities." Jasper watched him with narrowed eyes. "The man might not realize he has a daughter. Might be happy to claim her when he discovers the truth. This could very well backfire on Anice."

"I've no strategy. No thoughts on how to proceed. I feel as if the blind is leading the blind in this circumstance. I'm certain this is what Anice wanted. Falling into her plans is also not a good approach." Jason's hands were behind his back as he watched the girls skip along the path to the gazebo. He saw that Tessa hung back. Wondered if she would mention Anice's threats to her sisters.

Several pleasant evenings were spent in the gazebo with Tessa. He recalled them with great fondness. She had been so shy. Still, he'd never had a woman in his arms who soared so fast. Her passionate responses to his every caress were treasured. Jason turned to meet his brother's hard-eyed gaze head on.

Leaning forward, his glass dangling between his legs, Jasper appeared to study the amber liquid that caught the light from the sun shifting through the window. When he looked up his expression was one of deep concern.

"Who are your guesses?" Jasper asked after he tossed back a good swallow of the brandy he'd been studying a few minutes earlier. "We must begin with the most obvious then proceed from there."

Jason made a grunt of agreement before beginning to speak what he knew. "There is one man who I know of who could be Tessa's father. Don't know yet if he spent any amount of time with Anice twenty years ago." Jason failed to mention the name for a reason. He truly didn't believe that man to be Tessa's father. While there was a slight resemblance to the man, there was something innately wrong with the guess.

He was loath to let a condemning name fall from his lips. Knowledge could shatter Tessa into thousands of pieces he didn't want to pick up. Gather up those small fragments, he would have to do. The communication was knowledge she deserved. This information was also knowledge her father should have at his disposal.

"Who?" Jasper pushed the point. "Who are you leaning toward as being Tessa's father?"

Jason drew a large draft of air into his lungs before he spit out the name that had been plaguing him since Tessa confided Anice's plans to him. "Judge Miles Seymore."

His blunt mention of the esteemed judge brought crease lines on his twin's forehead then a lift to his dark brow. Affirmation that he needed to proceed with caution. Miles Seymore was a formidable man. Important. A man one did not take advantage of or blackmail. Jason didn't believe him a man to succumb to extortion or intimidations. He would meet the issue head on. Confront the man or woman. It could be that Anice understood that fact. It could be that Anice wanted to terrify Tessa.

"The judge you say. Why? Why do you suspect the man?" Jasper swirled the liquid before drinking again. "Never thought Miles would kowtow to blackmail. Did you? That would be unexpected."

Jason snorted then with a small chuckle he didn't feel, spoke, "That's two questions. Why? Because on first sight of Tessa, Miles called her Gracie. He thought Tessa was his daughter. Apologized for his *faux pas* within seconds of making the mistake. You do recall Gracie Murray is Miles' daughter? At that time the fact surprised me."

"Do the two women resemble each other?" Jasper asked, his eyes focused on him. "If that is the case, that might be enough proof to approach Miles as the possible father." Jasper scratched the back of his neck. "You say he played the father of the bride role at your wedding? Walked Tessa down the aisle. Could he have known or guessed then? He would only think Tessa might be his actual daughter if he had an affair with Anice twenty years ago."

"Not as if they are identical twins but yes there is a great deal of resemblance between the two women. The same light-colored hair, the same general characteristics. Enough so the judge mistook Tessa for his daughter. Their eyes are not the same. Gracie has the eyes the color of a summer storm, a little bit blue and a little bit smoky. They are not Miles' eyes. Tessa's eyes are a deep, rich blue, sapphire blue."

"You don't think Miles is the father?" Jasper answered his question. "Because of the difference in eye color? There are two parents involved. Remember?" that said with a touch of sarcasm in his tone. "I have no idea."

"He could be. However, you do recall he has an identical twin, Armstrong. What color do you suppose his eyes are? Smokey blue or sapphire blue. Hmm…you recall that while we both have brown eyes there are differences."

"Have no bloody idea. Never stared at the man's eyes," Jasper downed the rest of the drink in a gulp. "All you've said is correct. So, do we visit both men? Tell them what we believe then see if either man proclaims himself the father?"

"Gracie and Fletcher are coming to dinner in a few days. They accepted the invitation. They've both been here a couple of times. Gracie was a help to Tessa after we were first married. Showed her around the nearby village among other things. They took to each other as if they'd known each other for years."

"As if they were sisters," Jasper murmured.

"That among other things." Was something Jason wasn't about to elaborate. Those first few days were an eyeopener to him. Never thought anyone could be so naïve as Tessa. He wondered if Maggie had been that innocent at the beginning of Jasper's marriage to her.

"Perhaps you should include Miles as well as the twin brother…what did you say his name was?" Jasper asked. "Seems I've forgotten. Should recall."

"Armstrong," Jason told him with a thin smile. "Armstrong Seymore. Would be interesting to see how much they resemble each other. Haven't seen Armstrong for several years. They were good friends of Father's."

"You should include the twins. The invitation might shed light on our predicament," Jasper pointed out. "You don't remember because we were not very old when they were visiting."

"I'll need to run it past Tessa first. She's not that comfortable with strangers. Told me the girls never had friends. She doesn't know how to interact." His wife was doing better with each new acquaintance. The seamstress in the village loved her. While she didn't get a gown for the wedding, he made certain she would have whatever she wished for the celebration. Thinking of all that could go wrong put a lump in his throat.

"Fine with me. On second thought not all that certain it's a good idea. If the truth came out that night, the situation might be very awkward," Jasper pinched the bridge of his nose. "We'll need to pay both men a visit."

Jason's mind was roaming to his wife. He was eager to be with her again. These last few days she'd spent much of her day with her sisters chatting about everything. He needed her to himself. Didn't know what Jasper's plans for the remainder of the summer were. He hoped his twin along with his wife would return to Glasgow. He wanted Tessa all to himself.

If they were to meet with Armstrong, Jason felt certain he too would need to make a trip into the city. Just as well, Nellie as well as Fannie made it clear the city was where they wished to be as soon as the day after the party. He couldn't blame them. They had invitations. Nellie said something about a scavenger hunt. Interesting. Making the most of their time was important to them. At least these two now had friends. His heart went out to Tessa at all that had been missing in her life.

"We'll have to make a trip into Glasgow," Jasper spoke up, snapping him out of his thoughts of Tessa.

"What! Oh, yes, I was thinking along the same lines. Do you think we could do it in one day. Meet with both men somewhere convenient? A restaurant maybe or a bakery."

"I'll send both a message. Say, in two days. That will give us time before your reception to talk to the men. Don't believe you would want surprises that evening," Jasper said. "So, for now, do you think we could see our wives?"

"Would like to take a stroll with Tessa among the roses." Jason's mind was wandering to his wife. If she wasn't with him, he was always thinking about her.

"Do you think the ladies are still at the gazebo?" Jasper asked.

"Not all of them. Maggie returned a few minutes ago. One of her maids…or the nanny…fetched her. Certain she is with your son in the nursery," Jason turned on a heel to speak. "You don't suppose we can find a reason for the girls to return so I can have Tessa all to myself in the gazebo?"

"Can't imagine what would bring them running indoors on such a beautiful day. Not too hot or too cold. Perfect for whatever one wants to do."

“No, I don’t either. Imagine I should allow them more time together. Understand Tessa has missed them.”

“I’m off to see if Maggie needs anything,” Jasper said.

“I’ll write that message to the Seymores. Send it by messenger this afternoon.”

Jason watched his brother leave. Hoped there was nothing wrong with the baby. He was sure it was nothing. The boy most likely woke up cranky from a nap. Maggie would feed him. Jasper would play with his son. All would be well in his brother’s part of the world.

The last week he wondered about Tessa as well as if she’d find herself increasing soon. Jasper had his heir. He didn’t need one. Jason hoped their first born would be a little girl who looked just like her mother.

Ah, he should go find her. Touch her. He couldn’t do that in the gazebo while the sisters were chatting.

“Jason?”

He turned to the door. “Tessa!” He held out his arms. She ran to the exact place he wanted her. Within his embrace. He kissed her hard then deep. “I’m surprised to see you. What brings you back to the house. Did everyone return?” Jason couldn’t stop his grin from consuming his face. As if thinking about her would bring her to him.

“Hmm…no, Fannie and Nellie are still at the gazebo. I grew tired of listening to them talk about the young men they’ve met. Wanted to be with my man. Is that alright?” Tessa paused to search the room for something imaginary. “The door wasn’t closed. You’re not working, are you?”

“That’s a lot of facts to mull over. Should we concentrate on your question? The most important one?” His heart skipped a beat when he heard Tessa call his name. Her sweet voice rippled through him with a potency that he could never deny.

“You’re working. You want me to leave?” Tessa asked while she began to back from the room. “I don’t want to bother you. Keep you from obligations that need to be fulfilled.”

“Not working. Not unless it’s working on getting you pregnant.” He loved the soft flush of color that appeared with his words. “Come in. Lock the door. Don’t believe we’ve made love in this room.” His pulse shot forward, raced with anticipation.

With a few hesitant steps, Tessa shifted inside the room. Before she did as he asked then locked the door, she leaned against the wood for a few heartbeats. Her lashes lowered to her cheeks. He saw the swift catch in her breath…the rise then fall of her breasts. When she opened her eyes, they were dark sapphire, shimmering with raw desire.

"Sometimes you're outrageous," Tessa murmured as she watched the expressions change on his face.

"Sometimes?" he chuckled with a broad smile. "Hoped that would be all the time where you are concerned. I love to watch the color rise on your cheeks. You are so adorable. So sweet. I need to taste you."

"Well, when we're alone you say the most shocking things to me. I don't know how to react to your suggestive words. What you say always embarrasses me."

"You don't wish to carry my child?" Jason wasn't certain why he panicked. Why he jumped to the conclusion she might not want children. Tessa never gave an indication otherwise.

"That's not fair. Of course, I want children with you. You'll make a wonderful father. It's just that people don't talk the way you speak to me. They always skirt around the topic coming straight to the point with no diversions. You are blunt." Tessa looked to the floor where her toe seemed to trace circles on the rug.

She was nervous. He'd made her that way. To change her nerves to hot delicious passion was his intent. "A husband should be direct with his wife." Jason thought that was perfect to say. "Lock the door, sweet. I've a huge need to kiss you…among other delightful ideas about the two of us. I want you wet. Swollen." He needed to feel her softness surround him. "We both understand the direction kisses lead us. What did you talk about with your sisters?" By her hesitation, Jason figured the chat with Nellie and Fannie left her wondering about something that might be suggestive. Perhaps the conversation was centered around her father. He would need to put off her seduction until she got to the point. Tessa must have come here now because she needed to talk.

She smoothed her skirts then clasped her hands together. Drew a breath of air from the room. Tessa still hadn't moved from the door. "We talked about mother. Told them about her threats to my father. The father I have no name for. The father I've never known. Don't even *ken* what he looks like." She stepped farther into the room. "How or when will we know if she carried through with her promise to name me as his daughter?"

"Lock the door. We need privacy." No matter what they did, interruptions would not be appreciated. He needed more time with her. Jasper managed to help him understand she needed to know as much as he did. He didn't want her to be blindsided by unexpected information. Easing into the situation was the best way to proceed.

"Oh…yes…" Tessa did as he asked before she walked to him. "Are we going to talk? …or something else?"

To put distance between them, he'd retreated after their first kiss. Jason stepped around his desk, his arms open again. Before they spoke of the blackmail, he meant to get one more hug then a deep kiss, a not so chaste kiss. Perhaps they should make love first. No, if he seduced her first, they would not get to the discussion until tomorrow morning. He volunteered to write the missives to Armstrong as well as Miles. He decided he would have Tessa help him with the wording.

Tessa walked into his arms. She snuggled. Pressed her cheek against him. He felt the swift intake of her breath as he cupped her bottom with both hands, drew her against him. Knew she felt the evidence of his need for her. As soon as he touched her, blood raced to those parts that anticipated her hot moist channel.

He slipped his finger beneath her chin. Gazed into the sapphire of her eyes. The jeweled color became her. "I need another kiss first. After that I promise you we can discuss whatever you want." Jason's mouth claimed hers with scorching intensity. Sealed her lips beneath his. Ran his tongue across the crevice inviting her to open for his advances.

With no hesitation or thought, Tessa opened to his invitation. Touched the tip of his tongue with hers. He pushed deeper, parting her further. Inside her sultry warmth, she tasted of mint. He touched the silken area between her teeth and her lip. Shifted forward to move across the velvet smoothness of her tongue. Felt her shudder with golden tremors as she responded to him. Her fingers slid into his hair threading the strands between the sensitive flesh. He bit with exquisite tenderness.

Penetrated.

Retreated.

Wished he could complete this joining.

The sensual movement of her slim form against him fired lightning bolts to that part of him that needed her the most. Jason understood he should end the intimate contact while he still could. After she ran her hands down his back, held his butt with those tiny hands of hers, he groaned with the realization he should have never kissed her before the impending discussion. To end this now, would take all the willpower he possessed.

After his hand closed around her breast, assessing the weight, he knew passion would rule over conversation. The buttons on her blouse flew open almost as fast as the fastenings on his pants. She circled him with her hand. Tested him from base to tip. Ran her thumb down the shaft igniting him further. All he could think about was dipping into the soft hidden folds, damp with her mercuric passion. They would be moist with desire. Sultry with the sensual promise of her sweetness. Ready with heated velvet to surround him. Needed to feel her muscles kiss his swollen member.

Jason captured the tip of her unveiled breast in his mouth. Drew upon the hard crown. Circled with his tongue. Raked with his teeth to bite with gentleness. Listened to her purr of feminine pleasure.

He swept the few papers from his desk with one swipe of his arm. Set her there. Parted her legs so he could find the way between them. Her dress rose to her knees. He felt the ivory softness of her inner thigh. Cupped her, pressed into the swollen petals. Found the tiny hidden nub. Circled the tip with his thumb. Hungry rain poured down on his fingers. She clung to his shoulders. Arched with anticipation.

"Wrap your legs around me, sweet."

She did. He plunged inside the sweetness of his wife. He clenched his teeth trying to prolong the mating. Could not. His seed spilled into her.

Tessa cried out his name as her body fragmented. The mating was fast. Furious. Over before he could slow down enough to savor all of her. Above her, he brought in large gulps of air. He set his forehead against hers. Embarrassed at the speed of the climax that overtook him. She was everything to him.

"I will do better tonight." Jason pushed damp strands of hair from her forehead. "Sorry, little one. You deserve a man who can take his time with you. A man who has a slow hand. Who sees to your pleasure before his. Usually…" It was true that most of the time he was able to control himself. She ignited his passion with little effort.

"I needed you too. I found my pleasure. My sisters…" She breathed in deeply, touched her hand to his face. "Maggie has been talking to them. They've questions I'm too embarrassed to answer. Don't think Maggie does much better with their queries. Though, she has been married a year."

He fastened her blouse before he fixed his pants. Brought her skirts down to cover her legs. She was such a huge temptation, a living breathing enchantress. Even now he wished he dared carry her upstairs to their huge bed. "You shouldn't be uncomfortable. Though I do understand. This is all new to you. Your sisters do deserve answers. They should not be left so innocent they have no idea what is happening to them if they have a suitor who would take advantage of their naiveté."

"Seems Maggie left a lot out of her conversations with them. All I did was heat with mortification when they asked me if I enjoyed doing this with you." Her hands shook while she smoothed her skirts.

Jason hooted his laughter. Pleased she was being open as well as honest with him. Caressed her cheek with the back of his hand. He needed to understand her better. "What did you tell them?"

Tessa turned away from him to stare at the wall. He didn't wish for her to run from her feelings or hide who she was. Tessa was filled with passion. She should be able to speak with her sisters about sex. God, if they were as naïve as her. Hell, they had to be. Tessa told him their mother didn't speak with any of them about sex or their own sexuality.

The devil.

With as much gentleness as possible, he brought her around so she faced him. Tessa lowered her lashes before sweeping her small tongue across her mouth. After she looked at him, she spoke, her voice soft. "That it was nice. What we did together was pleasant." She gazed at him, her sapphire eyes shimmering with an emotion Jason didn't quite understand. "What we do together in much more than nice or pleasant."

He helped her to a sitting position. Couldn't bring himself to move from between her long white legs. She was so delicate. They dangled on either side of his thighs. The scent of lavender coupled with aroused woman lingered in the air, forcing him to concentrate on her words rather than pulling her into his arms again then creating the magic that always flamed in an instant. He wanted to make love to her again. They must have the conversation.

Control.

Patience.

Wasn't as if he was a randy boy with his first girl.

"Nice? Or…more than nice?" Jason questioned with a tilt to his lips as he studied Tessa. Thought her description was lame. "Nice? That was just nice? I would have hoped for something a *wee* bit more than nice. Maybe spectacular. Exciting."

Her flush of color deepened to a huskier shade of pink. "What was I supposed to say to them? That I scream your name when I climax? I didn't know that word or what it meant before… That you send me to the sun and back? That at the end, I shatter into thousands of tiny pieces that take more than a few minutes to put back together? I'm so weak and shaking that my arms along with my legs feel like jelly." She asked the question of him, drinking in a deep gulp of air.

He chuckled, loving what she told him. She was expressive. Honest. He felt the need to tease. "I do all that? You certain it's not a *wee* bit more?"

Her tiny fist surprised him when she connected hard with his shoulder. "Jason! Be serious." She scowled at him. He wanted to trace the tiny lines in the middle of her forehead. "How could what I feel be more than what I just described. Saying those words mortified me. You don't understand what it cost."

"I am serious. You are as red as a lobster. Love that color on you. Brings out the color of your eyes along with the cream of your skin." He stepped back a moment not wishing to give her space. Needed to feel her close to him. He held her hands within his. They were so tiny. She was fragile. He needed to take tender care of her. "Now, what is it you wish to talk about? Your sisters? You? Who your father might be? Want you to understand I still don't have a definitive answer." The tenderness for her overwhelmed. Caught him by surprise. He never expected to love this deep or this fast.

"My father? You know who he is?" She looked so eager. Her eyes widened. The sapphire of her eyes deepened to a dark blue.

"Guesses. Between Jasper and me we've got enough information to contact the two people we think know something. Two people who might be candidates for that position. I hope you will be pleased. They are outstanding members of the community. Though, if they knew of your existence, that fact diminishes who they are. If the one who sired you didn't know, that fact comes down on your mother. She might not have told the man."

"Who? I want him to know what might happen. If he doesn't know about me, mother could take him by surprise."

"Are you certain you can handle the information?" Jason asked, concern etched in every word he spoke. "I would not…" Perhaps this is not the right venue for this type of discussion. While he didn't want to hide her sweetness from his eyes, he began to pull her chemise together then to button her blouse.

"I can do that. Take care of myself. You've no need to…to dress me." Tessa seemed to have sensed his withdrawal. She brushed his hands from her bodice. "I don't appreciate being left in the dark. Don't welcome being treated as a child."

"Is that a yes? You can handle what I'm going to tell you?" Jason persevered needing to be certain. "You won't swoon?" he asked with a bit of a smirk. Jason understood her determination. Understood while she might be naïve, she wasn't a shrinking violet. Except for that one time at the jeweler's, he'd never known her to faint.

"Please." After he moved back, she slipped off the desk. "I've never fainted in my entire life." She paused. "Except that one time. What do you think? You believe I have to be treated as if…as if…" she choked with the words she had trouble with.

"I'll call for Clancy. We can have dinner brought to our room. Want you all to myself tonight. Don't wish to share you with anyone, not even your sisters. Doesn't seem we've had many moments of peace since your family arrived. We are, after all, newlyweds. Shouldn't have to sneak around to find time alone with each other."

"It's only a few more days until the reception. Will everyone go home after that?" She sounded as eager as he was to have the place to themselves. "While I'll miss my sisters…" Tessa left the sentence unfinished. "I feel the same as you. Sharing you is far too difficult than I could have ever imagined."

With regret, he was certain was written on his face, he shook his head. "Heard my brother's plan was to stay here for the remainder of the summer. Maggie will be here. As to Fannie and Nellie, I'm certain they will lobby to go back to Glasgow. If that's the case, living in the city won't be any more private than living here."

He almost laughed when he saw the look on her expressive face. "We should return to the city if everyone stays here. With your sisters in the house, we will have fewer moments alone. What do you think? After the reception should we go back to Glasgow?" He was eager to hear her response.

"Need to have more time with you. If we go back, will you have more work? If we return will Nellie and Fannie think they can go home too? Don't want any chaperone duties where my sisters are concerned. I would not do a good job. I would always be looking the other way."

"Yes. Nonetheless, I can still work at home. We will need to see who stays along with who goes. Not intending to watch out for your sisters either." Seemed they lost the train of thought that had them most concerned.

There was a knock. "Clancy here."

"Come in…a minute…" He forgot the door was locked.

When he opened the door for the butler, Clancy's grin was wide as if he understood why he'd not been able to enter. A wise man, Jason thought.

"We'd like dinner brought to our room. A bottle of wine, maybe two. After that, I don't…" Jason paused a moment, cast a glance at Tessa. "We don't wish to be disturbed for the rest of the evening."

Clancy nodded with a gamin grin. "As you like. Will have your order there as soon as possible. Ring the cord if you need anything else.

Someone will come."

"There..." Jason felt relief to the tips of his toes. He brushed his hands together. "We will eat. Talk. Make love, in that order. Don't you dare sidetrack me with your beautiful breasts. Can't see them without wanting to taste. If you flaunt them... Can't taste one tip without sampling the other. If you keep looking at me like that, I'm going to lock this door again. Damn, the food can wait. Need you. Now!"

She shifted. Her skirts swirled around delicate ankles. Breasts that shouldn't entice with every shift of her body, swayed. Called to every male part of him.

"Then..." She paused touching her chin with the tip of her finger. "You don't wish for me to wear..."

He knew what she was going to say. "No! Not until...yes, but wear a robe that is not transparent to cover yourself. One that is opaque will do the job of keeping my hands to myself...I hope. There are no guarantees." He breathed in a deep sigh of remorse. While they ate, he would love looking at her through the transparent glimmer of the lingerie, he bought with just that scenario in mind.

"As you like," she parroted Clancy's reply. "I will wear the dark blue robe that covers me from my neck to my toes."

"You damn well know that's not what I want," he growled, his voice hoarse with desire. "Needless to say, it is what has to be if we are going to have a discussion that lasts longer than the time it takes for me to see you wearing almost nothing then nothing at all."

Jason stepped up to her. Fastened a few buttons that were still askew. Despite the fact she could dress herself this afternoon, the job was done with trembling fingers. Several buttons were left undone. "Shall we go?"

Tessa slipped her arm through his, leaned into him as they walked up the steps. The curve of her breast pushed against him.

He groaned with impatience.

~ * ~

Tessa understood she might not enjoy the ensuing conversation with Jason. The need to learn the identity of her father overshadowed her fears. With a certainty, she understood from the years living with Anice, this would not be pleasant for any of the parties involved.

Especially not the men. She hoped the two men would never cave to her mother's greed. Her never-ending thirst for power. Prayed they could never fall to her blackmail.

They walked up the steps. She strode into her dressing room to change her clothes. Jason walked in the opposite direction to his separate dressing room. When they both emerged in the elaborate sitting room, he wore a long black robe that was belted at his slim waist. It was adorned with gold braid. She wore a sheer silk confection beneath an opaque robe that covered her from her neck to the tips of her toes just as she promised.

What she wore didn't seem to make much of a difference. He studied her with the dark shimmer of passion in his eyes. Tessa now, after being with the man intimately, understood what that intense look meant. Unless one of them stood firm, there would be no conversation tonight. He must be the one to stand firm. With one kiss, she lost the ability to think. She melted, flowing all over him. If she kept her distance…

This discussion seemed essential for her peace of mind. "Where do we want to sit?" Tessa asked. Nonetheless, she had ideas. Jason would want her on his lap. They needed to be separate from each other if there was going to be any conversation. He told her they would eat first.

"At the table," he said lifting the corner of his mouth in a sardonic smirk. "Were you thinking somewhere else?

"Touché," she murmured, thinking she didn't deserve the mockery. Where he was concerned, there were no rules. "The table it is then." A small table was covered with a white linen cloth. Clancy must have had time to set the plates made of delicate bone China. She loved the tiny blue flower pattern of the set. The flatware was silver. Anice never used the best dishes along with her silverware unless someone important was coming to visit. Tonight, it was just the two of them.

Jason pulled out a chair for her. After he pushed it in to finish seating her, she felt his hand glide across the back of her neck then down her shoulder. With the startling contact she gasped in a breath of air. Her shoulders tensed. Even through the heavy fabric of the robe, she felt the heat his hand generated flow into her.

"Are you hungry?" Jason asked while he sat himself across from her. "I'm famished," he told her looking pleased with his comment.

The twinkle in his eyes told her he understood what he did to her. Beneath the table, his foot slid next to hers. Her breath caught in the back of her throat. He pushed on the fabric of the heavy robe, made contact with her ankle then roamed higher.

"Jason…?" her voice quivered. He was taking advantage of every possible opportunity. Her heart sped.

"Yes?" As if he was the innocent his expression proclaimed, Jason uncorked the bottle of wine then splashed some into both glasses. "Did you wish to say something? What is it you would like? I mean to please." He continued his lazy exploration of her ankle. Switched to the other foot. Investigated.

"No," she muttered thinking it best to keep her thoughts to herself even while she tried to ignore the subtle caresses. She sipped the white wine Clancy must have chosen to go with the meal. "Nothing to say. Just waiting for you to… oh!" his foot moved higher. Touched along her calf. Again, the look of innocence crossed his feature.

"First we eat," Jason reminded her, his voice a soft silky purr with a note of huskiness that hinted of hungry desire. "Second, we talk. Third, we make love. Everything in order. Don't want you to think you can deviate. Though through all that time, I do wish to keep you aroused. Want you…damp."

Tessa didn't think they would make it through the meal before he seduced her. Her body jerked then quivered with every sensual contact. His knee touched hers. Pushed on that part of her until her legs moved apart. Unable to stop the impulse, she scowled at him. Beneath the table, his foot now ran along the inside of her thigh.

Advanced.

Retreated.

Aroused.

Retreated.

Moved higher to touch her more intimately.

Retreated.

Her body hummed with delicious rapture.

Clancy filled the plates before they were delivered. She tried to eat. He pushed her feet farther apart with his. There were no options except to stomp down on his foot. The act would do little good with slippers on her feet. What she needed was hard riding boots. The air she sucked in caught in her throat with the bite of chicken. Her fork landed on the table hard. His smile was mischievous. She wanted to throw the fork at him.

"Do you want me to eat?" Tessa retorted, feeling the heat growing along with the ache. The man knew what he did. He pursued with intensity.

"Yes. Are you having difficulty? Is the food not to your liking? I find it tasty. Might come back for seconds." Seemed nothing he was doing to her affected him.

"It's you. You're the trouble. Not me. It's your fault." Tessa sounded indignant. She was. He told her one thing, expected her to act in a certain way then made certain she was in need of him.

"It's me? I'm the trouble? What have I done?" he asked while holding his glass of wine to the light seeming to study the swirling liquid.

Leaning forward, Tessa picked up her fork then pointed the utensil at him. Shook it. "You know what I'm talking about. Don't play dumb with me. You need to stop this right now. Oh!" He was at it again.

His foot ran up her leg to her knee before pushing fabric aside to continue along the inside of her thigh again. She closed her eyes. Held her breath while she tried to keep the sensual contact from sending her body tumbling into an abyss she would never be able to climb to the top.

"I don't ever intend to play dumb. Understand that you wish to eat. I can feed you if you are having trouble. The fork you are directing my way needs to be used to spear your chicken as well as the rest of the food on your plate."

"You…! Stop!"

"Stop what?"

"You are playing dumb," she accused even though she wanted this as much as he did. They needed to talk.

He leaned back in his chair with his wine glass in hand. Drank. "Imagine I am. No apologies. Eat your dinner. We'll talk. After we finish with the discussion, don't expect to sleep. I hunger for you. Missed you the entire day. Must have more of you."

"You were deep inside me less than an hour ago. You can't be that desperate."

With a heavy, long-drawn-out sigh, he spoke. "I am…frantic…aroused to such a degree I ache. Don't believe I can get any harder."

He removed his feet from between hers. Cleared his throat. Stared at her as if he hoped for a confession too.

"I'm not at fault," Tessa retorted. "Did nothing to make you act so…so wanton. I covered myself from my chin to my toes."

His dark brow lifted to the ceiling as if questioning her statement. "You are as much the problem..."

"No! How?"

"You're too damn beautiful," he confessed his voice hoarse. "Too soft. Too ripe for the plucking. Some parts of you I wish to pluck more than some others."

His statement surprised her even though he'd told her before how he thought about her. Tessa didn't understand what that had to do with restraint. He made the overtures. Attempted seduction when they assured each other that wasn't going to happen until after they ate as well as talked. She did nothing to provoke. Covered herself from head to toe.

"So, you say. Even if that were true, it's no excuse for trying to seduce me from under the dinner table."

"Good enough reason for me." Once again, the smirk on his face told a multitude of tales. He wasn't the least bit reticent. If allowed the opportunity, he would do so again then again.

The remainder of the meal proceeded in silence. Tessa was able to eat even though she tensed with every slight movement Jason made expecting more of the unexpected. He appeared contrite. She knew the expression was far from sincere.

"I'm done." Tessa looked around for a possible place to sit where Jason would have no access to her. She didn't trust him. If given the chance, he would pull her onto his lap. When that happened, there would be no going back. They would never talk. Speaking of what was happening was a necessity that could only be put off so long.

"As am I." He rose then extended his hand for her to take.

She didn't feel as if she was given a choice. Don't panic. She gulped down the remainder of her wine. Jason filled the glass to the brim. She needed her wits. When she left the crystal on the table he brought both glasses with him.

With a nod, he told her where he wished for her to sit. A deep relieved breath of air filled her. He was looking at the two wing chairs that faced the fireplace. The weather was too hot for a fire. Though the room was cool. Tessa pulled the robe around her.

Jason handed her the wine. She set the glass on the table between the two chairs. "Talk," she told him, ready to learn what he knew. Tessa understood his reluctance. Why he was using every opportunity to put the revelation off. Knowledge of her father could turn her life topsy-turvy. The status quo was always nice. Life rarely remained the same no matter how much a person wished for that to happen.

"Tell me who you think my father is." She headed straight to the point. Something Jason usually did, not her.

The deep breath of air he sucked into his lungs told her she might not be pleased. The narrowing of his eyes told the same story. She was on tenterhooks waiting.

"Is it that bad? He's a convicted felon? A cut purse. Someone who beats women?" Her mind blasted at her in too many different directions. "He's a horrible human being. Tell me before I go crazy with the worst-case scenarios."

"The possibilities are endless. Your mother is a faithless bitch. I'm certain as you said once before there are endless possibilities. Nonetheless, Jasper and I have narrowed it down. We could be wrong."

"I know." Tessa watched his face for clues. "You don't believe you're wrong. I'm certain you've taken into account all the relevant facts. Between you and your brother I'm most positive you've deduced correctly."

"In this case, for a change, Anice might have good taste. One could be a renowned judge the other an outstanding peer of the realm."

She sucked in enough air to choke. In this case blackmail was very plausible. "You don't know for certain?" Beneath her ribs her heart thundered in anticipation. “One seems to be more likely than the other. You don’t know?”

“No.”

“Could be either man? Why?” Tessa asked confused by his curt statements. “Explain, please.”

He lifted the broad masculine shoulders she so adored. “They are twins. Identical. Just as I’m identical…”

“Like you and Jasper?” she questioned before he could finish speaking. “There are differences between the two of you. I can tell you apart.”

“Yes, and yes.” Jason was still contrite with the few words he spoke.

She drew air into her lungs wishing she could see into his mind. Wondered if he would name one of the men Anice tossed out to her. This had similarities to pulling teeth. “Which one slept with Anice? It can only be one.” Instinctively, she knew that wasn’t true. How could her mother have sexual relationships with two brothers…identical twins? Doing so would not be difficult for Anice. She would take pleasure in knowing she slept with brothers. Understanding they wouldn’t know until or unless she made the revelation.

“How? Thought you were no longer so naïve.”

Heat rose to her cheeks. He was right. Just because sexual talk embarrassed her, she was no longer innocent. Did the brothers know they slept with the same woman? How could they not? She didn’t believe Jason and Jasper shared names of their female conquests. Though Jasper knew about Sarah.

“I’m not that innocent. You are right.”

“Good. I won’t need to explain how they might both make love to the same female. They might never have spoken to each other about the women they were with. If that was the case, neither man would know what the other did. There is no way to know unless we ask. I doubt if either man will be forthcoming on the issue. Both are private individuals.”

Tessa was growing tired of the conversation. Needed for it to come to a close. “Do these two men have names? Would I know them if I saw them on the street or at a party?” She was impatient with his reticence. He didn't need to prolong any of this conversation. Jason should just tell her.

"Of course they have names." His answer was too calm.

She had the immediate urge to shake the blasted man until his teeth rattled. Instead, she shook her head at him, waiting for the words she wanted to hear for too many days to count. Tessa didn't intend to say anything more until he spoke. She folded her hands in her lap then drew her feet up beneath her. Watched him beneath the fall of her lashes. Waited. Knew he was reluctant. This was something that was not easy for him. She needed patience.

His grim expression told her he didn't like telling her the names of the men who might have sired her. He must expect something bad to come from the knowledge. This was something that was her right to learn. She sensed his feelings from deep in her soul. Knowing would change her life. Neither of them knew if that change would be good or bad.

"You remember our wedding?" Jason began, with something innocuous while his eyes darkened and his lips thinned. She imagined this wasn't pleasant for him either.

Of course, she recalled that day. "How can I forget? It was a momentous day in my life. One that will remain in my mind forever." Her eyes almost crossed as she felt a connection with what she expected his next words to be. Clancy wasn't a judge or an aristocrat. The only other male there was Miles Seymore. His was one name her mother listed as a possibility. Did her mother sleep with Miles? She thought he was a judge. Wasn't certain. Why would he lower himself to adultery? Maybe not. She jumped to conclusion. There might have been some extenuating circumstance. For some unaccountable reason, she didn't believe he was married now.

"You recall the man who walked you down the aisle. I see the knowledge written in your eyes. You've guessed before I can say the words. The memory is there. The wheels are turning in your very agile brain." With the tip of his finger, he tapped the side of her head.

"Yes, I remember. He was very nice, is nice," she corrected herself. "He stepped in to help when there was no one else. Is he supposed to be connected to me in some way?" She didn't like the notion. When she thought on it, the man was a better prospect than some. Better than the man who she'd always believed was her father.

"Do you recall that in the village he mistook you for his daughter, Gracie? You fainted when you heard his name. That was telling. For a few seconds the miscall stopped me." Jason seemed to be pointing out the obvious.

"Yes." Did she look like Miles' daughter? Is that the reason why he brought up the judge as a possible father to her?

"The two of you could be…," he began.

Tessa cut him off before he could finish. "No…" This reasoning was tainted with lies as well as deception. Gracie could not be her sister. She had her sisters. Didn't need anymore. "He can't be…" Muddled thoughts twirled in her head smashed together with force. Miles could be. She hated to admit.

"The man could be your father. In this case, so could his brother Armstrong. We, Jasper and I, will set up a meeting with them. While you were changing, I sent a quick message to the two men that I hoped we could speak with. Told them the meeting was important. Should come about as soon as possible. At first, I thought to have you help me word the missive. Changed my mind."

"They both slept with my mother?" She was shocked. On further thought she wasn't surprised. Anice would have pursued the twin brothers in order to muddy the water. "Isn't there something wrong with that?"

"I don't know, is the answer to both questions. Maybe, maybe not. We will discover the truth. I would make a guess they didn't sleep with her at the same time."

"Imagine either scenario should not come as a shock to me. My sisters and I were witness to any number of men coming through our house to see Mother. They always left with her for the night. She never kept her lovers secret." Bitterness seeped into Tessa's soul. The more she learned about her mother the more she lost respect.

"Your connection to Gracie is what brought the twins to my mind. Miles mistook you for his daughter. Your eyes are different from Gracie's, the color most decisive. You two are very similar in appearance. Enough so to give pause."

"I did feel as if I'd known her my entire life the moment I met her."

What about her other sisters? How were they going to feel? They would each gain another sibling through the connection to their mother.

"She might be another half-sister. Would you mind?" Jason asked, concern etched in his expression. He reached out to her then brought his hand back as if realizing touching her was too soon. They weren't through with the discussion. He could not risk touching her until the final period was put on the end.

"The question is would Gracie care if she was related to a bastard." While they'd met, Tessa didn't know her well enough to come to the conclusion. Neither did he. Her bitterness surpassed every other thought. Tessa despised the fact she was a bastard. Everything she thought she knew about herself along with her parentage was a lie. "He didn't care enough about me to claim me. The judge must despise me."

Jason cleared his throat before proceeding further. His thoughts did not bode well. "I doubt if Miles knew anything about you when he participated in our wedding. Do you think Anice would have told him he sired a baby? Maybe even then, Anice had plans of blackmail. Was thinking of a way to use you. Was waiting for the perfect opportunity."

"That would not surprise me. Would she have similar plans for the other three?"

Of course, the woman would have strategies. That was what she was all about. Getting what she wanted. Maggie thwarted her plans by running off with Jasper. He protected Tessa from the scenario she planned for his wife.

"We don't know if either man slept with her. One of them did though, I'm positive," Jason told her. "There are too many similarities to discount the possibility. The similarities are not a coincidence."

"What is the other man's name? The peer of the realm. Many aristocrats don't claim their bastards. Some did."

"Armstrong." Jason answered growing more concerned for Tessa. "After we meet with the Seymore twins, we'll have a better idea if one of them is your father. We could be wrong. If so, we are back to the beginning. Don't know where I would start if they both cry off as having never slept with the woman."

"If they both say they have?" Tessa didn't wish to think of that possibility. "Where are we then?"

"In either case, we are one step closer to discovering the truth. Now, we can play if you want. Come here." Jason patted his thighs. "Bring your wine. Let's get you a *wee* bit tipsy. You are such a delight when you've had a tad more to drink than you should to keep a steady mind. Not that it matters though. You are delicious every way you come to me."

Tessa hesitated. "I don't know. When did you ask to meet the two men? I'd like to be there. With you."

"Tomorrow or the next day. Understand they have a home in these parts. If they cannot come here, I'd like to go into the city." He patted his lap again. Smiled…his heart stopping grin.

"You'll let me come with you?"

The sigh issuing from his lips left him frustrated. It seemed she wasn't ready yet to play. "Yes," he said still moving his hand beckoning her to come to him. "Let's move on to the third part of the evening. What do you say?"

"Third part?" she questioned even though he was certain she understood his intentions. He wasn't subtle.

"More wine? Now that you don't need to think you can have as much as you like. The third part is to make love. To hold as well as explore all of you. All the parts I cannot get enough of."

"Maybe…?" she questioned as she walked toward him, fiddling with the three buttons that held her robe together.

"Take off the robe, sweet. While it's charming I believe there are other parts of you I'd rather notice. I have some tiny bows to play with. Bows I would like to undo. Need to see what lies beneath the robe along with the gown. It's been far too long since I've seen you. Start with the robe."

His comment sent flames to her cheeks. With cold hands she touched them. His wide grin sent more heat flaming to her face.

"Take off the robe. Undress just for me." His voice soft while he grinned. "Would you like me to do the honors? Taking clothing from your lovely body is always enjoyable. One of my favorite pursuits of pleasure."

For a few seconds more she fiddled with the buttons, twisting them as if she was having trouble. Tessa would understand as soon as the robe pooled on the floor, he would be able to see all of her. She planned this donning her most sheer gown. Nothing of her would be hidden from his view. He'd seen her many times before. Each time was special in its own way.

Turning her back on him, she unfastened the three fasteners at the top. Shifted the garment from her shoulders. The robe slid with slowness, she also planned, down her body to land on the floor. Lifting the sheer gown she now wore to her knees, Tessa stepped over the fabric. She wondered when he would insist she turn to face him.

Heard the small inhalation of air. Understood he was studying her. She gasped when his hands closed over her shoulders. Gulped when his fingers came around her to hold her breasts in his large hands. He set an inferno within her while his thumbs swept across the hard crowns with lazy abandon meant to seduce. He knew just what to do.

He ran his hands along her bare arms to her nape then back. His fingers wound into hers while he brushed his lips across the back of her neck then along the tops of her shoulders. She shuddered with the sensual pleasure his caresses evoked.

"Jason…" His name whispered from her. She didn't think she could say anything else or form a coherent thought. "Please…" It never failed to amaze her how swift her hunger rose when he wanted her.

"Tessa, sweet, sweet girl." His lips pressed against her shoulder. Teeth raked along her nape. Tantalized.

His teeth scraped there. Lips slid along sensitive territory. Silver flames of heat flitted in the depth of her core. One bow holding her gown in place fell to his questing mouth as he pulled on the tie. She shivered as the material slid downward. Caught on the tip of her breast. Hovered for seconds before continuing its freefall down the length of her body.

Another shudder rushed through her when he did the same to the second bow. When the fabric came untied, the gown slid to the floor. Little shivers of desire cultivated by the slight chill in the air caused goose bumps to form on her skin. She wanted to turn to him. Rub her cheek across naked flesh. He still wore all his clothing.

"You're cold." Once more, he ran his hands along her arms. Held her away from him so he could see her.

Impatient, he cast her into his arms then carried her to the big wing chair where he'd been sitting. She set her head against his chest. The velvet softness of his robe passed over her nipples. Sensations coursed through her at lightning speed. She needed to meet his flesh with hers.

A little purr of contentment ruffled in silence from the back of her throat. Tessa rubbed her cheek on the soft fabric.

"You're wearing too much," Tessa purred catlike, while she pushed at his robe, trying to help him get rid of the offensive clothing. She bit his chin then his shoulder.

With a few groans coupled with a grunt, the robe slipped from his shoulders. She untied the belt then pushed the fabric away. She was in a hurry to feel his skin next to hers. Needed his warmth to cover her.

"I want you, all of you," she pressed a kiss against the hollow between his collarbones. Caressed him with her cheek. His scent spicey as well as Jason. When she touched her tongue to his hot male flesh, she tasted salt. Her breath caught. Held for a few beats of her heart.

"This will be hot and messy. Can't wait a moment longer." He sat. Brought her with him. Ran his hands along her ribs. Spread her legs. Touched intimately. He kissed her nose. Rested his palm on the flatness of her belly.

"Oh!" She explored the hardness that was all Jason. Ran her hands across his chest. Touched everywhere. Placed kisses wherever she could reach.

His eyes smiled down at her, shining with raw passion. "I will still be the same in a few seconds. Waiting for you. Hard. Take your time. Remember, I told you I was going to savor every part of you. Take this joining as a serious lover should. We'll make this time slow…easy. My hand will be gentle." His hoarse voice resonated in the room. With a light willowy touch, he floated the palm of his hand across the crests of her breasts. Teased. Heated her from the inside out. "This isn't going to be like the desk this afternoon. Though, that held its pleasures."

Once the robe was opened, Tessa curled her fingers around him. She wished she dared taste him. Wanted to suck on that male flesh, play with him. Wondered if he would accept that boldness. He was so hard, so very smooth.

"Sleek satin," she murmured her voice in awe at what she felt. After she looked up, she asked, "Can I taste you? Here?" She looked down. Her voice was such a soft whisper Jason leaned forward. Their noses touched.

His Adam's apple moved up then down with the anticipation her words created. He kissed her forehead before setting his hand around hers. "Whatever you want. Don't know if I can last if I feel the sultry heat of your mouth on my sex. Taste. Savor. I'll try to control myself."

She ran her tongue along her lips as if she already treasured him with her mouth. Hesitant, she shifted her position to between his legs so she was kneeling in front of him. After that, she lowered herself until she could touch him with the tip of her tongue. Licked. A few ticks of the clock passed. His body tightened. She brought his member into her mouth. Sucked then drew harder. He growled. Tensed. She felt the pulsing of him, the vibrancy. Touched beneath to hold the soft spheres below his sex.

Her heart raced as his fingers slid into the length of her hair. Let the strands fall through his fingers.

"God, woman, what you do to me. Come here." He pulled her up so she lay against him. "I can't take any more just now. You will unwind me. I'll explode into your mouth. Must be inside you when that happens."

She felt the crisp dark hair of his chest pass across her nipples. Closed her eyes to better savor the moments. With a quick decisive twist of his body, Jason set her on the chair. Rid himself of his robe.

When he stood in front of her, she memorized him. Looked the length of him from his eyes to his toes then back. Before her studying gaze, his sex seemed to grow larger as she watched him with so much admiration it had to show in her eyes. "You're beautiful. I could look at you forever."

Sitting down, he brought her to straddle him. Her inner thighs felt the heat of his legs. She sensed him pulse against her. Was aware of the tip lying so close to the entrance of her core. It was hot and smooth. Throbbed proclaiming his need.

"Jason?" she queried with curiosity. Tilted her head to the side to better understand what he wished.

"Sit on me. Take me inside you. The control will be yours. You are in the driver's seat." His voice loomed like rich deep amber. Hoarse as well as throaty at the same time. The gold flecks in his eyes caught the fading light from the window, grew brighter as the light touched upon him. Then…they darkened with anticipation of the pleasure of their joining.

Tessa felt her eyes widen with the sudden realization of what he asked. His hands on her waist he helped her. Slow and easy, she lowered herself on him until he was deep inside. Filled her. Stretched her channel so he fit. She clenched her muscles, tightening around him.

"Jason…?"

"Hmm…" He helped her move on him.

"This isn't going to be slow." The start of her climax shattered as she brought her legs tight against his hips. Arched her back while she realized the command of this situation was lost.

He found the tiny swollen jewel. Circled the bud with his thumb. Thrust inside her passage. Once, twice. Touched her womb. She cried out with the pleasure, pulsing, milking his rod as he sent her to the sun. Filled her. Jason yelled out her name then sent his seed inside the molten heat of her secret depths.

Unable to move, Tessa lay against him. Heard the fast beating of his heart begin to slow. Listened to his breaths do the same. Running her hands along the width of his shoulders then down his arms, he was sweat sheened. Beautiful. All male to her female.

"Maybe when we are old and gray," she whispered.

"What?"

Her laughter was soft. "Maybe when we're old, we can do this slow. I don't care how. As long as I please you."

"I'm easy. As long as you find your pleasure. Still," he caressed her cheek. "I'd like to take my time. Want to kiss you everywhere. There will need to be a few rules for both of us for that to happen."

~ * ~

The meeting with Miles Seymore to Jason's great frustration proved unhelpful. Armstrong was in France on business. The younger brother was reticent. Didn't intend to offer information with his brother absent from the conversation.

"What do you know of Anice MacRae? Any data would be helpful." Jason jumped right to the point. Obvious to Miles he searched for news about Tessa not her mother.

Miles suspected there would be a meeting long before he received the message from Jason. He and his brother spoke of the possibilities before he left. Now the twins along with Tessa were sitting in the drawing room of the country estate located about ten miles from the Kenworthy home. Miles wished his brother might have joined them. Doing so was physically impossible for the older man.

"What can I do for you?" Miles asked as he tested the waters. He looked from one man to the other then on to Tessa. Tessa appeared tired, maybe a bit confused. Stress lines appeared around her eyes. While she sat on the edge of her chair, her hands were clasped tight.

As Tessa appeared tense, Jason had the air of a fully confident male. At first look, he appeared relaxed. On the second appraisal, his smile was predatory. The man would see to business first. No subtle innuendos would escape his notice. Jason Kenworthy was indeed formidable as was Jasper. It would be up to him to make certain his, along with Armstrong's scenario, was carried out.

He wished to know more in-depth reasons for the visit than what Jason Kenworthy wrote in the letter he received. Though Miles didn't have a difficult time making an assumption, he never appreciated guessing. When the twins discussed the situation, they understood it was only a matter of time before Jason along with Tessa would figure this out.

There were two relevant facts that would bring them to the conclusion. One was the similarities between Gracie and Tessa. The second was the fact he called her Gracie when he first noticed her in the village. He wouldn't take that back even if he could. Tessa was a beautiful young lady. To call her daughter or niece would be a pleasure. Miles resented the fact he didn't know if Tessa was his daughter. If she was, he intended to make up for lost time.

"Don't play dumb, Miles. We all," Jason gestured around the room, "understand the reason for this visit. We need to hear the truth from you as well as tell all that we know. There could be much at stake. Anice is a formidable woman with her own best interests in mind. She is not above blackmail."

"Alright, I understand more than I'm ready to admit. To gain the knowledge you're after will be invading mine as well as my brother's privacy. Not certain, under the circumstances, I'm ready to provide that information to you." Miles stood rocking on the heels. His hands were behind his back. His chin slanting in a determined position. In this, he wouldn't back down.

"I've a right to know if you're my father," Tessa blurted then turned to Jason as if asking permission to speak either that or seeking encouragement. She continued despite the narrowing of Jason's brows. "All my life I've wondered why I was so different from my sisters."

He shook his head giving silent warning to remain quiet, to allow him to do the talking. Miles thought the two must have rehearsed who would speak and who would not. Jason would have more experience in delicate conversations between men. Whether those be private or business, it didn't matter.

He wasn't about to acknowledge that right. Tessa was an adult now. Who her father was shouldn't matter that much. Tessa didn't know either his brother or him. Between his twin and himself, they decided the child was most likely Armstrong's. There was no way to be certain. A babe could result in one night of pleasure. He did take precautions. Nothing was infallible. Not the usual scenario though. Too bad there wasn't some type of test that could be given that would tell a man if he sired a child. Under the circumstances, it was possible Anice would know.

"Probably do. That doesn't mean I'm going to give up my privacy. I *ken* what the two of you wish to know. That is not something I intend to give out without Armstrong along for the decision. You must understand."

Miles watched her tiny fists clench in anger. Rose blossomed on her cheeks brought out by his refusal to cooperate. This one had a temper. One she held in check very nicely. His brother had more of a temper than he.

"What is that?" Jason asked as he sat back with the brandy Miles splashed into his glass a few minutes before. "What is it you're keeping from us?"

The man was conniving, weighed each question with care. "If I slept with Anice MacRae. Why don't the two of you ask her? Would she be forthcoming? Probably not. I doubt that woman gives out the names of her lovers unless doing so suits her."

Tessa's face flushed a deeper shade of pink. Ah, she understands who her mother is. That is good.

"My point exactly," Jason pointed out. "We must ask you along with your brother."

Just like Gracie's when she's embarrassed. A lovely girl. I wouldn't mind having another daughter. Don't think Tessa's is mine. She's Armstrong's. Has to be.

His twin slept with Anice for almost a year. They should have conceived in that time if no precautions were taken. He was certain there weren't. Maybe there were. His brother was a prudent man. Despite his effort to the contrary, he could have sired Tessa. Anice should have told him. He'd enquired a few times. After her adamant no, he forgot.

Before Armstrong left for Paris, they agreed nothing would be elaborated until they were both in residence. There would be nothing said. He agreed in principal that Tessa deserved to know her father. What he didn't like was admitting to her that he crawled into bed with the witch-woman. He imagined he needed to man up with the information. Not until Armstrong could be present to defend himself would he do that. He imagined Tessa would be disappointed neither he or his brother could shed any light on the information she wished to learn.

Tessa looked to Jason then back to him. She was asking permission to speak. With his nod, Tessa cleared her throat.

"Mother wouldn't tell me. I asked before when she threatened me. On this topic she is mute, except to tell me she will ruin my father if I don't do as she wishes. Since I've already defied her, we thought it prudent for you as well as Armstrong to learn about our fears."

"What did she hold over your head?" Miles asked becoming more curious now that new information was coming to light.

Her heavy sigh set his emotions rolling. "Your ruination…if you are my father. That's all. There is nothing else. I wouldn't wish to see someone such as yourself ruined because of me. Yet…" she paused a wistful look on her young face. "I've set the wheels in motion by marrying

Jason against her wishes."

"My ruination?" He squinted at her trying to see her expression clearer. Old age was nothing enjoyable. His sight grew worse with each year that passed. "How so? That woman does not have the ability to ruin me or my twin. Besides, you had nothing to do with your conception. This is not your fault. Never your fault."

"I guess…" she paused to look at Jason again a slight lift to her shoulders. "I guess by telling the good people of Glasgow, Scotland as well that you sired a bastard. Me. Don't know what else mother has in mind."

Miles chuckled. "Would love to have the likes of you for another daughter. Gracie as an only child would love to learn of a sister. Would never disown you if you were mine. Don't care what people think of me. If I sired you, I wouldn't be the first man to have a child out of wedlock. Doesn't make either one of us a lesser person."

"Then why?" Moisture shimmered in her startling sapphire eyes.

Eyes so similar to his twins. If nothing else convinced him she was Armstrong's, those eyes would.

He leaned forward, his arms braced on his thighs. "Armstrong and I agreed we wouldn't talk of this until his return. You are a lovely young lady. Any man would be proud to be your father."

"You don't think I'm yours." The disappointment in her gorgeous eyes was unmistakable.

Miles hesitated, almost telling her no, she wasn't his daughter. Caught himself. She was a beguiling little thing. Had a way of getting a man to open up to her even when he didn't wish to do so. He turned his attention to Jason Kenworthy. The smirk on the man's face gave credit to the fact he understood his wife's ploy.

Jason nodded. Miles thought if Kenworthy wore a hat, he would have tipped the brim in his wife's direction.

"Since there is no reason to stay, we should take our leave." Tessa rose. Her back stiff. Her smile only half of what it could be. "I understand why you won't say more on the topic."

The men stood.

She turned back to address him, "Will you be attending our

reception? Seems the man who stepped in for the father of the bride should be there."

"After today, do you want me there?"

"Yes. Gracie and Fletcher will attend. Maybe we can compare notes about our fathers," Tessa's irritation at his silence shone bright.

Chapter Seven

The day of the wedding reception started out with the sky covered in clouds. Dark. Dreary. Not the type of day Jason would have ordered for the long-anticipated event. This morning his wife kissed him on the cheek before dashing from the bedroom to spend the day with her sisters. She didn't even stay long enough to participate in their usual morning activities.

Sitting on the chair in front of the fireplace, Jason sipped his tea. Lack of knowledge about Tessa's parentage frustrated him. Coping seemed impossible. He waited for Jasper to arrive for a discussion on said topic.

He remained in the library until his brother's appearance. Together they would decide what was to be done with Anice when or if she came *sans* invitation to the party. Armstrong along with Miles agreed to attend. The entire village was invited. It would come as a surprise if Anice didn't discover the event then make all miserable with her appearance. No doubt, she would find a way to ruin the party.

They found all types of talent within the small scope of people in this rural setting. Musicians would play traditional Scottish songs. The food was traditional as well as coupled with some delicacies that were among Tessa's favorites including tiny lavender and spice cakes which she adored. The large cakes to be cut for the customary tastings were to be white with chocolate frosting, strawberries adorning the top as well as in between the layers would be featured. He was looking forward to Haggis along with Neeps and Tatties. For additional treats, he asked for shortbread.

The girls decided if Anice attended, she would be allowed to stay despite the lack of an invitation. Didn't wish to make a scene as long as her mother behaved herself. When she appeared, they would close ranks.

Protect the sisters from the woman's venom at all cost.

When he looked up, Jasper stood in the doorway. "Do you think Anice will be true to form and come?" Jasper asked while he poured himself a cup of tea then helped himself to a scone. He broke the bread, spread strawberry jam over it.

"If she stays true to form, then yes. Of course, Anice will put in an appearance. The question is when as well as what she will do to make life miserable for her daughter." Jason cocked his head toward his brother. "Who knows with the woman?"

"Anice would guess the Seymore brothers would attend since their country home is nearby," Jasper pointed out with a grimace. "She will wish to be present so she can gloat. Making an announcement tonight might be within her plans."

"She'll want to surprise us," Jason said with a bland tone. "Take us off guard. She'll guess we'll be expecting her on our doorstep. Maybe she won't make an entrance or spoil the special celebration. Perhaps she is capable of thinking of someone other than herself."

"Does that mean you don't believe she will attend?" Jasper asked. "Maggie is all a flutter. Doesn't want her sister's special event ruined by her mother. She does recall our wedding."

"Tessa is resigned. Seems to believe her appearance is inevitable. Just a matter of when not if," Jason said with thought. He trusted his wife was right on her assumption all the while praying she was wrong. A few prayers could be answered this evening. If so, he'd be a pleased man.

"Anice is a woman who weighs everything before she takes a step," Jasper said with a bit of angst tinging his voice. "She might want to make herself known on a different occasion. The woman wants surprise on her side. Enjoys the shock on a person's face when they realize they are trapped within her talons."

"All true," Jason's tone was bland. Too much time had been spent worrying about Anice MacRae's plans. Miles along with Armstrong were forewarned. Though neither man admitted siring Tessa, Jason understood the fact remained untold because neither man knew the truth. Even if Anice named a man, the accusation might come because of spite.

"Come…it's almost time to dress for the occasion," Jasper said as he rose. "While you would never wish to outshine your bride, you might wish to look presentable."

"The sisters wished to give her the traditional bridal gifts," Jason told his brother. "They are dressing together in Maggie's and my rooms. I took the liberty of putting my clothing in your rooms."

"Maggie is giving her the garter she wore the day we were wed. Do you think there will be a man out there to catch it? Will that bring good luck?" Jasper asked with a half-grin on his face.

"There always is a youngster to step into the fray. Do you know if she…" Jason found himself shaking his head. Tessa told him nothing about the wedding celebration plans? "Does Tessa have a bouquet to toss?" Maybe one of the sisters would catch the flowers. They were all about doing things the right way.

"Believe she does. Maggie would have seen to the purchase. They were in the village several days in a row cementing plans for this festivity. What have you been doing this last week? Seems you've got your head stuck in the clouds."

Jason looked up with a crooked smile. Lifted his shoulders a fraction as if his nonchalance gave him an excuse. "Haven't been doing anything if that is what you're implying. I bought her a sapphire necklace to match her eyes, earrings too. Her gown is of the same color. Tessa didn't get a wedding gown you know. Seems she learned from Maggie's mistake. Tessa didn't want to take any chances on the day of the wedding. What I regret is that the ceremony was such a speedy affair. There was no time to invite you and Maggie along with her sisters. Needed to take advantage of the opportunity that presented itself."

"Quite by accident her father might have walked her down the aisle," Jasper followed up on the idea. "That would be a nice touch since the man they all thought to be their father is in jail," he said, a wry touch of amusement in his voice.

"Might have been her uncle who did the deed. That's better than Clancy though my butler would have been pleased to do the honors. He might also have been pleased to be the father," Jason said with a masculine snort to end his words.

"The man is a good sort. He's been there for the Kenworthys since we traveled to Ireland to protect Maggie."

"Jasper?" Maggie stood at the doorway. "Are you free?" she questioned with a mischievous grin on her petite face.

Jason jumped, startled by the unexpected intrusion. He thought they would be alone for at least another hour. Should have closed then locked door before they began to talk. One would think they would learn from their mistakes. It was apparent he nor his twin thought to take the precaution.

"Didn't expect to see you for another few hours." Jasper rose to bring Maggie into his arms for a long hug.

The light kiss he gave her had Jason wishing Tessa would show up in the doorway unanticipated. Would appreciate a surprise such as the one his brother just had. A little play in the middle of the afternoon would be delightful, an afternoon delight. The diversion might hold him over until they could retire for the night.

Then again it might not.

His appetite for his wife didn't diminish with one encounter. Seemed to escalate every time they were together. This morning, she left before he could make love to her. Jason peered around the couple hoping to catch a glimpse of Tessa.

"If you're searching for Tessa, you won't find her behind me," Maggie said with a little giggle then a wink at Jasper. "She's at the gazebo seeing to the decorations there for this evening. You might…Tessa told me she'd like your input."

"I'm on my way," the younger twin said grinning as he strode from the house. She wished for his input. He could think of many different ways to do that. Input…hmm…

Shooing away any help Tessa had at the gazebo would be his pleasure. For a few minutes before guests started arriving and the girls left to dress, he needed to see his wife. Hold her. Fill her. If there was privacy, she would let him have his way. Tessa was never able to say no to him. That was one of the things he adored about his wife.

A pleased feeling in his heart, Jason strode down the pathway leading to the gazebo while he tried not to run. They played at the little piece of paradise in his backyard before the house was filled with an abundance of people. Now, he couldn't count on not having company even if they started alone.

When he reached the shaded summer place, Jason saw her sitting on one of the cushioned sofas. Her feet were tucked up underneath her. In front of her, she held a pillow, her smile angelic. She waved to him, beckoning him. He saw the deep rise then fall of her breasts. As she anticipated him, her eyes darkened. Tessa wanted him. The notion sent heat pulsing to every masculine part that could perform. He was eager. Excited to the tips of his hairy toes. She liked his toes. He couldn't figure that out.

He stepped onto the platform. "You invited me? I was pleased to hear you were at the gazebo," he told her while he wondered about her plans for the afternoon. Hope they were in tandem with his. "Did you have something in mind?" He asked, a tilt to his smile. There wasn't a soul around. To his surprise, no one was close. On his way here, he noticed the girls helping to put tablecloths over the many tables that would see their guests.

"Yes, and yes again." Her little half-smile delighted him. She ran her fingers through hair that tumbled to her waist. He wanted to do the same. Feel the cool silken strands slide between his fingers.

She was precocious. A little flirt. A delicious looking little flirt. Tessa was all his. Seemed she missed him as much as he missed her. "Are you being coy?"

"Perhaps." Smiling at him, she lowered her lashes, set her finger against her rosy lips. "I might be if that's what you would like me to be. Can do most any role. Name one."

"Can I sit?" Jason motioned to the couch where there was plenty of room for him to join her. He watched as she tilted her head seeming to consider his question.

"Yes. If you won't misbehave," Tessa told him with a demure lowering of her lashes. "You can't be taking advantage of me. I wouldn't like that if you did."

The little minx. "We both understand what is going to happen if I stay. You know I'll misbehave. Understand if I can find a way to take advantage of this situation, I will."

"Not used to not seeing you for several hours," she murmured while she once again lowered her eyes. Batted the long sooty lashes against the creamy whiteness of her flesh while she pretended to study the ground. "Needed to hear your voice."

"Is that all you needed?" Jason's voice was hoarse. His body filled with eagerness.

"No."

The gown she wore was made for comfort. The scooped corsage coupled with small sleeves would be easy to push over her shoulders then down her arms until he witnessed her beautiful twin globes as they swayed with delicious pretense. She would blush, coloring the rounded tops. Thinking of tasting her sweetness speared into his groin. He wished to treat the tips of her beautiful breasts as if they were his favorite candy. If she looked, Tessa would see the evidence he could never hide from her. He was hard. Ready to fill her. Taste her heat. Needed to kiss her everywhere. Not this afternoon. He would save that pleasure for their evening tryst.

"Are you sure you want me?" Inside the gazebo, they were alone. Where the festivities were being organized, there were people everywhere. Working to make this evening a success. Anyone could interrupt their private moment. The danger of that made this assignation even more arousing, titillating in the extreme.

Tessa nodded. Stretched her skirts over her legs. Hesitated before speaking, "I've nothing on beneath my gown."

He sucked air. Hit the side of his head with the base of his hand. His heart lurched while he thought, startled by her statement yet pleased too. "Brazen hussy," he murmured having not expected anything like that. He had no trouble imagining what she looked like beneath the fabric.

"You like me that way? Naked?" Tessa blushed, for the first beat since saying the words she appeared uncertain.

"Love everything about you. Your brazen side. The shy maiden. My wife who likes to take me into her mouth. Love every way you come to me. Keep surprising me. I can't wait to touch you beneath your skirts."

"I hoped you would." Tessa played with the skirt of her gown. "Didn't know what I'd do if you were upset with me. I thought…" She twitched her skirts, shuffling the fabric across her legs, giving him glimpse of bare feet as well as ankles.

Jason sat down next to her. Drew her into his arms for a long deep kiss. God, he wanted to make love to her in this idyllic setting. Serene but a dangerous place with all the people surrounding this tiny paradise. Pressing kisses along her shoulders he nudged the sleeves of her gown down one arm then the other. Only a few more nudges…

The creamy globes were rounded above the corsage. Ripe. Enthusiastic to be grasped. When he looked downward, he was rewarded with the sight of the rose color around her nipples. She relaxed into him. Gave him a puffy piece of air telling him she liked what he did. He rubbed his cheek across the tops of the soft globes that still needed their revealing. She gasped. Drew air into her lungs. He had minutes enough to slow his as well as her passion. Perhaps this would be the time they moved at a snail's pace.

Instead of moving too fast, he brought his mouth to cover hers. A measured caress. Languid in the extreme. Swept his tongue across her lips, urging her to open for him. Little encouragement was needed. Her heat flamed. She countered by penetrating the inside of his mouth with her tongue. Massaging his with the velvet softness of hers. Teasing him. She purred. He met her tongue with his. Fenced as they enjoyed the moments. He deepened the kiss.

Penetrate.

Retreat.

That was a pattern he capitalized on.

Pierce.

Withdraw.

Felt the low rumble of a growl come from his throat while her ribboned response of absolute pleasure entered into him. She tasted of sweet mint, of aroused heated woman. The dark sultry confines of her mouth set him on fire. Rocked him to his soul. He would never be able to experience enough of this woman. Knew there was more pleasure to be had with his wanton vixen. Her passion raged, simmered within his command.

Holding back longer was not an option. He needed to taste more of her. Sip on more tender sensual spots on her lush body. Create more after that even more magical enchantment. Without hesitation, he pressed her sleeves down her arms until the lush fulness of her breasts were freed. The tips showed her physical response to him. Jason moved far enough away from her to gaze at her. Watched as she responded to his sensual perusal.

The slight breeze beneath the covered gazebo floated across them. Whispered the fragrance of summer. Shadowed patterns of leaves laced the ground in intricate displays. As if in response to the cool air, the beautiful crowns on Tessa's breasts hardened further while his body heated then strained against the confines of his britches. The buds were tight, eager for savoring. With gentleness, he bent to sip on one then the other. Sucked the globe into his mouth. Tasted her delicate flavor. Savored. Tessa whimpered then arched against him giving him more intimate access. Her fingers tightened on his shoulders while she steadied herself. She pushed on his frockcoat. The fabric slid down his arms.

Beneath her gown, his roaming hand caressed creamy soft flesh of her inner thigh. Twitched higher to sense the soft hair at the apex of her thighs, a bit in awe of the moment, he spoke, "You didn't lie. Will you come to the reception tonight this way? Naked except for the gown you wear."

"If that's what you would like?" Her smile was shy.

He was surprised when she didn't hesitate in her answer. After thinking about what she accepted, Tessa might feel different when the time came to dress. She would be with her sisters. How would that go?

The snap of a twig. The clop of a foot falling on the path brought him back to the real moment at hand. Their privacy was invaded. With quick flicks of his hands be brought her gown to cover her breasts after removing his hand from under her gown. Bemoaned the fact he would not get to see to her pleasure.

Tessa whimpered. Her mercurial pleasure was being denied. Her voice trembling, she questioned his sudden withdrawal. "Why? Why are you stopping? We can have…no one is around." Eyes wide she gazed at him.

Jason set his forehead against hers. "I'm sorry. Should have known better. We've got company. Don't wish to share you with anyone. Doesn't seem I've a choice." He didn't regret the kiss that led to more. What he did regret was the fact she would not receive her pleasure. Relived his request. Smiled at the thought she considered it.

"Well, well, if it isn't my wayward daughter with her husband? Did I interrupt a dalliance? Ah, too bad. Went against my wishes to wed a Kenworthy rake. You'll rue the day you didn't listen to me." Anice's voice was cold, colder than he'd ever heard it before. Her eyes frigid with hate. The threat was all too obvious for his likes. This woman detested her daughter.

He turned to face the woman who birthed his wife. That was the only part she played in the upbringing of the woman he loved that was at all good. "What do you want? You do realize there is nothing here for you. You aren't welcome on my land." He wasn't surprised at the harshness he heard in his tone. Even though he expected Anice to show up, controlling his anger would be difficult.

Behind him, Tessa clung to him. Her small hands on his arms tightened as she came to realize all her mother wanted to do here was to create trouble. Her labored breathing did nothing to soothe his anger. The woman shattered their brief moment of privacy. He knew the others respected their time here.

"You've figured out who your father is?" Anice directed the question to Tessa. "How drole. I'm certain whatever you decided you are mistaken. You couldn't guess. Your father is obvious to anyone with intelligence." Her laughter sent a shiver through Jason. He wished he could signal someone to have her removed. They employed no one for that job. Hind sight. A few well-trained men placed around the perimeter of the gardens would have been wise.

The stiffening of Tessa's small body was apparent. Jason hoped her mother would answer. Anice didn't deserve a reply to something so horrendous that Tessa couldn't ever figure out who the man was.

"If more blackmail is on your mind, you can forget it," Jason told her, the smooth edges of his words belied his fury. Standing up to her was the only way to proceed in this matter. They couldn't allow Anice to believe she held the upper hand. Her threats would be unheeded. She would fail in her efforts. No one would believe her accusations.

Anice paled as if his words were a backhanded slap. “The man doesn’t want his name revealed,” she said as if trying to regain her footing.

“Her father won’t give you anything for your silence either. There will be no rewards for your threats,” Jason continued. After his meeting with Judge Seymore, he didn’t believe either Miles or Armstrong would care about the revelation Anice threatened. They both would claim Tessa as their daughter if given the chance.

“You don’t know that. Can’t understand what it is I hold over his head. I’ve spoken with the man several times. He is aware of his daughter. Doesn’t want anything to do with her. Doesn’t want his name out there associated with a bastard child, male or female. He’s made his wishes clear.”

This scenario didn’t sound anything like the Seymore twins. She was pretending, flaunting what she thought was the upper hand. Trying to make them believe her story. Why? To Jason there didn’t seem to be anything to be gained with dishonesty. “You’re grasping at straws, madam.,” Jason said deadpan. Yet the idea flitted through his head that neither Miles or Armstrong were Tessa’s father. What if all their guessing was for naught? He couldn’t bear the thought. Just because Tessa resembled another woman didn’t make them related. Just because her eyes were the same vibrant sapphire as Armstrong’s eyes didn’t make the man her father.

Tessa didn’t look like her mother either.

“I won’t be staying,” Anice purred as if she just caught a mouse in her sharp little teeth. Cats played with their prey. “Won’t interrupt your fun…yet. The two of you may party alone. You didn’t invite me. Won’t attend another event uninvited. The last one invited too many repercussions for my taste.”

With that said she turned and left them. Tessa’s face pressed against his back. He heard the difficult lumber of air into her lungs. “Come,” he said as he faced her. “You need to get ready. Wish to see you in that beautiful gown. I’m certain your sisters will be more than ready to see to everything you need. It’s almost as a wedding day should be. I would have you with a smile on your face.”

"Yes." It didn't seem she was too exuberant. With her mother's visit, she seemed to have lost the pending excitement along with the glow of anticipation that was on her face before Anice made an appearance.

"You know we shouldn't allow her to ruin this day." He lifted her chin to see into the beauty of her eyes. "We're going to enjoy all our friends. Laugh. Dance. Eat. Afterwards I'll finish what I started this afternoon."

This day was supposed to be perfect. Since the dreariness of the early morning, the clouds disappeared. Now the sun shone bright as well as hot. Looking out on the preparations, all was going with smooth ease. The musicians practiced. The sound of pipes filled the air. If not for Anice's appearance here, he would feel content.

"I'll walk you to Maggie's room. I hear your dress is there. First, however, I'm going to give you my gift to you on our wedding day."

"You brought me a gift?" she asked, her eyes wide, her hands set on his shoulders. She pressed. "I don't…I didn't know. Don't have anything for you."

He felt her distraught in every nuance of her small body, in every expression crossing her face. He hoped Anice spoke true. Prayed she was gone for the evening. Headed back to Glasgow where she could make all the trouble she wished. "You're all the gift I need. Don't wish for anything else."

When Jason started out to see Tessa at the gazebo, he put the small box in his pocket with the intention of giving her the necklace, her wedding gift after they made love. He reached for the package. Handed it to her. Tessa's eyes lit with vibrance, the blue twinkling. During her short life, she'd not received many gifts. This would be the first in many for her. His intention was to shower her with things she would like.

Her hands trembling, Tessa accepted the package. She seemed to be afraid to open the box. He was impatient. Beneath lowered lashes she looked at him. Still shy despite the changes in her personality over the last year. He would never tire of this woman. Just as he was certain Maggie would never bore Jasper. Tessa was made perfect for him.

The ribbons surrounding the gift fell to their feet then the box. Tessa held the glittering sapphires draped across her fingers. She looked at them then at him then back. Tessa seemed awed. Astounded. “They are beautiful. I’ve never…except for my engagement and wedding rings, owned anything so beautiful. Thank you.”

“You’re pleased?” he couldn’t help but ask. “I hoped you’d like the necklace. May I?” he held out his hand hoping to fasten the chain. Needed to see Tessa wearing the jewels that were beautiful, but not as lovely as her eyes.

“May you?” she questioned as if she didn’t wish to let go of the chain of sapphires. As if she didn’t understand what he asked.

“Fasten the necklace. You do wish to wear it.” His voice held a wealth of amusement. “I would help if you allow me. Push your hair to the side.”

“Yes.” Tessa handed it to him then turned, lifting her long hair out of the way. “Please. I doubt if I could fasten it by myself.”

After, he stepped back to look at her. “Perfect.”

Arm in arm the lovers walked back to the house. They were the picture of newlyweds. Jason walked her to Jasper’s and Maggie’s rooms. He was reluctant to leave her. Wished they could dress together in their suite. If that happened, they would never make it to the festivities in their honor.

Stopping at the closed door, he spoke, “Hear we are. Suppose I’ll see you downstairs in an hour…or…would you like me to come for you and we can appear at the celebration together? Make an entrance.”

“Together. Yes, come for me in one hour. We’ll weather the entertainment together. All of the guests,” her voice was tentative.

“Are you frightened?” Jason asked, wishing he could remove any fear.

“As I know I shouldn’t be, can’t help but have a little angst.”

Anice’s visit shook her. He could tell by her posture, by the slight downward tilt of her shoulders. “A deal. I’ll be right here in one hour.” He placed a chaste kiss to her forehead. “More? Would you like another kiss for courage?”

Deciding they needed more of a kiss to sustain themselves for the remaining hour, Jason didn’t wait for a response. He claimed her mouth with his. She parted her lips for him. Their tongues danced together in perfect harmony. Played until she moaned. Clung to him. Pressed her small body so there was no space between them.

She advanced.

He retreated.

With little effort, they lit each other on fire. When he finally withdrew, her lips were kiss-swollen, bee stung. Damp with the contact between them. He ran his hand along her spine to her cleft then back recalling with this intimacy she wore nothing beneath her gown. He was tempted to bring the fabric higher. Wanted to cup her delicious bottom with his hands. Was reminded of her words to him.

"You will appear this way for the celebration." He understood by the tone of his voice this was more a command than the question he meant it to be. Realized she might have a problem fulfilling his request.

Once more she must have decided to play coy. Lowering her lashes, "What way?"

His bark of laughter caused her eyes to widen. "You know what way. Don't make me elaborate. If that happens, I'll find the nearest empty room to show you how I want you. If that happens, we will be late to our party. Might not appear a'tall. Might get so sidetracked that we forget all about our guests."

"You wouldn't?" she dared as well as questioned him at the same time. Turned as if to open the door. An escape attempt would never deter him. He would do as he pleased.

"Don't think so?" He slanted her a dark look then grinned, a wolf's grin, showing his even white teeth. "You understand to do so would be my pleasure. I'm refraining, tamping down my desire, only because I assume you would like to spend the next hour with your sisters. Though…" He paused while he stroked his chin thinking, making plans. "We seem to ignite each other. A little romantic tête-à-tête in the library might not take more than a few minutes. The short, fast dalliance would please us both. Tell me what you think. Should I carry you off to the library?"

"You're speaking of more than conversation," Tessa announced as if he didn't understand that fact for himself. "I don't—"

"Yes," he interrupted with another sardonic grin molding his lips into a smirk. "If I didn't know your ripe little body so well, I would think you're still aroused. Damp in appropriate places. Ready for the dalliance I'm speaking of."

"I…I am."

"Are you wet?"

The blush she always wore when he spoke about sex deepened to a dark rose. He chortled, pleased with the knowledge she gave him by the swift rise of color. Thought perhaps they could ease each other, take the edge off. If he took her to his office, locked the door, cleared his desk they would both be in better condition to face the night ahead of them.

Supposed he teased her enough. "I'm going now. I will be here in an hour. If you're not dressed in the way you tempted me earlier, I'll do something about it. Fix the little *faux pas*. Do you understand?" The warning was clear.

He couldn't spell it out better. She would do as she intended. He would follow up on whichever path she chose to negotiate. Looking forward to the end of the hour along with what it would bring, he turned to leave. Whistling, he strode to his room to dress. However she turned up, it would end the same. Tessa would be naked beneath the beautiful sapphire gown she wore.

~ * ~

Every time Tessa thought to surprise Jason, he turned the table on her. Shifted his position so she couldn't counter with a different strategy. Thought the fact she wore nothing beneath her gown would delight him. It did. That wasn't the problem. Now, he asked, no, told her to do the same for the celebration.

When she was half-naked for him this afternoon, she knew few people would be around to notice. It would just be the two of them at the gazebo. Only the two of them who would know what she didn't wear. At the reception there would be over two hundred people milling about, looking at her. She didn't believe she could do that. Thinking about it caused heat to race through every nerve. If anyone else discovered her state of deshabille, she'd be mortified.

Tessa didn't doubt for a beat if he came to escort her and she wasn't dressed the way he hoped, he would do something to fix that condition. She fingered the sapphires at her throat then looked at her hand where she wore the beautiful rings he bought. Jason deserved all that he wished for.

The man was generous. She didn't need precious gems to love him. Love Jason she did. More than ever, with each passing second her heart beat faster when she thought about him. Understood even if doing so would embarrass her, she would do anything he asked.

Nonetheless, she needed the man to love her.

Knocking on the door to Maggie's suite of rooms, her breath hitched. He stood behind her, his hands resting on her shoulders, thumb moving in lazy circles. Teasing. Always inciting. Possessive. Deep inside she pulsed. Ached for him.

"Tessa you're here! We all thought you would…" Maggie left the rest of the sentence in the air when she saw the couple. Noticed the expression on her face.

Jason placed a lazy kiss on the back of her neck where the necklace was held together. Smiled. "You will meet me here in an hour. The way we discussed."

"Please." As if she could hear his thoughts, he was revisiting their earlier conversation about the state he expected her clothing.

Ignoring him, she focused her attention on her sister. Stepped into the room. Waited until the door closed behind her. She spoke the second most pressing item in her head. "Mother was here." Tessa didn't want to put a damper on the evening. Reminded herself it was her mother who caused the obstruction to having fun. Her mother who had the ability to ruin the evening.

"You saw her?" Nellie asked, coming up to the door to meet her. "She was outside with you along with Jason? I can't believe her nerve."

"She was. Still threatening me with the life of a father I've no knowledge of. Jason reassures me that all will be fine. He doesn't care if my parentage is announced to the entire world. He will stand by me. Don't know if the rest of you care about who your father is. I shouldn't care about the identity of mine either."

"We've been through the scene before. Remember my wedding?" Maggie stepped into the conversation with the question as she handed her a glass of wine. "Drink up. Seems you will need the fortification. Mother never brings out the best in anyone. If she says she is leaving, she will do the opposite. Count on the fact."

"Mother did tell me she wasn't staying. She made her appearance. Said that was enough. Now she is gone. At least that is what she said." The following hesitation provoked her to ask. "Do you truly believe she will do the opposite?" Tessa prayed she'd seen the last of her mother tonight. It wasn't as if she would visit Anice of her own accord or even if she was summoned again. Neither Keir, in Glasgow, or Clancy here would allow her entrance to the Kenworthy homes if the twins gave the order they were forbidden.

"You believe her?" that question coming from Fannie. "I don't. Agree with Mags. The woman will do the opposite. Always has, always will. It is not a question of if she will make an appearance tonight, it is when."

"Neither do I," Tessa said with a soft sigh of regret. "She'll wait until everyone is having a great time to do whatever evil she might have in mind. Even if showing herself just puts a damper on our fun, she won't be able to keep herself away from that bit of pleasure for herself."

"Forget about Mother. Whatever happens will happen. To worry about it now is a waste of time. Let's get you dressed." Maggie brought in the sapphire gown the village seamstress created for her. Held the dress aloft for all to see before setting it aside. "Matches your new necklace along with your eyes. Perfect."

Tessa touched the stones with the tip of her finger. "A belated wedding gift is what Jason told me."

The village seamstress created silk underthings that matched the gown. The elegant ballgown hung by the window. The underclothing was draped over Maggie's arm. She looked at her sisters then the garments. To tell her sisters she wasn't going to put anything on under the gown would mortify her. She couldn't do it. Must take her chances with Jason. She would dress in the normal way. Hope he didn't act on his request.

With any luck, he'd forget what he asked of her. Jason wouldn't forget something like that. Never in a hundred years.

"Why are you so red?" Fannie asked, curiosity in her voice. "It's not as if we haven't gotten dressed together before. Does marriage make you shy?"

"Maybe…maybe not. It's just that…that I did something this afternoon. Now, that act is coming back to bite me." *In the butt*. She didn't know how to tell her sisters how brazen she was. They would… what would they think? Maggie would understand because she was married to Jasper. Jasper must be much the same as Jason.

"What was that?" Maggie asked, a smile tilting the corners of her mouth. "Got to tell us. We've never kept anything a secret. Who better to tell something that's embarrassing to than your sisters in crime?"

"I told…" Tessa couldn't say the words that seemed to stick in her throat. Tessa cleared her throat giving her time to plan what she could say along with what she didn't dare to tell.

Drawing in a deep breath of air, she looked around the room. Her sisters were all waiting with anticipation in their eyes. If Maggie was the only one within hearing distance, she might be able to say the words. It wasn't just Maggie. Fannie and Nellie listened, seeming to hold their collective breaths.

"Go on," Nellie told her, nodding her head. She pulled the hairpins from her lips so she could talk better. "This should be interesting. Your eyes always speak volumes. Right now, they are as big as saucers."

Tessa gulped air which didn't do anything to tamp down the embarrassment flooding through her system. She thought she should just go ahead, blurt the words and be done with this conversation. Shaking her head. No, she meant to take her chances with Jason. She would dress in the way he expected.

A quick turn about in her mind had her blurting her thoughts. "I'm not going to do it," she warred with herself. Debated pros along with cons until she couldn't think. Her mind was a muddled mess. She was stymied.

"Do what?" Fannie asked with a slight twist to her head as if the new position would help her understand. "You *ken* it's not fair of you to keep teasing us."

"Not fair at all," Nellie echoed her sister.

Fannie was right. She shouldn't tease. Once they heard, her sisters would all understand her reticence to relate her thoughts.

"Jason doesn't wish for me to wear anything beneath my gown tonight. He pushed me to agree. I would test him by…if I don't do what he asks, there is not one doubt in my head that he will remove my undergarments." The hushed silence told her more than she wished to know. Nellie along with Fannie were flushed to the roots of their blond hair. Her words didn't seem to affect Maggie in anyway.

Maggie's snort then her trilling laugh sent a shiver down her spine. No, Maggie understood all too well what Jason hoped for.

Men.

"All men must be cut from the same cloth," Maggie laughed again this time with a soft chuckle. "At least the Kenworthy twins are much the same. Jasper is constantly implying, not at all subtly, that I go *sans* underwear. I've never done that for him. He has never insisted." Maggie laughed again at something she must be thinking. "Maybe we should both surprise our husbands. What do you think?"

The heat covering Tessa's entire body grew hotter. In Maggie, she sensed a kindred spirit. How could she tell her oldest sister she put the bug in Jason's head, not the other way around? Given a few more days with her, though, he might suggest for their best interest she go without benefit of clothing beneath her gown all the time. He would tell her, pantalettes along with her chemise would slow them down.

"You're turning even darker," Fannie pointed out with a snort. "Why on earth would men want their wives to go without underwear? Makes no sense to me."

"Why not?" Nellie countered, a mischievous look in her eyes. "They could—" she was cut off by the oldest.

"What do you know?" Maggie asked with concern coating her words. The oldest pointed a finger at her. "You haven't…"

"No, of course not. I've listened to your lectures. Made some assumptions of my own. Maybe I've jumped to a few conclusions, but…" She pushed out a curved smile that made her look years older. "What else would you believe?"

"After what you just told me, I might need reassurance that you haven't acted on a man's suggestions." Maggie told her.

Nellie retorted by waving her hand in the air. Then repeating her declaration in part. "Of course not. I'm going to wait until I've a ring on my finger and the vows have been said to sleep with a man. Besides, I haven't found a man I'm interested in enough to wish to marry."

The sigh between oldest and youngest sister was only acknowledged by the pair. There was nothing else to do. Maggie didn't wait but thought she had. Jason managed to have the vows said then the ring on her finger before he made love to her.

"How much time is left? Thought I heard Jason say he would be at the door in an hour," Maggie said as she set the underclothing aside. "I can barely wait until Jasper discovers what is not beneath my gown. I will memorize his face at the time."

Maggie was eager. She wasn't quite so enthusiastic as Maggie. Tessa realized the moment he made the suggestion he would take every available opportunity to get his hands beneath her gown. To entice. Arouse. He wanted her ready for his bed when they arrived later tonight. In a way this would be a wedding night. A second wedding night for them. Maybe for Maggie this would be a second wedding night for her too.

Tessa understood they would make love into the *wee* hours of the morning. The breath she held let go with a rush. She stood in front of the mirror, trying to decide if anyone would be able to tell if she wore nothing beneath.

"You can't tell." Maggie stood behind her looking at the mirror as if reading her thoughts. "Except for the fact the corset is missing. That part is obvious."

Swallowing a lump in her throat, Tessa murmured. "I can see my nipples. They're poking against the material of my gown. What if it's a little chilly out? They'll grow even harder and bigger. I can't…" She thought about how the crowns hardened with chilled air. How Jason could pass the palm of his hand across them and they would grow larger.

"That's what this lace shawl is for. You can wrap it around your shoulders. Tie it in front between your breasts. It will also hang down your back. No one will be the wiser," Maggie seemed to try to reassure. "I've one also. As Jasper wouldn't wish for anyone else to see me like this, I would presume neither would Jason. Smile, this will be fun."

Tessa wasn't as certain about the fun part as Maggie. Thinking about showing up this way sent her nerves crashing into each other. She felt naked. Jason along with Jasper would be at the door to greet them in five minutes. There was no more time to change. The ormolu clock ticking on the mantle beat a cadence that permeated in her head, became part of her.

Seemed to seduce.

Provoke. Awaken every female part of her.

Her sensuality exposed.

The knock rocked her. She gasped in a lungful of air. This was the moment. There was no going back. Not that going back would help.

"Are you ready, little sister?" Maggie asked, seeming eager to make her way to her husband. Her expression was wicked. As she walked, Maggie's hips swayed to show off her bottom.

The sisters stood behind them grinning, as if they understood all they shouldn't. Tessa hoped neither one had an idea about what was going on between the couples. Tonight, there would be a lot of touching. Caresses that would never be proper. Skims of hands over sensitive places, intimate places. While Maggie was looking forward to the secret, private moments she would garner with her husband, Tessa was terrified of the possibilities of each one.

Maggie opened the door. "Jasper…Jason…assumed the two of you would come together. Jason, your bride is ready for you."

Jason's grin was broad, all-knowing as he watched her step to him. When he held out his hand, she accepted. Heat burned through her at first contact. His gaze flamed. The heat of his touch speared higher. For several ticks of the mantle clock, he focused on the outline of her breasts. If not for the shawl, he would have noticed the hard outline of her nipples. He nodded, approval shining in his lovely brown eyes.

He brought her hand to the crook of his arm. Bent to speak to her. "You're beautiful tonight." His fingers grazed her skin when he traced the sapphires adorning her neck. Lingered. Swept across the fabric as if the material was offensive. "Why the shawl? The evening is warm. Would send your maid for it if you needed it. A man wants to see his woman, all of her."

In her mind she supplied the missing words. *Wearing nothing a'tall.*

"Thinking ahead. That's all." Tessa found that his words caused a shiver to rip up her spine. "You don't object. Do you?" She didn't know why she asked.

Jason was asking questions to discover the truth. He didn't need to ask. The way he studied her at first sight would have told him all he needed to know.

"How do you feel?" He squeezed her arm, let his hand roam from shoulder to wrist. When his exploring hand travelled back, he set his fingers beneath the lace. Hard knuckles passed across soft globes. She shuddered. Knew he felt her reaction. Understood he would be pleased.

"Nervous," Tessa told him, refusing to give away what he wanted to hear. She meant to deal with this predicament of her making the best way she could.

When he explored, they stopped walking. Jasper with Maggie walked around them. Tessa heard their chatter. Now that he discovered more truths, they continued on the path to the table that was set up for them. The walkway was lined with well-wishers.

She stumbled on an uneven cobblestone. He held tight to her. His hands dropped to her waist to assist.

"Everything alright?" he asked as he supported her. Held her close. He would feel more of her. Would understand more. She had nothing to hide. Nothing at all. She was open to any plans he might create.

His thumbs traveled along her ribcage. Touched upon the underside of her breast. She jerked at the silky, smooth caress of his long fingers. This night was going to seem an eternity if Jason continued in this vein. While he continued the calculated yet subtle assault on her person, heat flooded her face. She wished she dared cool them with her hands while his remained below the evocative covering of her shawl.

All he did was hidden from view.

"Fine," she tried not to stutter the word. Thought she succeeded until she heard the low vibrations of his laughter. The man understood he called her bluff. She needed to figure things out before she was drowning in deep water.

"Fine is good, very good indeed. Can you be more specific?" he inquired of her while the light of amusement shimmered in the golden specks of his eyes. Continued light strokes meant to incite. "I would learn more."

Tessa nodded toward the tables. "Believe the guests are waiting for us. Looks as if Jasper has poured champagne. I would like something to drink." She started forward. His hand closed around her waist.

"Not so fast, little one. I have something else in mind before we settle down at the table to eat. Tell me more about what you're feeling," he kept insisting. Appeared he would never back down until she told him what he asked.

Jason brought her close. Molded her form against his. He cupped her bottom with his large hands, drawing her close. So close, she felt the evidence of his desire. With this contact, he would know she wore no pantalettes. The motion of his fingers caused shudders to dance through her body.

His kiss was brief with a myriad of promises. The roar from the guests reverberated in her ears. Cries of 'more and again' coupled with ribald gests greeted the embrace. Continued even after he ended the kiss. With little distance between them, he smiled at her. His look of possession along with confidence told her she fought a losing battle of wills. His was by far the strongest.

"Yes," He murmured still focused on her. "There will be more of this, along with that," he whispered close to her ear as another tender caress on her bottom sent ribbons of pleasure to dark secret parts that only Jason knew. "Right now, I believe we'll be doing this."

Tessa tried to ignore the heat of arousal as well as the fire of embarrassment. She was certain there would be more of both before the night ended for them. His fingers didn't stop moving. Caressed. Molded. Enchanted. Even while they walked to meet Maggie and Jasper, Jason found ways to rush desire.

At the bride and groom's table, Jasper handed them the glasses he filled. "Cheers," Jasper told them. "May your life be blessed with everything you want as well as need. Children who will adore you. Along with every man's dream, a woman who can seduce her man, with a glance, a gesture, even the suggestion of nothing a'tall," Jasper's gaze traveled to his wife whose blush told him he knew what she was thinking.

Another roar went up surrounding them. “Kiss her! Kiss her!” The chant continued. “Kiss your bride.”

Jason cocked an eyebrow at her. A sharp crack of laughter followed. “Should we give them what they want? Won’t do anything without your go-ahead, sweetheart. What do you say? A kiss for our guests? Maybe one for the two of us.”

She didn’t think he meant to wait for her agreement. Yet, he paused until she gave him a nod of approval. Realized he would take the moment to pursue her with his charming ways. Tessa understood what he wanted.

Tugging her into his arms, he circled her. His long fingers were again beneath the shawl. Discovered. He was able to touch the outer side of her breasts. She knew if he extended his reach, his fingers could float across the hard tips. This time he wasn’t going to do so. He meant to seduce, arouse sensual flames one tiny bit at a time. Meant to tease until she begged. He would plead before she did.

This kiss was deeper as well as longer than the last one. He swirled his tongue around the inside of her mouth. Made no move to press her against his sex. Though he did hold her close. This go-around there was air separating them. His hand settled on her hip. Flexed as if testing. Glided. Slipped fabric upward along her legs before letting the skirt drop.

When she met his tongue with hers, she heard the hoarse groan rumble from him. At that instant she realized this evening would be just as long for him as it would be for her. He would also find himself aroused. He would never be able to hide the fact. Tessa meant to capitalize.

He released her with what felt like regret. Held their joined hands high in the air. “Eat!” Jason cried out. “Dance and enjoy the entertainment. My wife and I thank you all for coming to celebrate our wedding with us. Stay as long as you wish.” With that said, he seated her. Maggie and Jasper sat at the same table beside them. Maggie next to her.

“Does he know?” Maggie spoke with a soft voice.

“How could he not?” Tessa retorted with equal quiet, hoping neither man would hear all she had to say. “He’s touched me everywhere. Jason must have noticed within seconds of escorting me down the stairs. He’s a perceptive man.”

"When it comes to you. As is Jasper around me. He also realized within seconds my state of deshabille."

"Drink up!" Jason chortled next to her ear. Fondled with his tongue. Dared to explore. "You have no secrets from me. I know you respected me. Did what I hoped for. Did you know, I would not have done anything if you chose to ignore my wishes? There would have been no reprisals."

Tessa was startled he would admit so soon that he knew she followed his invitation. Shaken to hear he would have left her underwear on if she chose to wear them. She was left with nothing relevant to say. "Don't want to get tipsy," she muttered as she accepted a gulp of champagne letting the warmth slide down her throat to settle in her empty stomach. His male laughter echoed around her. Heated her.

"I love you a *wee* bit tipsy."

"What do we have to eat?" She tried to divert the topic to something that wouldn't cause her cheeks to flame. Nothing worked. She couldn't keep her mind from traveling in a direction where she didn't want it to go.

"Your favorite spice cakes as well as the lavender ones you've come to adore…almost as much as you adore me. Oh, but you need nourishment first. Must keep up your strength for later. I've a great deal planned for tonight. Sweets are for later. If you don't have them before the cutting of the big cake, they will be in our bridal suite when we return there. More champagne for us."

"You think of everything."

"No, you do." He clicked his glass to hers. "Here's to you, my wife. This man approves of all your naughty thoughts. Hope you never change." He kissed her cheek. A slow glide of the tip of his finger down her neck followed until the nail vanished in the valley between her beasts. "Would you like me to dish up a plate for you?"

"If you wish." She still held no coherent thoughts in her head. His last actions didn't help. His finger slid along the inside curve of one breast.

"I do wish for a great deal of things. How about you? What do you want?" He ran the tip of a strawberry between her lips. "Take a bite."

"Hmm…" The berry was sweet. Good. "You bite."

"Can I bite you instead?"

"Not here."

"Later," he promised. "I've lots of places I'd like to bite. Would you like me to tell you where?"

Tessa had no idea what she wanted. No, on second thought, she wished they were alone. Didn't need this party to feel well and truly married to Jason Kenworthy. Looking out on the guests, Tessa felt a bit whimsical. These people liked her. She never met most of them before a few days ago. She'd been introduced to Gracie and Fletcher Murray. They were also friends. They played a friendly game of lawn tennis though Fletcher tried to make it more.

They were friends. She now had friends other than her sisters. This was all new to her. Anice kept them secluded. Even their education was managed in the upstairs of their Glasgow home with private tutors.

"Where are you?" Jason waved his hand in front of her face. "You thinking about the after party? I am." He set his thigh against hers. Moved on her, stroking her with his leg.

Tessa thought to change position. Decided she would see if she could embarrass him. After all, he wore the evidence of his desire for all to see. A turnabout would be fair.

She pushed back. Heard the immediate sip of air, "Was dreaming about…" She sent her tongue across her mouth. Watched the way his eyes seemed to follow the movement. Pleased with her first endeavor. Maybe this was her second venture into seducing her husband.

"Dreaming about what?" was his hoarse question.

Unwilling to allow him to see her smile, she hid the silly grin behind her teeth. Her simple gesture affected him. "You…" With boldness that surprised her, Tessa set her hand on Jason's leg. Proceeded as she would have expected him to do if the roles were reversed.

"You, my sweet one, play with fire. I can give back ten times what you can't begin to imagine. Play away with my person. I'm a happy man. I'll be thinking of more ways to see color paint your lovely face."

Play she would. A few words that might be a bluff would never deter her now that she set her course for the evening. Make him wonder if his bluff worked. The coy look she sent his way brought a feral grin to his lips. The game was on. The war would be decided with each skirmish. Tessa didn't care who would win. In the end they both would reap the benefits.

Jason's hand came down on hers where she stroked his leg. He moved it higher until she felt the swollen evidence of his need. He pressed all the while he kept the focus of his attention on her eyes. Their gazes seemed glued to each other. To inform him he didn't intimidate, she rubbed her hand along his hard length.

"Witch." He brought her hand to his chest. Kept it there while he steadied each drawn breath.

"Did I do something?" The innocent question would never be believed. Tessa blinked a few times to help make her point.

Jason grunted. "I'll get even. Now use your fingers to hold your fork. As I said earlier, you need sustenance for the rest of the evening."

Deciding she won the first round, she did his bidding. Forgetting that she committed to seducing her husband. Looking to her sister, she saw Maggie was doing the same. Jasper's eyes seemed to cross then bulge. Maggie must be working her nimble finger on her husband's person. Tessa didn't want to guess where that was.

Jason fed her. She tasted his fingers. Bit. Licked. His eyes darkened. Glowed with desire. They toyed with each other until the dancing began. The first dance was theirs. A slow waltz filled the night air. She tied her shawl after Jason undid the knot to float the palm of his hand across the taut hard buds he seduced to perfection.

He teased her throughout the meal just as she tempted him with subtle movements of her body against his. Dancing, he pulled her too close. She was flush against him. When the dance ended, he maneuvered her to a secluded place behind the gazebo. They were masked in shadows. Clouds moved across the moonglow, lighting then darkening the small area where they stood.

His mouth flattened against hers. Softened. He penetrated. Retreated. Her needy response was fast. She opened for him. He deepened the kiss. The inferno flared. She wove her fingers into his hair. Scraped nails against his neck. Slipped her hands beneath his frockcoat to be closer to him. Against her palms, she felt the steady beat of his heart.

Moments later, her veiled breasts were cupped in his hands. He played with the hardened peaks until she moaned. Bent to take a nipple into his mouth. Savored with his lips as well as teeth and tongue. Little whimpers floated from the back of her throat. After he pulled away, the fabric was damp. Her nipple a proud hard peak. He blew at that place where he could see the tips. She trembled at the contact.

Ribbons of fire poured into her. Consumed every part of her. Surrounded. She knew he was just as aroused. Startled by the unexpected contact, she gasped when his hand roamed along the inside of her thigh. He pushed her feet apart. Cupped her. Felt the slide of his finger at the apex of her thighs. Fondling. Petting her. Arousing her more with each pass of his fingers.

Her head fell against his chest. Moaned as her knees weakened. She wobbled as fingers entered her, circled the swollen bud with his thumb. Moved within her. In then out.

"Jason," she moaned, her voice so thready she didn't recognize the sound. Her eyes closed. Lashes swept across the silk of his shirt. She needed more of this.

"Yes," his voice was a deep husky sound touched with raw passion. "Do you want me here?" he asked as he pressed further inside. Retreated before pressing another time.

"Not…" She gulped air unable to say more. She did and she didn't. Not here. He wouldn't dare.

"Not?" he questioned, his voice taking on a skeptical note. "This is not for you to dictate. Remember that. I will always triumph."

As if he knew she couldn't stand, he pressed his thigh against her, keeping her from falling while he continued to toy with her. Mercuric sensual passion swept. Encompassed all of her. His lips molded against hers. Just as his fingers penetrated her, so did his tongue. The two worked in unison to bring her to ecstasy.

Her disjointed pleasure, the broken cry of her release was captured inside his mouth. She arched. Pulsed with increasing frenzy. He continued with slow strokes, calming her. Held her close to his pounding heart.

Jason would tell her he won this round. He didn't. All the pleasure was hers. He received none.

"You…" She slipped her hand inside his pants, needing to feel the hard smoothness of his sex. To give back tenfold what she received.

His fingers wound around her wrists pulling her hand away from his member. Not before she grasped. Enjoyed the slow glide of her hand while he pulled her away. Heard the groan of starving passion that followed.

"No, not right now, little one. We won't be at this celebration much longer. I need you too much. Let's cut the cake. We'll leave our guests right after that."

"You won't put icing on my face." The words came out as a demand rather than a question.

"Not if you don't first," was his reply.

~ * ~

Maggie was having fun with Jasper. He was first shocked by her lack of clothing then delighted with the ability to touch so much of her. During the feast, he slipped his hands beneath her dress, petting her intimately. They danced. He pressed hands where ever he could. Brushed nimble palms across hardened crowns. Flattened his hand on her bottom when no one would be able to see. Pulled her tight against him so she could feel him pulse against her belly.

"A man's wife should always be like this. Unencumbered beneath her gowns. Available to him when the mood hits," he whispered next to her ear, bit with a gentle caress. Swirled his tongue around the center. "Shall we look for a private spot to continue our explorations?"

"Meant to surprise you. Keep you guessing," she murmured with a whisper of a sigh. "Does it work?"

She'd seen Jason and Tessa disappear into a wooded area. Knew what was on their minds. Perhaps as Jasper suggested, they could do the same. She wouldn't mind a *wee* bit more attention. He would set her on fire. She was already so hot, so very wet, she thought she must have touched the sun.

"Just go without underthings all the time. Doing so would please this husband. We would never have to waste time getting rid of clothing.

It could be done with more ease. Could raise your passion to higher plateaus. The sun is the limit."

"I'd like that. What about the servants?" She wanted to give him some problems to think about. This wasn't meant to be easy for the man. "They would always be underfoot. We might never find privacy."

"We have locks on all our doors. Could make some do not disturb signs. Keep one in every room of the house. Certain Jason would appreciate that too." He murmured while he pushed her shawl away. He placed kisses along the tops of her breasts. Pushed them together. Snuggled his face between them. With his teeth he pulled on the corsage until one pink nipple popped free.

The mewling sound rippled from her throat when his teeth closed around the tip. Maggie wanted this as much as he did.

"You can't…here…not." she whispered, struggled with the words on shaking legs while he continued his ardent attention to the tips. "Jasper…this is just pretend. You…oh…"

His questing fingers found tender evocative flesh, wet with her passion. Heat spiraled higher then higher still. "Go, some…where."

"I want you to purr your pleasure. Don't hold anything back. Within my mouth I'll drink your cries of ecstasy."

She didn't think she could take more of his hands fondling, stroking, petting. Her body hummed, pulsing with vibrant life. Inside where his fingers pressed, her muscles clenched.

Jasper's lips claimed hers. Tugged on the bottom. Slid his tongue inside. The velvet softness of his rubbing on hers sent a tempest of sensual pleasure flying through her. Maggie clung to him. He pressed and circled the nubbin between her folds. She flew. Higher. Almost. Not enough.

"You're very wet. Hot. Do you want me to finish what you started by your naughty misbehavior? Say yes or no."

"Yes…" she murmured as he sent her over the precipice. When she cried out her release the words echoed inside his mouth. Drained of energy, she fell against him. Clung to his shoulders. While she tried to breathe, her body shook with the aftershocks of this experiment.

Her head rested on his chest. Jasper ran his hands along her back. Soothed. Calmed the tempest he created with her wanton behavior.

When she was more herself, he adjusted the skewed clothing. Tied her shawl. Tapped her on the lips.

"Nothing we can do about your mouth."

"What?" Maggie brought her hand to touch where his fingers had just been. "My mouth?" she questioned.

"Your beautiful lips will tell the world what my lovely wife has been doing with her husband. They appear bee stung, well attended to by yours truly. Didn't you think of that?"

"My lips?"

"They are deep rose, swollen…kissed by me." His voice sounded proud. "They will stay that way for a time.

Cocky man. His suggestion puzzled her. She blurted the first notion in her head. "Why aren't' yours?" she asked, having never thought about that aspect of kissing before now.

"Yours were inside mine. I covered you. Just as I do…most of the time…when we make love. It's a man's goal to see his loving attentions on his wife's mouth. Just as I've placed a few red marks on the white flesh of your neck, even your delectable butt. Those places will tell the world you're mine. Only mine."

"Jasper…you're making this up. Be serious." With frustration simmering and unable to think of anything else, she poked him on the chest. Maggie understood he wasn't going to give her an answer.

He stepped back. Made a circular motion with his hand. Smiled seeming content with his explanation. "Turn around. Let me see if you're put back together correctly. Parts of you could be askew. That might be more embarrassing than bee stung lips." He made the pretense of rearranging clothing. Instead, he continued to charm her with his attention. Passing his palms across her nipples while he adjusted the corsage. Touching her bottom. Even raising her skirts to see if the fabric fell the correct way. She gasped with the startling contact.

After the little dalliance as well as a bit more caressing, arm-in-arm, the two walked back to the table. Jason and Tessa were staring into each other's eyes. Tessa's hair was falling from its pins. Her shawl was draped across one shoulder, not the other. Maggie understood much the same was happening to her sister. They were both finding themselves thoroughly seduced. She didn't mind. Not one bit.

"Have more champagne," Jasper suggested with a grin as he pulled out a seat for Maggie. After she sat, he caressed the nape of her neck. Ran his finger along her shoulder pressing fabric to glide to his whims. "The two of you look as if you could use some liquid pleasure."

"Help yourselves," Jason said as he smiled at his brother. "My glass is full as is Tessa's. We're just waiting for Clancy to bring out the cake."

"That wasn't planned for another hour," Jasper told them with a flat tone to his voice. "The two of you eager for a little privacy?"

"From what I'm seeing, no more than the two of you," Jason retorted with a wave of his hand. "What have you been up to?"

"Difference is, Maggie and I can go anytime we please. You have a few traditions to see to the end before you can retire," Jasper said as he sat himself next to Maggie. With his leg, he pushed against hers. Set his hand at the top of her thigh.

With a shivering response to his bold advance, Maggie punched him on the arm, "We are not going anywhere before the bridal couple leaves. Want to throw the rice at them. Want to see them cut the cake. Need to see everything. Do everything."

"Did we have rice?" Jasper asked. "Don't know why anyone would want to throw rice at other people." He squeezed. Cupped her as she opened for his encroachment.

Another punch brought him to heel. Though he continued the seduction of her body. "No and well you understand why. Mother…" she bit off with the slow glide of his hand along her thigh where he'd slipped his hand beneath her gown.

"And here I thought you forgot who I was. Not one visit since you've been back from Ireland. Would like to see my grandson," Anice stood in front of the table, posturing. She stared at the two girls then let her gaze move to their husbands.

Maggie stiffened. Between her husband's bold attack and her mother's sly grin, she wasn't prepared. The last person she wished to be anywhere near her son was her mother. To no avail, she attempted to push Jasper's hand from intimate territory. Now she tried to keep her rattled brain from befuddling her more. “No. No, you aren’t welcome anywhere near our boy! Don’t even try to see him. I won’t have it!”

“Why?”

“You’re not a stupid woman,” Jasper told her while he drummed the fingers of his free hand on the top of the table. “Figure it out. You shouldn’t need the words spelled out to you. You’re not welcome anywhere near my family.”

No, Mother wasn’t stupid. She was just incapable of rational thought. Either that or she persevered when she knew the answer would be negative. Maggie trembled at the thought of Anice having anything to do with her son. Anice was not a good mother. She wouldn’t even be a tolerable grandmother. Anice must have something in her head. A notion that would never be suitable.

“What are you doing, Anice?” this question from Jason whose brows were furrowed. “Seems I remember you telling Tessa and me that you wouldn’t intrude on our celebration. Despite all that, here you are.”

“Nonetheless, my companion does have an invitation.” Anice looked over her shoulder smiling at the man standing behind her. “I’m certain you would never turn away this family friend. Would you?”

Armstrong stepped up beside Anice. Clearing his throat, he spoke, “My apologies. This isn’t what you might think. I didn’t bring Anice MacRae to the event. Anice found me, coerced me to walk with her. Seems she has something to say that she hinted might concern both of us.” While he spoke, his voice was tight, holding back emotions that seemed to threaten to erupt. Trying to explain his presence with Anice MacRae. “She sought me out,” he finished on mumbled air.

“Oh, but of course, it’s exactly the way it seems.” Anice waved her hand. “He’s lying through his teeth. The man is sweet on me. Don’t you know. Has been for years. We’ve…” Anice held onto his arm, pushing her body against his, snuggling. “Though we haven’t spoken in about twenty years, give or take a month or two. Once we were very close. Close until I found someone I craved more, his twin.”

Maggie was appalled with her mother. Even more than usual. She flaunted this man for what reason unless it was to further embarrass or threaten Tessa. There was more here, unsaid, than met the first perusal.

Armstrong appeared mortified. Silent except for those first few words. "Explain yourself."

"Believe Armstrong and I will stick around for a while. Dance. Eat. Do wish to watch the cutting of the cake? Tessa should have her real family here. This is after all about my daughter," Anice spoke in a low voice before casting her attention toward Armstrong. Anice's slow-eyed approval of the man sent a shudder of revulsion through Maggie.

Even if he wasn't giving into the blackmail, he seemed embarrassed by Anice's attention. She clung to him. Purred his name. Stroked his arm. Pushed her breast against his arm. Anice wanted something from him.

"Where is Miles?" Jason asked while he held onto Tessa's hand. "Your brother? Didn't you come with the judge?"

The trembling of her shoulders was visible. She was shaking. Maggie wished she dared toss the champagne in her glass on her mother. Jasper's hand stilled as well as comforted her. She needed to tamp down her anger. This was not supposed to be happening. This was the celebration of her little sister's marriage.

Anice waved her hand in the air circling the entire yard. "Oh, Miles is somewhere around here. I'm certain he will show up to congratulate the bride and groom who he played the role of father of the bride for on their wedding day. Though it is startlingly close to the truth. One might make a guess. They would be wrong."

Maggie didn't have anything else to say. It was apparent no one else wished to speak to Anice. "We should go," Armstrong volunteered to end the silence.

"No. Absolutely not. I'm going to stay for a piece of cake. Want to watch my daughter along with her new husband cut the sweet confection."

Maggie understood nothing could drag her mother away.

Chapter Eight

The pathway was lined with villagers all the way to the Kenworthy back door. Laughing, the two of them ran the gauntlet of well-wishers. Everyone there held a bag of rice put together by the sisters. All tossed rice. Laughed. Yelled at the racing couple. The small white grains fell into his clothing. Slipped through the smallest spaces to land between flesh and fabric. Jason wondered where he would discover rice on Tessa. This would all be a new experience.

He looked forward to the process of discovery. Running, he held her hand. Urged her to run faster. Hoped the less time they spent beneath the shower of rice, the less they would have in their clothing. As they neared the back entrance, she gasped for air. He swept her into his arms. Cradled her small body against his. She wrapped her arms around him, clinging, burying her nose into his shoulder.

"I can't breathe," Tessa whispered with her nose in his chest. "I'm not used to running so far and so fast."

"Hang on…" He felt the vibrations of her heart, the rapid breathing as she struggled for each tiny bit of oxygen.

Two stepping the stairs, he crashed into the door. Fumbled with the handle then pushed it open. Stepped inside. With his foot, he kicked the door closed. Leaned against the hard wood with his eyes closed. Found he was breathing harder than he could believe. He enjoyed the way she felt against him. Her breasts curved on his chest. Through the fabric separating them felt the hard crests. She was ripe. Ready to be plucked.

"What do we do now?" Tessa's breathless rush of words sent fire blazing. "I would…" She tilted her head back as if to look into his eyes.

Jason held her gaze with his. Tried to hide the smile that threatened to erupt with the sweetest passion. "Recover."

"Oh."

Tessa squirmed against him. Rubbed her cheek on the skin where her fingers opened his shirt. Tongued his neck. Bit the tender spot at the base. Slid the velvet softness up then down. Excited him with her small teeth at the point where his heart pummeled. She continued with slow, easy strokes of her fingers, with her wet tongue. He groaned.

"You're going to be the death of me…" His fingers closed around a breast, weighed as well as measured. Ran his thumb across the hard, inviting crown. "If you keep this up, we won't make it to the bedchamber."

Good God, the response was fast. Urgent in the extreme. She arched against him as if strung as tight as a bow. Her small whimper told him how much she wanted him.

"Can we…?" She kissed him along his collarbone while her fingers fell to the fastening of his pants. Rice clattered to the floor with each unveiling. "You would need to carry me. Doubt if I can walk up all those steps."

"Find a room," he gritted out. his voice harsh when he wanted gentleness. "Somewhere…people will be returning soon."

"That one has a lock," she murmured as he sprang free from the confines of his trousers.

Caressing his length, his body filled with fire. An inferno that needed her dark wet sheathe. She would douse the fire in his loins. The flames would rise again. There might be a short respite. Her fingers circled him. Ran up then down. Repeated.

"Little witch, don't know if I can make it to the office if you keep that up. The kitchen table looks good."

Her fingers petted his hard flesh. Surrounded him. Continued the seduction. Rose then fell along his length. Jason couldn't hold back the groan of need, of raw hunger for this beguiling lass who wore nothing beneath her gown. She'd been a temptation for the entire night. He'd been hard the second he realized all she didn't wear. Now, he didn't need to hold back. He could have her. Could push into her magical channel.

Setting her on the table, he came between her legs. Pushed her skirt to her waist. Encountered bare flesh. Tested her secrets. He found her. Wet. Hot. Her honey rained down on his hand. With no hesitation he thrust inside. She gasped. Purred her satisfaction. Once sheathed to her womb, he held still for a second. Overwhelmed by need, he began to move.

"Jason!"

Taking this slow was out of the realm of possibilities. He'd been aroused for hours. Hard as steel since he first discovered she didn't wear her underclothing. Lightning shot straight into his groin with each contact between them. A fine sheen of moisture covered his skin. He wanted to do this with a slow hand. Never seemed to be able to accomplish that feat.

Penetrate.

Retreat.

Her tight, hot sheath milked his sex. Kissed his length with affection. Adored him. She arched with each hard thrust. He felt the beginning of her climax. Heard the changing of each breath. Small sounds rippled from the back of her throat to wind a ribbon of sensual need around them. He couldn't hold back. The next moment, he emptied himself. Cried out with a low, husky growl.

She ran trembling hands along his back. Slid her sharp little nails the length of his spine. When she unfastened all the buttons of his shirt he didn't know. When he pushed her corsage to her waist then slid her skirt to the same position. He didn't have the vaguest idea. He set his forehead against hers. Her gown was bunched around her waist. He stood between her thighs. Using her arms for support, she rose from the table.

Even in the aftermath of the fast, fierce lovemaking he was growing hard again. If he didn't do something now, he would take her again on the kitchen table. Once was a risk they shouldn't have taken. Twice could be a disaster in the making. He wasn't about to be caught with his pants down when the rest of the family trooped into the house. No one would suspect they weren't able to make it to a more private room.

"Hurry." Jason fastened the top of his pants, drew up the bodice of her gown slid her gown to her ankles. "We've got to get out of here. Now!" He was certain the noise from the festivities was now closer to the house than he wished.

The next second she was cradled in his arms as he raced to their rooms. With the door closed behind him, frantic, he let her slide down his length until she touched the floor. He panted from the exertion. Against him she was breathing with sporadic gulps of air.

"You want me again, now?" Tessa asked, her words thin as she clung to him still unable to stand. "I can't…don't think I can…" She fell on him. Used him to support her weight. "Parched. Need something to drink before..."

Jason knew he must tamp down his need for her. When he looked above her head, he saw the tray of food along with the opened bottles of wine. "It's alright." His fingers wound into her hair. Let the long strands slide between his fingers. "We've got lots of time. Have no reason to rise early. If you like, we can stay in bed all day. Make love whenever the mood strikes. What do you think?"

Against him, he felt her nodding her head. Heard the long deep breaths as she tried to drag more air into her lungs. One then a second after that a third deep breath, she seemed more relaxed. Her body molded against his. They were a perfect fit for each other.

As he looked down, he saw rice in her hair. A snort then a chuckle sent his fingers spinning through the white-blond strands dislodging hairpins along with the rice that was gathered near her scalp. One more time, he cast her into his arms. Carried her the necessary steps to the bed. Set her down. Her skirts rose above her knees. The hastily replaced bodice left the tip of one breast, popping free.

Damn she was lovely. Disheveled by his hands. Her lips were kiss-swollen. Ripe. He'd plucked the lower lip with his teeth. Sucked on the soft flesh that beguiled him at every turn. Discovered the satin skin inside her mouth. All of her captivated him. There wasn't a single part of Tessa that didn't tempt him. Lure him to the heat of the sun.

He needed to hold back at least an hour. She needed time to recover. Looking at her now, all of her was love-tousled. Her hair was undone. Hung around her shoulders across her breasts. Nothing she wore was in the right place. Pushing hair from her face, her breasts danced with the movement. He delighted in watching her.

He slipped off his frock coat then his shirt. Sat to get rid of his shoes along with his socks. If he removed the rest of his clothing he'd be inside her before she could voice a protest. Tessa would never complain. Never tell him no.

Clancy left a bottle of champagne on the table along with treats to eat during the night. As he looked at the food, his stomach rumbled. Eating was something they did little of during the evening. They were both too preoccupied playing with each other to put more than a few bites into their mouths.

Yes, he fed her then she reciprocated. When fingers touched the other's mouth other emotions took over. Sensations that could not be reversed flared to life. Jason concentrated on pouring champagne into the crystal glasses. Stared at the small bubbles floating to the top. Heard the soft intake of Tessa's breaths.

Sitting on the bed next to her, he handed her one of the glasses. Watched while she took a dainty sip of the bubbling brew. Thought about what would come next. "Would you like to get into something more comfortable?" The *wee* giggle following his question took him by surprise. "What?"

Tessa tilted her head to the side, a flirtatious smirk on her lips. Sipped again. Looked up while the liquid glided down her throat. "How could I ever be more comfortable? I'm practically wearing nothing a'tall. You've touched most all of me. What do you think? Should I don one of the filmy pieces of nightwear you've given me? There is no difference in comfort. However, one is made for seduction, the other is not. Is that what's on your mind?" She paused as if listening to the beat of her heart. "Well, maybe there is more of a difference. Nonetheless, it's of my opinion, you want to be able to see all of me through the fabric. Is that your preference? To see me?" With that said, she drank long and deep. Waited with wide sapphire eyes looking with appreciation at him.

The way she was looking at his chest didn't help his state of arousal. It was taking a huge effort to hold back the flames she created with her sultry heated glance. When her gaze dropped lower, he turned desperate. He still wore his pants. That was good. It would take longer to thrust inside her. Then, she swept her sweet pink tongue across her lips. Moisture glistened. He flamed to life. "You can't do that," he whispered as his sex leapt harder than he would have expected. "You can't flirt so outrageously then expect nothing to happen."

He thought he'd controlled his desire for her. When she seduced, she was a force to be reckoned with. He didn't stand a chance with her in the driver's seat. At least he knew she was recovering from their quick sex. They'd been married for more than a few days. She wouldn't be sore. There was nothing else he could call what they did. A name eluded him. Quickies. Well, that might work. He gulped the champagne, spilled more into his glass then hers too. Searched for time to get command of his most randy part. If not, he would be deep inside her, thrusting until she cried out her release. Until she split into hundreds of tiny shards.

"Thought you needed to wait for the second round. Had the notion you were thirsty. Hungry." He was ready to drop his pants to the floor.

"I do need to wait. Not ready a'tall," she murmured while she lowered her lashes, looking at him from beneath. When she met his gaze, she mimicked him again. "Not a'tall." After she looked over the rim of her glass her eyes were shining with humor.

"Even if you don't wish to don something more bedtime appropriate, I do." Unable to face her without tossing up her skirt, her one and only skirt, he headed for his dressing room. He sought a few seconds where he wasn't staring at her in beautiful disarray.

Jason had no idea how he would find Tessa when he returned. All he could think about was the here and now. He was on fire for his lovely wife. He'd taken her on the kitchen table as if she meant nothing. As if she didn't deserve the slow seduction that could be had in their bed. Making this right was his sole purpose for the rest of the evening.

The devil, so far in their short marriage every time they came together the joining was fierce. Faster than it should have been. Hotter than he'd ever expected. Messier than he'd ever thought possible. He had no idea how to slow things down. Wanting to do so now played no part in the process. While he knew he gave her pleasure, he needed to hear her beg for her climax. Needed for her to straddle the brink between pleasure so intense you might die along with the wanting of that pleasure. Every time he could, he would send her to the fire of the sun then back. The trouble in this was that her passion leapt with each caress of his hands.

He was ecstatic she was so quick to respond. Passionate to reciprocate. Famished for him. He didn't think she would ever deny what they had together. Even if she was angry because of something he might do or say, she would come around when he charmed her. Seduced in the only way he knew. They would mend their argument with hot, fast sex. He groaned thinking about the scenario in his head.

Slipping from his pants, he was still ready to seek entrance into her sultry heat. Hard. Stimulated as if this was his last opportunity for sex with the woman who meant so much to him. If he tried hard enough, he could be patient. Jason slipped on his robe. Rolled the sleeves to his elbows. Before leaving the room, he finished his champagne. Sauntered into the main room to discover the area empty.

Ah, she'd left to put on her negligée. He'd had three fashioned for her from the modiste in the village. All were varying shades of blue, of sapphire blue. The exact color of her eyes. They all sported tiny little bows at the shoulder he could play with. When she wore them, they made her eyes brighter. Bluer. He didn't think that was possible but the fact was true beyond a doubt. Blue made her eyes bluer. Jason was besotted with his wife.

On the bed, he stretched out, crossed his legs waiting for Tessa to appear. He leaned against the headboard. Watched. Thought to give her an unencumbered view of him when she entered by bringing his knee up then opening the robe. If she was continuing this game of seduction they began at the festivities, he would win.

They would both win.

Both would accomplish what they set out to do since their end game was the same. Pleasure. Ecstasy beyond conceivable. Jason found he enjoyed playing games with Tessa. Pitting their minds along with their wills against each other for mutual enjoyment intrigued him. She attracted him in so many different ways. He loved her quick wit. Her intelligence. On an equal level, she met him move for move.

Checkmate.

When she stepped into the room, his breath caught in the back of his throat. Framed in the doorway, she paused. Moved enough to set her unrestrained breasts dancing, the picture erotic. He was right about the games. She meant to win. As did he. She posed for him. Turned sideways then back to face him. Ran her sweet pink tongue along her lips, moved just right to make her breasts dance again. Tessa understood what to do with her magnificent body. He tightened with need. Hoped for restraint.

Didn't know how long she would wear this blue confection. Not long. Once she sat beside him, he would remove the thin veil of fabric.

From the beginning, he understood there would be nothing about her he couldn't see. The negligée was sheer, just as he planned, just as he'd seen before. The number of times he'd seen her in this filmy concoction of his creation never dimmed what the sight induced. With this appearance the resulting evidence of his need was obvious. Now she moved with provocative steps toward the bed. Her hips swayed. Trim ankles played peekaboo with the gown. Little witch. She understood what she did to him. His robe was tented where his sex leapt to attention. His arousal was something he could never hide.

Hands down, she won.

Hands down, he won.

Jason sucked in a gulp of Tessa scented air while he wondered what her next move would be. She could approach this from a myriad of angles. Anticipation sent more heat pulsing and leaping with wild abandon through him. Wild tempest surged. Flames galloped. She stopped once more to pose.

"Little siren, come to me."

Her smile was heart stopping. "You want me?"

"Yes. You know I do."

With hips swaying, breasts moving in opposition, she glided across the room. His need for her intensified tenfold. She was fire in his soul. They would burn together. Turn to cinders. Didn't see how he could get any hotter. What the devil was his little enchantress up to? Seduction? Conquest perhaps? He imagined he would soon discover the truth.

Tessa stopped to pour more champagne. Lifted the glass in his direction as if she meant the gesture to be a toast. The hardened pink crests pressed against translucent material. He sipped air. Hungered for a taste of the succulent buds. This round might very well be Tessa's. He would need to play the game with more care. Perhaps he could seduce better than the little temptress. Turn her machinations to work in his favor. Give her back what she asked for him to give. Surprise might work to his benefit.

She sat at the table where all the delicacies had been placed. Set her hands in her lap. She wasn't coming to him. Not yet. "I'm hungry," she said with a sultry sigh that sent more heat waves straight to his groin. Picking up a berry, she ran the mouthwatering fruit along her bottom lip. Her eyes shimmered, darkened with passion.

Jason understood she baited him. With ease, he could turn this around. Did he wish to change the direction of her passionate seduction? "Hungry for what, love? Cheese. Bread. Me?" he asked, despite the resolution he made to himself not to mention that. In the heat of the battle, he was losing. Taking on a more subtle approach would be a must. At this second in the adventure, he just didn't know how to go about subtle. All the notions in his head were brazen, straight to the point. Fast and furious.

"The berries are delicious." She cast him a sultry siren's smile directed at his groin that caused another shiver of flames to rip into him. Again, she ran the berry across her lip. Sucked on the juice. A small bead of red liquid on her mouth tempted. Would bring him to his knees if he allowed it. If he sat at the table with her, he would lick the juice.

He wanted to tell her she was playing with fire. Understood she comprehended that fact. "So are all the parts of you as ripe as that berry you're eating. Are you ready to be plucked. Succulent. Juicy. Should I test my theory? You could sit on my lap. Want your sweet juices to flow. We could see what happens."

Tessa jerked. Reacted unexpectedly to his sensual words. He was a bit crass. He knew that for a fact. She needed to hear his thoughts, all his thoughts. She was no longer an innocent to be sheltered with pretty phrases. Tessa started this sexual game between them. He meant to finish this in his way. Not hers. With the widening of her eyes, Jason sensed his win. From experience though, he understood she would never give up the game this fast.

"Plucked? Juicy? Juices flowing?" Her voice wobbled. Whispered. "What do you mean?"

He heard the hesitancy in her questions. She didn't understand what he wanted. It was time to put an end to this part of the game. He comprehended she would continue to play as long as possible. She enjoyed seducing him almost as much as he was pleased to be seduced. How to proceed? He pondered that for a few ticks of the clock. Watched her eat the fruit on her plate.

"Plucked," he agreed shooting her a feral smile, his eyes hooded. "Your nipples enjoy being…plucked…by my fingers as well as my mouth, my teeth. What else? What other part of you could be plucked. Hmm… Between your soft creamy thighs, that little knot of passion grows hard when I grasp it with my fingers, my mouth. You arch like a drawn bow when my thumb surrounds the tiny pearl of delight. What else would enjoy being plucked?"

With his brazen words she gulped air. The buds he'd been speaking of grew beneath the thin veil of fabric.

Jason needed her to wonder what he was up to next. While he wasn't certain himself, that fact by itself would keep her from the answers she wanted.

She hesitated, her eyebrows narrowing as she watched, waited for whatever might come next, seemed to wonder what outrageous sexual talk would be emitted. "What? What are you saying. That…" her voice held a slight waver. Her shoulders trembled setting other parts dancing.

Ensuing as planned, he sent her a smile that was all masculine pleasure coupled with victory. He slanted an eyebrow upward. Wanted her to question. "Figure it out. Know you can." He issued her a challenge. It was something he understood she would embrace. A test she would be certain to ace. With time she would understand if she didn't already.

Tessa would accept any challenge he sent her way. She brought in several deep breaths of air as if she was mulling over his sexual innuendos. A few more seconds passed before she spoke. "What if I plucked you instead? Would that be pleasurable for you? What, I wonder would I pluck?" Her gaze first rested on his chest then dropped to his groin. She ran her eyes over the hard concealed length of him.

"The devil!" He hadn't meant to say the words. She, once again, seemed to be winning the exchange of words between them. If this didn't stop soon, he'd be inside her. In one thrust he would expel his seed. There would be no slow hand. She would not beg for his entrance. Where she was involved, it didn't take much provocation for him to lose the restraint he needed.

This woman who tempted him beyond endurance was the same woman who was supposed to be quiet. Non-committal. No one, not even her sisters knew the depth of Tessa. She seemed to learn from listening. He'd taught her enough about sex that she seemed to understand the nuances of everything he said.

"Come eat," Tessa changed the subject. She took the moment to pour them both more champagne. More seconds to place food on a plate for him. "If you're going to pluck my sensual female parts you will need nourishment. I wouldn't want you to fail because you become faint." She tossed her hair behind her back before she winked at him.

"Yes, you're right." Jason threw off his robe before sauntering to the table naked as well as fully aroused. "Eat then pluck away? Is that the way you want this to go? I can accommodate all your wishes."

At her obvious shock, he hid his grin behind his hand. By coming to the table naked, he one upped her. The unexpected always seemed to take her by surprise. Just when she believed she held the power he up ended her. Turned her topsy turvy.

"What? Nothing to say?" he asked as he pulled her from her chair, her breasts pushing across his arm then his chest. Setting her astride him, he played with the bows at her shoulders. Watched passion grow in her eyes. Heard the soft moan she couldn't keep behind her teeth.

Before he ate anything from the table, he needed to see how she tasted. Tessa always tasted of sunshine and lavender along with the summer storms that swept through the highlands charged with electricity. He debated with himself what he longed to taste first, her sultry mouth or the hardened tips of her breasts.

When she allowed her weight to settle on him, he felt the humid heat at the apex of her creamy thighs. The feminine petals were swollen with her need. She was wet. The passionate sensual foreplay of words affected her as heatedly as they did him. With the bows untied, the filmy garment fell to her hips. He wished for her to be naked while they continued this game of words as well as wit. After she moved on him, he sucked air. Her soft swollen petals caressed his shaft. Fought for the ability to hold back. Her honey rained on his sex. As he said, her juices flowed. He almost slipped his fingers between her legs. Kept himself from doing so by a thin margin of pure concentration. Staying focused on his goal was imperative.

"I want you naked while we eat." His voice was so deep and raw he didn't recognize the sound. "Wish to pluck your ripest berries. Savor all your feminine secrets. See what comes next." Jason lifted her. Pulled the gown from her legs with a bit of help from her.

Tessa was once again astride him. The hard tips of her breasts danced on his chest while she adjusted herself. He tilted his glass. A few drops of the bubbly liquid spilled onto one hardened crown of one breast.

At the cool liquid contact, she sipped in air. The sapphire of her eyes widened.

He sipped on her nipple, plucked the tip with his teeth. His tongue swirled around the pink crest. His teeth raked across the tip. She arched with an urgency he understood. He ran his hand along the inside of her thighs. He wanted to taste all of her. Needed to slow his hand. The hard swollen jewel between her legs would soon need tugging.

He couldn't stop himself from testing her arousal. Felt pleased now that he held the winning hand. Once she was naked, Tessa had no chance of the win. She would surrender the game soon. All that…if she took his sex into her, he would explode. The game would end. He fought the flames of his desire. Needed to prolong this.

Jason slipped his hand between her thighs. Cupped her. Slid his finger through the damp petals. Plucked on the small pearl. Decided he would bring her almost to her climax, back off then repeat the process. He would be the one to decide when she would fragment. She would have no choice.

"Jason…please…" A broken sound filtered from her lips.

The game would end soon with him as the winner. "Please what? You are used to fast and messy. Let's make this slow and neat. What do you say?" He brought his hand from the sultry heat between her legs. Touched her cheek with the evidence of her need. Handed her the glass of champagne he set on the table earlier.

"I don't want…" Her eyes were closed. Thin lines around her mouth told of the strength of her awakening.

He would let her simmer before he burned her again. "You must drink before your pleasure," he told her while he nipped on her ear. Touched the lobe with his tongue then whirled it around the outside then inside. “Drink.”

Jason sat back, drank from his glass. Watched as she did the same. Without finishing the small amount, Tessa set the glass aside. He spilled more champagne inside the crystal. Filled the glass to the top. If she was a *wee* bit tipsy, this might take on a different edge. Jason needed to see every side of Tessa.

Taking the initiative, she pressed her lips against his. Opened for him, touched him with her tongue. He moved her back. Stared at her hard. His point needed to be realized. “You must drink it all before I see to more pleasure.” He held up a pastry. “Take a bite then drink. After that we will see how much energy you have.”

With her scowl, his laughter cracked. “Bite. Eat. Make love in that order. I will have this no other way.”

“What if I refuse?” she questioned, seeming not to understand the scenario. “I…” She seemed to believe she could seduce him.

She couldn’t. Not now that he found the restraint he needed. He was hungry to taste all of her but not desperate. “You won’t get your pleasure if you refuse.” Jason held out the piece of cake.

They continued in the same vein.

~ * ~

Tessa understood she would lose the exact moment he set her astride his lap. At that point she managed to seduce herself. She didn’t know how the tables turned on her so quickly. All she wished for now was her climax. With restrained purpose, he withheld that from her. She was both angry as well as frustrated after that provoked more than she’d ever been. With incredible intent, he was keeping them both from their release. She didn’t care about a slow hand. Had only one idea in mind. by his actions he was tormenting…torturing both of them. He must also be on the brink of desperation.

Near the third almost orgasm and now the third glass of champagne Tessa wondered if she could survive this slow hand of his. This new Jason was going to be the death of her. Each time he brought her higher. Burned her with more heat. Aroused to a blinding fever. At the very moment he thought she was on the precipice, he would set her aside. Give her more to eat as well as drink. He had yet to enter her, to fill her with his satin steel.

"Are you ready?" his voice whispered across her cheek. His words of sensual pleasure sent her higher still. The warmth brushing her, the mercuric scent coupled with sensual pleasure sent lightning deep into her. She quivered then whimpered. "Tell me how much you want me. Put your need into words." He rubbed the stubble of his cheek against her breasts, the column of her throat.

A broken sound revealed itself.

Nerves splintered.

She'd been ready for what seemed like hours. Thought she would die a thousand times over if he didn't do something to relieve the mounting tension, the ache that was centered in the moist, dark secret parts of her. Moonlight wafted over them as she sat, straddled on his lap. The light glistened in his dark hair.

"Please…" she moaned the one word she hoped would sway Jason from his resolve. Sweat sheened, she trembled with raw passion. Sent her tongue across her lips. Thought she'd never felt such heightened pleasure. Fire burned within. Tempest soared to greater heights.

His big hands were on her waist, lifting. The probe of his sex touched upon her softness. Teased her. She tried to move down, to take him into her. She tossed her head back, needing, wanting him to fill her. "You haven't said if you are prepared for me. I can't come inside you if you're not ready to accept me into your silken sheathe. Don't wish to hurt you, precious Tessa. Only one time, never again."

If he didn't know just how prepared she was he was not too bright. They both understood that wasn't the case. Breath caught in her throat as he bit with exquisite tenderness the tip of her breast. Still playing her even though he won the game she began. "I'm…" she could not get the words out through her parched lips. Tessa licked again then another time. Against her she felt the tip of his sex.

Jason, stop teasing.

"Maybe you need more food along with another glass of the bubbly. What do you think? If you can't talk, you don't have the strength for what I've in mind. Once begun, we might not finish until the morning sun rises." His voice was a husky low growl. His fingers cupped her slid into the folds between her legs then out. Circled the hard bud that brought her to the highest of highs. There wasn't one part of her that wasn't prepared for his entry. She wanted to butt her head against his to knock sense into the damn man.

"Don't need…just you…Jason." She leaned against him. Bit his shoulder. Still, he held her so they just touched. She needed him to sink into her. Make her complete. Needed to be joined together, to be one with each other. "What…what do you want from me?" her words were a thin wail veiled by the darkness of the room.

With his thumb Jason continued to circle the place that sent her soaring. Teased her with no mercy. "Tell me, love. Don't wish to do anything too soon."

It had been more than thirty minutes of sensual arousal. Torture when he teased but did nothing. Didn't act on his need or hers. She didn't know if he punished her for beginning this sensual play between them. It seemed he reprimanded himself every time he took her so fast the joining was over in seconds. He'd given her fair warning this time would be different. She would beg.

She swallowed the lump in her throat. Thought hard. Attempted the words he wished to hear. Formed the words in her mind. Forced herself. Wished she could find a way to surface for air then to tease him as he teased her. She could not. Perhaps another time. "I'm…ready…Jason, please. No more."

As slow as she thought possible, he allowed her to glide down his shaft. He filled her. Heated her from the inside out, the sensations delicious. When she expected him to thrust into her as his usual habit, Jason held still. She felt her body pulse and clench against his hard length. So adrift with aching need, she set her forehead on his. She gulped in a breath of Jason scented air. Her breasts moved against his chest. Inside she felt the raging of her body. As was the last three times, she was about to splinter. She might do so without him moving on her. With a slow hand, he continued to circle the small pearl he told her about. Explained to her how touching the knot would always bring her the greatest pleasure.

“You certain?” With his question she wanted to hit him. Instead, her nails raked down his back. She felt his shudder of mercuric passion.

“Yes!” She arched. Cried out with the tempest of pleasure igniting her.

He circled the tip of her breast with his mouth. Sucked the globe deep between his lips. Pulled on the nipple. Tweaked. She strained toward him silently asking for more. Still, deep inside her, he remained as if frozen. He let the nipple go with a loud sound that sounded like a plop. His mouth framed hers. As he began to move, his tongue repeated the rhythm. Penetrate then retreat. Over then over again as she was cast to the storm he orchestrated. Tessa didn’t think she would survive much more.

A heartbeat later she splintered. With greedy hunger for the end, she cried out his name. Pulsed then throbbed more while the fragmenting continued as she clenched him tighter. He thrust harder. Faster. She continued fracturing until she was drained. The orgasm seemed to have lasted for minutes on end. Breathing was too hard.

She wilted over him. Supported by his strong arms. Moisture from the intensity of what she experienced, filled her eyes. Shone on her body along with his. His sex slipped from inside her. She felt the loss. Cradling her in his arms, he walked to the bed where he set her.

He laid down beside her, pulling her against his chest. She nuzzled him, her cheek resting against his shoulder. This uniting of their bodies was better than anytime that came before. She was exhausted, shuddering still in the aftermath of her pleasure.

“Jason…” Tessa could barely say his name. The whisper was hardly a sound. She rubbed her cheek against him.

“Hmm…” Jason played with her hair. As his finger ran from base to the tips the strands fell against her. The sensation lazy in the reverberation of something far more intense.

“Why?” Tessa thought she might understand the why of it without his explanation. Before when she climaxed the fragmenting of her body was fast. Explosive. The duration short. She never thought to experience anything so long lasting. Vibrant. Powerful beyond anything she could have ever imagined. Maybe he was right about a slow hand. She would consider the options. Though both ways had merit.

"I think you understand, love. With patience everything is better. Even sex. You were so aroused. Your body continued the promise seconds upon seconds I started." He ran his finger through her hair. Seemed to enjoy the gentle petting that didn't arouse. "Promised you a slow hand. Though I had to work hard to achieve my goal. You were determined to have things your way. Rest assured, I will endeavor to control our lovemaking so both of us derive the greatest pleasure possible." He sounded smug, overconfident.

"What you did might have been too slow. Could we, maybe, find something in between to try? I never thought I could survive what you were doing." She understood there would be times when the sexual contact would be fast. Seemed to be in his nature. Hers too.

The expression he slanted her was a mischievous male smile. "We can try. Though I promise you that if I toss you on the kitchen table then explode within in you in mere seconds, the next time will be just like this one."

Mulling over his words, she decided to move on to something else. This was a second wedding night for them. Didn't wish to mar the rest of the evening with a discussion of her mother. Somehow felt her fears needed to be voiced. She would need to go against her wishes. Mar the tender moment with talk that would please neither of them.

"Mother showed up here for a reason. She never does anything that isn't calculated, well-planned. Why do you think she showed up with Armstrong? Not Miles? I'm certain she has her reasons. It's just that I don't understand."

The thought that Armstrong Seymore might be her real father both pleased as well as terrified her. Tessa wondered what type of life she would have had if the man bothered to claim her as his bastard. She might not have known her sisters. That would have been a horrible loss. Though she might have grown up with a cousin. Gracie Murray was the judge's daughter. That thought gave her a small measure of pleasure. She liked Gracie.

"I fear to guess on the possibilities," Jason said while he continued the slow glide of his fingers along her body as well as her hair.

While no one spoke of the possibilities to her, she made guesses for herself. Tessa understood that Miles and Armstrong were twins. Since she looked enough like Gracie for Miles to mistake her for his daughter, she assumed the possibilities of parentage. If they both had affairs with Anice, either one could be her father. Her biggest question was would either man admit to sleeping with her mother?

"Do you think one of those men is my father? Is that even out of the realm of possibilities?" Tessa played with the dark hair on his chest, winding the softness through her fingers. Thinking about moving her hand lower to more intimate territory. This time she wanted their loving to be fast. Over with fast as well as frenzied, messy and hard just as all the times that came before. "I wouldn't mind either man being named my father. Nonetheless, I would assume that Anice never told them of the possibility of a child. Neither man strikes me as the type who would ignore offspring. Even a child who was born on the wrong side of the sheets."

"Imagine not," Jason replied with a throaty noise then a snort. Holding on to the hand that crept lower as they spoke. "Armstrong had the appearance of a caged animal when he was with Anice."

"Does that mean…"

"Doesn't hold any value as something we can draw inferences from. Anice is filled with deceit. She isn't about to the tell the truth until she has milked everything as far as she can go. Once that happens, she'll drop the ball. All will be done."

"I don't know. There is something wrong here. I can feel her delight at the pain she will cause. Maybe you're right about her dropping the information when it will most hurt me. She loathes me. I've always known that little fact. She must detest both men." Admitting to that truth had been hard. Once she understood, she had to live with the information. At times she thought her mother's hatred was better than the fake love she cast out to wet her appetite for something more.

"Believe she despises all her daughters equally," Jason said, his voice soft as if he wished to take away some of the sting Anice caused.

"How do you feel?" Tessa asked as her hand began to roam lower still. Always intrigued by the path of his dark hair.

"Me…what?"

"About who my father is. Do you care?"

Jason sat up. Brought her with him. Held her face between his big hands then kissed her soundly, deeply. When he pulled away, he spoke with a soft cadence, "Who your father might be makes no difference to me. You are my wife no matter who Anice reveals as your parent. In the end, the name of the man who sired you will never change anything between us."

Tessa brought her lips together in a thin line. "You mean that?" She hoped and prayed his words were true. She didn't want to lose him to her mother's evil plans. Didn't see how blackmail played any part in this scenario. None of the men involved would deny parentage if labeled as her father.

His hands went around her neck then settled on her shoulders. Jason tried to further reassure. "Tessa, I mean everything I've said." He paused pressing a gentle kiss on her lips. "Do you want more champagne?" he asked while he laughed.

She gave an unladylike snort. "My head is spinning from the three glasses I had before we made love last time. Don't want food or drink. Need to sleep."

Exhausted coupled with satisfaction was the best way to describe the way she felt. He pulled her into his arms. The firelight was burning low. The candles had all been extinguished before they made love. She heard the steady beat of his heart.

"Should we sleep?" he asked.

Her lashes fluttered closed with the next deep breath. The next she knew morning sunlight slipped into the room. Jason wasn't beside her. He'd told her they didn't need to rise early. They could sleep the day away. Where was he?

"I'm right here, Love." His voice came from behind her. "Don't want you to think I abandoned you."

Tessa turned to see him wearing his robe, sitting at the small table. "You got up?" She questioned feeling a little disappointed. She'd expected to wake to his roaming hands. Thought they would make love as they had each morning since their marriage.

"Hungry," he murmured. "Had to get something to eat. How about you? Are you as famished as I am?" The question seemed to have a different meaning. The words not quite what she thought he meant.

"I, well," she looked at herself. The covers slipped to her waist. Tessa was surprised she felt at ease wearing nothing in front of this man she loved to distraction. Cool air tightened her nipples. "Yes, believe I am hungry. Would like a bath before I eat."

"Would you like me to remove my robe? No? You don't want to see me naked?" He lifted a dark eyebrow. "No, suppose that won't be a good idea. I foresaw your needs. Clancy will be in soon along with the servants bringing hot water. What do you say?" The knock on the door stopped his conversation for a few seconds. "Perhaps you should burrow under those covers. Naked, you might shock our stoic and very celibate butler."

Without a blink, that's exactly what she did. Buried beneath the blankets, she caught the scent of Jason. Held his pillow close to her nose. She breathed in deep the spicy aroma she'd come to love. While she listened to the servants walking in then out, the water splashing into the tub, she closed her eyes remembering all the exquisite pleasure from the night before. The slow loving. Yes, that had been nice in the extreme. What they shared was more than nice. The loving had been exquisite.

Together they slept. Woke. Ate bits and pieces that had been brought to them. Drank more champagne. She thought she should have a headache. She did not. They did finish off two bottles.

Beneath the covers, she listened to the chime of the big grandfather clock in the hallway. Twelve o'clock. Noon? She'd not expected to sleep so long. No wonder she was hungry.

"All's clear," Jason boomed as he lifted one corner. "You can come out now. We can play more if you like. We've the afternoon awaiting us. If the weather remains nice, we can frolic in the gazebo."

"Don't want the water to get cold," Tessa mumbled but she rose from beneath the layer of warmth that had been covering her. "Have to eat before I can play. As you said last night, nutrition is important."

"Very well," he told her before turning his back to walk to the table.

She'd thought he would ask to share the bath. He didn't. Puzzled she watched him, pushed hair from her face. "You're acting strange. What is wrong?" Tessa needed words. Something tangible to hold onto. His mind was preoccupied.

"Maybe. I've taken a bath. I know I told you we had nothing pressing. Seems I was wrong. Received a summons from Miles Seymore. While I doubt if it concerns anything about you and who your father is, I intend to visit him sometime today. When, is all that remains to be decided upon."

"Don't you think I should tag along? If it does concern me…" She didn't know what else to say. Perhaps it was best if she waited for Jason to return. The summons could be nothing. She was tired, didn't need another disappointment. Could sleep another hour or more. If she did, she would never get to sleep tonight. Not that sleep made a difference with Jason. Last night wasn't the only night they made love more than once; woke up to have his arms wrapped around her in a tender, sensual embrace.

"If you wish, of course you can tag along." He picked up the paper to scan the front page before he settled on an article to read.

Tessa had a myriad of different thoughts about following Jason to the meeting. She decided she would rather wait. Hear secondhand what Miles had to say after he returned. A leisurely brunch then a walk to the gazebo sounded relaxing. She would take a book along to read. The warm summer air would feel refreshing. The scent of summer flowers would fill the air.

"You go on. I'd rather wait to hear if this meeting has anything to do with the identity of my father. As you said, this visit might not be anything at all." Tessa paused for a few beats while she listened to the pounding of her heart. If she told Jason she didn't care, she'd be lying. "I'm afraid. That's all. While I wish to know who the man is who sired me, I've spent too many years believing I was legitimate. If I'm given a name, I'll be a bastard. It's not something a girl…or anyone wants to learn."

Tessa felt moisture clog her throat. Tears threatened. The last few words had been difficult to say. He was beside her in an instant. Jason wrapped her with delicate sensitivity within the warm embrace of his arms. He set his chin on top of her head. She absorbed the moment of gentleness.

"Good. While I would never protest your presence, I find I'm relieved you've decided to stay home. Don't wish to have you subjected to anything that might go wrong with this interview. Enjoy your bath as well as your breakfast. I'll dress. The sooner I get going the sooner I'll be back to share the rest of the day with my lovely bride. Will you be in the gazebo? I'll meet you there."

His grin was handsome as the very devil. Hair so dark, eyes so golden brown. He kissed her forehead as he strolled by her to the dressing room. Tessa rose from the bed to go to the bath. Jason peaked out from his dressing room to watch her. The grin she witnessed widened. He looked all mischief paired with daring.

She turned to him. Twisted her hair into a coil then a knot on top of her head. Knew he watched her. His eyes darkened, lingered on her breasts then roamed lower. She posed for him. Set a hand on her hip, understanding he might not leave right away. Swept her tongue along her lips before letting it hover on the top. There would be no complaining from her if he stayed to make love.

The long whistle of air from his lips were followed by the soft words. A curse. "I can't…" he told her. "Nonetheless, after I return, we will make it fast and messy if that's what you might like. I'll save the slow hand for tonight. What do you think? Is that a date combined with a promise of uncontrolled pleasure?"

"Your restraint is admirable," Tessa told him while she thought about the quick encounter on the kitchen table the night before. Both ways of making love were wonderful. She would never complain when his hands along with his mouth moved over her. Touched her with hungry tender care.

With a long sigh of ecstasy, Tessa slipped into the hot water. Soaked up the warmth. She heard the door close as he left. Thought about how fortunate she was to have found a man so magnificent. Breathtaking. While he hadn't yet told her he loved her, she could wait. She knew he cared for her. His care was all she needed at the moment. He would do anything for her. Give her anything she asked.

Care was good enough for the present. It was a fine word. Care, she rolled that around in her head for a few moments of thought. Was not good enough though. She needed more than care when it came to Jason.

Soon, she hoped. Soon he might tell her he loved her.

At least thirty minutes passed before she was dressed and ready to seek out the gazebo. She hummed a tune she learned in Ireland. Today would be a good day. Looked forward to Jason's return in an hour or so. At the bottom of the steps, Clancy seemed to be waiting for her. His smile of welcome looked grim. Her heart skipped a beat. His brows came together in a snow-white line of what appeared to be concern.

"Lady Tessa," he held out his hand with an envelope resting on his palm. His voice was one of apprehension. "This letter came for you. It's from your mother, Anice MacRae. Don't know if it's urgent. Thought about waiting to give it to you until Lord Kenworthy returns. If you'd like to read it with him present, then I'll wait."

"What could Mother want? No, I need to see it now." Her breath quickened. A premonition of doom swept into her. She needed to find her courage. Seemed bravery was elusive. She always did lack nerve. Was always willing to hide behind others.

"Imagine you will need to read the letter before you can have an answer to that question," Clancy told her, his voice holding an edge of amusement. "Are you certain you wish to see it now?"

"Imagine that," she said deadpan while ice swept down her spine. She reached out for the missive. Gulping a large dose of oxygen for courage, "Yes, I wish to read it now. I'll be in the gazebo. When Jason returns, tell him where I am and that I'm waiting for him." *For news.*

Reading a letter from her mother was among the last things she wanted to do. No matter what it said, Tessa knew the morning tranquility would be ruined. Something in the words that were penned would be caustic. She didn't want to believe this might ruin her life. Her mother never did anything that would benefit her personally.

Holding the paper beneath her chin, she tugged in several deep breaths of air. "Thank you, Clancy. I appreciate…" Tessa didn't want to talk to anyone.

"If there is anything I can do?" The butler appeared worried. Frown lines marred his forehead as he seemed to study her. "You should reconsider. Wait for Jason. He would want you to do that. Wait for him."

"Not right now. I'll let you know." Clancy was right. Jason would like her to read the letter with him beside her. She had to know what her mother penned.

Feeling as if the world was closing in on her, she walked into the backyard, heading for the private sanctuary she was coming to love. Sunshine gave her spirits a bit of a boost. The tabby cat who frequented the back of the house shadowed her while she tried to think what her mother would have to say. Flowers blossomed along the walkway. Bees sipped nectar. Her heartbeat matched the rapid flutter of a hummingbird's wings as it supped on honeysuckle blossoms. Seemed after last night and her mother's intrusion to her wedding celebration enough had been said to last several lifetimes.

She curled up on one of the plush chairs. Bringing her legs beneath her, Tessa held a pillow in front of her with one hand, the letter in the other. Sweat broke out on her forehead. Feelings of terror she didn't understand swept through her. With unmeasured instinct, she recognized the news would not be good. Nothing good, kind or beautiful ever came from her mother. She thought to put the missive aside. Thought better of waiting. If you wait, you'll be just as everyone thinks of you. A woman with no backbone.

Get this over with.

Do it now before you lose the courage.

She took the seal off the envelope then pulled out the parchment. It was folded in half. With fear in her heart, she unfolded the sheet of paper. Stared at the written words for a few minutes before seeing the letters. Stole oxygen from the air. Looked to the cloudless sky, her pulse quickening.

My dearest Tessa,

This is written with the heaviest of hearts. I'm telling you of your true father. I should not have waited this long to apprise you of his name. Should have said something the first moment you showed interest in Jason Kenworthy. Though at the time I wasn't positive about your parentage. Waiting has caused more pain to you. This is all wrong. All terribly wrong. At your marriage celebration, you looked at him with such love in your eyes. The sight of you so vulnerable hurt me. I digress.

Tessa, darling, you cannot continue with this ill-fated marriage of yours. You must end the debacle. By now you will not be able to ask for an annulment. You might even be with child. This is so horrible. I can't tell you how terrible I feel. I never thought you would marry the man. The deed was done before I knew. The two of you never invited me to the wedding. So, I had no idea how you felt. If you had invited your mother, I would have been able to put a stop to this untenable marriage with a few words. Have Lord Kenworthy file for divorce. An ending to your marriage is the only way to escape this horrific dilemma. Haste is what you need. Tell him today. Have the divorce filed quickly before you are enceinte.

Tessa sipped in air. Her head spun. What was she up to now? How dare her mother send something like this to her? *How dare she?* The letter sat on her lap, her trembling hands still holding onto the paper. She didn't think she should finish reading. Anice's words were all drivel. All that was said sounded as if doom would come her way and Jason's. The end of the marriage was what she'd wished for all along. Anice wouldn't win without a fight. She tried threatening. That didn't work. Now this bizarre letter.

After another deep breath, Tessa turned the paper over. With trembling hands, she began to read again.

You are probably confused. As was I when I heard via second hand of your wedding. I'm telling you this because the truth is for your personal good. The marriage must be ended. You and Lord Kenworthy cannot continue to live in sin. I fault myself for not having the courage to tell you sooner.

Tell me what, Mother? Get to the point. You are beating around the bush, never saying anything useful. You have repeated yourself to no end.

I'll get straight to the point. I comprehend that you are wondering. The two of you are brother and sister. Your father is Lord Kenworthy's father, Simon. While that fact didn't affect Maggie, it does you. I had an affair with Simon twenty years ago. Yes, he was cheating on his wife. Yes, I'm an adulteress. That is something you've always known, no surprises there. I detested my husband who was not the father of your sisters as all of you know. I'd been hoping...nay...praying that Armstrong Seymore was your father. Alas, he is not. Discovered that after our talk last night. Until then, I had not been certain. Armstrong couldn't be because we stopped seeing each other shortly before you were conceived. I also had a one-

night dalliance with Miles but it also was before you were conceived. So, you see, there is no other possibility except Simon. Previous to the finalization in my mind as to your father, I did guess at Simon as a possible candidate. He was quite the brilliant lover. Was disappointed when he abruptly stopped seeing me. I do believe he guessed I was with child. He was not honorable. Miles along with Armstrong would have claimed you as theirs. They are both decent as well as moral men.

Come home to me. I'll help you find a suitable husband. I'll take care of you. With my help, you have nothing to worry about.

Your loving mother.

Tears dripped on the paper, spreading the ink in places into blurred lines. Her heart slowed. This couldn't be true. Why? She dropped the letter on the seat. Held her hands over her eyes sobbing out her despair.

This had to be a lie. All lies. This cannot be true. Can't be. With the backs of her hands, she wiped the tears away. Stiffened her back. Mother is horrible.

Tessa knew the letter would not bring good news. She had never thought of anything like this. Anice was right. They couldn't remain married. She could never have Jason's child. Her hand settled on her belly. What if she already conceived their child. Her breath caught. Broke. More tears slid down her cheeks.

Jason is my brother.

No! How could that be?

I must leave here. Don't have anywhere to go.

Still in denial, Tessa staggered from the chair she'd been sitting on. Knowing only that she had to get as far away from the reminder of her love that she could. She loved Jason. She couldn't love him. Couldn't stay here. Couldn't see the look on Jason's face when he discovered he'd married his sister. How could this happen? Time and again, she asked herself that question. How? Why didn't anyone guess before they made this fatal mistake? What they did could never be undone.

No...no...no!

Didn't dare go into the house. If Clancy saw her, he would question her. Would see her tear-stained face. Would send for Jason. She had nothing to say to anyone. Ashamed and vulnerable, Tessa made her way around the outside of the house. In a blind stupor, she walked. Headed toward the village. Plans had to be made. Saw nothing she could hold on to. Hated words rang in her head. She continued walking in an unreasoning daze. Didn't know what to do except go to the village. Maybe someone there would help her get back to Glasgow. Jason would look for her there. She should go to Inverness or Edinburgh. Disappear into a city…any city…somewhere he'd never find her.

She'd heard of a woman in Glasgow who helped women in trouble. Daryl was her first name. She would go to her. The woman owned a bakery. She would work for her. What if Daryl didn't need help at the bakery? That was a milestone she would need to cross when she found her way to the city. Glasgow it was. She could go nowhere else.

If she sold her wedding and engagement rings, she would have enough money for a few days. She could catch a coach into Glasgow. That's what she would do. She would take only enough of the money from the sale to tide her over for a few days. Certain the jewelry cost Jason a small fortune, she could not take everything. Must leave most of the money from the sale for Jason. She wouldn't steal. In time, she would pay him back.

~ * ~

Anice expected her daughter any minute now. Tessa would have read the letter this very morning. As gullible as her youngest was she would have believed every word. She grinned thinking about her creative endeavor. What she did was bold as well as optimistic. She along with Lord Abernathy had plans for her youngest. If she admitted to the fact, she didn't know if either Armstrong or Miles was the father, she couldn't be certain. One of them was the sire, of that she was positive.

What she knew for a fact was that Simon Kenworthy never bedded her. Never cheated on his wife. Never created a child with her. From the first moment she saw Simon all decked out in formal attire, she was smitten, besotted with lust. She approached the man only to be rebuffed. From that moment on, she wished for vengeance. No man shunned her then got away with the rejection. Now retribution was hers. Tessa fell into her trap with innocence. Didn't matter. Anice supposed her daughters felt the same way about the Kenworthy twins. The two men were every bit as handsome as their father.

She snorted, smiling laughter rising up from inside. This was all she'd ever wanted. The youngest daughter had always been a thorn in her side. Glad she would get her comeuppance as would Jason Kenworthy. The Viscount of Townsend, Lord Abernathy was still unwed. She would see what kind of deal she could make with the man. A profitable one she hoped.

Ah, she understood very well that Nelson would never take a used woman as a wife. He could set her up as his mistress. He would enjoy the power over the wayward girl. Would teach her a few lessons in comportment that needed to be learned. Tessa would come to know who was her master.

Tessa, as Nelson's mistress, would be acceptable to her. As soon as Tessa surrendered herself into her mother's safe keeping, she would hand her over to Nelson. She owed the man for the mess up with her oldest daughter. She would send a quick note to Nelson to meet with her as soon as he could. Would give him the opportunity to find suitable housing for Tessa. Her daughter would stay under lock and key until Nelson came to claim her.

Sitting back, she sipped her glass of wine. Enjoyed the sweet Bordeaux. Proud of the coming together of all her plans. It had been an accomplishment to come up with Simon as the name of the unknown father. Simon was dead. The poor man was in no shape to defend himself. If she got the letter off quickly, maybe Nelson could visit with her tonight. They could finalize their plans. Tessa would not get away from them.

Yes, she mused again, the poor man wasn't alive. He couldn't defend himself. Jason along with her daughter would never learn the truth. Jason would live the rest of his life believing his father cheated on his mother. Not that she didn't try to get him into her bed. Simon was a handsome devil. Time and again, the man refused her overtures.

"What?" Anice looked up to see her butler. He never interrupted her solitude when she was in her private room. "What is it?"

He bowed smartly just as she drilled him. "Lord Abernathy is here to see you. Says now would do for him. Nothing less. Doesn't wish to wait."

That bit of news shocked her. Surprised by one of the objects of her thoughts coming to her without an invitation. Pleased as her plans for her youngest was coming together with little effort.

"What should I tell him, ma'am. Understand you don't like to be surprised with unexpected guests. Told him he most likely wasted his time by arriving without a proper request. Should I send him on his way?"

Her smile was feral. This was good…very good. No wasted time. Anice waved her hand. "Send Lord Abernathy to me. We've quite a bit to hash over. Bring my best brandy. He will be thirsty." With the thoughts swimming in her head, her mind roared to life. This was so unexpected. Soon, very soon, she would hand her youngest over to this handsome man with a slight cruel streak. If she behaved…ah, that would be the test. Tessa would have no say in the surrender of her body. Nelson would take whatever he wished to take. Whenever he wished to take it.

In her private sitting room, she rose to greet Nelson. Her arms outstretched for the hug he would give her. After the quick embrace, he kissed both cheeks. Held her by her shoulders to peruse her.

"You're looking pleased as well as beautiful. What has happened?" Nelson asked as he stepped back. "I'm certain I'm going to like whatever news you have for me."

"Tonight, you must have been tuned into my mind. I was about to write a quick note asking if you could see me as soon as possible." She opened up her arms grinning. "Here you are. How fortuitous?"

"Was thinking about you. Thought I would pay a visit after news of Kenworthy's wedding to Tessa made the rounds this evening. I did not expect the wedding. Was still hoping to have the wayward chit in my marriage bed."

"Her marriage will end soon. Jason will ask for a divorce. There is no other course for him. With tears in her eyes, Tessa will sign whatever is put in front of her. Should take no more than a week or two to accomplish the end of that marriage."

His sly smile told Anice he understood she'd done something untoward. An action that would benefit both of them. "Just…how did you accomplish this feat?" he asked while she poured him a snifter of her finest brandy. "Interesting that a newlywed couple would suddenly wish to separate, file for a divorce."

"Not so surprising when one understands the incorrect facts I've set in motion." She rolled the snifter of brandy between her hands, watching the amber change color.

"Glad I'm not your enemy," Nelson muttered while he took a chair facing her. His eagerness began to show. "How?" he asked again. "Tell me all the sordid details. What did you put in motion? That cannot be undone?"

"Genius…my actions were pure genius. I am a mastermind of deception." Anice licked her lips then drank. Held the brandy in her mouth for a few seconds before she swallowed, let the liquid burn down her throat.

"Explain," he said as he relaxed, one leg crossed over the other. "I'm too curious to play games with you."

"My youngest daughter's father was Simon Kenworthy. At least that is what I've led her to believe. Tessa is so gullible she will credit me with the truth. Even coming from me, she wouldn't consider the words a lie. So, you see, the two will believe they are sister and brother. The marriage will end. There is no proof otherwise."

"A stroke of brilliance!" he cried out to her, grinning as if he conquered the world. "Would have never thought of it by myself. Does that mean I will have *carte blanch* with the girl. She is beautiful. I've wanted her ever since you made the suggestion. By God, I can't wait to have her in my possession. First, the little trollop will pay for all the trouble she has given me. My mind spins with plans of revenge."

"*Carte blanch*," Anise agreed with a half-smile. "You can do anything you wish. First, she will come here. I'll send a message as soon as she arrives."

"I've a place in mind to put her up. It can be readied by tomorrow evening. When do you expect her?"

"If I know my daughter, she will not stay with Jason a moment longer than need be. She will flee. Since she has nowhere to go except home to me, I might see her first thing in the morning. Possibly later tonight, depending on when she read the letter I sent her." Beneath her chin she tapped her fingers while she thought.

"I will pick her up tomorrow…say…around five o'clock. Would that work for you? She will be here?"

"Perfect. I will be looking forward to giving her to you for your personal use. I do owe you. Now I'll consider our debts paid in full."

Chapter Nine

"Where is she? Where's my wife? I have news. Good information!" Jason walked past Clancy as he headed up the steps to the bedroom expecting her to be resting, waiting for news upon his return. One foot on the top step, he stopped. "Upstairs?" He looked over his shoulder for a second glance at the butler while he anticipated an answer.

Clancy's lips were thinned. Lines that appeared to be stress radiated around his eyes that seemed to wrestle with anxiety. The old butler shook his head while he focused on the back door, seeming unwilling to give a reply. "Sir."

"Yes?" Jason started back down the stairs. His steps fast-paced. Stopped in front of Clancy. "What is it? Is there something wrong? My wife?" He sensed the nervous energy in the air. Found his pulse quickened. Clancy would never have this look of distress if he also didn't sense something was wrong.

Jason was eager to see Tessa. Needed to get to the crux of this problem whatever it might be. His news would delight her. At least he hoped the information would. Armstrong admitted to being her father. Felt at the time twenty years ago that Anice should have told him she was with child. Armstrong felt certain Anice withheld the information as her way of getting revenge for his sudden withdrawal of affection. While he couldn't guarantee beyond a shadow of a doubt that he sired Tessa, he was as close to positive as a man could be under these circumstances. Armstrong couldn't even be certain she wasn't seeing other men at the time. Though he spent so much time with the woman she would not have had much energy left over for another man.

Clancy cleared his throat. For unknown reasons, he was stalling. This time he ran his hands down the legs of his pants. "Lady Tessa walked to the gazebo a few hours ago. She has been there ever since. Thought she might have grown tired or hungry. Expected her to return before this. She told me to send you there when you returned from your visit," Clancy told him while he watched the butler shuffle his feet.

Trouble came full force to the front of his head. Jason didn't have to be a mind reader to understand. The hair on the nape of his neck stood on end. "There is something else?" Jason asked, while he watched the nervous twitch of Clancy's eyes. "What? Out with it! Tell me everything." Clancy never minced his words. He was always straight forward. "Tessa? Did something happen to her?" Jason found that he wasn't making guesses. His stomach rolled then spasmed. Clancy needed to spit out the truth before he was forced to shake him.

"Lady Tessa…yes this involves your wife. Didn't want to say anything. With you gone, didn't believe there was a choice. Couldn't go to you first to consult. I gave her a letter from Mrs. MacRae. She took the dispatch with her to the gazebo. Said she wanted to be alone when she read her mother's thoughts. Believed she might want to wait for you. Told her as much. Your wife declined the offer." Once the information was given, Clancy seemed to relax.

His mind numbed. Froze. What the devil would Anice be writing about? There must be something clandestine in this. He turned his focus on Clancy. "A letter from Anice? That can't be good," he murmured, turning for the back of the house in an urgent run.

The chill that swept over him with the information Clancy gave him stopped his heart for a beat then another. He prayed there were no lies in the letter. He wouldn't put anything past that shrew of a mother. Prayed, Anice only meant to congratulate her on the marriage. Congratulations were in order. It was what a mother should do.

By the time Jason reached the gazebo, he was breathing hard, sucking in air. Stopped to look over the small area. When he saw the place empty, he cursed. Told himself that it didn't mean anything. Where the devil was Tessa? Searching for her, turning in a full circle he rubbed his hand across the back of his neck. Swore again. She has to be nearby. Where would she go? Clancy would have kept an eye out for her. He would have known if she returned to the house.

He sat down on the couch. Brought the pillow to his chest. Caught her scent. Lavender coupled with sunshine along with summer storms. Closed his eyes while he inhaled the potent fragrance. Tried to calm himself. Needed to put himself in Tessa's mind. Doing so was impossible. He saw her when she teased him before her bath. Posed for him with no shyness. Recalled last night when his slow hand brought her pleasure. Remembered the fast messy coupling on the kitchen table. Thought of the small giggles after she drank one glass of champagne too many.

Where was she?

Had to be close.

Clancy would have known if she was in the house. He would never send him to the gazebo if she wasn't supposed to be at their private sanctuary. After giving Tessa the letter, he would have kept a look out for her. Clancy understood the precarious position they were in with her mother. Until she conceived, she would still be vulnerable.

Jason didn't know what to do. He needed to find her. Needed to understand what was happening. Maybe he was jumping to all the wrong conclusions. Everything was fine. Tessa must have gone for a walk. That was all. If he started for the rose garden, he would find her sniffing roses. She loved to touch the petals to her cheeks.

What was in that letter? Where was the missive? He needed to see what was written. What Anice said. If he could see the printed words, he would have a better idea how to proceed. Found he was frantic with dread.

This wouldn't be the first time Anice MacRae did something to harm one of her girls. He was certain this would be bad news for Tessa. He didn't know what that pain could be. Thank God, he possessed good, important facts for her. She would be pleased to discover the identity of her father. Happy the man was Armstrong Seymore. Content that he'd never known about her existence. Armstrong told him he would go through with the paper work to claim her as legitimate offspring. She would no longer be a bastard.

Restless energy consumed him. He rose. Paced the length of the gazebo then back. Sat. Stuffed his fingers through his hair. Walked to the pathway leading to the house. Strode around the shelter. Found nothing except emptiness. He discovered no trace of Tessa except the soft scent of lavender on the pillow.

True to what Clancy told him, she'd been here.

Where did she go?

Why wasn't she at the house or here? He was wasting valuable time.

His head in his hands, he sat back down on the cushion. Closed his eyes wishing he had some way to contact Tessa. Thought of her. The way her smile lit his heart. The way her sapphire-colored eyes turned dark with her passion. How she wrapped her long white legs around him when he made love to her. Needed to figure out a means to learn where she was.

A sixth sense told him she left. Left him. What did he do? Believed she was happy. Thought she trusted him. Knew she enjoyed their love making? What words of his could have driven her away. Again, he tamped down that fear. He would walk back to the house. Find her resting in the bedchamber. Clancy might have missed her. Anything was possible. He was getting ahead of himself.

The letter would be the impetus driving her. Without Anice's written words, he had no ideas. She should have waited for him to read the letter. Waited for him to stand by her side. Support her if Anice said horrible things to her. What possible news from Anice could send her running away from him? He stood again. Ran his sweaty palms down his pants. He picked up each cushion. Wanted to throw them. Didn't know how to go about finding his wife. He needed air. Must have advice. Jasper might have an idea what he should do. Maggie could understand what drove her. They both might have guidance.

They would be on their way to Glasgow. Business called Jasper back before he planned. His brother wasn't going to ask him to see to the work when they were just wed. The sisters traveled with his brother and his wife, eager to resume their entertainment. There was no one at the house for him to seek advice.

Hell!

He threw the pillow he was still holding. It landed on the cushions where he'd been sitting. A flutter of something white was swept from the couch to the floor, caught his eyes. His attention focused on the paper. A lump caught in his throat. For a few beats he was afraid to look.

The letter.

He most likely sat on the thing. Picking it up he smoothed out the wrinkles. Stared at the tear-stained words. Was able to read the missive even through the blurry ink. Swore. Cursed several times. Reread the words that sent Tessa running. Where the hell would she go? Not back to her mother. She would never be so stupid. Her mother never had in mind what was best for her. The lie was obvious though. Anice expected her daughter to run to her. Expected to receive some compensation for her troubles.

Lord Abernathy...

Tessa didn't believe this drivel written here. Did She? The question filled his mind with despair. His father never cheated on his wife. Never. Not even when she was sick with fever. At ten years of age, he was old enough to see his father's grief for his wife, for his mother. A woman such as Anice MacRae would never appeal to his father. He believed in truth combined with honesty. His integrity was undeniable. Anice possessed none of those traits. His father wasn't here to defend himself. Simon was an easy target.

Lies. All lies.

Tessa didn't know his father. Had no idea who Simon was. What he believed in as basic human characteristics would be different from what she was used to. Tessa might well believe most people's beliefs were closer to her mother's. Didn't understand how honorable Simon was. Even after his mother's death he never sought out women. It was the way he felt about Tessa. He wasn't interested in any other woman now or in the future. If she died... He wouldn't think about that now. If that happened, not even Sarah would appeal to him. Not after learning Tessa. Knowing her scent, the silken feel of her flesh. The taste of her breasts.

Jason read the end of the letter.

Come home to me. I'll find you a suitable husband. I'll take care of you. With my help, you have nothing to worry about.

Tessa wouldn't go to her mother for solace. Would she? Anice wasn't going to find Tessa a husband because he would never file the necessary papers for a divorce. Anice would not be looking for a husband for her, she would be handing her over to the viscount to use as he pleased. Abernathy wouldn't accept the wife of another man as his own. All their plans would be for naught if Tessa went home to her mother.

Bloody eyes! Tessa was his wife!

Think.

Jason brought in a big dose of oxygen that seared his lungs, burning deep, scorching. Tessa would believe she couldn't stay here. She would go to the village. For her there was no other option. What would she do then? Look for a means to leave. She would feel the sin of sleeping with her brother. Would feel humiliated with the fact.

Running one more time, Jason raced to the stable. Saddled his horse. Someone in the village would have information about his wife. The jeweler would be his first visit. She might try to sell her rings. Money for a coach would be a necessity. Tessa didn't have much. If she left the house before going to her room, she had only the clothes on her back along with her rings.

Maybe he would discover where she went. Must have gone back to the city. In the distance, he saw someone riding fast. Dust billowed behind the horse's hooves. As the boy approached, they both reigned in.

"Sir? Lord Kenworthy?" The lad was breathless, breathing hard from his race. Held out his hand. "Here. This is for you."

He recognized the young man, the son of the village jeweler. Freckled face along with his red hair, the boy slanted a half-grin his way. He was lanky. Now, appeared to be all arms and legs. His eyes were a deep green. Would grow into a handsome man. "From?" Jason hoped this was from his wife. Instinct told him the message wasn't. Prayed this would give him insight into Tessa. Where she could be. Someone must know something.

"Mr. Callahan, the jeweler, my father. Told me to get this to you fast. Rode as hard as I could. Said to wait for your reply."

Holding his breath while he read, Jason understood Tessa must be doing her mother's bidding. She would go to her. After reading, he wadded the paper into a fist. Drug in a deep breath of air, holding the oxygen until his lungs burned.

I'll kill anyone who hurts Tessa!

"No need to send a message with you. I'm going to see your father." With that said, Jason didn't wait for the boy. He urged his horse to run. Dust kicked up behind him. Hooves pounded the hard dirt road leading to the village. Time seemed to stand still while he raced to catch up with his misinformed wife. Alone she could find trouble. She had no one to protect her. Tessa was beautiful prey to any predator. Abernathy was not the only hunter in this world. Jason dreaded what Anice had in mind for her youngest daughter. Beyond any doubt, Jason understood Tessa, once in her mother's care, she would find herself handed over to Abernathy. His gut rolled then cramped with fear.

In front of the shop, he leapt from the horse. Jason knew his mount wouldn't wander off. Knew his stallion would wait for him. Left him untethered. Long sure strides took him inside. The door thudded against the opposite wall with a horrendous bang.

He recalled the day he bought her the rings. Remembered how Miles thought she was his daughter Gracie; they looked so much alike. Miles agreed to attend the wedding. Miles would be Tessa's uncle. She didn't know that fact. Wouldn't know Armstrong was her father. Must have believed her mother. Left to save him from the mortification of learning he slept with as well as married his sister.

Tessa was wrong on all counts.

"Lord Kenworthy!" Mr. Callahan greeted him. "Must speak with you. Lady Tessa was so distraught when she was in here. Tear streaks ran down her cheeks. Stubborn lass that one. Must have your hands full. Tried to discover the problem. She remained mute. Wouldn't explain a thing. After she handed me her ring, she refused to take all the money."

"Was my wife unhurt?" Jason stepped forward to accept the one ring into the palm of his hand. The worst-case scenario was beginning to unfold before his eyes. She didn't sell both. Must have kept her wedding ring. His heart skipped a beat.

"Yes…yes…no she wasn't hurt. Tried to talk her out of leaving. She didn't tell me where she was going, though I tried to find out. Knew you would want to know. The two of you seemed so much in love."

Love? I do love her.

"Sent my boy after you as soon as she left. Knew you would want to know what happened."

"Money?" Jason pinched the bridge of his nose. Stared at the ring

Mr. Callahan gave him. Understood what she did.

"Your wife sold back her engagement ring. Said she only needed enough for the coach then a bit for food," he continued. "I…I didn't know what I should do. Hope this helps."

"You've done fine." Again, he focused on the ring sitting in his hand. The sapphire gems caught the light. "I'll pay you back what you gave her. She is going to need her rings. She can't just sell…" The devil this was getting worse by each beat of his heart. Tessa kept only enough to pay for her ride somewhere as well as eat for a few days. Nothing more. The ring was hers. The money was hers. Tessa wouldn't see it that way.

With the ring in his pocket, he ran to the station that sent coaches out to the cities. Two coaches left in the last hour. One to Glasgow and one to Edinburgh departed at approximately the same time. The man at the desk didn't know which coach she took. Told him they were busy.

Which city did she go to? He was only an hour behind her. If he made the wrong decision, he'd be days behind her. A decision had to be made.

How much trouble could she find in a few days? More than he wished to think about. She didn't have a means to survive unless she went to her mother. Jason found himself shaking, his entire body trembling with fear. Tessa would realize her mother didn't harbor good intentions where she was concerned.

Edinburgh or Glasgow?

As it stood now, he couldn't race his horse to either city. He would need to return to the townhouse for their coach. More wasted time. After several deep breaths of air, Jason changed his mind. He had no other recourse than to follow her now. The coach would travel faster. His stallion was winded. He'd raced him hard to get to the village. He couldn't run his horse to the ground. He would need to take care, take time to let his horse recover. Doing so would still save time. Jason strode to the stable in town. Rented a horse. Decided two horses might be faster than one. Decided on renting a third. He could race the entire distance.

Jason wrote a letter to go to Clancy, explaining his plans. "Here, can you have your boy take this to my butler?" He pulled out a few coins to give the lad. "There is no hurry as long as Clancy gets this today. There is nothing that can be done." As soon as he found Tessa, he would bring her home. Perhaps he should first explain what he learned.

Jason understood he'd been rude to the man. He would apologize later. There was no time now. Hoped that if he got off to a fast start, he would be able to intercept Tessa's coach. Realized, doing so would be near impossible.

Miles peeled away from the village. He saw nothing in the distance. No dust from the wheels. Didn't see a solitary soul. Now that he had more than one horse he could gallop. He didn't need to hold back. As the sun began to set and the city of Glasgow neared, he lost all hope of catching up to her. The first place he intended to look would be the townhouse where Tessa grew up. He didn't care if he intruded. Information needed to change hands. If Anice wouldn't let him in, he'd break the damn door down!

By the time he reached the MacRae home, the hour was late. Dark clouds threatened rain. In some ways he prayed Tessa was here. If she was this would all be finished. He would collect his wife then explain the truth of her parentage. He was furious with the out of hand situation. He should be dining with Tessa, experimenting with new ways to make love. Instead, he was searching for his wife because of lies penned by her damn mother.

When the door opened to allow him entrance, he walked past the butler, pushing the man aside. Jason knew if he wasn't straightforward, he would never be allowed to see the woman. If thwarted, he'd break every damn door. "Where is Anice? Is my wife here?"

The man dashed around him in an attempt to head him off. Tried to block the way with his thin body combined with a commanding tone to his voice. "You can't come in! You've no invitation!"

"I can do whatever the hell I want!" Jason roared back. His hands were fisted ready to prove to this man he didn't need to be invited. "Where is Anice? For that matter where is my wife?" His words echoed around the entrance. He sucked in air. Anger wasn't going to get him what he wanted. An air of cold, calculated calm swept over him.

"You've misplaced your new bride? How drole?" Anice now addressed her butler from behind them. "You can relax. I supposed I would need to speak with Lord Kenworthy. Come into the drawing room. Have a brandy. We can talk about the pending divorce. Tessa says she won't fight the dissolution of your marriage since you are her brother." Her cat-like smile sent his already frayed nerves stretching. His fists tightened. Shaking this woman would be a delight. Strangling her even better.

"There will be no divorce! Tessa is coming home with me now! Where is she?" Jason's demand seemed to give Anice another reason to smile. He understood the woman meant to prolong the situation. She enjoyed everything about provoking him.

"Have a seat, Lord Kenworthy. We can talk about this…er…situation. Of course, there will be a divorce. A man cannot remain married to his sister. In this day, that just isn't done." She glanced from him to the nearby chair.

Frustration built despite his attempts to tamp the emotions down. For Tessa's sake he needed to remain calm. "There is nothing to talk about. Tessa is coming with me. My wife will live with me. Tessa is not my sister. She is my wife!" All Anice said was a lie.

"No…no…you're wrong. Tessa is your sister…well…half-sister. You must file for a divorce with haste. The gossip will tear both of our families apart. I won't allow my daughter to live in sin with you." Her sweet smile meant nothing.

Jason didn't know how to combat the lies except with stark truths. "You are a bold audacious liar, Madam. My father never slept with you. You're detestable. He would just as soon sleep with a viper as you. Tessa's father is Armstrong Seymore. She is the spitting image of Gracie, Miles' daughter. Tessa has her father's sapphire eyes. Armstrong's eyes. Armstrong told me about his affair with you. Once he saw Tessa, he was as certain as Miles was that she is his daughter. Told me he would have claimed her if he'd known about her. Would have never allowed his daughter to be brought up by a witch-woman such as you."

"That doesn't mean anything. Lots of children don't look like either parent. The resemblance is a coincidence. Your father came to me. Wanted me desperately. I agreed to sleep with him even though he was still married at the time. At first when I declined, Simon begged." Anice lifted her slender shoulders. "How could I refuse such a man. He was devilishly handsome. Told me all the right things to get me into his bed.

What say you? Have you lied to Tessa. Told her all the right things to get her into your big bed?"

Jason found himself shaking his head in frustration. He was furious with Anice. Needed to find Tessa. Take her from this horrible place. "All Kenworthys have dark hair combined with dark brown eyes. Some eyes have flecks of gold. Tessa hair is nearly white. She has Seymore eyes, not Kenworthy eyes. Any fool can see the resemblance. She looks nothing like a Kenworthy." His arguments would go nowhere. Jason understood that fact. He needed to search the house then leave with Tessa.

Anice waved her hand in the air, dismissing his words as if they meant nothing. "No…no…Tessa is definitely Simon's bastard daughter. He knew all about her. If he said different, he lied. Told me he didn't want the world to learn how he cheated on your mother. He was protecting his family by denying her. That's what he said. He supported her throughout the years. Sent money for gowns as well as tutors so she would receive the best education possible. I took the money, agreeing to keep the secret. So, you see," Anice straightened her skirt. "He cared in his own way."

Discussing this with the woman would get him nowhere. She would never bend. "Never mind." Jason wasn't going to wait for an invitation to find his wife. If he had to, he would search every room in the house. Setting off through the door, he headed up the stairs.

Anice reached out to stop him. She grabbed his arm. Furious, Jason shook her off with a fierce thrust of his arm that sent her pummeling into the door. He didn't care if he hurt her. He would do worse if she continued this act much longer. If he gave into his first thoughts, he would wring her skinny neck.

"There is nothing you can do to stop me."

Jason heard Anice tell the butler he needn't go after him. He slammed into each room he encountered. The pounding of the doors shook the house. The girls, at one time, had individual rooms. Similarities to their rooms at the Glasgow townhouse told him whose room was whose. By what he saw, they were given everything a young girl could wish for, except love.

Stepping into Tessa's room, he stopped. Caught his breath. She wasn't there. What had he expected when he crashed his way up the stairs slamming doors in his wake. Tessa wouldn't hide from him. She might have heard the commotion. If she believed her mother, she might go somewhere else. Jason continued his search. Room after room was surveyed. He strode to the third floor. Found nothing.

Tessa wasn't here.

His quick descent seemed to catch Anice by surprise. With no hesitation, he pushed her against the wall in her private quarters. His hand wrapped around her throat.

"Where is she?" he growled. "I've lost what little patience I had. I could strangle you without a blink."

Her wide eyes surprised him. The flush of her cheeks turning ashen was a wonder. She was startled. Appeared to believe him. "I don't know. Haven't seen her since we spoke at the celebration. Maybe you should try keeping better track of your wife."

Suspecting she was telling him the truth, he let her go. She gasped. Touched her throat. Coughed when she tried to bring air from her throat to her lungs. "You had no right!" Her voice roughed out.

"I've every right." The force of his words created another startled gasp from the woman. "You lied to her for your own means. Don't know what you planned. Though I have guesses. Mark my words, I will find her. The truth will come out along with all your lies."

"As you just saw for yourself, Tessa isn't here. I don't know where she is."

"If Tessa does come looking for your help, send for me. If you don't, you won't like the consequences." Jason didn't know what he would do. He would figure something out.

"Is that a threat?" she whispered still holding her throat with a hand.

"A promise."

Jason headed out. The door shut behind him with a significant explosion.

Where is she?

With no other place in his mind to search, he headed home. When he walked in the door, Keir met him.

"We weren't expecting you. The others arrived around noon. Is

Lady Tessa with you? Can I get you something to eat? Drink?" No one here knew what transpired today. Keir acted surprised but went about his business as if nothing was wrong.

"Need to see Jasper. Maggie too if she's available. I'll just help myself to a brandy in Jasper's office. Tell him where I am. Tell him this is an emergency."

Maggie must have some idea where Tessa would go. He didn't have one tangible clue. He already used up his one thought. Though he was more than relieved she didn't go to her mother seeking help. That would have resulted in disaster. If she had sought out Anice, by now, she would have found herself with Nelson Abernathy. The thought of Abernathy forcing himself on Tessa brought his stomach to a roll. He found the decanter of brandy. Filled his glass. Stared at the amber liquid.

Not too many ticks of the big clock in the hall passed before Jasper greeted him. "What is it? Didn't realize you were coming home today. Thought you and Tessa wanted some alone time for yourselves. By the way, where is your wife?"

"Tessa is gone. Vanished." As he spoke, Jason waved his hand in the air. The sinking feeling that she was lost to him mounted. "Don't have one notion as to her whereabouts."

"I'm not sure I understand."

Jason reached into a pocket then handed him the letter. "Read while I try to steady my nerves."

He stared at the expressions on his twin's face as the words were absorbed. When he looked up his face was a contrast of emotions. "You can't believe this nonsense."

"No, of course not. Every word is a lie. Problem is…Tessa believed the drivel."

After Jasper finished, he whistled through his teeth. Poured himself a brandy, consumed half in one long gulp. With a snort, he continued, "I assume you went to see Anice first. It's what I would have done."

Jason nodded, knowing he was out of clues. Only another sister would be able to see into Tessa's mind. "I need Maggie. She might know of some place Tessa could have sought refuge. A place only the sisters knew about. Hope she's not retired for the night."

"Maggie was exhausted from the trip. She's sound asleep. The baby cried most of the way. She is with child again."

Hell!

What was he going to do now? He couldn't ask his brother to get her up. That wasn't something he was willing to do.

"In the morning you can speak with her. I'm trying to understand your frustration combined with the fear that must eat at you. Can you think of anywhere Tessa would go? Anyone she might have known?"

Jason found himself pacing the floor. One way then another until he could bear the tense silence no longer. He stopped at the window looking over the gardens. Wished he could see her walking down the path. He saw nothing but silent, still shadows.

"Tessa and I do not share fathers," Jason said as if he thought he needed to reassure Jasper. He turned, "We both understand that is not the case. Father would never bed a viper such as Anice MacRae. Never!"

"I know. Tessa has the look of the Seymores not the Kenworthys. Anyone who has eyes would see the similarities. Don't quite understand how Anice could think to get away with this lie."

"Tell that to Tessa. She must have believed her mother. There is no other logical reason I can see for her to run from me. Tessa sold one of her rings to book passage on a coach to somewhere. The man selling tickets at the station couldn't tell me if it was to here or Edinburgh or even Inverness. What if I made a mistake?" His stomach was tied into knots. His hands shook with terror for his wife. "What if Tessa picked Edinburgh or another city?"

A mistake wasn't something he could afford.

Jasper held up a hand. "Wait! I do have one idea. Reminding you won't make you feel better. However, what I have to say will take us one more place. I'll go with you."

"What is it?" His hopes rose a fraction. "One place? If Anice contacts Abernathy, he might search there too."

"Yes, you're right about Abernathy…the homeless camp. He was there the night we found Maggie," Jasper said with a blunt tone to his voice. "Yes…" he continued, "That's where we found Maggie. I know the girls knew what she did. Though Maggie didn't tell them beforehand. Afraid Abernathy would or Anice would be able to get the truth from them if they knew her destination."

"Let's go!" Jason felt his heart speed. Hoped for the positive. He was out the door before he heard his brother hold him up.

"Give me a moment to leave a note for Maggie in case she wakes. In this instance a minute won't matter."

God, he didn't want to wait a moment. If Abernathy found her, a minute would make a hell of a lot of difference. Shocked, he never thought about the homeless camp. He should have visited there first. Tessa had to be there. She'd be cold tonight. Clancy told him she never returned to the house. She would not have taken anything with her. All she had were the clothes on her back. That wasn't the way to run away. She should have taken more time. Should have packed something. Taken more money. Should have gone to Edinburgh.

If she'd done any of the above, he would have caught up with her before she bought the ticket. Tessa would have known she would have to act fast.

Pacing the foyer, it seemed as if Jasper took forever to write the note. At least it wasn't winter. That's when Maggie chose to flee her home in the middle of the night with no coat to wear. No money to her name. Were all the MacRae girls this impulsive?

"I'm ready. Brought one of Mag's shawls for Tessa when we find her. We will find her." Jasper ghosted him from the house to the carriage which waited for them. While Jasper was writing his note, he sent Keir to order the carriage brought around. They were ready. In what condition would he find his wife?

"Easy, little brother," Jasper warned. "We both understand Tessa might not be there. If she isn't, we will talk to everyone we can find until we have another clue as to her whereabouts. There will be indications. Someone will give us advice. It's just a matter of time until you have her in your arms again."

"I won't feel calm until I'm holding my wife. Not until we come to an agreement that the words Anice wrote were cruel as well as lies. Words meant to harm not help."

Jason watched the scenery pass by while they rode through the streets to the homeless camp. Nothing more needed to be said between the two men.

"Told Keir to send another coach with baskets of food along with firewood. It's been months since we helped the homeless women. Should have done this sooner," Jasper told him as they approached.

"That's a good idea. Makes questioning those at the camp easier. With food in otherwise empty bellies, the people will be more responsive."

"Is he going to send blankets too? Even though it's summer, the nights can get downright cold," Jason said, his thoughts now centered on finding his wife. "Wouldn't want to be stranded here."

~ * ~

Tessa paid for a cab to the bakery. All her hopes were centered on finding help with this woman. Heart in her throat, she stepped onto the sidewalk. The cab left. She hissed out a breath of air. Shocked, she stared at the building. All the lights were out. The closed sign hung in the window of the door. *No…what else can go wrong?* There would be no shelter tonight, no food or the promise of a job on the morrow. She would need to be patient. The bakery would open early. Somone would be there before dawn to begin baking. She only needed to spend one night in the open.

What she'd been thinking eluded her. She believed this place would be open? Tessa didn't know the time. What she did know was that it was late. Of course, the place would be closed. A bakery opened early in the morning, closed early in the evening. Her stomach rumbled. She'd not eaten anything since this morning. Since before her life fell apart.

My father is Simon Kenworthy. Can't be Simon Kenworthy. It's not possible. Mother wouldn't lie about something like that.

How could it be possible. Well, she knew how. Now that she was married, she understood. Her hands settled on her stomach. Prayed she wasn't increasing. The thought sent nausea to her throat. She gulped in an attempt to control the rising sickness. Couldn't tamp the queasiness down.

She rushed to a spot at the side of the store. Tossed up nothing. Heaved until her throat was raw. There was nothing in her stomach to lose.

Yet her body continued to protest. When she was finished, she sat back on her legs. Wiped her hands across her face. Looked to the sky as if that would help. Nothing happened. A slow breeze rustled leaves in the tree above her. The moon was clear. The breeze chilled her flesh. Wished she'd not dismissed the cab. Even if she didn't, where would she go?

Despair filled her with uncertainty. Goose bumps prickled along her arms. To find some place where the chilled night breeze didn't sweep into her was her next destination. From here, she didn't know where the homeless camp was. The site where Maggie took refuge. She might have gone there. Didn't want to risk walking alone in the dark. The women who brought food always had body guards. She'd learned that piece of information from Maggie when she explained what happened to her the night of the Christmas Eve ball.

Tessa started walking. Hoped there might be a backdoor to the bakery where she could find a bit of shelter. Knew the woman who owned the establishment to be nice. Under the circumstances, she didn't think Daryl would mind if she used her backdoor as protection from the night's cold chill. The owner of the bakery brought food to the homeless. Had done so for years. If she found her at the backdoor, she wouldn't kick her out. Prayed for that. Still hoped for a job at this business. While she couldn't bake worth a damn, she could clean. Everyone could clean.

At the back door of the bakery, after testing the door, the lock held firm. Resigned, Tessa curled into a ball. She hoped tomorrow would be smoother. Wrapped her arms around herself as if that would keep warmth inside her. When she closed her eyes, she found herself assailed with the words on the letter.

Jason is my brother. Simon Kenworthy is my father. No!

She found herself shivering. Freezing. Tried to move as close to the door as she could. She hunched. Curled tighter. Wiggled against the wood. Nothing she did warmed her. When she finally fell asleep it was as if her body gave up. Her mind was immersed in dreams. Imaginings that would never come true for her. Jason was in front of her, teasing. They made love on the kitchen table. After that he brought her with exquisite slowness to climax while she straddled him. Her dreams faded then seemed to merge together. She cast about with no destination. Saw more vague pictures of Jason.

Again, he kissed her. Made love to her. The images made her smile. Hope filled her.

She couldn't have him. He was her brother. What they did together was a sin. Marriage to a brother was wrong. Everything was all wrong. She never knew.

The tenor of her visions changed. Lord Abernathy took the main stage. He laughed at her. Pointed in her direction. Told her she was his now, his little whore. She was put on this earth for his pleasure, nothing more. He wouldn't ever let her go. Too bad she wasn't a virgin any longer. He would never take anyone for a wife who wasn't pure, chaste as new fallen snow.

"Wake up!" Someone shook her. His voice was unforgiving. Angry.

Her head lolled back. She tried to open her eyes. So cold, she couldn't rouse herself. He slapped her across both cheeks. Shook her again. Pain ripped through her.

She'd hoped the voice belonged to Jason. Her husband wouldn't hit her. Tessa didn't recognize the sound. "Little whore, a slut that's what you are. Bitch! Gave yourself to your brother," he snarled, then the man shook her again. Her head banged against solid wood. "Time to wake up, whore! Now! Open those blue eyes of yours!"

Tessa pushed against the wall behind her, needing to free herself from the rough hands shaking her.

"Open your eyes! Damn you!" Again, the man shook her slapped her face. Hit her hard. One more time, her head hit against the wood behind her.

Visions filled her with terror. She did as he commanded. With wide open eyes she saw her nightmare. Lord Abernathy kneeled in front of her, hands on her shoulders. Fingers bit into her bare arms. His leering grin told her he was pleased to find her. Told her she would regret running from him. When long hard fingers closed around her wrist then yanked, Tessa knew this wasn't a dream.

"Oh!" She cried out startled by both the pain as well as the surprise of finding herself yanked from the porch. "No!" She wrenched back. Dug in her heals. Despite her meager effort to fight him, he pulled her to her feet.

"You're coming with me, now! You're mine bitch!" His eyes darkened, his lips thinned. "You've no choice in this little matter. Your mother gave you to me. I can do with you whatever I please. Need to see to your pain before anything else. You betrayed me. No one betrays me!"

"Leave me be!" She struggled. Fought. Clawed at his face. Left a line of blood on one cheek.

He cursed. Grabbed her hands to hold behind her back. Her breasts pressed against him. "Stop fighting. You won't win. You're only going to hurt yourself," he growled in a low, cruel voice.

She kicked hard at his chin. He lost his hold on her. She lurched forward in an attempt to run past him. Needed to find her way to the front of the bakery. Her feet whirled with the effort. She would run as far as she could. Even with the first few steps, she understood she would never get very far. He was too big. Too fast. He would catch her. His curses shadowed her flight. Cold sweat slithered between her breasts.

Then what? She should have never left the country. Should have sat down. Talked this out with Jason. He might have had some idea what to do. How to protect her. Her impulsiveness cost her this encounter. Might cost her even more if Lord Abernathy had his way with her. Jason would never want her back.

Nelson grabbed her skirt as she tried to rush past him. Yanked hard. "No, you don't! Not going to get away from me this time. You are mine, bought as well as paid for."

She stumbled backward. Landed awkward. Turned. Tried to crawl on her hands and knees. Tiny rocks bit into her hands. In front of her, he blocked her way. She looked up into cold eyes. "No!" God, what was happening to her. She wanted to die before she went with this man. "No, I'm married! Leave me alone! You can't do this! Jason will come for me." She spoke the words even though she knew Jason wouldn't care. Not now. Not after she ran from him. Not after he learned she was his sister.

"Not for long. A woman can't be married to her brother. You're mine, slut. Anice gave you to me just last night. Told me I had *carte blanche* with your perfect little woman's body. Do you understand what that means? If you don't, I'll be pleased to show you. Been waiting for just this opportunity for a long time. Can do anything I wish with you. There's no one to stop me now." He grabbed her wrist. Pulled her against him. Her breasts pushed on his chest.

Carte blanch?

Tessa would rather die than let this man touch her as Jason touched her. "Mother can't do that! Give me to anyone. I'm not her property." Tessa tried with fierce determination to yank her arm free. His hand tightened on her wrist. Held tight.

Abernathy set his head back, hooted his laughter. "You're wrong." Bent his shoulder. When his body hit her waist, she gasped for air. Found herself slung over one shoulder. Tessa pummeled his back with her fists.

"Put me down!" His arms around the back of her knees kept her from kicking. He didn't seem to feel her fists on his back.

"What is going on here?" A voice from behind them had Abernathy swirling so fast her head spun with the motion. "What are you doing? Put the lady down. It's obvious she doesn't want to go with you. Come inside have a cup of tea, a pastry. We can talk. Resolve this argument." The woman started toward them, a towel in her hands.

"Ah…just collecting my wife. No need to bother anyone. She…well…we had a disagreement. You see." He tossed her into the waiting coach. Closed the door. "She is a handful at times," he said with smooth confidence. "She enjoys playing games with me. You see, she runs. I find her then bring her home. We make love until the *wee* hours of the morning. When she gets bored again, the process is repeated. I'm sorry if we disturbed you. No need for a cup of tea or food. Have plenty at home." Nelson leaned against the carriage door, his arms crossed in front of him, blocking her possible escape.

Tessa was peering out the window of the coach. Banged on the window, hoping to discredit Abernathy's words. Mouthed words the lady didn't see.

"You…" The woman looked at Tessa's face. Stepped forward as if she understood Tessa didn't wish to be where she was.

"I wouldn't do that if I were you," Abernathy's voice filled with ice stopped the lady from moving farther. "This is not your business. The lady is my wife. She will come home with me. She will do what I ask when I ask it of her. The lady vowed to obey."

"Why?" she challenged. "Just thought to get a confirmation from…your wife. If she doesn't wish to be with you, I could…"

Under the circumstances, there wasn't anything the woman could do to change what was happening now. Tessa cursed herself for sleeping past dawn. She'd been so tired. Abernathy found her. How? How would he think to try the bakery?

"She wants to be with me. Loves me with all her precious little heart. Sometimes, my woman has a strange way of showing that adoration. We are going home." He left the lady gaping when he jumped into the coach.

"No…" Tessa cried out, hoping her denial would reach out to the woman. Hoping the lady could do something to help her. With a sinking heart she realized, just as Abernathy said, there was nothing the woman could do to change her plight.

The carriage swayed when he sat down beside her then pulled her close. His hand covered her mouth before she could say anything more. She tried to shake off his fingers. Strained to bite down. He was too strong.

"You little bitch," he whispered close to her. "You've cost me a wealth of time. Not going to allow you to have your way. You now are in my control. Once I've had you beneath me, your husband will no longer want you. Don't expect an unexpected rescue. That won't happen."

A hot breath of air brushed across her cheek. Disliking the scent, she tried to turn from him. His fingers bit into her face while he held her still. When she tried again to bite his hand, he held the fingers far enough away to stop her.

The coach lurched forward before settling into a smoother ride. After Abernathy let go of her, she pitched herself toward the door. Cold fingers clasped onto the handle. Had to get out before the coach picked up speed. Before she would hurt herself if she threw herself from the moving vehicle. Before she could open the door, he caught her hair.

"No!"

"Yes, you, my dear little whore are all mine."

Abernathy yanked her back against him. Her hands flew to her scalp trying to keep him from hurting her further. She tumbled on top of him. “I’m not yours. You’ve no right to kidnap me. Take me back.”

“Thought you were the quiet submissive sister. Glad to find out you’ve got fight in you. Love to tussle with a woman in my bed. Gives new meaning to the sexual games we will play together. You know you can never win any round with me unless I allow the win.” His fingers wound tighter into her hair. Turned her head so she couldn’t look away.

The scent of him made her gag. The stink of brandy combined with a smoky odor did not sit well with her stomach.

“You’re going to play it this way? Well, now I understand I’ll have to lock you in your room. Don’t want you to get away from me until I’m bored with you. Believe that might take years. Anice advised me to do that until I tamed you. She gave me a few more pointers on how to deal with you. Said withholding food always made you submissive. I can do that with ease.” His leering smile sent a shiver of revulsion down her spine.

To no avail, she tried to look away from him.

Tightening his hold, he forced her to face him. She closed her eyes. His fingers wound fiercely into her hair. She cried out when he jerked her so hard her head was sent flying backward. “Open your eyes, whore!” He jerked again. “Look at me. Don’t ever look away if you know what’s good for you.”

Tears filled her eyes, slipped down her cheeks. She looked at him with defiance. He could hurt her. Might try to bend her to his will. He wasn’t going to succeed in making her a submissive creature. She would outlast anything he tried.

“You refused marriage to me. That fact turns out to be a mistake. Decided to give yourself to your brother instead of me. I would have worshiped you. Put you on a pedestal. Revered the very ground you walk on. Now, you’ve been defiled. You are dirty. No longer clean. Imperfect. Now, you’re going to be my beautiful little harlot, my slut, my whore. I can dress you up anyway that pleases me or dress you not at all.” His sneer sent a shudder through her. “Thought at one time to make you my beloved mistress. After this show of defiance that will never happen. When I’m finished with your sweet, perfect body, Jason Kenworthy won’t want you back, not even as a beloved sister. He won’t even wish to protect you.”

At his loathsome words, she shuddered. There was nothing for her to say. She wouldn't make this easy for him. Fight him every step of the way was the only way she could move on. Jason would come for her. No, Jason was applying for a divorce. From that direction she would have no help. Now she had only herself to rely on. Jasper would come for her because Maggie would insist he do so. How would they learn that Nelson Abernathy kidnaped her? The man was a braggart. Given enough time the information would slip from his lips. By then it would be too late to save her from eminent rape. He meant to force her.

Her sisters would search for her. They would care about her. Yes, Jasper might look. Though he would feel for his twin. He might believe whatever happened to her she deserved for deceiving Jason. She didn't misinform anyone. She'd never known the truth. Maggie would explain all that to him.

The clatter of the wheels on the cobblestones, the pounding of the horse's hooves all filled her head. She no longer wanted to think. Wished she could block out what was happening.

His fingers eased from her hair. "Are you going to behave yourself?"

The wild look in her eyes must have told him her real feelings. She didn't have to say anything to the man.

"I've a home for you," Abernathy was telling her as he sat back. Kept her hand within his. Stroked her wrist then higher. "It's rather nice. Nicer than you deserve the way you've acted this morning. As soon as you adjust to your new position, it will be easier for you. Don't wish to lock you in the bedroom forever. Until I can rely on your loyalty to me, that's what I'll do. I've a trusted man who will be there to guard you night and day. Bring you food along with something to drink when it's meal time."

He ran his knuckles down her cheek. The soft caress made her shudder with revulsion. She loathed this man. He wanted her. Moisture filled her eyes. Tears slipped down her cheeks. He caught the moisture on the tip of his finger, brought it to his mouth. Tasted then leered.

"I do enjoy a woman's tears. Salty. Does the rest of you taste this good? Hmm…I will discover that truth in time. Spread your legs. Savor you between your white thighs. Not tonight. Tonight, I've somewhere else to be. To my misfortune, I will need to leave you alone. What a pity. I always enjoy a bit of a fight from my women coupled with her fear. I can smell your fear. Love the aroma. Female struggles do intensify my pleasure. Though…" He ran his finger down then up her arm. "I would wager tomorrow you will be just as fierce a little warrior as you are at this moment. We will see. Can you wait until tomorrow to feel me surge inside you? Ah…you will have to wait. There is no other scenario here."

Her shudder of revulsion didn't go unnoticed by Abernathy. His crack of laughter was vile. Spoke to the character of the man. Even if doing so killed her, she would find a way out of wherever he was taking her. Tomorrow, she would either be dead or somewhere safe.

Through the window Tessa saw that he circled around to the back of the house. For a moment he studied her. Lifted his shoulders before sending her a wicked grin, "Don't wish for the neighbors to see. Gossip will not serve my purpose. You going to come willingly? Do I need to put you over my shoulder? I'll do whatever is necessary."

Her answer was to put her chin into the air. She didn't intend to say anything to this disgusting, despicable man.

"I see. Have it your way this time." Abernathy looked as if he was enjoying himself.

As if she was a sack of grain, he yanked her from the coach then tossed her over his shoulder. His hand came down so hard on her bottom, more tears formed. He squeezed where his hand lay. Pain leapt through her. He laughed when she cried out from his next assault with the flat of his hand. If she continued to defy the man, he would beat her.

Tessa decided to save her struggles for when he left. Needed energy in order to escape. Escape she would. She had all night to figure out how to leave this place. If he put her on the third-floor, bolting would be more difficult. She would find a way. Go out the window. Anything to be rid of him.

On the second floor, he opened the door. Bending over, he set her on her feet. Still holding on to her, he waved his hand around the room. "This little piece of paradise has all you need. I've left a bottle of wine for you. Had your guard bring a tray of fruit, cheese, bread, meats for your consumption. There is a negligee on the bed. If you get tired of the clothing you are wearing, put it on. More clothing will arrive tomorrow. Thought to have everything ready by five this afternoon. To my misfortune there were a few delays. I will see to them."

She pressed her hands against his chest trying to distance herself from the lecherous gaze that roamed her body, lingered on her breasts. His eyes were so cold. She shuddered at the thoughts flashing through her head.

"I must have a sample of what waits for me tomorrow. A little piece of you will warm my heart when I can't be with you." His hands on her shoulders, Abernathy pulled her to him. His mouth came down hard on hers. Fierce. Vicious. Determined. Within his embrace she struggled. Fought to remove herself from his mouth. She kept her lips shut tight. Didn't allow him the entrance he sought. With his teeth, he pulled with malicious intent on her lower lip. She understood what he wanted. Meant to keep herself closed to him as long as possible. His tongue passed by her teeth forcing them to part despite her efforts.

Tessa bit down hard.

The yell of pain brought relief to her as he jerked from her. Eyes flashing anger, he stared at her for a beat of her heart. His violent slap on her cheek sent her head reeling. Without his hands to hold her up she stumbled. Fell to the floor.

"Don't ever do that again!" his words harsh with the pain she caused. "You will feel far more than a mere slap to your face if you ever do anything to hurt me. That's a promise. Treat me right, I'll be good to you. Act like the hoyden you are now, I will make your life a living hell." His growl brought her chin in the air. She wasn't going to bow down to his dictates. Noticed her mistake by the glint in his eyes.

She backed away. He pulled her against him. "Let's try that one more time. Open for me, little bitch. Open then give me your tongue. Let me play with that sweet tender part of you. You will taste my blood just as I do. Savor the thought. The remembrance will be something you can think about until tomorrow. Don't forget. If you hurt me, I'll be certain to cause excruciating pain to you. I have the means as well as the knowledge to do so."

He didn't wait for a reply that wasn't going to come. His lips spread across hers. He probed with his tongue. Found his way inside her unwilling lips. She held her body still. Frozen against the fevered assault. Didn't intend to give him anything but the frigid ice in her veins. With the merciless slap, she learned a lesson. His words of reprisal told her more. The only way to fight this man was to revile him with no response.

When she didn't struggle or respond in any other way, he shoved her so hard she staggered, landing on the floor again. She braced herself. Scrambled to her feet in hopes of deterring another round of punishments.

"Whore! I'll teach you manners if it's the last thing I do. You will respond to me. You might have ice in your veins but you will give me all that I want. If you deny me, I will torture what I need out of you. Give me your sweet body without a fight. Without holding anything back. Your coldness will never keep me from tasting you, filling you, giving you my seed. Savoring every part of what belongs to me."

The door banged shut. His footsteps echoed down the hall. She was about to rush to the door when a key turned in the lock. Her breath caught. A broken sound of despair followed.

Tessa put her face in her hands then sobbed for all she lost, all she might need to endure. Her life would be a living hell if she didn't find a way out of this dilemma.

Maggie, please look for me. Jasper please...don't forget in all ways that matter, I'm still Maggie's little sister.

After Lord Abernathy lost Maggie, it had been his intent all along to bring her to heel. If she didn't act with haste, he would rape her. By his admission, she had until tomorrow at the latest. If he grew bored with whatever commitment he had tonight, he could return. She didn't trust his word.

Several minutes passed while she gulped air. Once she felt as if she possessed a small amount of control, she stood. Even though her legs wobbled, she was able to take stock of the room. She didn't move. Listened to the sounds from inside the house. Heard a person rattling around downstairs. Seemed to her there was only one man, her guard. Heard no chatter. The viscount must have left the house right after he left her.

Even understanding the bedroom door would not be an acceptable means of escape she tested the lock. When nothing happened, she continued her perusal of the room. Found the French doors leading to a patio.

Her heart skipped a beat. She and her sisters spent good times escaping their house through the balcony from Maggie's room. Maggie was the only one who had a verandah. There was a sturdy trellis attached to the balcony. It was easy to climb down.

She weighed more now. Wondered if a trellis would hold her weight. First, there would need to be one. Outside, she discovered there was nothing of that sort. Nothing to make her descent easy. Thought for certain, she could hang on to one of the posts that kept the porch attached to the house.

Counting on Nelson not returning anytime soon, Tessa returned inside. Found the food Nelson left for her. Poured herself a glass of wine then ate. What she couldn't eat, she wrapped in a napkin before placing the uneaten food in the pocket of her dress. She did feel better now with a full belly. She still had a little money.

Beyond taking more chances, she couldn't afford to waste food. Didn't know how to get back to the bakery. Remembered the sign, 'Daryl's Bakery.' Not original but easy to recall. Someone must know where the place was. Would be able to give her directions. She could walk.

If she was gone tomorrow when he came for her, would that be the first place he would look? Most likely. Nonetheless, she had nowhere else to go. If she found her way to the Kenworthy townhouse, would Jasper give her shelter. She needed a roof over her head. Needed to find someone she could trust not to send her back to Abernathy.

Jason would never hurt her even though they were related too closely to be married.

This was the time.

Now or never.

Standing at the edge, her hands on the railing, she felt dizzy. Her head swam. The ground seemed too far away. While she had reservations, she reminded herself what awaited her if she didn't take the leap. Well, she wasn't going to leap over the edge. What she was going to do was shimmy down the pole until her feet touched the ground.

If she was still ten, she wouldn't think twice about the mini-adventure. Years had passed since she and her sisters climbed trees then wobbled down them or fell out. None of them were ever hurt. That thought didn't help her now. During her younger days, there was no fear. When she peered over the edge, the ground threatened to rise up to meet her.

"Now or never," she muttered to herself. "Now or never." The air she inhaled stuck in her throat. Burned through her.

Tying her skirts so they wouldn't hinder her legs, she hoisted one leg over the edge of the railing then the other. Her muscles knotted. She groaned. Looked down. Saw the earth whirling. She closed her eyes. Bit her lip as if that would give her the needed courage.

After a few giant gulps of oxygen, she lowered herself until she could wrap her legs around the post. Felt the cool wood against her thighs. Pressed her face against the railing. With slow movements, she eased herself toward the ground. Second by second, she made her way, searched for her goal, the earth against her feet.

"What have we here?"

The words startled her so much she jerked. Felt sudden pain that she hadn't reached the ground before she was discovered. The voice sounded familiar. Couldn't place it. Knew the man wasn't Lord Abernathy.

No!

"I've got you!" The words were hard. Furious. He didn't have any reason to be angry. She did. "Don't be afraid. I caught you before you could hurt yourself. Will have to tell the boss that you put yourself in danger. He won't like that. He will decide to punish you. Going to settle you on the third floor until he can figure out a way to keep you in the bedchamber where he wants you. Doesn't like walking to the third floor every time he wants a little poke or two. Imagine I'll be asked to install another lock on the patio doors. If that's the case the third floor won't be necessary."

He's got me. Who's got me. It wasn't Lord Abernathy's voice that came from below. Good, God, the man had his hands on her bottom. Her waist. He must be the guard. Hope sunk to the pit of her stomach. She was going to be locked in again. This time with no means to escape.

~ * ~

Nelson's grin warmed Anice's heart. She knew by the way his lip turned up in a half smile, half sneer, he found her daughter. She'd sent word to him as soon as Jason left her home the evening before. Told him he needed to make haste if he were to find the little runaway before her husband found her. Gave him a few ideas as to where to look. Hoped her input would help.

"Spent all night searching for Tessa. The energy expended was worth the effort. The girl is just as appealing now…no she is more fascinating. Now she has fight in her. Won't be an easy conquest. Didn't wish for easy. Tessa is perfect in every way. A woman who fights back is more exciting. Makes my sex swell with anticipation." Nelson poured himself a glass of brandy before making himself comfortable. Sipped. Swallowed. His eyes focused on her. She nodded for him to continue.

"Where did you find her? Tell me all about it. Everything. Don't leave one detail out." Anice found she was sitting on the edge of her chair she was so eager to hear about the hunt then the capture. She needed to calm herself. Even to a friend one should never appear too eager. Never show a weakness.

Nelson did a slow drag of assessment looking her over as if he was savoring the next words. Clearing his throat, he began. "The back door of Daryl's Bakery. Just as you said, Tessa would try friendly faces. Daryl, we both know, is the lady who feeds the homeless. Maggie or Jason would have mentioned the fact to Tessa. They did find Maggie at the homeless camp."

"Tell me what happened. What did my daughter do? I'm certain she didn't comply with ease to your wishes. Tessa has changed over the last year. I find I like her better the way she was before. She was much easier to manage. Imagine you have the opposite feelings toward Tessa."

"No, she didn't comply. Yes, I enjoy the fight in her. Will enjoy the struggles more when sex is involved. Might need to restrain her. Tie her hands so she won't do me damage when I'm having my way with her." He paused long enough to adjust his pants which looked to Anice as if they were getting tight. "Tessa was asleep when I saw her all curled up by the back door of the bakery. She was half-frozen with the chill of the early morning air. At first, she didn't know it was me shaking her. I enjoyed that combined with the terror in her eyes when she realized who was in front of her. Not her milksop of a husband. She knew she was well and truly caught. Understood there would be no escaping. Though the stupid girl tried to get away."

"Cold night. Yes, she would have been cold, hungry too. Whenever I needed the girl's compliance, I withheld food. You would do well to remember that little piece of information." Anice decided she would visit in a few days. Give Nelson time to teach Tessa a few lessons in comportment. She would relish seeing the change. Catalogue the event as another victory for her.

"She fought just as you said she would. I do enjoy a good scuffle with a woman. When a woman fights me…well…" Nelson's grin would make any woman weep with fear. "I obtain more enjoyment from the act than simple submission. The battle of a woman's will against a male's is one that brings joy to my heart."

"Thought you did. What else. I know there must be more. Your lip is swollen. Hope you paid her back for biting you. Was that the beginning of the lessons?" Ah, Tessa had been a thorn in her side from the beginning. When she was a baby, she should have given her to Armstrong. If she had, she would not have this fun now. No, this way was for the best. Given enough time with Nelson, her Tessa would give her no regrets.

With a crack of laughter, Nelson continued. "Yes, she bit me. I slapped her hard. Tessa will be bruised for a while. I'll take pleasure watching the colors on her cheek change." He ran his thumb over his swollen lip, "After that she was a good little girl. She will pay more for the bite she gave me. Haven't begun to punish her for the transgression. When I found her, I had to get her out of there fast." He paused a moment in thought. "No, that's not quite right. Tessa played the cold bitch. She let me inside her mouth. There was no feeling exhibited. She played the cold little harlot. Can't allow that to continue. Told her I wouldn't be back until tomorrow. She believes she has a respite."

"You're going back this afternoon? Can't say as I blame you. You waited a long time to have her. In my estimation you've been a patient man," Anice said with a trilling laugh. "You will shock my youngest when you show up before planned. She's always believed in a man's word. After tonight that won't happen again. Her naïve being will float away as if the characteristic was dust in the wind."

"Yes, I have waited so long for her. Don't intend to delay another day. Do want to see her expression when I unlock the door. The first thing I'm going to do is rid her of that horrid gown she was wearing when I caught up to her. The second thing I'll do is…" Nelson stroked his jaw. "Not at all certain of the second. Imagine what happens next is how she responds to being naked in front of me. The girl will try to cover herself. They always do. Not that it matters."

"She will be…shocked." Anice paused, taking a sip of her brandy, letting the warmth slide down her throat. "Wish I could be there to see you take her. Give to her what she deserves. You understand Jason didn't believe his father was also hers. If he finds her before you can cover her, with or without force, he will convince her that she is Armstrong's girl. You must take her before Jason finds her. If you do, the man will never want her back. The divorce will go through. He will wash his hands of her. She will be yours until you no longer want her."

"Why not come watch? I've a peep hole that looks into the room. Have always enjoyed examining my mistresses when they don't know anyone is looking. Tells a man a lot about the woman. You can come with me tonight. The observation room is set up for two to three people. I'll have a bottle of wine along with some tasty pastries brought there for your viewing pleasure. I might watch with you before I go to see her. I'd like to see how she is taking her confinement."

Anice clapped her hands together delighted by the promise of the evening. She couldn't help the giggle of delight that left her mouth. "Witness my final triumph over the youngest MacRae bastard. While Maggie is out of reach for the time being, the other two are not. We can put our heads together. Make some plans for Nellie and Fannie. You do have friends, I assume."

"Yes, friends who think the same as I do. There is a pimp I know, Craig Halsey. Believe he would enjoy having one or both girls in his stable. Tonight, you will witness my triumph. I've coveted Tessa for more than a year. It's about time my patience pays off. *Carte blanch* while you are watching. How could anything get any better? I find I'm eager to explore everything about Tessa. How long will it take you to get ready?"

"Not one more second."

~ * ~

"If you try to fight me, I've got permission to use force to keep you in line." Her guard set her on the ground. Took her wrist in his hand then started toward the house. "Don't dally. Need to get you out of sight. In this neighborhood there is always a risk of some good-doer thinking he can rescue a little slut."

He was a big man, tall as well as broad shoulders.

Lacie Stewart the Duchess of Southcliff, studied the situation. The man's hair was a light blond. She couldn't see his eyes, but his jaw was sharp. There was something wrong with this scenario.

The girl dug in her heels. Tried to dislodge the man's hand from her wrist. Pushed on his confining fingers. "No! I'm not going back in that house with you! No!" she yelled as if she hoped someone would hear.

She bent over. Bit the man on his hand. He yelped. "You little bitch!" He slapped her hard. Her head jerked back. "You're just as Nelson told me you'd be. Never expected you to climb down from the porch. Nelson did. Told me to be ready for anything. I did what he said. Caught a pigeon before she could fly. You're not leaving now or ever. Believe he'll want you for quite some time before he grows bored. You're quite the pretty little thing, a fighter too. He relishes a woman with fight in her bones."

She managed to free herself from his grip. The girl turned to run. The man caught her by the hair then dragged her against him. He tucked her beneath his arm before starting for the door. "No, you don't. Not going to be the one to tell the boss I lost you. While you're not going to be where he put you, you will be in a room you can't escape from."

"Don't hurt her," Lacie called out with the intention of stopping the man. "I'll see you thrown in jail if you do." She shook her fist at him. "Put her down. She doesn't look as if she is willing to do what you're requesting."

"If I do your bidding, the boss will have my head. Not putting this little lady down until she's locked in a third-floor bedroom."

"Too bad," Lacie looked to her husband. Wasn't certain what to call the expression on Leslie's handsome face. At this given time, he seemed unwilling to let her take care of the situation. Didn't appear to wish to step into the fray. That was unusual. He must not sense danger to this lady or he'd take over. Since he wasn't helping out, Lacie cleared her throat. "You're going to go about this my way. Put the girl down. Set her on her feet. Let her go. I'll call the authorities!"

"Can't do that, ma'am."

"Please!" the girl yelled. "I don't want to be here. Lord Abernathy kidnapped me! Abducted me right off the backdoor porch at Daryl's Bakery! I went there for help!"

Nothing the girl yelled came as surprise. Nelson Abernathy was not a good person. He was known to take women with brutality. Lacie imagined the bruise on her face spoke to the truth of that assumption. "Did you give the girl the bruises?"

"No."

When Lacie stepped forward, her husband, set his hand on her arm. "That's far enough, m'dear," he growled from deep in the back of his throat. "Guess I need to put in a few thoughts myself. This man won't back down with a woman's soft voice urging him to go against his wishes. It's obvious he fears his boss' retaliation more than your commands."

"Do you want to return to that house?" The Duke of Southcliff asked the woman, stepping between his wife and the man. "If not," he turned, his attention directed to the man, "I suggest you let her go. Set her down now. She is not a sack of flour to be hauled around at your whim."

"Suggest all you want. The girl's going back to the house. I'm returning her to her plush environment. This one won't want for anything."

"Except freedom," Lacie said.

"He's going to rape me!" The *lass* yelled while the man swiveled to face the house. "Don't let him take me in there. I don't belong. I'm not Lord Abernathy's mistress. Don't want to be…" she blurted out in a rapid fire of words.

Leslie Stewart, Duke of Southcliff wasn't a man used to having his commands ignored. His voice was soft. Lacie understood that was a danger sign to all who knew her husband. The gentler his voice the more dangerous he was. "Put her down. Now." His words remained calm, deceptive.

"Or what?" The man challenged.

"This…" the quiet in his voice was more threat than anything. With one hard swing, Leslie hit the man on the jaw. He crumpled to his knees then his face hit dirt. On the ground, he lost hold of the woman he'd been carrying. The girl scrambled to her feet. Started running.

"Stop!" Leslie cried out.

Lacie hoped the one word would deter her from leaving.

The girl did turn, her eyes wild. Her white-blond hair tumbled around her shoulders in disarray. Frantic with her fear, she was looking for a place to go, her breasts heaving for air.

She understood when Leslie used that tone a person would be wise to steer clear of his path. She wasn't surprised by what she saw. Lacie sucked in a gulp of air as she watched the lady stumble then stop for a moment. Imagined if the woman wanted to leave, she could. Nonetheless, Lacie held the distinct impression this particular lady needed help. A great deal of help. With her encouragement Leslie would bring her back to the fold.

Lacie agreed with the woman. Leslie pushed the guard with his foot. He was out cold. When the girl tried to run a second time, the duke caught her by the arm. Whirled her around to face him with answers to whatever questions he might have.

"Not so fast. Think we have a few things to talk about before you run off to find yourself in more trouble than you know what to do with. Seems that if Lord Abernathy found you once, he can find you a second time. Whether you wish to admit to the fact, you need me. If he has to chase after you, from the gossip mills, I would guess you'll be sporting more than these few bruises," Leslie told her while Lacie held her hands clasped tight beneath her chin. "Who are you?"

"Who are you?" The girl bristled. Her chin going up in defiance.

"Leslie Stewart, Duke of Southcliff," he turned to the woman, "My duchess, Lacie." He paused still holding her by the arm. "Your turn."

Leslie was grinning, showing a wealth of even white teeth. He was a handsome man. Older. Still in good shape for a man of his age. His hair was lighter than when she first fell in love with him with a few strands of white around the edges giving him a different appeal. Lacie would term the look regal. Leslie would snort then disavow the notion. She would always love this man with all her heart. Now they had to figure out how to help the girl who didn't appear to want their help. The woman was terrified. Leslie was using his grin to charm this woman. The woman needed to trust in her husband. From what she'd been through, trusting a man might be hard to come by.

Her chin still in the air, she spoke, though her words were soft. "Tessa. My name is Tessa. That's all you need to know. I can't go with you. I don't know…never heard of you. Don't dare trust."

"What were you doing climbing from the window?" Leslie asked. He must hope for more information, a clue. He needed to find someone who might care about the young lady.

"Lord Abernathy locked the bedroom door. It was the only way out of the house. Wasn't going to stay until the Lord returned. He meant to force me. I'm not…" she gulped air. "Not a whore."

"No, I don't suppose you are. Don't have the look of one," Leslie said appraising her as he spoke.

"Come let's get you away from Nelson's home. If you're climbing out the window then down the post, it means you aren't here by choice," Lacie said with quiet conviction. "With us, you've nothing to worry about. We have nothing to gain by befriending you." As if guessing her thoughts. "Nothing to lose either. Neither of us will hurt you."

The duchess held out her hand. Tessa accepted the proffered invitation. Together they walked down the tree lined street. Three houses down, they turned.

"This is our home," the duke told her. "You'll be safe here forever how long you wish to stay. However, you will need to help us if we're going to help you. Is there anyone we can send word to that you are here? A mother? A father? You aren't very old. Do you have a husband? We could contact—"

Tessa blurted before Leslie could finish. “All I want is a job. If you can give that to me, that’s all that is necessary. Otherwise, I have no one. Will work to earn my way.”

Chapter Ten

Jason sat in his office, a glass of brandy dangling in his hands. The big clock in the hall chimed twice. He and Jasper had been to the homeless camp. They searched through all the people there, talked to anyone who was still awake. Handed out food along with blankets. Asked questions no one had answers to.

Discovered nothing.

Had no clues as to where Tessa could be. The night was cold. She wore no coat. Had no food. His stomach rolled with terror for her. All this because of a letter filled with lies from her mother. The woman had no conscious or soul. The lady was a despicable human being.

"We'll find her," Jasper said as he sat down in a chair facing the fire. He let his head fall back. Rested on the soft cushion behind him. "I know we will. One of us will think of something or someplace she might feel safe."

"Maggie?" She was the only one who could help. To be able to speak with her they needed to wait until morning. She was with child. Was drained from the drive into the city. Couldn't risk the baby. Jason was too pumped up with energy to succumb to exhaustion. He was both restless as well as impatient. Needed answers that he couldn't begin to guess at. Without Tessa by his side, he wouldn't be able to sleep.

"Yes, or Fannie or Nellie, the girls share everything. One of them might have an idea or two as to where to look," Jasper meant to boost his sagging spirits. "I've gone over what I know about Maggie a million times. She told me she had no friends in the city. There was one girl she was close to but decided not to go there. Her home would have been the first place Anice would search. She wasn't stupid."

All that would give him hope he would be able to find her. He wanted to race around the city. Search in every nook, every horrible place he could find. Anything could happen to her on the streets. He threw the crystal at the stone fireplace. The glass shattered on impact. Brandy flew through the air. Drips of amber ran down the rocks. He fought the chaotic energy simmering. Fought his mind that held his fear intact.

"It's only a few hours until dawn. Tessa probably found a nice warm place to sleep through the night. She'll weather this storm. Maggie is an early riser. As soon as she is up for breakfast, we'll talk."

"We'll talk. Will that shed new light on her whereabouts." With each beat of his heart, Jason's fears grew. The sound in the hallway caught their attention.

"I heard…" Nellie stood in the doorway clutching her robe. "What?" She stared at the fireplace. Brought a deep breath of air into her lungs. "Something's wrong."

"Have a seat. I'll pour you a sherry. You and Fannie were out late. We didn't get a chance to speak with you about your sister." Jasper looked the personification of a calm man. Jasper was always composed when he was not. Imagined the unruffled state came from being the oldest, the heir.

But then…his wife wasn't missing.

"Maggie?" she asked, looking up the stairs to the rooms there, her lips thinning. For a few seconds she murmured something to herself. Jason didn't understand. "Nothing has happened to the baby? Has it?"

Jasper handed her the glass of sherry. "No, nothing has happened to the baby. Maggie is tired. She went to bed early. My wife needs her rest more now than before." So much said. So much left unsaid.

"Oh…" Nellie turned to Jason then back to the fireplace where brandy still dripped off the stones. Her face paled. She would understand that left the only sister Nellie couldn't account for. Tessa. "What? What has happened to Tessa?"

Nellie would think of Lord Abernathy. All thought Tessa safe from the man now that she was married. Jason pinched the bridge of his nose thinking about what could as well as what could not be told. For a few seconds, he closed his eyes. Didn't want to make this worse. Didn't wish to tell the sisters he lost Tessa. Had no choice. Nellie might know something. Might be able to provide a clue.

With a long breath of air, Jason spoke. "It's Tessa. She's missing.

Lost her yesterday. Don't know where to look for her. Don't even know if she is in Glasgow." He couldn't bring himself to say anything more. Couldn't tell Nellie what her mother did. It was a scene created from nightmares.

The girls should understand what Anice MacRae was capable of doing. Not tonight. Tonight, he couldn't bring himself to explain. Had trouble acknowledging a mother could be so horrible to her children. In time they would learn what a despicable person their mother was. Nellie along with Fannie would also need round the clock supervision. The girls would rebel when confronted with the hard facts. They were becoming used to their freedom.

"Missing? How can Tessa be missing? She is supposed to be with you. Why would she go anywhere without you?" She was clutching the glass in her trembling hands. The question was logical. She sipped the drink. "Where is Tessa? You…"

"If we knew where she was, Nellie, she wouldn't be missing, he wouldn't be tossing crystal glasses filled with brandy against the fireplace," Jasper replied with slow precision. His soft voice coupled with his easy manner would surprise anyone watching. This was why he was the heir. This was why he was meticulous in everything he did. Jasper didn't make mistakes. He would have never lost his wife.

It was just as Jason had said before. This was a nightmare of Anice's making. What was it that Anice wanted from her girls? Oxygen caught in his lungs. His reply was raspy as if he needed air. "Tessa is not with me. She misunderstood something we've been discussing. Made an assumption that was wrong. Left before I could explain. Do you have any thoughts about where she would go? Did she know anyone here in the city. We need to find her." Yes, they needed to find Tessa before Abernathy did. By now the man would know she was vulnerable as well as unprotected. She would be easy prey.

With a blunt voice, "We don't have friends. Didn't back then. Fannie and I have friends now. That won't help you discover our sister's whereabouts. Tessa doesn't know any of the people we do. For the last year, she has spent all of her time with you or brooding about you." Nellie plopped down on the sofa spilling a few drops of sherry on her hand. She licked the drops. Her long sigh seemed to tell all their emotions.

Nellie's words sounded like an accusation. Guilt inundated every pore. He was guilty. Damn guilty. He should have taken her with him to see Armstrong. He'd been afraid of bad news. He hit his forehead with the heel of his hand. *Damn!* A list of things he should have done muddled his brain. He tormented himself with all his bad judgements.

Jason felt swamped from fatigue. Tension radiated through his body, flooding him, breaking new territory with every tick of his heart. He was angry with himself. Furious for not seeing this as a possible outcome. Anice would do anything to hurt her girls. She wallowed in deceit. What did they ever do to her to cause such hatred?

Where?

Where could she be?

Jason began to pace again. He walked outside to stand on the porch. Inhaled a deep breath of cold air into his lungs. As he blew the air out, oxygen tightened in his throat. *Tessa.* The weather could be colder. Could be the end of December. At least this was summer. Tessa would never freeze to death. He needed to be with her. Hold her. Keep her warm. She would snuggle into him.

Jasper was beside him, his hand on his shoulder. Squeezed as if attempting to give encouragement. "She's a fighter. All the girls are. You must believe in her. She's not the meek girl all thought her to be when we were in Ireland. Go to bed. Get some rest. I'll wait up in case there is any news."

Jason turned on his brother. With curt words he explained his feelings, "If it was Maggie out there, would you go to bed? Could you rest? Sleep while your wife might be hurt?" Jason snarled at his brother. News? There would be no news forthcoming before dawn. Nothing. They wouldn't know anything more in the morning than they did now. All, it seemed, he could do now would be to pray that Tessa would exhibit a bit of common sense. Find shelter. Pray she would come here so she could be with her sisters. Under the circumstances, Jason understood he was the last person she would wish to set eyes on. She would feel embarrassed by what she thought to be truth that was lies.

"Point taken. What do you plan on doing?" Jasper let his hand drop to his side then roughed his hair.

"Worrying."

Jason couldn't do anything except try to keep the nervousness about his wife at bay. Her laughter, he would never get enough of the soft ripple of sound when something amused her. The way she walked, hips moving one way, her sweet breasts dancing in front of her the other direction. When she touched him, she lit a fire that went straight to his heart as well as... He couldn't resist her smile, the shimmer of her deep blue eyes. The way her brows drew together when she was thinking about something. The soft moans of pleasure she made when he was deep inside her heat.

"I'll stay up. Worry with you," Jasper offered with a slight lift to his shoulders. "Maggie snores when she's with child. Won't get much rest for the next months. Might as well keep you company."

"No, go to your wife. Try to sleep. Though I don't believe you when you say she snores. More than likely it's you who snores. When she wakes, the two of you can join me at the breakfast table. We will need food in our bellies to make it through tomorrow. Believe it's going to be another long day. If I think of anything, I'll leave a note."

He watched his brother walk up the stairs. Poured himself another brandy before he started for his office. Sipped the potent drink. His mind still a blank slate. His brother would tell him he tried too hard. He would tell himself he didn't try hard enough. His mind no longer seemed to work.

At the entrance to his office, Jason leaned against the doorframe. Between his hands he twirled the crystal. Smiled. Thought of making love to Tessa on top of his desk. He could clear it with one sweep of his arm. Needed to get her back to do that. Convincing her that his father was not hers shouldn't be too difficult. He had solid information now. Hard facts that couldn't be disputed. If he made his case in an orderly and logical manner, she would believe him.

The letter sat on top of the desk. After he sat down, he read it again. He needed to burn the damn thing. Kept the letter as a reminder of how foolish he'd been. Of how naïve and believing Tessa was. She should never trust her mother. Never. He crushed the tear-stained paper in his hand. Tossed it.

Through the remaining hours, Jason listened to the tick of the clock. Heard the breeze ruffle around the eaves coupled with a limb of an oak as it rubbed against the roof. Dozed. Dreamed of Tessa. Thought hard on where she might go to feel safe. Nellie said she had no friends. Even if there was someone, a friend, Anice would know about that person. Tessa would never be safe anywhere except with him.

Near dawn he heard her calling to him. Maybe that was all in his head. A dream. Needed to believe she wasn't hurt. He felt her chill almost as if he was lying next to her. He couldn't believe in dreams. Could only believe in facts.

His imagination worked overtime.

Keir was up, walking through the house, speaking with the servants. Jason asked for a bath. A hot bath combined with a change of clothing would make him feel better. He needed a shave. Needed his wife more. Tessa wouldn't have any of these comforts. His wife needed to swallow her stubborn pride, come home. If not to be with him, to be with her sisters.

Sinking into the steaming water guilt washed over him. Tessa wouldn't have a hot bath to help her feel better. She wouldn't have breakfast. He hoped his worst fears were not true. A shiver of apprehension washed through him. She might be someplace safe.

Hoped Abernathy hadn't found her. Understood Anice would have notified Abernathy that he was missing Tessa. Would have informed him his wife ran off. Jason was certain this had all been orchestrated to put the two of them together. If Abernathy found her first, it might be difficult to get her back. The man would never admit to having her. He could hide her away as long as he wanted. Jason hurried with his bath then dressed. When he looked at the clock the time was eight.

Jasper told him Maggie was an early riser. So was Tessa. The day looked better when he walked to the breakfast table. Maggie and Japer were eating. Jasper had the newspaper open. A pot of hot tea was on the sideboard along with an assortment of food. He poured himself a cup of tea then helped himself to a plate filled with more than he could eat. Hunger was not something he felt.

"Think of anything?" he asked Maggie, believing Jasper must have said something to her. "Anywhere your sister might seek refuge."

Maggie grimaced before she shook her head. "Nothing. Haven't a clue as to where she would look for help. The homeless camp was a good idea. Abernathy would have looked for her there too. Could he have gotten there before you? Found her? He would have taken her some place he could keep her with no one knowing. He has the means. Know he owns more than one home. He always has at least one mistress."

Those were his fears too. He put jam on his scone. With a shrug of indifference he didn't feel, he spoke. "Don't see how. Went to the camp as soon as I left Anice. If she informed Abernathy, it would have been after I left. Didn't see him there. Spent a couple of hours chatting with people. Was in every room of her house before I was satisfied Anice wasn't hiding Tessa."

"Let's talk this through," Maggie spoke softly, her expression sad. "Maybe we'll make sense of something."

Jason could see the worry lines on her face. This wasn't good for the baby growing inside her. God, he hoped Tessa conceived. Had to find her. Needed to protect her from Abernathy. He was failing to do so.

"Alright. I'm open to anything." If talking helps, then he would talk. He needed a clear head. That was something he didn't have. "Ask me whatever comes to mind. I'll see what I can remember."

Maggie tapped her nails on the teacup. Nervous energy seemed to occupy her. "You went to the camp last night. Searched for her. Did you find or see anything unusual? You recall I traded my dress for a rag so Abernathy wouldn't find me. Perhaps she was there all along. If she ran from you, she wouldn't want you to find her. Could have obtained help from any number of people."

Jason ran those words over in his head. He felt certain if Tessa was there, she would not have been able to hide from him. "Spent over an hour at the camp, searching. Closer to two." He bit into the scone. Chewed then swallowed waiting for the next bit of inspiration. Maggie was doing well. Pointed out things she did to hide. Praying enlightenment would come. "Who's counting? Maybe we should return. As you say, might have missed someone. We've no other leads. Nothing to go on."

"You spoke to everyone. Were the ladies from the bakery there giving out bread? They swing by most nights." Maggie asked as she watched both her husband along with him.

Jasper's face looked as blank as he felt. He had no memories of ladies handing out bread. "Ladies from the bakery?" Jason asked confused for the moment. There seemed to be a blank space in his muddled brain. Felt he should recall them.

"The ladies who bring day old bread to the homeless every night. Do you remember? They were there when the two of you found me." Maggie mentioned the women again. "They are there most every night. Have been doing the same for years and years. Everyone knows of them. Did you forget?" Maggie turned her attention to her husband. "How could you?"

"Never paid too much attention to the ladies. Was more interested in you. I know who they are. Yes, I do recall their mission of good." Jason looked to Jasper for an answer. Tried to remember the night they found Maggie. If they were an institution he should remember. His memory needed more of a nudge than what Maggie was giving him. "You know about these women?"

"Not very well. Know of them along with their efforts to help the poor people of Glasgow. As Maggie pointed out, they've been bringing food to the needy for years. Don't know if I would recognize any of them."

"Did Tessa know about these women?" Jason asked, feeling the first light of hope he'd felt in hours. "Would she have gone to the women for help?" His mind was full of unanswered questions.

"Yes, I told my sisters about them. Never talked a lot to the ladies. If you recall, you and Jasper found me first. Helped me. After we returned from Ireland, I was married. Do you think she might have gone to the bakery?" Maggie asked them. "Find her. I don't want to have to worry that Abernathy discovers her whereabouts before the two of you do."

"Would she *ken* where to find the bakery?" Jason asked as he waited for a few more answers.

"Anyone in Glasgow could tell her. Daryl is the sister to the Duchess of Southcliff. There is not a person in the city who doesn't know where Daryl's Bakery is located."

"Let's go!" Jason was on his feet headed to the door, Jasper behind him.

A half hour later, with accelerated hopes, they walked into the bakery. The little bell above the door announced their entrance. The hour was too late for the early morning breakfast crowd. One woman worked the counter. Jason could hear another singing from the back room. The scent of fresh baked bread stirred his senses. Even though he'd eaten, his stomach growled with anticipation. He wondered if Tessa had anything to eat.

"Can I help you?" The woman asking was pleasant to look at.

No, she was beautiful. Slim still, even though she must be nearing forty. Her vibrant red hair showed no sign of graying. Jason stepped forward. "Information is what I need. I'm Jason Kenworthy," He paused to look over his shoulder. "This is my brother Jasper. I'm looking for someone important to me."

"Of the serious type, I suppose. I'll see what I can do to help." She tilted her head a bit sideways studying the two men. "Believe I remember the two of you. You've helped out at the homeless camp a time or two." Her eyes sparkled. Sunlight slanting in through the window brought a beautiful sheen to her skin.

"How did you know? We are serious. Now that I see you, I do remember you from about a year ago."

"Lucky guess. You look as if you could slay dragons. I'll do my best to help. Been a bit of a trying day." She blew upward to dislodge a lock of hair that had fallen into her eyes. "Maybe this will be a better variety of news."

"No dragons here that need slaying. I'll get straight to the point," Jason wondered how her day had been trying. Couldn't get into that. He needed answers.

"…And that is?"

The point he was going to get at, yes. He was interrupted.

"Do you need any help out there?" a woman from the back room called out.

Jason could see her watching from the window. The second lady started for the door then hesitated at the threshold.

"All's fine," The woman shot back before focusing on him, giving

Jasper an ardent look that asked if she knew the older twin then back to him. "Now…what is that point you wish to get at? I'm busy. Have to get ready for the lunch crowd." She looked at the sun which was almost to its highest point.

He couldn't help the grin when she realized they were twins. "Yes twins. I'm looking for a woman," Jason said moving his shoulders while he tried to ease the stiff muscles. He'd been up worrying what seemed the last two days. Sleep had been elusive. Until he found Tessa it would remain that way. He thought of her fingers massaging the kinks from the back of his neck.

"Aren't they all," she laughed. The sound was musical. "Good thing I'm taken. You two are of the handsome variety. Don't believe Donal would take kindly to the two of you. He is rather possessive."

"My wife," Jason amended with a bit too much emphasis. "I'm looking for my wife." Damn he was possessive too. Could understand how a man could become obsessive with a woman. Until Tessa he never believed that man could be him.

"You've lost your wife." She drummed her fingers on the counter. "Seems a man should take better care of someone he loves. Doubt if I can help you out. Aren't any lost wives in this bakery."

"She ran away," he said as he cleared his throat then immediately regretted giving out the information. This lady didn't need to know anything about the difficulties he was having with his wife's mother. Anice caused all this. Why the woman could be so bitter about her daughters was beyond his imagination.

"Been a lot of that going around today. Just this morning in fact," Daryl said with a bit of a snort. Said something beneath her breath. "Had some misgivings about that particular situation. The lady didn't seem to be too eager to be caught by her husband. The man told me it was a game they played. Apologized for getting me involved. The game never involved other people before."

With that mentioned, Jason's heart lodged in his throat. He prayed this wasn't Tessa and Abernathy. "What did she look like? The woman? Her hair? Her eyes?" He understood he showed way too much eagerness. This woman, Daryl, would question that. Might even doubt his sincerity.

If she only knew the circumstances. He handed her Tessa's most arresting features before she could answer his earlier questions. "White blond hair, eyes the color of sapphires. Slim. Yet…" He didn't need to go into her shape or size or the way her breasts felt surrounded by his hands. Didn't need to tell anyone about the way her scent of lavender coupled with sunshine always greeted him when he was close.

Daryl hesitated. "Yes, that would describe this woman perfectly. She looked worn out. Cold to the bone. Her hair was disheveled. I tried to stop him from taking her. Said she was his wife. Since that was the case, there wasn't anything I could do to stop him. The lady wasn't this man's wife. Was she?"

"Him?" At that instant, Jason understood he was too late. His problems multiplied. Tessa was in more trouble than she could deal with on her own. He would need to call on the constables for help. Had to find her first. Might never find her. Luck was not on his side.

"Do you know him? The man who said Tessa was his wife?" Jason could still hope. Could pray there was some minor misunderstanding between a couple. Hell, Tessa wasn't the only woman with the characteristics he described. White blond hair was rare.

She tapped her pencil on the ledger in front of her. "Who doesn't? The man is known throughout Glasgow. Didn't know he was married though. Must have been a recent wedding. Funny, the two didn't have the air of newlyweds. Though…I don't keep up with the comings and goings of the gentry. You say…"

"What did you say his name was?" Jasper asked. "Certain my twin is growing more impatient with each passing second."

"Lord Abernathy. Nelson Abernathy, I believe."

"He said he was married to Tessa?" Jason gasped, unable to hide the trepidation in his voice. "Tessa is my wife. Abernathy kidnapped her right off your back porch. Wants to make her his next mistress. Has the notion she'll be biddable to the idea. She won't. Despises the man."

"Do you have any thoughts on where he might have taken her?" Again, Jasper jumped into the conversation.

"Took her in his coach. That's all I *ken*. She was trying to mouth words to me. Didn't understand what she was trying to tell me. I wish I'd found a way to stop them. You say the lady is your wife? Best you hurry. Before they left, her cheek was bruising. The man must have hit her hard. The girl wasn't happy about going with him."

"Thank you." Jason turned to his brother. "We're no better off now than we were when the morning began. We still don't know where she is. Don't have a solitary clue. What can we do now? Can't leave her to Abernathy's whims. He won't take her to his personal residence. That would be foolhardy. He must have another home set up for a mistress. How the hell are we going to discover the location?"

"We could visit Abernathy at his home. Give him some made up story. Have to think on that one," Jasper offered with what seemed to be reluctance. The hesitation in his voice spoke volumes.

"Surprise the man. We can shock him. Show Abernathy we *ken* what he is up to. Inform him there will never be a divorce filed," Jason added to his brother's thoughts. "Threaten his very existence."

"What?" Jaspers dark brown brows drew together. "Surprise? As in the element of? What do you have in mind?"

"Nothing at the moment," Jason grumbled still trying to think of a good offense to this horrifying situation. He turned to Daryl, "Thank you for your help. Don't shoot the messenger. Didn't appreciate the news though. If you hear anything send a message to Jason Kenworthy." With little hope of anything coming from this, he wrote down the address of the townhouse he shared with his brother. Now that they were both married, he should look to buying a home of his own. "Tessa is my wife. If she remains with Lord Abernathy, she will suffer at his hands. He's evil where women are concerned."

The woman caught her bottom lip beneath her teeth. "If I hear anything, I'll be sure to send word." She lifted the paper then nodded at the two men.

The bells eerie ringing when they left sounded a death nell.

"What now?" Jasper turned to Jason.

"We set up surveillance in front of Lord Abernathy's home. He's got to come out sometime. When he does, we can follow him."

"Should put someone in front of Anice MacRae's home too. The two could be celebrating Abernathy's early win."

~ * ~

Going with the duke and duchess might well be another mistake. She'd made so many in the last twenty-four hours, Tessa didn't think she could keep track of them. This couldn't be another blunder. Lacie Stewart was nice enough. Leslie intimidated her stockings off. Terrified her by the way his eyebrows drew together when he searched her face. The pair offered safe shelter. She hoped they spoke the truth. What she did understand was that she couldn't stay on the street. She needed a protected place where she could gather her wits. A place to stay that was warm. Last night she thought she might freeze to death. This was a gamble she must take. For her, choices were limited.

As soon as they were inside the home, Lacie took her by the arm. Led her upstairs. Ordered a hot bath for her. The room was decorated in light blue tones. Everything about it appealed to her. Pleasant sunlight filtered in through the open window. A soft breeze ruffled the pale blue curtains. The scent of rosses wafted into the room from the garden below. Her fears decreased even though she warned herself to caution. It would never do for her to become complacent or too trusting in this new environment. A fugitive of sorts, Tessa understood the need for caution. Even though the place appealed, she held back.

Lacie squeezed her elbow, a pleasant smile on her face. They stopped in the middle of the bedchamber. "Do you like the room? While you are with us, you can use this space for your privacy. Though I hope you will share a bit of your story with us. Think about doing so. We might be able to help. I'll be back in an hour with something for you to wear. I'll send out to my siblings. See if any of their daughters are about your size. You will need a few gowns along with underclothing to get started. This gown you wear now has seen better days. If you leave the dress outside the door, I'll have a maid pick it up. Have it washed if you like." She hesitated, a wry look on her face. "...or could burn the gown. What do you say?"

Tessa stood with her hands clasped in front of her. Her breaths were shallow...too fast. Afraid to speak. Terrified of what happened to her.

Perhaps in following Leslie and Lacie, she jumped out of the frying pan into the fire. Time would tell the story. At the moment, overwhelmed as well as terrified, she was unable to form a coherent thought. "Lord Abernathy? He won't think to look for me here? Will he? I don't…I can't…he kidnapped me right off the porch. You won't hand me over to him. Will you?" At the repugnant thought ice slipped down her spine. She shivered. Wrapped her arms around her trembling body. Thought her knees might give out. She fought the moisture forming in her eyes. Tessa thought she told this sweet lady too much then not enough.

"The nasty man wouldn't dare come here then accost you. While the man wields some power, he is not the duke." Lacie laughed then smiled at her as if hoping to reassure. She touched her arm. "Tessa, the man would be taking his life in his hands if he thought he could waltz in here and take you. Abernathy might knock on the door. My husband might escort him to his office for a short debriefing of this situation. That would be the extent of the hospitality we offer that horrible man. You, my dear, are under the Duke of Southcliff's protection. No one, I mean no one, will get to you. If there is anywhere in Glasgow you will be safe, your safety lies in this home."

Reassurance by the duchess helped somewhat. Tessa swallowed the fear in her throat somewhat relieved by the duchess' words. Lacie wouldn't understand how conniving the man was or how evil. If Abernathy wished to find a means to take her from this house, he would lie through his teeth to do so. He already told the lady at the bakery she was his wife. If not for that, Tessa thought the woman there might have helped her. She might have called out for help. There must have been patrons in the bakery.

She tried to smile. Found that she couldn't. Still, "Thank you. Don't know what I can ever do to repay you. I intend to find a way to manage my life. If Abernathy claims I'm his wife, know that I'm not." Tessa found herself staring at the floor. Wishing she was not the sister to Jason Kenworthy. She didn't know how to proceed from this point forward. She had no one. In this world, she was alone. Her sisters couldn't help without jeopardizing their lives. Jason would despise her for what they'd done together. Under the extenuating circumstances, would never allow her to stay with her sisters. Confiding in this nice lady would be good for her soul.

She couldn't tell the duchess her sob story. That was just what it was. A sob story. One with no merit.

Lacie looked at her with an interesting smile. As if Tessa could read her thoughts, she was asking for the truth. The truth was something she couldn't be free with. There was too much at stake here. What she needed from the duchess was a job, nothing more.

Appearing to give up on the truth, Lacie spoke, "Just relax in the bath for now." The duchess pointed to the bed where a dark blue garment had been set. "You can wrap yourself in the robe when you are finished. It will take me at least a half hour, probably an hour to find something else for you to wear. There is an open bottle of wine on the counter in the bathing room. If you are hungry just pull the bell cord. A servant will be right up to help you. Remember, you are a guest here."

A guest? How could that be?

While she watched, wide eyed, hands folded in front of her, the duchess disappeared. The breath of fresh air that was Lacie vanished. The water in the tub was hot to the touch. Steam rose into the air. Looked inviting. A towel was warming by the fireplace. She felt dirty. Used goods. Felt vile from Abernathy's touch. Was afraid to remove clothes. Had the horrible thought of Abernathy walking through the door to accost her. The way he looked at her this morning caused her skin to crawl. It seemed he wanted to devour her. At the time, she felt used, abused by his wandering eyes. The way his mouth slanted when he stared at her breasts made her skin crawl. Remembering caused her to shudder.

Don't be a fool. You're safe here. The duke knocked out the man Abernathy left to guard her. After the fact, he grinned as if he enjoyed himself. For a few seconds, Tessa caught the amused gleam in the duke's eyes. The man would know who the duke was. The guard would tell Abernathy where she was.

Lacie said Abernathy wouldn't dare show himself here. Implied he would be taking his life into his hands if he approached her while she was under their protection. The duke did defend her. Tessa remembered how the duke downed her guard with one blow to the chin. As if lifeless, he fell to the ground. Assumed the duke must have known the exact spot to hit the man. She didn't know what type of man the duke was. Sheltered as she was when she lived with her mother, she knew very little about the royalty or near royalty who lived in the area. What she did believe was the duke enjoyed the small skirmish. He might have wished the fight to last a *wee* bit longer. The duke did end the fisticuffs with one blow to the man's chin. Took care of the situation before it could escalate.

Understanding she didn't have much time before Lacie would return, Tessa stripped then settled into the hot water. She closed her eyes. Comforting heat washed over her, swirling around her. Oh my, this felt good. Eased tense muscles. Until now she'd been so cold. So very cold. The bath oil scent was of roses. The soap held the same fragrance. She was in heaven. It seemed so long ago she bathed.

These people were nice. What would they want from her? Would they demand something in return for their generosity? If she could, she would repay them. All she wished for was a way to earn a living. She told them she wanted a job. Neither replied that work might be a possibility.

So, what now?

She was so tired. Exhausted. Her eyes closed. Dreams of Jason flooded through her head. Recalled the last time they made love. Her hand on her belly, she prayed she didn't carry his child. The child would be…ostracized his or her entire life…another bastard in an unforgiving world. She would love the baby. Care for the boy or girl. She needed to make her case with more strength to the duchess. She was desperate for a job. Frantic for a place to call home.

Scrubbing all of herself she dipped under the cooling water. Used the extra pail of warm water to rinse out her hair. The huge bath towel was warm. She wrapped the cloth around herself. Draped another smaller one around her head to help soak up the excess water in her hair left from the rinse.

The light knocks on the door caught her by surprise. She'd been immersed in thoughts about Jason. She loved her husband so much. Now she needed to love him as a sister would love her brother. Didn't seem right. How could she have ever believed she was so fortunate to meet the man of her dreams. To fall in love.

"Tessa?"

It was the duchess. Not much time had passed since she left to seek out clothing. She looked to the clock on the mantle. Realized she'd been in the water longer than she thought. Lacie's soft voice was clear as well as sweet. She was so beautiful. No surprise the duke seemed to enjoy looking at her. After years of marriage, it was obvious to anyone with eyes he was still smitten. Tessa wondered how long the two had been married. Where were their children? They might be close to her age. Lacie wasn't that old. She couldn't be more than forty or so. Maybe not even that. She must have been very young when they wed.

"Come in." Tessa stopped her musings to smile. It was a half-smile, no more. She tried. "Sorry, I'm not ready. The bath was divine. Thank you. I needed the hot comfort of the water. Was cold last night." Something else she shouldn't have said.

"Brought you a couple of gowns to try on," Lacie said as she seemed to study her again. "Take whatever fits. The girls can no longer wear them." One at a time, she held up three gowns. Shook each one out for her to see. "What do you think?"

The dresses were lovely. "They are more than I deserve." She didn't have anything so nice, though Jason tried to purchase gowns for her. It was her past that stopped her from buying more than she needed. He tried to insist. She resisted. Not too many days ago he told her he would commission more clothes to be made for her. He would bring the seamstress to her if she kept protesting. That wasn't going to happen now. She needed to learn to make do with what she could afford.

"Oh, that's too much. I can't pay you for any of these. All I wish for is a job." Tessa didn't want charity.

"Nonsense, you must have something to wear. The other dress needed to be burned. It would never do again even with a good washing." Lacie pointed to the dresses she'd set on the bed. "These are all hand me downs. They would have gone to charity. You can use them until we figure out where you should be, along with what you should be doing. I know you've a story to tell. Would be so much simpler if you would help us out." The duchess let out a long deep sigh as if the small exhale of air would change Tessa's mind.

"I need a job. That's all you need to know about me. If you can't help me, I must go to someone else who can. Don't want to…" Tessa found moisture clogging her eyes. She sniffed. Pushed on the towel around her head.

Lacie waved her hand in the air obviously annoyed by the words. "Nonsense. We are going to figure out your story. You don't have anything to fear." The duchess held up her hands again. "Leslie has men on your story as we speak. Won't leave a stone unturned. You've left clues even though…"

"No!" Panicked she cried out. "No…you can't…you don't understand." Beneath her ribs her heart raced, beat a hysterical staccato.

"What I do understand is that you have secrets you don't wish for anyone to learn. How you came to be in Nelson Abernathy's possession is beyond the pale. It is clear to anyone who has eyes, you are a well-born lady as well as a wife to some adoring man. Your husband must be desperate to find you. In case you didn't realize you still wear the symbol of a marriage. There is a wedding ring on your finger. A very expensive one if I don't miss my guess. One that matches the color of your eyes. The ring was picked out with you in mind." Lacie seemed to pause for breath while she stared with pointed interest at the ring she described. "What happened? You're not married to Lord Abernathy. Who then loves you so much?"

Tessa gasped before hiding her hand behind her back. She was at a loss as to what to say. "I can't tell you. You can't know. No one can. It's a sin," she blurted without thought. As if to stop more unwanted words, Tessa put her knuckles to her mouth. The fact she couldn't bear to sell her wedding ring might lead to her downfall. Though doing so was hard, she did sell the engagement ring.

"Can't tell me what? Exactly what sin?" Lacie persisted. "Who you are married to? Someone with enough groats to purchase that ring…and I'm certain an engagement ring as well. The wedding band is circled with diamonds along with sapphires. If so, the man must be well-connected. Has legitimate means to pamper you. He must think highly of you." One more time she pointed out the reality of the symbol on her hand. "The sapphire in that engagement ring matches your eyes."

Her heart in her throat, Tessa sat down on the bed. Lacie was far too intuitive. She and the duke must have spoken about her. Exchanged stories. Come to conclusions about her. All based on the ring. She didn't want to give both of them up. As somebodies' servant, they would question how she came by such expensive jewelry. They were hers. Given to her under false pretense. "I'll try these gowns on. You are right. I can't wear the other one I arrived wearing. It's a mess. If you bring it back, I'll launder the gown. Clean the gown up so it is wearable."

"No," Lacie told her adding a charming smile to the mix. "You will choose one of these. Dress then meet me in the parlor with Leslie. We will then go over your story. What you will tell of it. The part you are reluctant to tell us we will puzzle out on our own time. Rest assured we will discover all your truths. In order to help you, Leslie told me he needs a few more details. He is very good at ferreting out important facts. Life would be easier for all of us if you quickened the process. We could have you back in the loving hands of your husband in no time. Nonetheless, I do understand your fear of the unknown. So far, in whatever way, you've been treated badly."

It started with her mother. She treated them all with unforgiving malice. The deep breath of air Tessa inhaled stuck in her throat. She didn't like this one bit. Imagined that the two thought they deserved a few answers for their help. She would tell them what she could, nothing more. There would be other places to look for jobs. Since Lord Abernathy found her at the bakery, she imagined that place was out.

Three gowns for her to try. They were all beautiful. Jason wanted to buy her gowns such as these. Tessa was relieved she didn't allow that to happen. Imagined that as a bastard sister to the Kenworthy twins, she had no rights where the family was concerned. They would never wish for the shadow of her parentage to be known.

Another knock, this one surprised her. She didn't expect Lacie to reappear so soon or at all. Tessa wrapped the robe around her. Tried to sound more confident than she felt. "Come in," the sound of her voice was a whispered croak.

"Miss…" The lady curtsied. Smiled. "The duchess sent me up here to help you with your clothing. You might need help with the corset or the fasteners in the back of the gown. I was to escort you downstairs when we are done here. Oh…your hair is so beautiful. If you wish, I could style it for you. I'm very good at arranging hair. If I do say so myself," seemed she was gushing the words.

Tessa nodded, surprised that help was sent to her. She never expected that consideration. The duchess would have known she couldn't fasten the gown by herself. Felt as if the duchess was reeling her in to the fold, potent scrap by potent scrap. "Thank you."

"I can do your hair too if you like," she repeated as if doing so was most important to her. "I'm good with hair. Yours is so lovely. Such an unusual color," she continued to chatter. The girl fussed with the remaining gowns, hanging them in the armoire. She couldn't be more than seventeen or eighteen. Still so very young.

"Thank you. What's your name? I'm Tessa in case the duchess didn't tell you." Tessa was overwhelmed by the young lady helping her with the gown as well as her hair. She'd never had a maid who did her hair.

The little maid wore her long dark brown hair in a bun fastened at the nape of her neck. Her body was slender, just beginning to blossom in womanly curves. With dark brown eyes that seemed to take everything into account, she seemed fragile. Too fragile to be a maid of any sort. Tessa wondered if she could do that job for some lady of wealth. She had no experience. Again, her mind returned to cleaning. What did one need to know about cleaning a home.

"Betsy, Lady Tessa, Betsy Callahan. That's my name. What do you say? Should I do up your hair?" Betsy asked again.

"I don't have a title. Just call me Tessa. Please," Tessa murmured, seeming overwhelmed by the situation at hand.

"Oh, I couldn't do that. You are a lady. Every *wee* little bit of you. You're a lady for certain or my name isn't Betsy Callahan. Sit down. I'll go to work. Get you ready in no time at all."

When Betsy finished, she stepped back to admire her handywork. Crossed her arms beneath her small breasts pushing them up. "Believe you are ready to chat with the duke and duchess. They are just the nicest people in the whole wide world. You will see. They never put on airs. Give me time off when I need it. Also, the duchess gives me little presents to take home to my younger sisters."

"Yes, they do seem to be very nice. I've just met them. Didn't know them before a few hours ago. They took me into their care without knowing who I am. Not many would do that." Tessa was wondering about all kinds of things. Such as if they had children. They must. The pair seemed to be very much in love. Appeared at times to be able to read each other's thoughts. She was starting to read Jason's thoughts. He was easy to read. All she needed to do was look at the expression on his face or into his golden-flecked brown eyes. Seemed he always wanted her.

"Do you know the way to the drawing room? No? I'll show you. Follow me. I won't let you get lost," Her cheerful voice had a way of easing Tessa's emotions.

Betsy didn't even wait for an answer. "No, please show me. Wouldn't wish to wander some place I shouldn't be." There was amusement in her voice when she spoke. The girl was eager to please. Was this how she would need to act when she became a servant? Didn't know if she could be that jovial all the time. Most often, she was too serious by far. She'd find herself fired for being too glum.

Tessa followed her down the long winding steps of the Stewart's home then into the drawing room. Lacie was pouring Leslie a drink when she entered. They were chatting about something the duke bought. She was half afraid they would be talking about her. Maybe they'd done that already.

"Welcome," the duke said as he accepted the brandy from his wife. "You look much better than the last time I saw you. How's the cheek. Should I send for a physician?"

The way he looked at his duchess, Tessa thought he must be thinking about tugging her onto his lap then pursuing other pastimes. It was the same look in Jason's eyes when he thought of kissing her, touching her in all the wonderful sensual places he found on her body. With her knuckles in her mouth, she stifled her groan. Lost love was difficult to deal with. She told herself she had no right to think of Jason as a love, lost or otherwise.

"Would you like a glass of sherry?" the duchess asked before she could answer the duke's questions. Lacie's smile would light up any room. "I'm having one before dinner. I'll pour you one too."

"Yes, that would be nice," Tessa murmured. At the mention of dinner, her stomach growled. It would never do if she seemed too eager.

"Have a seat," Leslie waved his hand toward a seat facing him. "We've a few things to talk over before dinner is served. Let's get back to the original questions. How about one at a time so you don't feel so overwhelmed. First one, how is your cheek?" he nodded to her. Sat back as if he waited for her to answer.

"It's sore, yes. If I don't touch the bruise, it doesn't seem so bad. All my teeth are intact. No, I don't need you to go to the trouble of calling on a doctor. I'll be fine."

"Good…good, let's move on to more important topics."

"If you don't mind," Tessa said her voice soft, submissive. Hoped the duke would understand. "I need a job. If you can help me, I'll repay any debts I accrue. Given some time, I would be able to pay for the three gowns lady Lacie gave me."

For a blink, Tessa imagined she saw the duke scowl. Couldn't image why he would do so. She said nothing that should bring up that harsh expression.

"No, you are prevaricating on unimportant topics. What you want is important to your life. A job is not one of the essential things for your future. I would like to know more about the young lady I'm helping. The one who caught the soft heart of my wife. Don't wish for a scandal to be following you. Don't want my wife to get stabbed in the back if you are not what you seem. In case you've failed to notice, I'm very protective of my duchess."

"Scandal? Stab in the back? Never!" she questioned then understood a woman married to her brother would create a scandal. Her face fell. Blood seemed to vanish from her face as she gasped a pint of air. The gossip would run through the society. Jason would be ostracized. The duke and duchess might also become the recipient of gossip if it was known they helped her. Abernathy would make certain the facts were known. He'd most likely revel in bringing the duke down a peg or two if that was possible.

"Yes, scandal," the duke repeated, his voice knifing through her. "My wife would be hurt if you are not as you seem. Don't like Lacie to be hurt in any way." The duke was repeating himself. Was that for her benefit? Undoubtedly, yes.

Fear flooded her. Tessa set her glass on the table. She stood, her knees quaking. "I should leave before more damage is done. Yes, everyone who is associated with me will be hurt. The duchess has been good to me. She doesn't deserve to be hurt in the reveal of my truths." Tessa turned to Lacie, "If you'll get my old gown I'll go. Don't wish to bother the two of you. I'm sorry for the inconvenience I've put you to."

"So." Beneath his chin the duke drummed his fingers together. "You aren't as you seem. A gently bred young lady married to a man of wealth. Who are you, Tessa with no last name. Don't bother to make one up. I will discover the truth," he sounded angry now. Furious with the lies coupled with deceit. "I always do. Your case won't be any different."

"A truth for you. I'm not married. At least I won't be for long. My husband is filing for a divorce as we speak. He has no choice in the matter." She wanted nothing more than to run. There was nowhere for her to flee. Thought she might be here for a few days. Long enough for Lacie to help her find a job. That wasn't going to happen.

Tessa didn't know if what she disclosed was true. Nonetheless it was what Anice told her he would need to do. Since they consummated the marriage, he couldn't seek an annulment. Jason would have no choices left to him except to end the ridiculous marriage.

"Sit down," he told her though ice-filled words. "You're not going anywhere until I understand everything about you. I will learn all the mazes and the puzzles you present."

"Why would your husband, who clearly adores you," Lacie stared at the wedding ring, "file for a divorce? You are not making sense, dear. We only wish to help you sort through your difficulties. You're making doing so devilishly hard."

Sweat slipped between her breasts. Tessa struggled to breathe. For a beat of her heart, she thought she might faint.

Since they wanted the truth, then so be it. She would deal with the consequences. "Because," Tessa began with a shaky voice, "I'm my husband's half-sister. At the time of our marriage, we didn't know the truth. There can be no marriage." In this case she didn't intend to give out a last name. Jason would be better off if these nice people didn't know.

Shock, that was what she witnessed on both their faces. "No…I don't believe it," Lacie said as she shook her head. "Why do you say something like that? Don't lie."

"We didn't know the truth until yesterday morning. I'm not lying. My mother wrote me a letter illuminating the truth. You see," Tessa lifted her hands in the air before letting them fall to her lap, "I never knew who my father was until the horrible letter. I'm a bastard. Now I know. He is the same man as my husband's father."

"Is that how you fell into Abernathy's waiting hands?" Leslie asked, while he rubbed the back of his neck, rose, then walked around the room. He stood at the window looking into the garden behind the home. His hands were clasped behind his back while he seemed to be absorbing the ambiance.

"In part. I left my husband. Didn't want him to kick me out when he discovered the awful truth. I was frightened. Horrified of what I did." She shuddered in a breath of air that stuck in her throat. "Didn't have anywhere to go. Thought for a blink that I might seek help from the nice lady who runs the bakery." Tessa lifted her shoulders in a shrug that wasn't heartfelt. That notion didn't work out at all. "By the time I got there the bakery was closed for the night. Don't understand why I never thought about that simple fact. Just expected the business to be open. Hoped I would find a job there, maybe even a bed for the night."

Tessa didn't need to volunteer any more information. She'd already said too much. By the looks on their faces, she might have made a terrible blunder. The two must know something about the bakery.

"Have another glass of sherry. I'll be right back." The duke walked out of the room with a determined pace. He no longer seemed to be at lose ends.

Lacie spilled more sherry into her glass. "Drink up, dear. Dinner might be delayed. I know you're hungry. Need to put something in your stomach. How long has it been since you ate?" The duchess walked to the door. Called out to the butler. Spoke for a few seconds then walked back into the room to sit down with her.

Tessa didn't understand what just happened. It seemed the few words she spoke set off an explosion of action. She tried to think of a reason. Couldn't put two thoughts together in her head. What she reasoned was that it had to have something to do with the bakery along with the lady who owned the establishment.

"While you sip on the excellent sherry, I'll tell you a little story," Lacie suggested, her voice soft as if lulling her.

Tessa wasn't at all certain she wanted to hear this story. She nodded as if she did. "You'll tell me whether I want to hear it or not," she mumbled while she swallowed the sweet drink. "Go ahead."

"Feel free to add facts about your interesting life as I begin to talk. Soon you will have nothing to hide from me. The two of us will be best friends," the sound of her voice was far too cheery. "Think of me as your mother."

Tiny drops of sherry flew from Tessa's lips. She touched each one with the tip of her tongue. Her breath made an audible hitch.

"Maybe not your mother," the duchess was quick to take back her recommendation. "A trusted sister, perhaps?"

Until that moment, Lacie almost reminded her of the maid. Too cheery by far, "That's what I'm afraid of," Tessa said with a parched throat. She sipped again. "My mother is not motherly at all. You are a much nicer woman. My sisters and I have always been close. We told each other everything that was important to us. I miss them already. It's only been a…"

"I'm the youngest of five siblings. The youngest girl." The duchess paused as if she expected Tessa to chime into the conversation. "We are all close too. We see each other whenever we can. Which usually is quite often."

Tessa supposed nothing she said here would make a difference in the duke and duchess' plans. "I'm the youngest girl of four, not one brother among us. A brother to protect us would have been nice." She coughed when the sherry went down the wrong way. Sputtered a few more drops onto the back of her hand which she held to her mouth. "We're all bastards," she added before she could think better of expounding on the dreadful news.

"Bastards one and all. That doesn't matter to me or my husband, the duke. I grew up without a mother or father. My oldest brother, Flynt, raised us." She grinned as if she was thinking of those years. "He wasn't always the most attentive guardian. He had ideas about how his time was spent. Those notions didn't include babysitting or chaperoning as he got older, four girls."

"I gather he didn't pay much attention to his sisters." Tessa gave a tight laugh that left a bitter taste in her mouth when she thought of her family. "Might have been nice to have a brother. On second thought no, he would have been a bastard too. My mother didn't care much for her husband. Found her fun with her other lovers." Again, she said too much. What did it mater. She was still alone in a world that had trouble forgiving accidents of birth. Lacie couldn't change that fact. She couldn't give her a real father. One who would care what happened to her. Her father was dead. She'd never even met him.

Lacie cleared her throat before she continued the story of her childhood. Tessa wondered where she was going with this. The moisture in her eyes telling Tessa that Lacie was caught up in Tessa's story.

The duchess' smile was tight when she began to speak again, "We, the sisters, all wed my brother's best friends. Every time one of us fell in love, Flynt, that's my brother, ranted and raved. Threatened his friends not to lay a hand on us. He couldn't stop love from happening. Suppose what we felt first was lust." She giggled behind the back of her hand. "They were all bad boys and proud of the well-won label. Of course, they all ignored my brother. Did as they pleased."

"Bad boys?" Tessa joined in with a small smile. Couldn't bring herself to laugh. Understood, the duchess was hoping she'd blurt something more of her less than perfect life. Beneath Lacie's scrutiny coupled with her tender heart, Tessa found herself unraveling one tiny strand at a time. She'd already said too much. "Believe that's what my husband and his twin are. Bad boys. Every hard inch of them." Oh, no…at the narrowing of Lacie's eyes, Tessa understood that was more knowledge than she wished to put forth. The sought after information was a means to identify her. For a few beats of her heart, Tessa lowered her lashes. Stared at the floor wishing it would swallow her up whole.

"Your husband has a twin. I see…there aren't that many wealthy twins in this area. Your husband must be the youngest or he would undoubtedly sport a recognizable title. I know the Seymore twins. Miles is a judge. Has a daughter whose name is Gracie…Murray I believe is her married name. Do you know either of those twins?" she asked with pointed curiosity.

The probing question took Tessa by surprise before she drew in a breath and thought about her answer. Tessa looked at her beneath lowered lashes. She didn't want to give an answer. This was getting the duchess far too close to discovering all her truths. The duchess had this way about her. She drew her into the conversation.

"How did you meet your husband?" Tessa asked. This time she wanted to be the one questioning. Not the one saying too much. Thought the story the duchess was telling her an interesting one.

"Through my brother. I don't remember how old I was when Leslie first kissed me. The kiss was in the stable. Not a very romantic setting, was it? The incorrigible man chased me from the third floor of our home. Of course, I wanted him to catch me." Lacie smiled with what must be a fond memory of that day. "I wasn't old enough for him to court. Nonetheless, I knew he was the man I wanted to marry. He had to wait a few years before he could do more than tease me with subtle innuendos I didn't understand. Was always jealous when I saw him with another woman."

"Why? Why was there a chase? From a third floor?" Tessa was far too curious now. The duke didn't fit into that persona. In her mind, she couldn't see that man chase anyone. Of course, he was younger then. Lacie was so beautiful. He would want to capture her for a kiss.

"My sisters and I were hiding in the room where the young men were playing cards. Each one of us was enamored of one of them. They all took exception to the fact they were being watched by young girls. They chased after us. Leslie ran after me. Caught me. Kissed me. The rest is history."

"How did you meet your husband soon to not be your husband," Lacie asked with a nonchalant air as she refilled the glasses. "Was he as daring as my husband? Is he conventional in his courting?"

"In Ireland…" oh my, well…what does it matter. She still doesn't have a last name for me. "I was invited to my oldest sister's wedding." Tessa couldn't tell her about the Christmas Eve party when Maggie escaped the engagement planned for her to Lord Abernathy. Wasn't about to tell her how Maggie ran into Jasper Kenworthy at the homeless camp.

"Ireland, you say. Why was the wedding there?" Lacie set the sherry down. Clear to Tessa she still groped for answers to the question of Tessa's last name.

"No," Tessa held out her hands as if to ward off further questions. "No, don't want to say anything more about me. I've said too much as it is." The duchess was getting too close to the truth. A few more questions she would have all the answers she needed to give her a last name. From there, the duke and duchess would bring Jason here. He wouldn't come. Would he? He would disavow her. They were related, too closely to be married.

"Afraid of the truth?" One of Lacie's eyebrows traveled toward the ceiling.

"Yes."

The duchess ran her thumb along the stem of her crystal glass before she said anything more. "I will tell you something else about my family. Something that might be important for you to comprehend. Daryl, as in the Daryl of the bakery where you sought employment, is one of my sisters. The gown you are wearing belonged to one of her daughters. When you brought up the bakery, Leslie sent a man to interview my sister. I'm not certain why he hasn't returned yet. It would only take a few moments to send a trusted employee. Because of his work with the Scottish government, he keeps men on hand for whatever surprise might end up at our door. You, Tessa, are a huge surprise."

"I don't understand." The tale being woven around this woman grew more complex with each moment that passed.

"My husband used to be a spy. Very good at his work if I do say so myself. Leslie hasn't quit the government. What he's done is cut back on dangerous assignments. Now, how much longer do you think your secret will remain?"

A spy…

Tessa found herself shaking her head. “Your sister doesn’t know my name. Knows only that she saw my kidnapping by Lord Abernathy’s hands.” She said the first idea that entered her head. It was the first thought. The second consideration was that Daryl would know she was kidnapped by a man. She might have been the woman watching. Might have been the woman who came out to confront Abernathy. The question was if Daryl knew Lord Abernathy. Stood to reason she would have a name for him since the duchess, her sister knew his name. Abernathy owned a home near here.

“No, you are right about that. However, one clue always leads to the next. While we’ve been talking you’ve told me quite a bit about yourself. So many truths that belong to one woman only.”

Tessa understood she’d been out maneuvered as well as out thought by this beautiful woman.

“A lot that I’ll put to use to discover what I need to learn.” The duke walked into the room, a broad smile highlighting his eyes. He bent over to kiss Lacie’s cheek then stood behind her. His hands rested on his duchess’ shoulders. “You could make this easy,” he addressed the statement to her.

She could but she wasn’t about to make anything easy for this couple. Lacie tricked her into confessing more than she wanted. “You were listening in on our private conversation, standing in the hall. How dare you?” By the tightening of his features Tessa understood she spoke out of line.

He lifted broad shoulders that strained the fabric of his coat. Seemed to brush off her mistake. “That’s what spies do. Is it not? A spy must be able to infiltrate whatever group or person he deems necessary.”

“Yes,” she muttered under her breath disliking the fact she agreed with the duke. “Imagine so. What do I know about spies? Nothing.”

“My sweet wife tells me I’m a very good spy. Says I’m good at other things that make her blush.” He grinned at the ensuing color flushing Lacie’s face. “What we do now is sit back and wait. Shouldn’t be too long before things start to happen. Must be patient. Won’t do a’tall to rush to conclusions. Who will arrive first? I wonder? I’m betting on your husband.

All the clues have been laid at his doorstep. With a little push in the right direction, he will figure it all out."

~ * ~

On the way to Abernathy's townhouse, Anice sat back in the well-sprung carriage. Enjoying the ride and knowing the next scene she witnessed would give her more pleasure than a climax with her latest lover. She was excited by all the possibilities. Enthusiastic by the prospect of watching sexual play by other people. That was something she'd never witnessed before. The thought in and of itself aroused her to the point of needing more attention than she would get here with Lord Abernathy. Ah, she would need to make do some other way.

"You look like the cat who swallowed a canary," Abernathy said with a bland tone to his words. "Your eyes are dreamy. You just moistened your lips for the third time. What are you thinking about? I might like to taste your lips. An older woman has endless potential." He sat forward, his forearms resting on his thighs. "Are you so excited by the prospect of your daughter under my control that you're licking your lips? The look of pleasure radiates on your face. After I've bedded your daughter, we could enjoy a threesome. You. Me. My new whore." He ran his finger along her naked arms. The gesture sent a wealth of goose bumps into play.

"You know I am excited. The little trollop will be fun to watch you command as well as manage. As to a threesome, I'll give the notion some consideration. Never done that before. Rather the threesome would be with two men and me. Would one of the guards like to join us? Who would be on top?" Thought of his hard youthful body blanketing hers. The vision sent the sensual play of her core into vivid, stark contractions.

His laughter cracked as he studied the mother of the woman he was about to lead to his bed. A very unwilling woman. "My whore. Be careful what you say about her," Nelson warned with an unforgiving tone to his voice. "I'm the only one allowed to hurt what is mine. To call her insensitive names does not please me. You gave Tessa to me, *carte blanch*. You've no hold over her or me." He tapped his long, slender fingers together as he watched. "We could see if the man guarding Tessa is up to you along with me together at the same time. If not, I'm certain one of my friends will be up to the sex. It would be…hot and messy. Nothing soft or gentle about the coupling. What do you think?"

Nelson was a handsome man. Well-put together in all the ways that counted. She would never turn down sex with a younger man. She would need to think about threesomes of any kind. If the sex involved her with Tessa, her daughter would be mortified. Revenge would be even sweeter. Tessa defied her wishes too many times. Decided she would give both a try. New sexual adventures would always stimulate.

"We could try it both ways. Not tonight though. She is yours of course. Wouldn't want this any other way. If you get tired of the struggle that will ensue, come to me with your guard. We will give this threesome a try." Anice watched the grin grow on his sensual lips. Thought of kisses, needed to see the man naked. When she stared at his crotch, Anice noticed the bulge growing with each passing beat of her heart.

"After I've covered her a couple of times, I'll come get you. Be ready. Tessa will be thrilled to see me leave. Though I'll be back to her once we are done." Nelson was staring at her breasts as if he could devour them right now.

Anice was pleased her breasts were still firm rounded globes of sensual pleasure. Thrusting them out in a carnal pose she mastered years ago, she waited for what? Anice wasn't certain. Understood Nelson would react with a promise of his making. She dropped her lashes for a moment. Thought if she uncovered herself, he might begin to drool. "I'll be ready whenever you come for me."

The low growl in the back of his throat promised a reaction to her posturing. "Show them to me," his command startled her out of her own perusal of his body.

"Show what to you, darling?" Anice loved to play coy. Watched his eyes darken with a warning of some potency. She wasn't sure if the darkening was from sexual awareness or anger. Either reaction would do. She didn't think Nelson was a man who was used to questions from women. Even playful non-threatening ones.

Anice gasped, startled when she was pulled onto his hard thighs. She felt his erection beneath her. His long fingers brushed her gown from her shoulders before pulling the fabric to her waist. He slipped the ties to her chemise out of the eyelets. Tugged the silk apart. The corset she wore pushed her breasts up. Pink around the tips showed. He flicked more fabric down to uncover her.

"Pretty." He licked the tip. Sucked hard as well as savored each one.

A shattered, shocked sound broke from her when he bit. She curved. Twisted within his hold. The bite was not exquisite or sensual but hard, demanding a response. The startling painful sensation dashed straight to her core. Filled her with hot liquid fire. What Anice knew was that she'd never become so aroused during a first hard encounter with a man. It would be a long time before she grew bored with Nelson Abernathy. Anice hoped his stamina was up to par.

She curved for him. "More," she moaned as she held onto his head. Ran her fingers through his hair. Pushed his face against her aching breasts. "Wicked…"

His hoot of laughter startled her too. Just as fast, she was sitting across from Nelson again. "Too much too soon," he said, his words soft with a hint of danger as well as promise. "Why haven't we done this before?" he questioned watching her pull her garments back into place. She showed him a slow-eyed grin all the while taking her time with her clothing. Taunting him as he teased her with a promise unfulfilled. Anice understood men. Nelson possessed some different characteristics from what she was used to dealing with. She intended to learn how to use those traits to her advantage.

Once her clothing was in place, she tapped her lips with the tip of her finger. "You bit me hard," she accused with a sultry voice that made his eyes cross for a moment. "Dear Tessa won't like that."

He gave her a slow grin. "Count on more of the same with you as well as your daughter. You loved what I did. You were twisting, begging for more. Don't try to deny anything. I have strong needs. Gentleness isn't one of them. Best you understand before you…bite off too much." Nelson stretched his arms across the back of the seat while his gaze remained on her mouth.

She stared hard at the bulge. "I could bite hard…" Anice was thrilled with the grimace on his face.

The carriage rambled along. While Anice didn't know where the house was, she thought it might be close. Nelson wasn't the type of man who would appreciate waiting for his pleasures to be met. Driving was a waste of time for a man with needs.

"Are we close?" Anice asked.

"Impatient?" he shot back her way. "I am too. A little bite of you doesn't go very far. Afraid your daughter might be in for a rough ride this first time. You've wetted my appetite. I'm aroused to a painful place. Don't mean to taste you again until I'm sated with Tessa. After that we can proceed as planned. What do you say?"

In answer, Anice did a slow-pass of her tongue across each lip.

"Temptress." Nelson grinned, seeming pleased with the arrangements they made. "Believe after a few times with mother and daughter you will no longer owe me. Tonight, might well be one of the best of my life. Mean to continue in this vein for months. Doubt if either of you will bore me any time soon."

"You might come to bore me." Anice knew this man's sexual prowess might never bring her to boredom.

The carriage rolled to a stop at the back of the house. Nelson helped her down. Led her into the house.

"Sir…" The guard he assigned to watching his newest acquisition rushed to them. Panting, "Lord Abernathy, if you please, a word. Must speak to you. This is urgent."

"How did you get that bruise on your jaw?" Abernathy asked, impatient to begin the sexual games he anticipated. "Is everything as it should be?"

Anice stopped still. Instinct coupled with the look on the guard's face told her all was not as it should be. The looks being sent to Nelson were far from anything good. The man's brows were furrowed. His lips thinned.

"Oh, this…doesn't matter." The guards hand rested on his cheek. "Come inside where we can talk in private."

With precise movement, Nelson closed the door. Leaned against the frame, his arms crossed over his broad chest. “What is it?”

“Your new lady is gone.”

“Gone!”

Chapter Eleven

Jason found a quiet place across the street from Nelson's townhouse to watch. His body was tense with worry, coupled with fatigue. His mind at times muddled to a fine blur. He sipped in a quiet breath of health renewing air. This home which held his interest sat in an expensive part of Glasgow. Shade trees lined the street, each house with well-manicured lawns. The area was quiet. Much to his liking. Fear for Tessa knifed through him. Hate for her mother met the same fate.

With practiced caution, he'd been able to follow the carriage from the mother's residence to this one. Otherwise, he'd never would have been able to find the home. Anice was with Nelson which didn't surprise him. He'd seen her through the open window of the transport. After reading the letter, Jason understood Anice would wish to see her daughter brought down. Would revel in the humiliation forced upon Tessa by a man she loathed. He'd never understood how far she would go to mortify her daughters.

Another thing Jason didn't understand was the venom in the letter. The hatred that surfaced in the last year ever since Maggie's escape from Anice's plans of wedded bliss for her oldest daughter. Perhaps the animosity had always been there. Perhaps the tiny bit of motherly love she showed was all an act. Fake love. How could a mother wish for her daughter to be with a man as repugnant as Nelson Abernathy?

He felt disgusted with the turn of events in his life. By Tessa's standards his life had been sheltered. Understood his wife must be in that house across the street from where he stood. There was no other place she could be. He wasn't certain. Couldn't figure out a lawful way into the inner sanctum. At the door, he'd find himself held back. Thoughts of creeping in the back had its moments. If nothing else transpired he would need to creep. If he had to enlist the police, more scandal would erupt. Abernathy would never call this place his primary residence. Though with a new woman in his bed he would spend tonight here. Most every night after that until he grew bored with the newest possession. The thought of his wife at the mercy of such a man soured his stomach. Set his nerves screaming with pain for Tessa.

Jasper was on his way. He'd arrive soon. His twin couldn't do any more than he could. They could commiserate together. Plot a way to get to Tessa. The fact that Abernathy was here now, told him he had minutes to conceive a plan. Didn't know how Nelson would proceed with Tessa. Slow? Fast? Indifferent? He would torment then torture. Rumors had it few women enjoyed the attentions of this man.

Nelson stood on a balcony. Looked over the side. Anice stood beside him, her hand resting on his shoulder. He turned to her. They seemed to be arguing. The man shook his fist before slamming the palm of his hand on the railing. Even from the distance separating them, Jason saw the flame of red on Abernathy's cheeks. He was certain he could see the strained tick of his jaw. For a few seconds Abernathy leaned on the rail, his arms crossed. Anice paced the perimeter of the small area.

What was happening now was not what Jason expected to see. It was clear Nelson Abernathy was furious about something. A sudden instinct caught in his mind held for seconds while he assimilated the thought. The man might only be that angry if his prey slipped away before he brutalized her. A long, relief of air slipped from his lungs. How did Tessa find a way from the confines of the townhouse? Abernathy must have left someone to watch her. Either that or he would have made certain the home was locked up tight. He would not allow her to walk away. Must have known if not sensed she was not with him because she wanted to be.

Tessa wasn't daring. What she was, was smart. Her intellect was sound. Miles Seymore was a brilliant judge. Armstrong a politician of renowned astuteness. They were related by blood. She would understand she needed to escape this man before he returned for her. Tessa might try anything. She must be desperate enough to climb down from the balcony. Abernathy would not have been so stupid as to leave her access to the verandah. By the way the pair were acting, that must have been her means of escape…if she did escape.

If Tessa wasn't in the house…she could be anywhere in Glasgow or Scotland.

Anywhere.

That sent him right back to the beginning of his chase. The thought terrified him. His mind ached with the all-encompassing fear. Thought about his day coupled with the information he recovered through interviews. After speaking with the lady at the bakery, he was positive he didn't guess wrong. Tessa was in this city. Abernathy kidnapped her. She should be in this house he was watching. For the startling reason Nelson was furious, he didn't think she was there. Somehow Tessa managed to escape Nelson Abernathy. While he was proud of her, he was also terrified that she would again be in desperate need of help. A woman alone on the streets was not in a coveted position. Better than being caught in Abernathy's torturous web.

Nelson was bending over the railing staring then pointing to the ground. While Jason couldn't hear the exact words, by the tone of his voice he understood vicious anger. A large man, the guard Jason assumed, pointed not at the ground but down the street. Did that mean Tessa left in that direction? Who lived down the street where she might find assistance? He didn't know anyone. Was certain his wife did not know anyone. She told him she and her sisters had no friends. Was this a good Samaritan of some sort? He could hope. Pray. Have faith that she didn't fall into someone's hands who meant to hurt her.

Tessa would be frightened. Hungry. Terrified of the coming night. Darkness would surround them all too soon. If the chill during the day was an indication, this evening would be colder than last. There were no clouds to threaten rain. She still had little to wear. His wife had been missing for more than twenty-four grueling hours.

Jason started for the house. If he needed to storm through the doors to get information, that was what he intended. For a fraction of a moment, he held back. Drew in a deep breath of air, rethinking his actions. Thought better of the foolish plan. No one there would be inclined to inform him as to Tessa's whereabouts even if they knew.

He needed more information, more hard facts before he could continue with any rash foolishness on his part. Getting locked up for breaking and entering would never give him back his wife. He didn't need to make the situation worse. "Foolish woman," he murmured under his breath. She could have waited for him before she took off without a penny to her name. Tessa understood why he went to see Armstrong. With the letter in hand, she jumped to a wrong conclusion.

"The devil," Jason muttered with savage fierceness hitting his fist against his palm, "Where the hell are you? Curse your beautiful hide." The conversation on the balcony was still raging. The sun was dipping lower on the horizon. He'd hoped to find her before darkness descended to blanket the land with cold air. She didn't need a second night alone as well as terrified.

Anice set her hand on Abernathy's chest. Stood on the tips of her toes. Told him something that didn't seem to displease the man. With his hands on her waist, he held her. Jason wished he was close enough to know what was being said. Anice would be no more pleased than Abernathy at the unexpected problem. They would seek a way to find her. Perhaps not.

The hand on his shoulder startled. He jerked. Heart racing, he whirled ready to do battle. The man's grin stopped him cold. "Who are you?" All his instincts told him this man was a friend. They also told him to be wary. This man might not wish harm, but he was dangerous. Could tell by the hard set to his jaw coupled with the shimmering darkness of his eyes.

"That's my question to you. Why are you watching Lord Abernathy's playhouse with that haunted expression in your eyes? Why have you been swearing and muttering about foolish women?" The man's voice was warm yet the words insisted on an answer.

"Playhouse?" Jason swallowed hard while his gut twisted every which way. He wasn't ready to give out information to a stranger. This was too private. There could be unforeseen danger here for his wife. "What do you mean by that? Playhouse?" The question he asked came out before he thought.

The man nodded in the general direction of which they were speaking. "That's where Abernathy keeps his newest acquisitions. His mistresses. Some willing. Some not so much. His playhouse is a blight on the neighborhood if you ask me. Everyone who lives near this home understands its purpose. Would love to see this particular viscount drummed out of the aristocracy. Even though he keeps women there for his pleasure, there have been no complaints from the ladies. They all have known who butters their bread. Or…they have been threatened with their lives. So, to my question?"

"Who are you?" Jason repeated, thinking he should know this man. He was certain he'd seen him before today. Where? "I would know if your intentions are good…or bad. Would understand why you are interrogating me." Jason's mind told him there were explanations waiting. The man didn't seem in a hurry.

"Not important who I am. Why are you watching the house? Looks as if everyone standing on the balcony are at odds or furious, perhaps both. You've been observing for a while. What do you think?" The man stood back, staring across the street. His hands were behind his back, relaxed.

"Don't believe you've the right to know. What I'm doing is private business. Rest assured, I'm not intending to cause problems for this community," Jason bit out as he turned his attention back to the house, the balcony in particular.

"Making it my business. My neighborhood. Important to me what the people here are engaged in. If anything illegal is occurring, I would see to charges being placed. Never did like the man." His casual calm voice didn't impress Jason. The man knew that for a fact. The smile didn't change. Nor did the relaxed easy demeanor of a man who knew he was directing the conversation. A man who understood control.

Jason realized this man wasn't going to go away until he had answers. Might not leave then. "A misunderstanding brings me to your neighborhood. Need to correct the mix-up before anything untoward happens."

"That doesn't tell a person much. What kind of confusion. A mix-up? A mistake? Something interesting I hope," he said as he focused his attention back to the people arguing on the balcony. "Those three aren't solving any of their problems. Look," he pointed in the general direction. "Seems as if Nelson wants to throw the other man off the balcony. The woman has reminded him of something. She must be purring into his ear. Wonder what she's saying. Doing."

Jason turned his attention back to the two people he loathed more than anyone in the world. After the fact, Nelson grabbed Anice. She screamed at the sudden vicious attack. He tore the bodice of her gown to her waist. Her breasts revealed. She arched, seeming to search for more of what he wanted to give. The guard helped Abernathy get rid of her clothing. Ripped at the gown until she was standing naked for the entire street to see. She wrapped her legs around Abernathy's hips. The other man stroked her back. Kissed down her spine. Abernathy sucked a breast into his mouth. They both heard her cry of pain or pleasure. Jason didn't know which. Didn't care. The scene was decadent. Should play out in privacy not on the front yard balcony.

His breath came out in a ripping sound he couldn't stop even if he wanted to. "I've seen enough," Jason muttered, certain Tessa was no longer at the home. If she had been, she would have been the recipient of Abernathy's lust, his sexual perversions. Now, she was no longer in danger of Abernathy. Still in danger from her foolishness though. Where to look was now the most potent thought in his head.

While the scene enfolding in front of him was worthy of note, he didn't care. Before he could react again, the threesome on the balcony were headed into the house. A bedroom, Jason assumed. The room where they stashed Tessa until she managed to elude them by climbing down the balcony.

"Where the hell is she?" he muttered again, forgetting the man who stood so close to him. "She can't be that far. Didn't waste time finding the home." He shuddered in a long drugging piece of air.

The man held out his hand. The smile grew. "I'm The Duke of Southcliff, Leslie Stewart. If you are who I'm hoping you are, believe I've important information for you. Trust I know something that will answer your question as to where the foolish woman is. If she is who you are looking for, yes, she is foolish. However, she is also brave. Courageous. Managed to escape the prison meant for her."

"That's why I thought I knew you. The Duke of Southcliff? What kind of information?" He'd been on tenterhooks for more than twenty-four hours. He didn't need someone to tease him with innuendos. His nerves were wired, ready to snap at the slightest provocation. Hard cold facts were what he needed. Information that would send him to his wife who was in need of a stiff lecture. "Don't beat around the bush. Tell me what I need to know." Jason was tired. He flexed back and shoulder muscles that were too sore to notice while he tried to ease them. He felt as if he'd been run over by a team of horses. His head pounded from lack of sleep. Exhaustion nagged at his brain while he tried to make sense of this encounter. He still had to find his wife who must be in worse shape than he was.

"You don't look so good." The duke told him on a bland note. "I might know of a cure for what ails you. Not going to give out information without incoming facts. The gift is too precious to give to anyone who doesn't appreciate what he has. Do you understand what I'm driving at?"

"Apparently not…no, I don't understand what you're getting at. Don't tease with impertinent facts." His exhaustion overwhelmed him. He didn't need to waste any more time on guessing games along with puzzles. "Spit out the truth."

"First give me your name. Unless, of course, you've something to hide."

"Nothing to hide. Just cautious with information." If he didn't tell this man what he wished to know this conversation might go on forever. He needed to give the duke what he wanted. Realized he needed to trust in this man. Hell, what did he have to lose? Nothing. Nothing except his wife.

Seeming to understand he was about to capitulate. The duke took over the conversation again. "Which Kenworthy twin are you, Jasper or Jason?"

"Jason," he blurted, understanding he had no choice.

"Thought so. Understood the first born was wed a year ago to Maggie MacRae. Seems my wife helped her out that night she ran. Had to be the second born she was talking about this time. The MacRae daughters seem to find trouble without looking for it."

"She?" He questioned hoping the duke would elaborate.

"The woman you are looking for. I gather she doesn't expect you to want her back after the…misunderstanding the two of you had. Hope you…" For a few seconds the duke seemed to think better of continuing the conversation. "What did you do to her. What did this misunderstanding entail?"

"Nothing," Jason grit out between his teeth. "The misunderstanding was all on Tessa's part. She didn't wait for me to get home to explain. Just took off in a blind rush. I've got to find a way to convince her the truth she thinks she knows was concocted by her mother in hopes of inspiring a divorce. What her mother told her is so far from the truth it's laughable. Though what occurred between us because of the lie is no laughing matter."

"Tell me about what happened to send her scurrying away from her husband," Leslie said with patience. "If I learn some of the details, perhaps I can help do the convincing."

"You, judge and jury? Not going to give me back my wife unless I prove worthy of her? Do I have that right?" Jason asked, while he examined the man who withheld the woman he loved. His bitterness was evident to anyone with ears.

"Yes, I need to know if you hurt her. She's been silent on most aspects of what happened. My wife…" He stopped to grin with clear pleasure as he thought of the duchess. "Has this way about her. She was able to pry a few truths from Tessa's lips. One was that she was married to a twin. Between the two of us we could only think of the Seymores along with the Kenworthys. The Seymores are too old for a young woman of her caliber. Though I'm not stupid. Women do wed older men. She doesn't seem the type."

"Armstrong is Tessa's father," he told the duke with bluntness that surprised him. "She won't believe me when I tell her that truth."

This tid-bit brought a raised eyebrow from the duke. He cleared his throat before he said more, "She believes with all her heart that your father is also hers. How are you going to prove to her she is wrong?"

"Been battling that gigantic problem for more than twenty-four hours, all the time she has been missing. The letter was a ploy by her mother to get her away from me then into Abernathy's filthy hands. My father was never Anice's lover. He was a married man, wed to his one true love, my mother. He would have never cheated on her with any woman, especially a woman of Anice's caliber."

"There can be no proof one way or the other that will guarantee your words. Do you know about the relationship between Armstrong and Tessa's mother?" the duke pointed out the obvious.

"For starters, she has Armstrong's sapphire eyes. While she doesn't look like the man, thank God, she looks enough like Gracie Murray for them to be sisters." While Jason understood that argument might not be good enough, it was all he had. Tessa would need to believe him before she would come back to him.

"Gracie is Miles' daughter." Once again, the duke instructed him on the obvious. "Tessa might not listen to reason. What else have you got?"

Jason through up his hands in exasperation. "Nothing. That's my problem. There is nothing else that would convince her unless Anice recanted her story. That is something I don't expect her to ever do."

"Could you bring Armstrong along with his twin brother to speak to Tessa? Explain the relationships that went on between her mother and them. They are identical. Are they not?" the duke tossed out the question for his opinion.

"They are both willing to discuss the situation. Yes, just as my brother and I are identical there also subtle differences. Armstrong is not proud of the fact but he had an affair with Anice that lasted for more than a year. If she learned she was pregnant before he became fed up with her antics, Anice never told him she conceived. Armstrong told me he would have taken his baby girl into his home. Legitimatized her. He still will if she will acknowledge him as her father."

"That's a big step. Could Miles be her father?"

The question stopped him cold. "Why do you ask?"

"Gracie and Tessa look alike."

"As you just reminded me, the men are twins…identical twins. I'm certain there will be some resemblance between Jasper's children and mine." Jason was thinking she might have conceived. The fact was something else she would be worried about. She wouldn't want to bring a bastard into the world. She wouldn't because he didn't intend to ever give her a divorce. "One more thing, Tessa doesn't have the look of the Kenworthys. No Kenworthy ever had hair the color of hers. We all have golden-flecked brown eyes. Dark brown hair so dark the shade could be called black. She doesn't look like her mother. What do you think?"

"You've convinced me. Believe the lady is a Seymore. You're right. Tessa doesn't have the look of a Kenworthy."

"Good!"

"I'm not the person you need to convince."

"I *ken* that little fact. She's far too stubborn. Once she gets a notion into her head, she runs with it blind." Jason was sweating bullets trying to figure out the best way to put forth his case. "Persuading her to my way of thinking might take more time than I wish to spend. Are you going to take me to Tessa?"

The high-pitched scream not only stopped the conversation but the noise turned their attention back to the Abernathy home. Pain was the first idea that popped into his head. While Jason understood he should care if Anice was being abused, he didn't. The woman deserved what she wanted her daughter to feel at Abernathy's hands.

"Did you hurt Tessa in any way? You haven't answered yet. I must know before I can justify taking you to her." The calm voice asking the question jerked Jason back to what was most important.

"No. Would never hurt Tessa…or any other woman."

"When confronted by you, her eyes won't lie. That fact will tell anyone watching the truth," the duke warned.

"She isn't going to be pleased to see me. That much I'm certain of. The reason is not because I hurt her. I haven't. Would never." Jason looked back to the balcony. Anice was sitting on the railing, naked, her legs spread around Abernathy while he took her for everyone to see. The guard stood nearby as if in line for sex. Must be waiting his turn. His stomach dropped to his feet. Would those two have been doing that to Tessa? She would never have survived.

The duke looked away before he spoke again. The scene at the Abernathy home seemed to be too much for either man. "Lacie is entertaining your wife with stories of her past. All the while seeking out information that would lead me to you. Finding you here was an unforeseen bit of luck. Though I did anticipate what I would be doing if my wife was missing. Would have searched Glasgow for all possible clues."

"Is Tessa at your home?" Jason removed himself from staring at the scene unfolding on the verandah. He couldn't stomach what the three were doing. Anice's cries filled the air. "Have I proved myself to you?" The fact Tessa was under the protection of The Duke of Southcliff pleased him, released him from his fears. She was not wanting for anything. The man possessed a stellar reputation. Even though the time spent conversing with the duke kept him from seeing his wife, he was content with the situation. Even if the duke wouldn't allow him to see her today, she would be warm tonight. She would not want for anything. Tessa would have food.

"She is at my home." The duke's tone gave him more insight into the situation. "Tessa will feel betrayed by both me and my wife. I've not a doubt that in the future she will forgive. Nonetheless, she will also be angry with the two of us. Though by now, Tessa must realize she has inadvertently provided more than enough information for me to find you then bring you to her."

"Undoubtedly. Can we go now?" His impatience brimmed to over flowing. Tension ripped through his muscles along with every nerve he possessed.

The duke's hoot of laughter put a scowl on his face. To Jason there was nothing amusing about his wife thinking they were related.

"I'll go ahead of you when we reach the house. Warn Lacie that the two of you will be in need of private conversation. Believe the library would work out best. Private for the conversation that needs to be said."

"Whatever you say. I'll take my cues from Tessa. How is she? I would know that she doesn't want for anything."

"She's been given every consideration," the duke said, his voice soft. "Lacie is generous in every way. Your woman was given a hot bath, a clean gown, food along with wine for her comfort. After that, conversation with my adorable wife."

Jason stopped walking. As if surprised, the duke turned to look his way. "How did Tessa come to be with you? Should have enquired sooner. Why? She didn't run to your door. As far as I know, before today, she had no idea who you were."

"I'm certain you recall the balcony where the drama was being staged." Leslie paused a moment. "Do you think they were doing that for our benefit. No, perhaps not. Nonetheless, Nelson must have known we were watching the house." He paused. "Back to the question at hand. The guard caught your wife going down the pole holding the upper floor patio to the building. Bet she did that as a child." This time he cleared his throat. "At the time, my wife and I were taking a leisurely stroll through the neighborhood. At Lacie's bequest, I convinced the man it would be most prudent of him to allow me take the girl with me after Tessa told him she wasn't pleased to be in his company."

"Oh…how?" Jason had some ideas about a few different ways. None of them polite. All of them included violence of some sort.

"A quick right to the jaw. I know precisely where to strike. The man crumpled." The duke's succinct reply gave Jason a reason to smile that he hadn't felt for more than a day.

"Oh…so most of the rumors about you are true." Jason snorted the statement. He'd heard quite a bit about the Duke of Southcliff.

"Never heard rumors about me. Gossip is for women. You shouldn't believe everything you hear. Most of it is unfounded. Not true."

"Just bet you haven't," Jason said with amusement lacing his words. "No one would dare spread gossip about the Duke of Southcliff."

The rest of the distance to the house was spent in silence. Jason ran over all the things he needed to say to Tessa in his head. Tossed out a few ideas that had no substance. As Leslie said, he went inside first. Escorted Tessa to the library while he waited in the entrance to their big home. Tessa would understand something was going on when she was left to fend for herself in the library with a closed door.

The gentle hand on his shoulder surprised him. He turned to encounter Leslie's wife. "You're the husband. Do you have a name?" Lacie asked while she kept him company. "Suppose you do. Certain you gave it to Leslie before he had any intention of allowing you to speak to your wife. She loves you."

His surprise would show on his face if he didn't school his features. Tessa never told him she loved him. "Under the circumstances that's nice of you to point out. There were times over the last day plus hours I had my doubts." To his ears, he sounded gruff, rough around the edges. Enough so he needed to temper his emotions. Didn't want to come across that way to the duchess. Least of all Tessa when he finally got a chance to speak with her. "She did run with very little provocation."

"Tessa told me you're her brother…half-brother…different mothers. That fact is enough enticement to leave. Is there any truth to that? Brother married to a sister is frowned on by most societies."

"None whatsoever." He found he was shaking his head. "Preposterous."

"You're certain?"

"Couldn't be more positive. Armstrong Seymore, I believe is her true father. All the facts lead to that conclusion. Though Miles could be her father. Anything is possible. They both had relationships with her mother at the time of her conception. Armstrong's dealings with Anice lasted a year."

"You don't doubt it. Why is Armstrong the best candidate?"

"Yes, the man, Miles, was only with Anice one night."

"Anice MacRae? The woman whose daughter fled for her life at the Christmas Eve party? I remember that night. Had a brief conversation with the girl, Maggie. Is Tessa her sister then? Interesting."

"The one and the same. Maggie is wed to my brother, Jasper. They are happy." He didn't understand why he was pouring out his thoughts. He barely knew this woman. Ah, he remembered Leslie's words to him. Lacie had a way of drawing people into conversations. Enticing them to reveal truths. That's what she'd done with Tessa. He imagined he should be pleased with Lacie's gift.

"I gave her my card. Told her to keep it close. If she needed anything she was to come to me. Never heard from her. Hoped she got away from the man. When I learned she married Jasper Kenworthy, I thought that was well done of her. The two of you bad boys have a way of finding trouble, now, don't you?"

"Is that a rhetorical question?" Jason asked monotone. He never looked for trouble. Never expected Anice to butt into his and Tessa's business.

"No, it's a fact. Why isn't Miles the father? Did you tell me? Must not have been listening too well."

Yes, he'd already told her. Went for a different approach. "He slept one night with Anice. Decided the time was not spent in a good way. Told me he took precautions. At the time, he didn't know his brother had been sleeping with her for over a year. The relationship might have developed for one purpose…to confuse issues that might or might not have been planned. It's possible Anice knew at the time that she conceived Armstrong's child."

"With that woman anything is possible," Lacie agreed.

"Tessa is waiting. Scared. Understands something is going on behind her back," the duke said as he entered the foyer where he waited. "Don't give her that scalding lecture that is pounding around in your head until you've made love to her at least once, maybe several times. She won't appreciate the verbal tongue lashing. She was doing what she thought best for you, not for her."

"I'll take your advice."

Stomach rolling as if he was on a storm swept ocean, he stepped into the library. When he saw her, his breath caught behind his teeth. She was such a beautiful sight to him. Could have lost her. He swallowed hard, telling himself she was more nervous than he was. He saw the trembling of her shoulders. A few beats of his heart passed with lightning speed. Her chin tilted upward. She was now showing her stubborn side. He wasn't certain how to begin the conversation. Reminded himself he promised to forego the lecture.

Jason wished to rant at her for being so damn stubborn. "There is not going to be a divorce. You can get that little fact out of your…out of your female brain and keep it out." Jason didn't like the way he sounded. His voice was too harsh. His words too demanding.

~ * ~

"We can't remain married. You're my half-brother. Things like that are just not done. You must file for a divorce. We have no choice."

"You have a way of tempting me to throttle you. Shake you until you see some reason." Jason paused while he stared at her hard. Ripped air into his lungs as if that would calm the steaming tempest inside him.

"Simon is not, I repeat, is not your father. He is mine as well as Jasper's. He's fathered no girls."

Tessa's chin tilted higher. In defiance, her eyes blazed while she spoke in the most commanding voice he'd heard from her. "Mother said she slept with him. Why would she lie about that when she knew the falsehood would break my heart?" Her breath caught in her throat when she said the condemning words.

His brows shot up. After that little acknowledgement of surprise, he stepped forward. He was so close she could watch the rise and fall of his chest when he breathed. "Anice lied. Why, you ask? She does want to hurt you. Needs to have her way in all things concerning her daughters. She must owe something extravagant to Abernathy. Paying that debt off when Maggie married Jasper must have made her desperate for her youngest daughter to be with him."

"You don't know that. Don't know any of that." Tessa was surprised with the conviction she heard in her voice. For over twenty-four hours, she told herself the same story. While there might be conviction there, moisture clogged her throat. Threatened to spill from her eyes if she couldn't keep tight command of her emotions.

"The reasons…I know my father loved his wife. Understood he would never disrespect her with another woman in his bed. Just as I would never do the same to you. He believed in as well as kept his marital vows."

Tessa hoped with all her heart his words were true. There was no way to confirm the accusations or to deny them. "This is all too confusing. I…I'm not certain of anything. Jason…" Her legs shaking so hard she didn't think she could stand a moment longer; she slumped onto the sofa. "Please."

"Look at what is obvious to the eye." Jason tossed his hands in the air as if exasperated by her reluctance to believe her.

Her gaze shot to him. Under the conditions as they stood now, she asked herself why she was so willing to trust her mother. "What is that? What is obvious to the eye? What does it have to do with proving who my father is?" She wanted to understand why he believed as he did. "I don't know what you are getting at."

"Anice wanted the divorce so she could give you to Abernathy.

What better way to get her wishes than to concoct a lie? The woman has no motherly feelings toward any of her daughters. She doesn't care a wit about her offspring except for what they can do for her. The two of you, Maggie and you, were able to find a man to marry without her advice. Abernathy still covets you. That is a proven fact."

"When we were still in Ireland everyone believed me to be the next target." Her voice softened, wavered with indecision. "We thought that when you married me, I would be safe from Abernathy. It's obvious that's not true. That still doesn't prove Simon isn't my father." Tessa was trying to go over everything in her head that had happened.

"All true. Doesn't prove that he is. There are other facts that point away from my father and directly to the Seymores." He dipped into his reserve of patience. "You are safe being wed to me unless you fall into her plans then run off with nowhere to go. Thought you went to your mother as the letter suggested."

"Are you lecturing me?" Her whispered question made his eyelids flinch. "You're yelling. I don't need that right now."

"No, sorry, promised I would refrain until I have you in my care again. The duke also told me you weren't going anywhere with me unless it was by your choice. So, we should move forward with caution. I do want you to come home tonight. Want you in my bed. Need to hold you in my arms. Reassure you we are not related by blood. Give comfort as well as receive security. I'm not in such great shape myself. Have not slept since you disappeared. Do you wish to spend another night alone? Scared? Looking over your shoulder? Even here you are close, too close for comfort to Nelson Abernathy."

Her smile felt good on him. Needed more of the same.

"The duke is very protective." Tessa couldn't help but lift her shoulders in a tight shrug. "Even of me. Suppose I should be grateful. He understood I needed help. With his wife he reached out to me. Found you. Brought you to me. Not so positive I was pleased when I understood what he did."

"No more protective of you than me. When I thought of what your mother planned for you, I shuddered. Raced all over Glasgow to find you. Searched the homeless camps. Went to the bakery. Thought as the letter suggested, you might have gone to your mother's. I went through every damn door of her house looking for any sign you were there or had been there."

A breath caught, stuck in her throat. Jason looked up when he heard the sound. Mother couldn't have been too pleased. She doesn't like to be interrupted at night. Tessa watched Jason as he paced the room. It was clear how agitated he was. "You tell me Simon can't possibly be my father? I know you went to Armstrong. What did he say?"

"While you still have doubts, I don't have one about my father not being yours. Armstrong thinks you are his daughter."

"Why?"

"He shared a bed with your mother for over a year. Unless one takes precautions, there is usually a child. Odds are stacked in favor of Armstrong. Miles slept with her once. Says he took precautions. Knows he's not the father. Couldn't say he wasn't disappointed. Decided that was one time too many. Believe your mother wished to compare twin brothers."

"There is no proof."

"True. You have the look of a Seymore not a Kenworthy. My mother's hair was near black just as my fathers. They both had brown eyes. Chances of blue seem very slim don't you think? Especially the sapphire of yours. It's clear to anyone looking at you, you possess Armstrong's eyes. The pale blond of your hair is known in his family. His mother had the same color hair as yours. There are other similarities. Coincidence…maybe, but I doubt it."

"Oh…" She felt struck dumb with too much information.

"Come here," he said, his voice gentled. A husky, rough sound of need followed. Looked at her with the slow burn of hunger in his eyes. "Please." Jason held out his arms to welcome her. "I won't bite. Believe you've tamed me."

His eyes darkened. Using the arms of the chair to support her weight, she stood. Her legs still wobbled. What she understood more than anything, she needed Jason to hold her. She wanted to believe him right about her parentage.

After she stepped toward him, Jason closed the distance between them. She found herself pulled hard against his chest. His warm arms locked around her, supporting her. She snuggled against him, understanding how much she needed this man.

Jason stroked her back, with slow precise moves, he touched each bone, lingered for a beat of her heart until he moved down to the next then the next. Both hands closed around her rear. Pulled her until she felt his need against her belly.

He lifted her. Held her tight against his chest, “We can’t make love in the duke’s library. Someone might walk in on us. Though I doubt either the duke or the duchess would interrupt our discussion. Can’t take the chance.” He raised her as if she weighed nothing then sat on the sofa where she’d been before she came to him.

His mouth captured hers. Mated. Brought back all the memories she never wanted to forget. His scent so familiar, she would know the spicey aroma anywhere. Her tongue met his with a heated response that sent vivid sensations all the way through her to her toes. He ran his hand along her side to cup a breast. She made a husky female sound of pleasure as he deepened the mating of their tongues.

Pulling away he stared down at her. Repeated the words as if had to remind himself. “We can’t do this here.” Still his kiss deepened. Touched everywhere. When he pulled away. “Are you coming home with me?”

“I don’t know yet.”

“Does there need to be more convincing?” He questioned while his thumb stroked idly across the tip of her covered breast.

He knew what he did. His intentions were far from pure. They were self-centered. “What if you’re wrong about Simon…Armstrong.” Even she heard the hesitancy in her words. She so wished to believe everything Jason told her. “What if Anice…” She broke off when he unfastened the front of her gown enough so he could caress tender, sensitive flesh with the palm of his hand.

“I’m not wrong. Come home with me.”

“What will happen if I accept the fact that Armstrong is my father?” She still had genuine questions.

“He will make you legitimate. You won’t be a bastard any longer,” he told her as his hands continued to find more sensitive places.

Her ability to think seemed to vanish with each stroke of his warm hands. "No." She stopped his hand from moving beneath her skirt even though she'd spread her legs in silent invitation. "Not here. Not now. We…what if Miles is my father?"

"You have Armstrong's eyes. True fact," He found tender flesh of her ankle. Treated it to slow strokes of his fingers. "Have I convinced you?"

The knock on the door startled both of them. Jason pulled her gown closed. She fumbled with the buttons.

"Everything alright in there?" The duke stood at the door.

His voice brought Tessa back to the reality of what they were doing. While she didn't believe the duke would be surprised, she didn't wish to be caught with Jason's hand beneath her skirt.

"I'm fine," she said with what she hoped was enough volume to be heard through the heavy oak door.

"Feeling pretty good myself," Jason chuckled as he understood the implications that he put forth. Leslie would understand.

"You've reached an understanding I assume?" he questioned. "Lacie wants to know what's going to happen. Always the little fixer, she has to make plans for the evening."

Jason's snort of laughter took Tessa by surprise. "Come in." He looked at her, adjusted her hair the best he could. "Don't enjoy talking through doors."

"Jason."

When Tessa moved to get off his lap, he pulled her back. "A united front," he whispered next to her ear. Touched with his tongue. "With you sitting on my lap, your hair disheveled and your face flushed that will be all the evidence the duke needs to come to the right conclusions."

His warm breath moved tiny strands of hair along her cheek. The tickling warmth sent little sensations causing goose bumps along her arms.

"I'm sitting on your thighs."

"I know. It could be better. You could be straddling me. Could be deep inside you, giving you pleasure. The duke would understand. Would back out of the room."

His male laughter caused more blood to rush to her face. She punched him on the chest just as the duke stepped through the door, his duchess peaking around him, hidden by his huge male body.

"You've got all the kinks worked out?" Lacie asked as she danced around her husband to stand in front of him.

"Not yet," Jason told them while his hand caressed the curve of her hip. "Plan on that later tonight. All the kinks will vanish."

"Tessa is convinced I take it?" Those words coming from the duke. "You can stay here the night, Tessa, if you still have some doubts."

"She doesn't wish to remain here though the hospitality was wonderful for her," Jason chimed in before she could respond.

"I do have some doubts. Not like before. I'm mostly convinced. In any case there is nothing that can be done to prove beyond a shadow of a doubt who my father is."

"I might spread some light on this. I am the oldest." Jasper stepped around him. "If you're wondering how I discovered you, the duke sent a message to me. I was waiting across from the Abernathy house wondering what happened to you. Afraid you tried to rescue Tessa by sneaking into the house. Was glad to realize you were safe and sound."

"Sorry. Things happened so fast I didn't have a chance to—"

"All of you will stay for dinner." Lacie stepped farther into the room. Her hands on her hips she continued to take charge of the moment. "I insist. We can talk more after our stomachs are full. What do you all say?"

"Would like to take my wife home."

"By Tessa's own words, she is not yet convinced," Lacie reminded them.

"Said I could lend a helping hand," Jasper said as he studied the couple. "If I'm staying, does anyone mind if I send for Maggie?"

Lacie clapped her hands together. "Would love to see Maggie again. We did have a nice chat that evening before she got away from Abernathy's men. Gave her my card. Told her I would help if she needed anything. Do you think she remembers me?"

Jasper spoke up with a warm smile as if remembering something from his past. "After she snuggled her little nose against my chest to warm herself, I was smitten. All she needed then was help from me. Must have fallen in love with her that very moment."

"You will have such a wonderful love story to tell your children," Lacie said while she held onto Leslie's arm. She pressed her head against him. "Won't they? Just as we have stories for our grandchildren."

"You going to tell them about that first kiss in the stable?" A dark eyebrow shot up. "I wouldn't tell them about some of the other things we did either."

"Oh, my, suppose you're right." Her hands were on her hot cheeks. "Best we go have a drink before dinner. Seems she is recovering."

"I'll send the coach for Maggie," the duke spoke up.

~ * ~

Anice had no idea what she'd gotten into when she agreed to have a threesome with Nelson along with his guard. The guard's name was Charles. He had stamina, more than any man she'd been with. Nelson was asleep on the bed. Charles sat against the headboard, his big hands behind his head ready to go at it again.

"You want to go another round, sweetheart? I love sex with a beautiful woman, willing or not," he asked as his gaze roamed the length of her naked body, lingered on her breasts then lower until it touched upon the apex of her thighs. "Have you had enough? I haven't."

"I'm sore. Not used to anything this decadent," she told him honestly. Though the pleasure was more than she ever expected. The man was rough, hard around the edges. Nonetheless, he knew how to give a woman just what she wanted. There was nothing about either man that bored her.

Charles sipped his wine, seeming to watch the play of her breasts as she moved. "Your daughter is a sweet little thing. Disappointed we lost her. Would have enjoyed using her when Abernathy was through with her."

"Yes, a sweet little thing," Anice said with a shimmer of anger intoned in her voice. She rose to pour herself a glass of wine. Walked to the door of the balcony.

Nelson took her on that railing with Jason and Leslie watching.

The two weren't immune to deviant sexual play. Anice rummaged through the pocket of Nelson's frock coat. Found a cheroot. With it between her fingers, she walked to Charles.

He grinned while he lit her smoke. Walking back to the door, she tugged in a long drink of smoke. Held the taste in her lungs until she needed to breathe again. When she turned to face the man, "I still have two daughters left. Unmarried. They might be candidates for a wife for Nelson. Doubt it though. If he catches them alone, unguarded he will bring them here for his use. He's perverse that way."

A wealth of ideas slammed into her. None of them good for her daughters. What did she care? They were all sluts. Deserved to be treated as such. Nelson would pay for their virginity. After he took what he wanted most, he would keep them as he intended to keep Tessa or…she knew people who bought as well as sold women. The trade was lucrative. He would sell them to the highest bidder. She knew a pimp who might want to help, Craig Halsey. Hmm…that was a thought. She would set him to watching her daughters. If they made a mistake either one of them…or both…might be his. What did she care? She tried. Found an excellent husband for Maggie. She refused her advice. Tessa did the same.

She would need to get to them fast. Both Nellie along with Fannie were playing with the social group that represented aristocracy in Scotland. They were both beautiful women. Neither would have difficulty finding a man to wed.

With her youngest along with her oldest, she failed to bring them to heal. She couldn't fail again.

Epilogue

"Are you satisfied?" Jason held Tessa in his arms. The sweet scent of lavender coupled with sunshine filled his senses. He knew even after a year, she still harbored a few doubts about her parentage. What he didn't know at the time, the duke also sent for the Seymore twins who joined them at dinner that evening.

The evening was a memorable one. So much information was exchanged, he thought his head would explode. By the end, everyone conceded the fact that Armstrong was the father of Tessa. Now they had a child, a boy. He looked the spitting image of himself. Brown eyes, flecked with gold, dark brown hair that was nearing black. Maybe if they had a little girl, she would inherit the sapphire eyes of her mother. He didn't understand how characteristics were passed down from one generation to another. They just were.

"Yes, Armstrong's testimony gave me reason to believe he is my father. I'm glad. I do like the man…both brothers. Armstrong made me legitimate. Can't quite come to call him father though he deserves the name."

Tessa sat up, her breasts brushed across his chest then his arm sending a bolt of flames lashing his body. He needed to set his emotions aside to deal with the very real fact she put herself into danger by running off without seeking help from anyone. Over the last year, he never got around to the lecture she deserved. She always found a way to distract him. Just as she was doing now. The distraction was pleasant…no…more than pleasant.

Seeming to understand what was on his mind besides making love to her again, she ran her finger across his lips. Her wide smile held a wealth of information. She meant to make the lecture more difficult. Tessa curled her fingers around some of his chest hair. With the tip of a nail followed the line to his erection. Closed her fingers around him. Played with all the knowledge she gained over the year. Touched him with her mouth. Slid her tongue down his length.

"You're toying with fire."

"I know," her female purr of awareness sent his nerves into a tailspin. "You don't want me to stop." She looked up then followed her fingertip with small nipping kisses down his chest back to his pulsing need. "You know you don't. I don't wish to stop either."

They didn't cease until they were both sated.

He sent his hand through her hair, letting the cool silken waves unravel between his fingers. Her scent floated around her. After the lovemaking, Tessa snuggled against him, relaxed. Breathing softly.

"Are you ready to have another baby? We haven't taken precautions the last few times." Jason touched each bone that went down the middle of her back. Touched each one as if learning about her for the first time. "The boy is only four months. Is it too soon?"

"Yes, I'm ready. Our son needs someone to play with. Another boy, I think, would be nice."

"I want a girl. Could we have twins?"

"Anything is possible."

"I do love you, Jason Kenworthy."

"I love you too… Tessa, you are my life. Always will be."

COMING SOON
by the author
at
Rogue Phoenix Press

Fannie
Good Girls Book Eight

Chapter One

Glasgow 1833

Fannie MacRae stared at the march of vehicles parading down the length of High Street. The steady clop of horse's hooves became a constant. From the harbor the sound of orders filtered into the other noise. If she wasn't so sick, she wouldn't be very angry with her sister. Nellie disappeared with her beau. Left her by herself.

The River Clyde flowed to her left and the Cathedral of St. Mungo to her right. Cold winds blew off the river. She coughed, wheezing as she tried to guzzle air from the busy street. Her throat was sore, raw. Tears filled her eyes as she battled the cold wind. She didn't want to be here. Should have stood firm against her sister's imploring way. Wished she was home in her nice warm bed sipping on a cup of warm mulled cider. Didn't understand how her sister, Nellie, managed to talk her into this scavenger hunt. She'd been the third wheel as her sister was paired with her new beau.

As soon as she was able to sweet talk some man out of a monogrammed handkerchief, she could go home. *A damn monogramed handkerchief!* How the sweet devil was she to do that especially when she disliked speaking to strangers? Could never figure out the necessary words. A blast of cold air swept her hat from her head.

"Oh no!" Too late to stop the event, her hand flew to the top of her head to catch air. "Stop!" What utter nonsense as if her hat could understand what she was yelling. Fannie ran after the tumbling hat as it danced along the sidewalk then careened into the street. She bent to retrieve the wretched thing. At the last second, she pulled back. "No!" A passing carriage ran over it crushing the hat flat. Her arms whirled, holding her back from falling into the path of another vehicle. With her hand pressed tight against her chest, she sucked in a gasp of city scented air. "Never liked the blasted hat anyway," Fannie muttered to no one in particular. She pressed her hands against her chest attempting to fill her lungs.

Letting out a slow breath of air, she was relieved she'd not dashed into the path of the vehicle. Thankful, her spinning arms stopped her. Her hand once again hovering over her chest she felt the pounding of her heart. Without clear thought about what she was doing, Fannie walked turning down one street then another. She didn't know where she was headed. In a daze, Fannie stopped a few people to ask if they would mind handing over their monogramed handkerchief for a good cause.

Each time a crack of laughter would follow her question then the one word "No. You have got to be joking." One man even called her a little bitch after her query. Exhausted from the evening, Fannie leaned against the brick wall of a building watching traffic on the street pass by. Closing her eyes for a moment, she listened to the rumbling of the wheels. Heard the chatter of people as they rushed to get home from a long day of work. Realizing she wasn't certain where she was, she fought the rise of panic. The people she now saw were mostly men. The women strolling the street were dressed to show off their bodies. Even in this weather, they were scantily clad. She thought the women must be ladies of the evening. That brought her mind to attention.

What did she know about ladies of the evening? Nothing. Did she wish to learn about them. No. Still, she was a bit fascinated as she watched the different ladies approach various men. They would posture. Sometimes money would exchange hands then the lady would go with the gentleman.

She was shocked to watch a man pull down the bodice of a

woman's gown then fondle her. The lady pushed her bare breast forward. With his other hand the man pulled her skirt up. The woman wiggled seeming to enjoy the contact. A deep flush of heat crept up to settle on her cheeks. Pressing her cold hands on her skin didn't eliminate her heat flushed face.

This place is not somewhere I should be. No kidding, I should be somewhere safe.

Nellie would be at the home where all this started. The various couples would set out all the objects they gathered in order to figure out who won the game. Her sister would be drinking punch, chatting with her new beau.

Hah! Here I'm still out here in the cold. I should stop this nonsense and go home. I don't know where I am. Just keep moving. Put one foot in front of the other. You are bound to see a landmark you will recognize.

She turned in an attempt to retrace her route. Dear Lord, she was tired. Her cold wore her down. Her throat ached. With dazed eyes, the buildings along her route swayed, swirled with terrifying speed. Fannie placed her hand on the wall to steady herself. Looking up then down the street, she searched for a cab. There was a row of them down the street a bit. They were lined up in front of a large three-story home. If she could make it there, she would be on her way home to her warm bed.

Where was her sister? Fannie couldn't recall where she was supposed to meet Nellie and the other couples on this hunt. Was it where they began this ridiculous game? She didn't understand the why of this game. The purpose eluded her. There didn't seem to be any reasoning behind asking people to hand over their belongings. Told her sister several times she didn't wish to participate in the scavenger hunt. Nellie begged. She needed a third person so she could be with the young man who captured her heart this week. Nellie never stayed with any man for long. Nellie would explain to her she was looking for another Jasper or Jason. There eldest sister married Jasper, the youngest was wed to Jason. They were both madly in love with their husbands. The two middle sisters were still single. They made a pact not to settle for anything less than true love.

For a few beats of her heart, Fannie closed her eyes hoping when she opened them the world would no longer be spinning out of control. To her dismay, opening her eyes the desired results were not in play. The road seemed to undulate. The hacks carrying people were hazy. She didn't know if she could put one foot in front of the other. The line of cabs seemed farther away.

Which way to go? She pushed away from the wall holding her up. Swayed on her feet for a second before she pulled herself together. Just take one step then another one. You can do it.

Wetting her lips she looked up then down the street where she stood. Had no earthly clue as to which way to go. She was lost, acknowledged the fact standing in this spot would never get her home. She could ask if anyone knew how to get back to the cathedral. Everyone in Glasgow would know where the church was located. She could try to walk the blocks to the home where the hacks were lined up. Seemed that was her only rational option. Wished one of those vehicles would see her then come pick her up. Why would they? The drivers would believe she was a lady of the evening.

In the very least, she could hope one of the cabs would take her home. How did she get into this mess? What she wouldn't give to see someone she knew.

The horrible smell caught her attention before the words. "Look what I found. Just standing here all pretty like waiting for the two of us to come along. What do you think? Will she do us for *wee* bit of fun? Do you think she's as pretty with all her clothes off. Would like to have a taste of her." A burly looking man spoke with his friend.

The voice was too close to her. The rancid scent of sweat filled the air. She caught the odor of liquor on his breath. She couldn't seem to swallow a lungful of rancid air. Fannie cringed against the brick wall, wishing for a way to melt into the stone. Her hands shook. She balled her fingers into fists to steady herself.

"A pretty lady…too lovely for the likes of us. *Tha i blasta*. She is too tasty," the man mumbled, his voice gruff with emotion.

Fannie wished she understood what they were saying. No one talked that way anymore, at least not in the city.

"Tasty morsal if I do be sayin' so myself," the other offered, touching her cheek with the back of his hand. She pushed against the brick wall. "You be comin' with us, little lady. We'll be showin' you *feasgar math*. That would be a good evening for you. For us too."

"Don't want a good evening with the likes of you," she muttered as one of the men in front of her blocked her path. His beefy hands were placed on either side of her head while his stomach pressed against her.

"We want you for the night. Not giving you a choice. You're going to come along with us. We got a room just down the street. The bed is ready and waiting. We'll share you."

Fannie shook her head. She did understand a bit of Gaelic but not much. These men were raw, hard looking, too strong for her to fight. Their clothing was ragged. Both wore beards. Must be straight off the docks. In that case, she might not be too far from the river. If she found the river, she might be able to find the cathedral. "No!" Panic glued her to the wall. No, must get to that line of carriages.

"Ah, *tha blasta eun bheag*," the second man said as his grin widened. His hands were still on the wall on either side of her head. She felt the heat of his body pushing against her. Fannie tried to swallow the lump of dread caught in her throat.

A tasty little bird? Is that what these men thought about her?

Deep in her chest Fannie's heart thundered. Seemed she couldn't catch a breath of air. She tried to slip beneath his arms. He caught her by her shoulders. Shook her, her head banging against the bricks.

"You dinna be sayin' much. I do like a woman who doesn't talk a lot. Now come along with us. We'll be showin' you a good time."

"No," her voice held a calmness she didn't feel. Understanding the importance of this moment, she needed to get away from these two men before she became their evening's entertainment. "No!" she reiterated as loud as her raw throat would allow her. "No…don't want… I'm not what you believe."

Fannie closed her eyes for a moment thinking of ways to remove herself from these men. Breathing in the tainted air surrounding these two, she steeled herself to move fast. With a quick jerk of her knee, she brought it as hard as she could between the man's legs. The shriek of pain coupled with the loosening of his fingers on her shoulder gave her the chance she needed. The man cursed then fell to his knees. She lunged away. Raced down the street. Didn't bother to look over her shoulder to see if the two men followed. Headed straight for the line of carriages in front of her.

"Bitch!" one of the men called out as he gave chase. "Stop right there! You're going to pay for what you did to my friend."

No, she wasn't going to pay. Getting caught by these men was not her plan. Running, she headed for the well-lit house where she could hire a cab. She ran for about five minutes. Raced around two people who were chatting in the middle of the sidewalk to plow into another man. She hit him with such force, she fell back to land on her rump. She sat, her hands at her hips keeping her upright. Breathing hard she looked into a handsome face…a too handsome face…a pretty face. She shivered. The man was dressed in black evening attire. The white shirt beneath the frock coat heightened his prettiness. He twirled a cane then leaned on it as he looked at her from head to toe. Her stomach twisted into a knot of revulsion.

The man was…pretty, slender for his height. His blue eyes twinkled as if he just found a present. Fannie shuddered. Didn't wish to be this man's present. The smile he flashed her was wicked, his teeth white. He looked as if he wanted to devour her or feed her to the wolves. Well, the wolves were after her. At least with the men chasing her, she understood the danger. With this man she did not. What did he want with her? Whatever it was she didn't plan to have anything to do with him. Fannie didn't have one doubt he had something in mind. The look the man graced her with reminded her of Lord Abernathy when he stared at Maggie.

"This *Caileaag bheag* is ours," her first attacker said with a low growl.

The handsome man looked at her a sly expression on his too pretty face. He pointed to the men. "What do you say, little girl? Are you theirs' for the night? If not, you will come with me. I've a cab waiting."

"No! No to both of you." Fannie felt as if she must be jumping from the pan into the fire. There was no other recourse. She scooted back, distancing herself. Her gaze shifted from pretty face to the burly seamen. "I'm not anyone's plaything. Not for sale. Not going with any of you." With those words she realized what both men thought of her. They believed she was here to sell herself to them.

"You're one against two!" The man she kneed in the groin shouted from a short distance while he shook his fist in pretty face's direction. "You can't stop us from having what we found."

"Seems this little girl packs a wallop. Besides, you lost the little girl. Didn't you. She says she doesn't wish to have anything to do with the likes of you," the man told her pursuers as the man she kneed in the groin limped up to them still holding himself.

"She's got to pay for hurting me."

"No, I'm not leaving her with the two of you. You lost. I won. I've got the little girl with me. She doesn't wish to go with you." He turned to her. "My name is Craig, Craig Halsey. Do you wish for me to save you from these two thugs? Speak up. I don't have all night."

"Yes." She did wish to find herself safe from these two men who wanted her for themselves. Fannie also needed to keep herself safe from Craig. She didn't trust him. This man was smooth which made him a dangerous agent. She wasn't a whore. They believed she was. What else could she do? Accepting this man's help went against the grain. This man who she didn't know could mean her harm. She needed to deal with one hazard at a time.

"Come along then." Craig took her by her hand then helped her stand. "I'll get you somewhere out of the cold. Give you something nice and warm to drink along with a place to sleep. After that we can see what will happen. Got some plans for you. Something I believe you will appreciate."

His hand held her elbow tight as if she might run. The row of carriages was still in front of her. Perhaps she should try to get away. Where would she run to? At least this man didn't have a horrible stench around him. No, but he did smell of too much cologne, a sweet scent, cloying in the extreme. Her instincts told her she needed to flee. This man didn't mean her well.

When Fannie looked in front of her, she realized why the two men allowed her to go with Craig. A carriage waited for him with a driver along with a second man standing by the door to help them inside. He was taking her away. She couldn't go with this man. Where did he intend to take her. What the devil was going on here?

Mother? No, she was seeing things. Her mind was fogged over. Her mother wasn't sitting in the vehicle

Fannie dug in her heels. Pulling back, she said with strong definition. "No! I will not get in that carriage with you." She would fight until her strength left her. Prying at his fingers, she tried to free herself.

Craig looked to her then back to the two men who accosted her. "I see. You wish to go back with these men? You would like to become their entertainment. I can tell you they won't pay you as well as I can." He told her one eyebrow arching as if he knew the answer ahead of time.

So, Craig wanted her for the same thing as these two. She wasn't a whore. Wasn't selling her body to any man. Was that truly her mother sitting in the carriage? Abernathy? Could he be there too? Her mind was playing tricks with her. Swallowing her fear, "No just tell me in which direction the river is then I will be on my way. There is no need for you to bother with me. I can find my way home." By the look in his eyes, Fannie acknowledged the fact Craig wasn't going to allow her to leave him. She needed to think of something else.

"I'll take you to the river in the carriage. No need for you to walk." One more time he held her elbow. Pushed her in the direction of the waiting transport. "It will be much more comfortable for you in my vehicle. We will be able to talk about your future. You are lovely. Will command top dollar I've no doubt."

She was both annoyed with the man as well as terrified. Her options were limited to one. "No…" Fannie wrenched away. The man lunged for her. Caught nothing but air.

"Little bitch!" He swore as he started after her.

In that split second before she jerked her arm lose, Fannie realized Craig held no good intentions toward her. If she stepped inside that carriage, she would be his for whatever purpose he decided. She didn't know what that was. Nonetheless she felt as if his purpose was not one she would like. If that woman was her mother, she would find herself in Lord Abernathy's bed. Gasping for oxygen Fannie ran as hard as she could. Stumbled once then a second time. Heard the pounding of Craig's feet behind her. He had to be gaining on her. Would catch her. She pushed herself harder asking for the last bit of strength she possessed.

That light in the house she first saw what seemed like hours ago, beckoned to her. She had to find safety there before pretty face could catch up to her. Fannie didn't know what would happen at the house. Had to be better than what was going to happen to her here. Well, it couldn't be any worse. She needed to take the chance there would be a welcoming committee that would give her the necessary aid…a nonthreatening welcome…a safe shelter away from the elements acting against her. Tearing down the street then through the gate into the backyard, she flung herself up the steps.

"Help!" Her fists pounded on the door. Craig was close behind her. The only reason he hadn't caught her yet was because she surprised him. "Help! Please!"

"Bitch! Come back here! I'm not letting you get away from me." Craig passed through the gate just as the door opened.

"Help me," Fannie bent over at her waist gasping for air almost fell into the room. "Please…please don't let him get me. I..."

A huge man, his skin as black as midnight stood in the opening. Muscles in his arms bulged. When he stared at her, she saw a light of compassion in his dark brown eyes. "Halsey, what brings you here? Suppose it's this little lady you're panting after. She doesn't look as if she wishes to become part of your stable."

A petite, redheaded lady stood behind the huge man, a broom in her hand. Her eyes blazed blue fire while her ample bosom heaved with indignation. She stepped forward. Swung the broom down on Craig's head. "Get the hell out of my yard and off my steps, Halsey! You're not welcome here! Be gone! Pimping little girls who say no to you is not honest. She looks to be too sweet for the likes of your clients." She hit the man again then again as Craig staggered down the steps to land hindside down on the gravel walkway.

"She's mine!" Craig yelled shaking his fist at the woman who defended her. "You'll see. I'll get her back. Just you wait. She will be mine." He stood, dusted off his pants then walked from the yard.

During the altercation the huge man ushered her into the home. He seemed to be a gentle giant. She stood in the kitchen not knowing what to do with herself, shifting from one foot to the other. Delicious scents of food wafted around her. To Fannie's mortification, her stomach rumbled.

"You hungry? We've got lots of food," the woman asked with a charming smile lighting up her features. She was probably in her late thirties. Seemed to have a motherly streak in her. "I can feed you then we'll see what else I can do for you. Sit down. You can tell me why this horrible man was chasing you." Kindness was written in her expression, in her eyes the way she looked at her.

A monogramed handkerchief. Who would believe?

As if magically, a bowl of soup appeared in front of her. She sipped the broth letting the warmth soothe her raw throat. Found pieces of tender beef along with vegetables within to help satisfy the hunger rumbling in her stomach. She didn't even realize she was hungry. Fannie ate until she could hold no more. Her throat still felt raw, though the soup soothed. She rested her hand on her throat. The proprietress of this house was patient. While she ate no one spoke.

The woman sat down across from her. "Now, I'm Hannah. In case you didn't realize, this house is a brothel. You don't look like a woman who would be seeking a job here. Halsey, the man who was chasing you, is a pimp. So, what can I do for you besides keep you from his filthy hands?"

Fannie had a few ideas about what a pimp was. She wasn't certain she could ask Hannah. Made no difference. Her throat was now so scratchy she couldn't speak except in a painful whimper. She tried to tell Hannah she was lost. The words came out in a croak. If she could speak, Hannah might put her on one of those carriages outside her home.

"You need a doctor, I see." The woman strode to the hall. "Angus, send for Saint. The lady needs some doctoring. Seems she can't speak a word without sounding like a frog. I'll give her a good dose of laudanum so she can rest. Sometimes on a Friday night Saint is busy until the *wee* hours of dawn. He might not return my summons right away. We need to put her in a bed where she can rest."

The big man nodded. "Aye…I'll send Jacko for Saint. He'll make good speed. I'll help you get the little sparrow to a room. We've that empty one at the end of the hall last door on the right. Will that do? Too bad she's not in the business. This one is a pretty thing. No wonder Halsey was after her. She'd make a mint for him. What do you suppose she was doing in our neck of the city."

"Thank you, you are right about this girl. We could use someone like this one. She's as pretty as a peach. Would guess all the gents would want her," Hannah murmured then turned her attention back to her. "Come with me." She held out her hand. "Angus and I are going to put you to bed. Perhaps in the morning after seeing the doctor, you'll be able to tell me who you are. You *dinna* have a thing to fear. I'll take care of you. Can send you home as soon as the doc gives you a clean bill of health."

"Here is the laudanum," Angus appeared with a glass of water. "She needs to drink the entire glass."

Fannie didn't understand why she trusted this woman. She did though. She drank the glass of water. The panic she'd been feeling ebbed as the woman was taking care of her. Angus picked her up in his arms then carried her up a long staircase to the second floor. Trusting this man, she set her head against his shoulder. Angus set her on her feet by the big bed in the room. Except for a chair by the fire and a huge armoire the only other furniture was a copper tub.

"I'll send up a hot bath for you. Might help you relax. Your shoulders are tense. Of course, after what you've been through tonight, there is a good reason for that. Suppose I only know half of what happened to you this evening. Don't understand why you were in this part of town. You're lucky you picked this place to seek refuge. Believe all the other establishments around here would have put you to work on your back. Ah, don't suppose a fine born lady such as yourself *kens* much about working in the bedroom. Glad you're not going to learn. Do you have a name?"

She tried to croak out her name. What she said was far from sounding like Fannie.

Waving her petite hand in the air, Hannah said, "Never you mind. Maybe in the morning we can figure out how to get you home. If you can talk, it will make the chore much easier."

Hannah rummaged through a large armoire. Brought out a scarlet dressing gown. "You can wear this. It's clean. Make yourself comfortable. The bath will be here in about ten minutes. Don't know how long until the doctor can get here."

Nodding, Fannie tried to tell her thank you. Mouthed the words.

Hannah held up her hands to stop her. "You're very welcome. Don't try to speak. Doing so will only serve to make your throat hurt more. Now you just relax. I'll put a rush on the bath. By the look in your eyes, you're going to be asleep before the bath water heats."

Fannie watched the madam stride from the room, her skirts swishing around her feet. Hannah seemed to be a nice lady. The sound of a hot bath sounded divine. The thought of a doctor even better than heavenly. She eyed the scarlet dressing gown thinking about disrobing.

She was in a brothel. She shouldn't take off her clothing. Didn't seem as if anything good would come of disrobing in a brothel. If she was going to take that bath, she would need to be naked.

With her hands folded prayer style beneath her cheek, she laid down on the bed. Closed her eyes wishing she dared try for comfort. Squirming, she changed positions. Her skirts bunched around her hips. All her clothing felt tight and damp from the misty fog of the evening. Hannah would never allow anyone to bother her in this room. Told her she was safe. Trying not to think too hard, she slipped out of her gown and underthings to don the scarlet dressing gown. It was made of silk, soft…comfortable. She tied the belt around her waist.

She lay back down on the bed, closed her eyes waiting for either the doctor or the hot bath. She must have dozed. Her mind seemed to be a muddled mess. When she opened her eyes, a man was standing framed in the doorway. He strode into the room. Smiled at her. He must be the doctor. His shoulders were broad. Didn't look like any doctor she'd seen before. He was by far too handsome. Doctors were old. He was Saint. Or…was he a saint?

Beside her he sat on the bed. His golden fox eyes shimmered in the candle light. He cleared his throat a couple of times before he spoke. With the back of his knuckles, he touched her cheek then her forehead. "Downstairs, Hannah told me you don't talk. I can appreciate that. A chatterbox can be annoying."

When Fannie nodded, she set her hand on her throat in an effort to tell him where she hurt. "C…c…ant ta…" He set his finger on her lips, shaking his head.

"Soft. You look flushed. Is it too hot in here? I can open a window. Angus must have built up the fire too high." The man set his hand on her forehead again. "Not too hot. We're you going to take a bath? I'll wait for you. Go on. Take your bath while the water is hot. I'm not going anywhere." His smiled flashed even white teeth. "I'll just watch." He slipped off his jacket then undid his cravat so it hung lose down his chest.

Fannie didn't understand what he told her. Swinging her legs over the bed, she eyed the hot bath water with eager anticipation. She could imagine the heated water closing around her. The scent of lavender rose with the steam. She liked the scent. Looking over her shoulder she saw the doctor sitting on a large chair, his long legs stretched out in front of him. He'd poured himself a glass of something golden…just like his eyes.

When she thought of a doctor, Fannie envisioned an older man with silver hair and eyebrows. His eyes would crinkle with tiny age lines when he looked at her. This man's hair held no hint of silver. He was dressed in evening wear. The cut of his black suit fit his broad shoulders to perfection. His white shirt contrasted along with the dangling cravat he untied. The cut of his britches molded to his muscular legs. She blinked several times wondering if she was imagining this man. Her heart skipped a beat then another.

"Don't hurry on my account." The doctor motioned toward the tub. "I've nowhere to go tonight. I'll wait for you to finish. I'm certain the hot water will feel good."

As she turned her back on the doctor, Fannie let the dressing gown slide down her body to pool at her feet on the floor. Disrobing while the doctor looked on seemed a bit strange…different from the norm. Tonight was far from normal. Must not be real. Because of the laudanum her mind must be playing tricks on her. Once before she'd had a dose of the drug. Her imagination toyed with her mind that time also. She stepped into the steaming bath, sinking down to her neck. The water curled around her, rippling around her. The tips of her breasts hardened when they bobbed out of the water to meet the cool air. She soaped a sponge with lavender scented soap.

Fannie ran the sponge along one arm then started on the other. The doctor kneeled by the tub one finger swirling in the water. His eyes focused with hers. Nervous with him so close, she swept her mouth with her tongue then heaved in doctor scented air. Her stomach was doing flip-flops. "Let me help with that. The washing will go much faster if I give you aide. After you're done here, we can get on with the business at hand." A strange ache blossomed deep within, a sensation she didn't understand.

The doctor took the sponge from her shaking hands. This didn't seem quite right. He did wash her. Didn't seem interested in anything except finishing the bath for her. When she watched him, he gave her an encouraging smile then nodded toward the bath towel.

"Stand up." He held a huge bath towel for her. "This will also feel nice. It's been warming by the fire. Hannah thinks of everything. Do you need help drying yourself?" His soft chuckle seemed strange in the light of his efficiency in washing her. She pressed her hands on his shoulders to help her stand.

First, she shook her head then nodded. She didn't comprehend what she wanted. Her limbs felt weak. Her mind in disorder. Fannie thought this might be what people talked about when they spoke of new discoveries in medicine…a personal touch. Before she could give a more definitive answer, he rubbed the towel across her shoulders then the rest of her. For a few ticks of the clock on the mantel, he cupped one breasts, ran his thumb across the hardened tip. In response to the intimate caress, she shuddered. Pressure pulsed within her then seemed to ache. He held her hand then led her to the bed.

"I'll get you a drink. The brandy will sooth your nerves. You are shaking. Don't be afraid. I won't hurt you. There is no reason for you to be nervous." He walked away from her, found a second glass, then splashed brandy into the crystal glass. Strolling toward her, he held a glass of brandy in each hand. His small grin reassured. She nodded to him thinking the drink would be nice.

No, Fannie didn't think he would harm her in any way. Didn't he take the Hippocratic oath? She stared at the dressing gown on the floor that seemed a mile away from her then back to look into his golden fox eyes. She could drown in those eyes. She lifted a hand to touch his cheek then let it fall back.

He chuckled again. His smile caused her heart to weep. She'd never seen any man so beautiful. "I can't work my magic if you've clothing on, even a dressing gown. You, my fine lady, need to be naked. Slip under the covers just the way you are. Drink some of the brandy. After you've finished the first glass, we will see what transpires." He tossed his loosened cravat on the chair near the fireplace.

She did what he told her. He handed her the glass of brandy. With special care, Fannie sipped a small portion. The liquid warmed her throat along with her stomach. The potent drink also soothed her aching throat as well as diminished her stretched nerves. When she finished, she held the glass up for more. He obliged, tossing more of the amber liquid into the crystal she held out.

After she finished the second glass, he set it aside. Touched her cheeks with the back of his hand then smoothed his hand down her neck. Lingered where her blood rushed in a thunder of fast hard beats. Good, he understood her throat was raw. Bent closer until she felt his warm breath against her lips then the sweep of his tongue. She shivered, strange new sensations coursing through her body. He caressed her mouth with his, taking tender concern. With his potent touch to her lips, she jerked startled by the contact that was unexpected though quite nice.

"Easy now…open your mouth to let me inside. I need to feel your warmth, the heat of you," he told her without blinking an eye.

Fannie did what he asked then said, "Ah…" understanding he would want to look at her throat. Hannah must have told him about her inability to talk. Pleased she wouldn't need to explain what was bothering her.

The doctor cracked a chuckle as he leaned back to look at her. He held her chin with one hand. The other rested on her shoulder. His fingers were warm. He squeezed as if to encourage her. "Not so wide, sweetheart. Just enough so I've access to your warmth." His lips closed over hers. The taste of brandy coupled with warm man filled her senses. Fannie wasn't all certain what was happening. One of his large hands skimmed down her arm then back to her shoulder. The other held her head in place while he explored her mouth. She felt his tongue rub against hers, testing. Yes, he was discovering how hot she was. Treated this foray with hungry exploration. She heated from the tips of her toes to the top of her head. Felt each breath of air as it entered her lungs. Pressed against his white shirt, her nipples hardened.

She felt his tongue slide over hers once then twice. Rubbed. Increased the pressure. He repeated the process while he changed his position. She moaned as his hand once more caressed her shoulder then her arm. He stopped his exploration to speak. "Give me your tongue, sweet one. Put yours in my mouth. Need to feel you inside me."

Understanding was beyond Fannie's imagination. She'd never had a doctor ask such strange things. She wondered if he could tell what was wrong with her throat when their tongues clashed. In her life, she'd had few doctors. None of them asked her to… Well, they always wanted her to open her mouth then say ah. When his mouth framed hers again, she did as he asked. Felt the soft, silken texture inside his mouth along with the raw heat emanating from him. A small whimper rose from the back of her throat. The penetrating sound rippled into his mouth.

His large hand rested beneath her breast right where her heart bellowed with the frantic tempest he created. Fannie wasn't certain that was something he was supposed to do. He must need to listen to her heart. *With his hand?* She closed her eyes reveling in the feelings encompassing her. The brandy joined with the laudanum in her system to relax her to the point of no return. She was sleepy as well as disoriented. Unable to hold a clear thought in her spinning head. With each touch of his big hands, she burned from the inside out. Her body arched as his lips moved lower, touched upon her belly. She felt wet in the dark secret parts of her. His hands examined places she never thought a doctor would touch. His fingers slipped between her thighs, parted her. Touched upon a sensitive part of her, lingered there as her hips bucked in opposition to his fingers. She needed something she didn't understand. Spiraling higher then even higher, she arched against him.

Fannie cried out as her body catapulted into hundreds of different directions. He rose above her. Set his mouth upon hers again. "Just a second." She watched as his clothes vanished to land on the floor beside the bed. Her doctor came over her, entered inside her. She jerked with the sudden pain. He told her he wouldn't hurt her. Moisture filled her eyes, tears slipping down her cheeks.

"A virgin whore…" He brushed the tears away with his thumbs. "I won't move for a few seconds. The pain will fade. After that, I'll give you more of what you want. You're new to this profession. I understand."

How the hell did he know that?

With no more warning, her doctor was on top of her, deep inside her. He filled her. She tried to register the words he spoke. Attempted to make sense of something that didn't make any sense at all. Her brain was too befuddled by the brandy coupled with the laudanum to sort through this. Without notice she'd felt the heat of him. He was right. The pain did vanish. Within her, he began to move, slow at first, then hard and fast. His finger touched upon her with intimacy. She spiraled with the renewed contact. Her body convulsed as he filled her pushing into her deeper each time. She was outside herself. Beyond her mortal body. The ripples of pleasure consumed. When she shattered, his mouth crashed against hers while he rocked her. Warmth filled her.

He was above her now, smoothing her hair away from her face. "I'm sorry. I didn't know you'd never been with a man before. All Hannah told me was that you weren't a chatterbox. She never said anything about virgin territory. I'm pleased I was your first." He set his forehead against hers.

Still not comprehending what happened, she nodded. Her lashes drifted closed. She fell asleep feeling the weight of his body on top of hers, blanketing her with life giving warmth. Felt the heat of the man penetrate through him into her. As Fannie drifted into oblivion, she realized she liked the way his big body fit with hers. Enjoyed the way he covered her. Wished this dream had been real.

When she woke, she slept on top of him. Her breasts pushed against his chest. Her legs sprawled across him. Fannie didn't understand why her doctor was still here. While she felt better, she still couldn't speak. Her mouth was dry. She ran her hand across his chest. Stopped to feel his nipples then run her fingers through the spattering of dark hair on his chest. Followed the line of hair to his waist. She was fascinated by the differences. Wanted to feel what made him so distinctive from her. He stopped her with his large hand on top of hers.

"If you aren't too sore, we can do this a second time. Otherwise, your questing fingers will need to stop. I can only take so much foreplay before I lose control."

Sore? Lose control? Fannie questioned but she stared at him. While she wasn't certain what he meant she did feel an ache between her legs. A sensation different from anything she'd known before. She shook her head her long hair spilling around him, curling around his shoulders. Words still didn't form. She didn't wish to croak out the one word.

"Good…" Her doctor filled her again. She clung to his shoulders, her nails biting into his flesh. "I find I need to feel your warmth surround me. You are soft. So very wet. I like that…" He kissed her. Set his lips against hers. Swept his tongue inside her.

She experienced him deep inside while she felt the same amazing feelings erupt within the secret place. The same as happened last night. Arching her hips she brought him deeper into her. He pulled her legs around his flanks. He thrust deep. Cried out when she erupted so hard she felt certain she flew to the sun. Her nails scarred his flesh. He collapsed beside her, rolled to his side bringing her with him.

Next time she woke, she realized she needed to leave this place. Her doctor was asleep. He was beautiful. She swept a strand of hair from his eyes. Wished she could see his eyes, his fox eyes. She would never forget those eyes. The effects of the brandy along with the laudanum was gone. Fannie's mind was no longer befuddled.

With sudden despair, she understood what had happened to her. What she didn't understand was why. She didn't intend to stick around to discover the truth. Didn't wish to see this …doctor…ever again. She must have put her trust in a woman who was untrustworthy. This man couldn't be a doctor. She'd just lost her virginity to a man she didn't know and hoped she would never see in her lifetime. Fannie didn't even know his name. Didn't know the name of the man who took her innocence. She inhaled a deep, ragged breath of air.

Fannie had to find her way home. Couldn't stay in this brothel a moment longer. Didn't wish to face the consequences of last night. Rising from the bed with quiet stealth, she stared at the man who claimed her virginity. Recalled the scavenger hunt that eventually brought her here. The men who attacked her. Halsey who wanted to take her to his home or someplace. The woman she saw in the carriage who she thought might have been her mother. All this because she was looking for a monogramed handkerchief. She remembered the carriages lined up in front of this home. Maybe they were still there. She did have money. Kept a small reticule in the pocket of her coat. She could hire a hack to take her home. She would be safe soon.

Looking at the man on the bed, she groaned, a soft sound vibrating in the back of her throat. She would never see him again, thank God. Didn't know how she would ever face the man if she did come across him. Knowing what he did to her, how he played her body, mortification would set in.

God, she didn't even know his name. Didn't want to recall what she'd done with her doctor. He couldn't be a doctor. Who was he? It was true. She was no longer a virgin. What she wasn't was a whore. What if she got pregnant from this encounter? What would she do? She would need to tell Jasper, her guardian. Dear Lord, was she just like her mother?

Anice slept with countless men.

Shaking off her thoughts, the potent need to flee this place rushed into her in waves of degradation. She didn't belong here. With fluid fast movements, Fannie dressed then grabbed the dark brown bag sitting by the door. The bag Nellie must have given her to keep the items from the scavenger hunt safe. In the next second, she was out the door, racing down the steps. To her relief there were two hacks in front of the home. She rushed forward. Gave her address to the driver then paid him. She was on her way home.

~ * ~

For Fox Taggart the evening could not have gotten any better. He started out with five thousand pounds then managed to increase the sum to fifty thousand in a few hours of gambling. He supposed a bit of luck went his way. Sitting at the table, gazing over the room, he sipped his brandy, felt the heat slither down his throat.

More than pleased with the outcome of the evening, he decided to celebrate his good fortune with a no strings attached dalliance. Thought about going to the widow he'd seen last night. Decided against that idea. Release was on his mind. Needed to ease his taut nerves. He'd been to Hannah's before. The brothel as well as the girls were clean even sweet. The establishment was an honest one unlike some of the others in that part of town.

After tonight, he now had enough money to make improvements on his logging adventure then buy more land. Last winter's storms were hard on the ranch. He tried to be self-sufficient. He owned several head of cattle, would like to increase the herd. The plans he made would now come to fruition. His ensuing grin reached deep into his heart. Jake Taggert, his father had nothing to hold over his head. He could no longer induce him to remain in Scotland. Jake wanted him to play a role in his business adventures. Wanted him close. As Jake told him, Minnesota was too far away.

Jake encouraged him to give up on the land. Fox couldn't. The land along with the mountains was in his blood, logging was all he ever wished to do. His logging camp would always be a part of his heart as well as his soul. He could have sold the ten thousand acres spread of timbre for a huge profit. He didn't want to sell. What he wanted was to live there, to bring up a family on the land who would appreciate the world he loved as much as he loved it. Clean open mountain air with none of the problems of the city. His children would be able to roam the land without fear. They would inherit the empire he planned to build.

"Well, you got what you wanted." His father slapped him on the back, grinning. Fox felt certain his father wasn't pleased with tonight's events even though he smiled. "Got everything you need to hide out in Minnesota for the rest of your life. No telling what you'll find there besides hard work from sunrise to sunset. You could have sold the land then come to work for me."

"Got exactly what I want, Dad. No thanks to you. Don't wish to work for you or live in the city. Want to build an empire my children can inherit." He did love his father, the ultimate manipulator that he was. Fox respected him too. He'd earned his money from the ground up. Their problems stemmed from the fact they didn't want the same things.

"You do understand I would have lent you the money. Told you that fact a couple of times." His father chuckled as he patted his back again. "Though I would rather see you stay here in Glasgow instead of hightailing it back to the states. I do understand that's what you want. What you don't know is that I do respect your decision."

"With interest." Fox understood what the interest would be. He'd find a woman for him to wed. By doing so, he would owe no interest on the loan. No, that was also something he had no interest in doing. He didn't want a wife who was handpicked by his father. He was looking for love. If he couldn't find that elusive factor by the time he was forty, he'd marry the first attractive eighteen-year-old who came his way. Forty was young enough to start a family as well as a dynasty.

"I'm a businessman," Jake reminded him as he nodded to a passing friend. "What else would I do besides charge you interest?"

Fox also nodded to a few people as he walked through the gaming hall. He lived in Glasgow half his life. The other half was spent in the wilds of Minnesota. He knew his preference for the land. "I won't be home tonight. Don't wait up for me. Plan on doing a little celebrating before I head back to my home. Once I'm back on the land, there will be work…hard work until all is as I want it to be." He thought of the journey. The devil he despised sailing. Hated the sea. The overland trip would be difficult but more enjoyable.

"Ah, seeing to your needs," Jake said, grinning. "Wouldn't need to pay for a whore if you had a wife. When are you going to settle down? A good girl would be just what you need. I do know of a couple of sisters. Either one would make a fine wife. They've been brought up well. Travel in all the right circles. Do business with their guardian."

Fox pinched the bridge of his nose hard reeling from his father's interference in his life. "I'll marry when I find a woman who will love me more than she loves herself or my father. Don't wish to meet anyone you might pick out for me. If they were bred in Glasgow, they might not wish to live on a homestead in the wilds of Minnesota. Need a woman who won't dissolve at the sight of a warrior. He meant the words. He'd been in love before, even had a fiancée. Strange how his fiancée, the woman he believed loved him, married his father. She still flirted with him each and every time they were in the same room. Offered up her mouth for kisses as if he would oblige. God, he felt bad for his father. The woman chased everyone who wore pants.

"You should pay more attention to your bride," Fox tossed out with growing agitating. "She might set her claws into some other man. Turn the tables…" Seeing the look on his father's face, he let that statement die a lingering death. While he felt certain Jake loved Beryl, he didn't believe for a beat his father's wife loved him. Perhaps his feeling were sour grapes. The woman betrayed him with an older man. Jake was old enough to be her father. What the hell did she see in him?

"Discussion of Beryl is off limit to you, son. Our relationship is between us." His voice was ragged. Fox heard the pain in Jake's voice. Knew he shouldn't bring up the past. What was done couldn't be undone. Jake understood exactly who his wife was.

Fox acknowledged the fact he hurt his father. Didn't like himself much for doing so. After what the man did, he shouldn't give a damn about either. He raked his fingers through his hair. "You're right. What is between the two of you is not my business." That was all the acknowledgment he was going to give his father. "Don't wait up."

"I wouldn't. Not when I've a wife as beautiful as Beryl waiting for me in my bed." Jake chuckled; his voice soft.

The words made Fox flinch. Hell, he didn't understand why. Knew he was better off without the lying little bitch. Still, the thought hurt. A man didn't appreciate the fact he lost his fiancée to an older man. Once Jake thought she was happy with him. Later she told him she couldn't bear to live in Minnesota. Didn't like the isolation. Needed what a city could provide for her. Wanted to go to balls, dance the night away. Hold dinner parties as well as flirt. She could do none of that in Minnesota. There would be times during the year when the winter snow would keep them isolated in his home.

Outside, Fox hailed a cab, gave directions to Hannah's place then he sat back to redirect the conversation he had with his father. After he decided there was nothing else he could have told the man who sired him, he set his mind to making lists of the improvements for his property. He let his head lean back on the seat. Listened to the sounds of the night. The carriage slowed then stopped. He drank in the scent of the chilled air. Caught the aroma of fresh cooked food. Hannah's place was well-known for its cuisine. He wasn't hungry for food. What he needed was a woman who would place no demands on him. Someone who wouldn't talk his head off.

Taking a few seconds for thinking, he stood in front of the three-story brothel. The lawn surrounding the building was manicured with precision, the paint fresh. During the ride some of his ardor cooled. Fox wasn't certain this was what he wanted. Maybe his father had a point. A wife would have been nice to come home to. He didn't have a wife nor were there any possibilities on the horizon.

"What the hell…" he muttered almost to himself. "I'm here. Might as well take advantage of the opportunity. He pinched the bridge of his nose. Maybe some of the tension he felt during the long hours at the gaming table would lessen. Who was he kidding? Most if not all the tension in the back of his neck resulted in his conversation with his father. The man tried to manipulate. His ploy wasn't going to work.

With a drawn-out sigh, he stepped up to the front door. Music blared all around him. Scantily clad ladies entertained gentlemen in the parlor. A few seconds later, he was greeted by the big bodyguard Hannah employed. "Angus," he said as he stepped into the foyer. "Nice to see you. I'm here for a bit of pleasure. Do you have a girl who isn't going to talk my head off? Don't want a chatterbox tonight. Not in the mood for conversation. Just need to…" He broke off with the rest of his thoughts. Why else would he be here if it wasn't to relieve his needs?

Angus tossed his head back then after a crack of laughter. "Follow me. Got just the right gal for you. Doesn't say much unless asked a question. That only to be polite. Has untold secrets. Come on in. She is new here. I'll let Hannah know who you want. She'll send you to the right place. You'll have a nice enjoyable evening with the little lady. She is fresh down from the highlands. Fairly new to the profession."

"Thanks…" Fox followed the huge protector of the house to the office where Hannah worked. He stopped at the door. The lady must be in her early forties. She was still pretty. Her smile welcomed him.

"You're back, Fox. Missed your handsome company. Where have you been all these months? Not across the ocean in that heathen place they call the United States? Ah, see the truth in your eyes. You like the wild land better than this fair city. Can't say as I blame you. Doubt if you've got pimps in those mountains of yours." Her laughter trilled around her. "What can we do for you tonight? Got lots of beautiful girls. A new lady, young, might be perfect for you."

"Angus says you've got a lady who won't talk my ear off. Don't want a chatterbox. Will most likely stay the night. What do you say? Can you put me in the loving hands of a lady who will keep her mouth shut?" He did have his preferences. Women who spent the entire time talking were not to his liking.

"Got the perfect lass for you. Go on up the stairs, her room is the at the end of the hall, last door on the right. Just give a little knock then go in. She will be expecting a guest so you won't frighten or startle her. Guarantee, she will be ready for you. I won 't even ask for you to pay more for the silent treatment." Hannah laughed again before sending him on his way. "Don't be a stranger. You're a true gentleman. We like having you here. All the ladies appreciate your talent."

After he opened the door, Fox took in the ambiance of the room. Two candles burned on a counter flooding the area with a warm tone. If this wasn't a whore's bedroom, the sight might have been romantic. The whore was pretty, perched on the bed, her feet tucked beneath her. Long blond hair curled around her shoulders before falling to her waist. She wore a scarlet dressing gown that molded to all her curves. Flickering shadows from the candles played along her body, giving her face a golden quality. He imagined her naked. Thought to taste her breasts, savor until the sound of her pleasure rippled into him. He could see the imprint of her nipples on the dressing gown. With that thought, he swelled against his britches. Jesus, it had been months since he had sex. He didn't want to explode before he could give her pleasure. He ran his hand along the back of his neck.

Hours later, lying in bed, he recalled the first time with her. Thought of the moment he crashed through her maidenhead. Her cry of startled pain reverberated in his head. She'd not expected pain. At least it didn't seem to him that she did. Hannah should have told him the girl was a virgin. He might have treated the moment different. Maybe Hanna didn't know. That might not be something a lady new to this profession would tell the madam of a brothel. Hell, he didn't know her name. His arm lay across his face, shielding his eyes from the light of the candle.

A virgin whore.

The second time with her was better than the first. She was responsive. He didn't imagine the raw passion she poured into her lovemaking. The way she whimpered then cried out when she reached that coveted pinnacle. Fox knew women. Understood what they liked as well as how to caress their feminine parts to make them wet as hell. He enjoyed the ride with her. It was one that might last him until he reached his home. He planned on leaving within the week. Jake wouldn't be too pleased when he discovered his intentions. His father mentioned a dinner with the two sisters he hoped to introduce to him. Wished for him to marry one of them. Hoped for an engagement.

Fox wondered where his little virgin whore got herself off to. If she'd been in the bed, he would have considered another round of early morning sex, something he enjoyed with the right woman. The lass wasn't in the room. Supposed she could be just about anywhere in the building. He could use a hot cup of bitter coffee, American coffee, the stronger the better. Ah…he was in Scotland. They drank tea. He needed coffee to spark early morning energy. Didn't enjoy beginning his day without the bitter brew.

The knock on the door startled him to a sitting position. The whore wouldn't knock on her door. Who the hell was it? His sheets fell around his waist. Another knock followed the first one. What…?

He didn't intend to answer. Whoever was there would let him know what they wanted.

"The doctor is here. He's ready to see..." There was a long pause then she continued. "Says he is sorry for taking so long to get here. Seems he had a busy night," Hannah called out. "You decent?" She stepped inside the room. Eyes widening with surprise, her gaze stuck on him.

"What the hell?" Fox muttered deep under his breath. A quick search of the room found his pants on the floor near the tub. "A doctor, who needs a doctor? I don't. You must have the wrong room."

Hannah's face paled when she recognized him. He still didn't understand. Fox saw her swallow a lump in her throat. She cleared her throat before beginning. "The more prevalent question is what are you doing in this room? I sent you to the…" she stopped talking for a few seconds. Passed the palms of her hands along her gown. "This could be bad, very bad. Always do get my right and left mixed up. This was not the room I sent you to. Couldn't be. This was the little lady's room. She was sick."

"You sent me to the last door on the right. Tell me what's going on." Fox didn't enjoy feeling as if the world was not turning the right direction. He was angry about the intrusion, angrier about the fact the lady went missing. What did she need a damn doctor for. "Are you telling me I'm not with the girl I requested. You know, the non-chatterbox? The whore who wasn't going to talk my ear off."

Clearing her throat again, Hannah began, her bosom heaving with each drawn breath, "Did you have sex with her?"

"The lady is a whore. Of course we had sex. That's what I paid for. It's what I came here for. What? Did you think I would pay for sex then not take the woman?" Fox didn't think he was going to appreciate what was coming next. The look on the madam's face was not the expression of a pleased woman.

"The lady might be a whore. That is true. I doubt it. She was sick. I gave her this room because she couldn't talk. Needed a safe place to rest. In her condition, I couldn't send her back on the street. Called for Saint but he wasn't able to make it here until now. Where is she? What did you do with her?"

"How would I know? The bed was empty when I woke." Fox pushed the sheets off intending to dress. Wasn't surprised to see the blood on the sheet. Neither was Hannah. The madam made a face at him. Looked from the bloody sheet to his member. He twisted with the unwelcome urge to cover himself. He didn't like the way this inquisition was proceeding.

"The lady was no whore. She was a virgin…" Hannah turned to head for the door before spinning back to face him. "You had no right…" Once more she broke off as if she understood she was wrong to berate him for something that was not of his making.

"Christ, lady," he pushed his hands through his hair. "What did you expect? I'm not a saint," Fox looked to the doctor. "This is a whorehouse, a very nice one. Nonetheless, the ladies who work here are expected to be whores. Expect to be paid for sex. Didn't know she was virgin until I broke through."

Fox had his pants pulled on and fastened. He realized then his bag was missing. "The lady might not be a whore but she is a thief!" He pointed to the spot by the door where he left his bag. "She stole my satchel. Best you know where to find this virgin whore." His voice was harsh his feelings crueler. If he ever found this virgin whore he'd strangle her thin white neck. "I want that satchel back."

"Was the bag so important?" Hannah asked but the expression on her face told him the question wasn't necessary. "I don't know her name. If you recall, last night she couldn't speak. Of course, I don't know where to find the lady. She is a lady. I'm certain of that fact. What she was doing in this part of the city is beyond the pale. Though she was running from Halsey."

"Contained fifty thousand pounds…" he gritted out between gnashing teeth. "I want the money back. You need to do all in your power to discover who this lady is as well as where I can find her."

Hannah threw up her hands, shooting him a look of disgust. "Can't give you something I don't have. How do I know you're telling the truth? This could be a ruse on your part. No…" Hannah paused one finger pressed against her chin. "You would never make something like this up. Fifty thousand pounds should not be much of anything to a man of your standing."

"Don't doubt me. Thought this place was honest. The money was meant for my business in Minnesota. If you haven't guessed, it's my father who has the considerable bank account, not me." Inside he was sweating. All his dreams of rebuilding his home along with his business had just gone up in flames. "I'll call the constables. They can rake over this house with a fine-tooth comb. Search every square inch of the place. Maybe we'll find the girl."

Hanna swiveled to confront the burly bodyguard. "Angus, search the house. His satchel of money has got to be here. Don't believe that little lady is a thief. She couldn't have taken it with her. Did you set the bag down somewhere then forget about it?"

"See that you do search every inch. I would not set the bag down out of my sight. That was my future inside the satchel." Fox was tucking his shirt into his pants. His anger was overflowing. His hopes along with his dreams dying. This was not what he expected upon waking up this morning. With his money safely in the bank, he intended to leave town within the week. Hell, that was most of the money he had in the world. He no longer had the five thousand pounds he began gambling with. He didn't have another five thousand pounds for another night of gaming. Should have forgone the brothel. Hindsight was always the very devil.

Hind sight.

Two hours later, bathed and with a change of clothing, Fox sat in the breakfast room of his father's townhouse, sipping strong black coffee. His dreams vanished because he needed a whore. He despised himself.

"My, my, you don't look as if you got up on the right side of the bed," Beryl waltzed into the room, poured herself a cup of tea before adding cream and sugar. She bent over to kiss his cheek giving him a bird's eye view of the valley between her breasts. He jerked away but not in time to miss the dampness of her lips on his cheek.

"Stuff it, Beryl. Don't want anything to do with conversation or you." Fox was not in the mood to speak with anyone, especially not this woman.

She made a face at him then smiled while she tossed her hair over her shoulder. "Now, is that anyway to speak to your stepmother. Should show me respect."

"Supposed you earned whatever you get flat on your back while spreading your legs for my father. No baby yet? How is father taking that?

Jake wants an heir. Since I don't wish to have anything to do with living in the city, the old man wants a second heir. You're going to need to do better or Jake might find another woman half his age to bed." One dark eyebrow arched toward the ceiling. He shouldn't speak to her that way. Couldn't help himself. This morning his entire world crashed down around his shoulders. He would start over. Would work for his father until spring. Win the money back.

Beryl stood behind him, her hand resting on his shoulder. Fox shrugged the offending hand off. She set her fingers back. He didn't intend to play any of her games. "Try being nice once in a while," she said, her voice sweet with stinging venom.

Fox pushed her hand from his shoulder.

She bent close to whisper in his ear. Touched the tip of her tongue to the lobe. "I'm always nice to you. Feels so good to be nice. If you would allow me, I could be even nicer."

He stood, knocking his chair to the floor with the force of his movement. Picked up his coffee. Fox needed to speak with his father. Jake would be in his office now. That was where he was this time of day, every day. So predictable it hurt. Fox hated predictable. Loved the spontaneity of his life. One never knew what would happen from one day to the next. He thrived in that atmosphere.

The door to the office was open. Fox strode inside. Shut the door behind him. Brought up a chair in front of the big desk where his father sat. His father didn't show his age. Except for a few gray hairs around his temples, he could be thirty instead of almost fifty.

Jake tapped his finger on the cherrywood. His eyes narrowed as if he knew this would be bad news. "What do I owe this visit? Thought you'd be upstairs packing since you are so eager to get away from me as well as the city." He leaned forward, his forearms resting on the desk. The pads of his fingers tapped on the surface. "You have a change of heart? Are you staying longer? If so, you'd make an old man happy."

Fox lifted one shoulder in a shrug meant to be carefree. He didn't want Jake to realize how devastated he was. "Lost the money. So…one might say I'm staying a *wee* bit longer."

The tapping stopped. Jake's brows drew together in a frown. His lips thinned. Silence heaved around the room stretching Fox's nerves to a snapping point. His stomach lurched. Jake sat back, his hand forming a steeple beneath his chin. The pose was thoughtful.

"How? Don't like to hear something like that. You were smug last night after your win. What changed in less than twelve hours?"

"Stolen by the little whore I bedded. Guess what I intended to pay her for the night wasn't enough. She wanted everything I owned." The bitterness in his tone was still there. Wouldn't go away for a long time if ever. He didn't like confessing to his father that he was done in by a virgin whore.

"What are your intentions? I gather you are not planning on leaving the city until you've managed to get the money back. Don't understand how the lady could get away. Doesn't Hannah just hire regulars."

"One way or the other I'll find a means."

"I see. When you can, you will find the gaming tables again. You could lose."

"True. Will work for you until I've enough money for another game of chance. Mean to win the money back. Start over. You know I'm skilled at games of chance. Need to be in Minnesota by summer." Fox lifted his shoulders, trying to shrug off his disappointment. Didn't work.

"You will understand if I'm not disappointed by the news. You're better off here in civilization than pursuing this ridiculousness…" Jake cleared his throat seeming to think better of spouting his opinion.

Dreams…I'm pursuing my dreams… They are not ridiculous.

"As well you know, to me…Minnesota coupled with my dreams are far from ridiculous. I belong out there just as you belong here. I love the clean air along with the open spaces. One can look for miles and see only the mountains along with the trees. Timber is my livelihood." Fox didn't wish to get into an argument with his father. The two of them had been over this topic too many times to count. They didn't need another go around. Nothing would change.

Jake's fist landed hard on top of the table. Papers jumped. "Hell! You could die in a snow drift. No one would know for days…months…" Jake waved his hand in the air clearly frustrated by his desire to live in the untamed land.

"My men would find me." He leaned forward, his forearms resting on the desk. Met his father's gaze with hard determination in his eyes understanding there was no compromise between the two of them. "I'm not stupid. Not going to die in a snow drift. Would never take chances that would have me in that situation."

"You could be shot by outlaws," Jake pointed out. "There are any number of ways to die out there."

"Could be run over by a carriage on High Street," Fox, in turn, pointed out, his tone bland. "Don't get your hopes up that I might stay in Glasgow to help with your business. That's not going to happen. One way or the other, I'll find the money I need to leave in fine style. If I'm unable to raise the funds on my own, I plan on looking for someone willing to invest in my company. Don't mind another partner if he is honest. Though I would plan on a buyout clause."

"Very well, if you plan on working for me, I'll need you to accompany me to a dinner meeting I've arranged. Are you going to stay here?" Jake studied him. "Work for me? You will be my right-hand man."

"Yes. What kind of dinner meeting?"

"With a wealthy friend of mine. Jasper Kenworthy is his name. He's a marquis. Has a twin brother name of Jason."

"What's the business?"

"The man wishes to branch out, to invest in my shipping line. You do recall we've a lucrative trade between Virginia and here. We supply Scotland with good Virginia tobacco. Believe the man might be interested in your plan. Probably won't appreciate a buyout clause."

Fox wondered how much of this shipping line would be part of his inheritance. His father told him he would lend him fifty thousand. He didn't want his father's groats. Needed to make this deal by himself. Didn't wish to be under Jake's thumb.

"He wants to invest…" Fox pondered those thoughts for a few ticks of the clock sitting in the hall. He didn't care one way or the other. His father would pay him a salary. He would do whatever it took. "A dinner meeting in two nights, you say?"

"From tonight."

"I'll be there." He sipped from the cup of coffee he brought with him from the breakfast room. "Anything important I should know?"

"Jasper is the guardian of two young ladies. Very inappropriate…the females live in the townhouse with him. Though there are a few extenuating circumstances to take under consideration."

"How did that come about? What are these extenuating circumstance? Something I should learn about?" Something about that made him sit up with interest. He found himself curious "Not the best thing. Though doesn't seem as if the house is a bachelor's residence."

"The ladies are his wife's sisters. Maggie is his wife's name. She is the oldest of four. His twin Jason is wed to the youngest, Tessa. Maggie will be there with. Beryl will also attend. Don't know who else will be in attendance."

"If you are planning a bit of matchmaking, I'm not looking for a wife. Nothing to hold me here in this part of Scotland if that's what you had in mind. Besides, a Scottish wife would never keep me here. I'm going back to Minnesota. If I wed, which I'm not for the foreseeable future, my wife would go where I go. I need a woman strong enough to live in the backcountry, one who will love the mountains as much as I do."

"Beryl burned you that bad." Jake held up his hands in surrender. His old man understood Beryl was not a good topic of conversation between the two men. "Should not go there. I've no regrets where it comes to my wife. I love her. Loved her from the first moment I set eyes on her. It has never failed to amaze me that she wanted me."

"The woman wanted your money," he said with a snigger. "Beryl is a gold digger. You were the better catch. Better than a dirt-poor timber baron. Besides when I met her, she pretended to love the ranch while all the while she begged me to move to the city…any city."

"You weren't poor until you lost the timber in a flood," Jake pointed out. "You're not poor now. At least you wouldn't be if you sold the land."

No, he wasn't. Nonetheless Jake had more money than he could spend in a lifetime. Even if he lost a ship, his financial status wouldn't be fazed. That was what Beryl wanted. Fox understood he shouldn't belittle his father's relationship with his ex-fiancée. He should be happy for him.

"What is my salary?"

"Let's negotiate this later. The money will be substantial. While I don't wish for you to leave, I'm not going to try to keep you here with a meager amount of money. I appreciate a man's worth. You are worth far more than rotting on land away from people who love as well as appreciate you. Even though you don't wish to be part of my business, you know it well."

Fox hands fisted. He bellowed. "Leaving is what I want! My land is what I want."

~ * ~

"Fox sent a constable to oversee the search of Hannah's brothel. We left nothing unturned. The brown satchel he claims to have come here with has vanished. The money disappeared with it. The girl had to be the thief. As he explained, there was no one else in the room." She ran her hand along the back of her neck while Angus looked on, a sad expression in his deep brown eyes. Hannah stiffened her shoulders determined to make the best of this situation. "Don't believe for a moment the lass stole the money. I'm a good judge of character as you've always told me. Her life had been threatened. She sought refuge here. What did I do for her? I failed to protect her interests. Sent a man to her to take her virginity."

"She is a lady. The way she was dressed…her speech. Wouldn't have need of the groats. She comes from wealth. That much was apparent," Angus acknowledged her sentiments. "The rawness of her throat was also not a pretense. The lass was sick."

Hannah felt desperation down to the tips of her toes. She wished she could find the money so she could return it to Fox. "This little incident could ruin our reputation. Wreck us. What are we going to do? Can't have people believing our place of business would employ girls who were thieves. Don't know how to find her. The little gal never gave us a name. Poor wee lass couldn't speak."

"That's Halsey's business. Cutthroats along with whores. He pimps everything out. His girls seldom last more than a few years. He rides them hard, uses them up real fast. When you dared to talk with the man, thought he might have some clue as to the name of the girl. When the lass was mentioned, he got this gleam in his eyes. Thought then and there he was lying through his teeth." Angus stood at the back door starring out at the wanning light of the day. "Remember when I heard her pounding on the door begging for help. The little gal was frantic to get away from that man. Of course, at the time she didn't know what lay in store for her with Halsey.

"Halsey didn't know the girl's name either. Hoped when you

lugged him over here, he could give us some type of clue about the lass. Nothing. Think he's lying. I'd wager the man knows more than he's telling us. He had that look in his eyes." Hannah repeated her earlier sentiments about that encounter. She set the tip of her finger on her chin. "Yes, Halsey had that look in his eyes when he's after something or someone. He was after the girl for a specific reason. The question is why. Other than he needed a fresh new face in his stable. I'll wager there is something else behind this."

"Told us he rescued her from the hands of two seamen. Rough sort…she ran right into him. Landed on her little butt right at his feet. Seems pretty convenient to me. Mumbled something about a monogramed handkerchief. What could that be about?" Angus asked as he turned back to Hannah.

"She didn't leave anything behind as a clue. Who the hell is she? The rich sometimes go on scavenger hunts. A way of playing with each other. A monogramed handkerchief might be what she was after when she strayed into the wrong part of the city. She must have been lost. Why the hell was she alone?" Hannah was pacing the tight confines of her little office. There are only a few blocks between the better part of town and this district. Might have been possible for her to wander here without knowing where she was.

Hannah couldn't afford anything to happen to her business. She'd fought to keep her girls safe from men like Halsey. Fought to make certain all her girls were taken care of. Saint was on a retainer. He doctored the ladies if they were abused. Delivered their babies when their precautions didn't play out. She tried never to allow a man to abuse the women she employed. Angus helped her see to that. Oh, abuse happened once in a while. The abusers were never allowed back in her front door. She always made certain Saint saw to the gals.

"Why would the girl steal Fox's money? To me that's the bigger question. A brown satchel could not have been on the list for her game. Fox told us he gave her brandy. The drink mixed with the laudanum would have left her mind muddled. She might not have known what she was doing. Do you think that's possible?"

"Anything is possible. The lass wasn't feeling up to snuff. Could it be conceivable she didn't know what was in the bag? Maybe thought the satchel was hers," Hannah asked feeling more than puzzled by the missing bag rehashing all she recalled from the night before. She felt as if she grasped at straws.

"When she opens it, she will return it here or send it with a messenger. Would hope the girl has enough common sense not to bring it herself."

The girl was a mystery. One she'd love to solve.

Also by the author
at
Rogue Phoenix Press

Don't Hustle Letty
Good Girls Book One

She's a good girl...

As tempted as Scarlett was, she had too many secrets to let someone enter her world—secrets that would send any reasonable man to the farthest ends of the earth. Bobby was far from reasonable and despite her desperate attempts to hold him at bay, he would not let her past destroy their future. With her escort service, Scarlett used men and their insatiable lust for women to capitalize on the means to survive and prosper. She vowed to never wed, to never put herself in the control of a man.

...nonetheless he has other ideas.

Lord Robert Munroe, with his newly acquired title of marquis goes to Scarlett's for training on how to comport himself. The marquis, better known as Bobby, knows how to pick a pocket as well as get into a bloke's home to steal them blind. What he doesn't know is how to be a gentleman. When he sets his sights on the prim Miss Scarlet, Letty, to his way of thinking, he decides she is the woman he wants to call his wife. He tempts all that she is with sweet words and tender coaxing until she is unable to refuse all he hopes to give her.

Only Caro's Baby
Good Girls Book Two

The Scheme

Genius botanist with theories of inherited traits, Caroline

Kenworth desperately wants a baby. Finding a suitable father won't be easy. Caroline's super-intelligence makes her feel pushed aside, unwanted as a woman. As a bluestocking she is determined to spare her child the suffering that plagues her life. Which means she must find someone very special to father her child. A person very...well...ignorant.

The Target.

Duncan Murray, the Earl of Downsberry, well known for his lack of intelligence as well as his rakish ways with women, seems as if he is the flawless man to fulfill the role. His amazing good looks and Scottish brogue are misleading. Caro learns too late that this debonair earl is a lot smarter than she first thought—in addition he's not about to be used then abandoned by any woman who has schemed to steal his sperm.

The Detonation

A dazzling solitary woman whose desires to learn what it would be like to become a mother... A man who is in control of all he does never allowing anyone to usurp his role will settle for nothing less than surrender... Can lust coupled with physical attraction drive two strong-minded yet vulnerable people to a completely unforeseen love?

Honey

Good Girls Book Three

She's a good girl...

Born a bastard, Honey McRae is taunted and bullied by her half-brother most of her life. Branded with a tattoo of the Saber and the Rose by the men's association, she is desperate to be free and escapes the country estate where she was held prisoner. Resigned to a passionless life devoid of men, she fights the nightmares that haunt her. Despite her past fears, she accepts the fact she will never be able to give herself wholly to the man she loves. Until that man, bold and breathtaking, decides he will find a means to woo her into his arms.

Nonetheless...

Stolen at birth and sent to live in the bowels of London, Billy–once a pickpocket and thief–discovers he is actually the Duke of St. Aubries. He is determined to win the woman he fell in love with the first time he saw her, the lady with a tattoo on her breast, a woman who has been cruelly used. He disputes her notion that men are only capable of inflicting pain...instead he binds her to his heart with his gentle and patient loving.

Betsy Be Good

Good Girls Book Four

AN ENGLISH ROSE

Sweet Betsy Darling, the oh-so-prim and innocent tutor for children born of rich aristocrats, is a woman on a mission—she has but a short time to lose her standing as a respectable spinster. Arriving in Glasgow with skirts flying, parasol pointing, and plump mouth issuing demands, she understands only one thing will save her form losing all she holds dear: complete and utter disgrace.

A BRAW HIGHLANDER

Known throughout the city as a bad boy with more money than he needs, Evan Murray has lost his temper one too many times, and now he's suspended from teaching at the university he loves as well as Halstead & Family the financial firm owned by his family. An apology which he refuses to issue is one of two things that will restore his career. The second is his complete and utter respectability! Now he's been coerced into escorting the bossy, parasol toting Miss Betsy Darling, and she's hell-bent on chasing down a tattoo parlor, dressing in skimpy clothing and worse...lots worse.

Gracie

Good Girls Book Five

She's a good girl…

During a tempest, Gracie Seymor flees the hands of an abusive fiancé to find herself tossed from her horse. The blow to her head causes the loss of her memory. In the shelter of a wayside inn, she meets a man who steals her heart. From the moment the handsome man, Gordan Murray, lifts his dark brown eyes to meet hers, they are drawn together, spellbound, into each other's arms then into the night of passion that claims her innocence sending her on a course that will change her life forever.

…Nonetheless he steals her heart

So dependent on the man who claims her virginity, Gracie becomes his mistress even though she understands she should refuse. She's a good girl. Good girls don't become men's playthings. After the night spent with Gracie in his arms, Gordan takes her to a cottage near his home. Here they will confront the specter of her past and discover Gracie's identity. It revolves around a tangled web of secrets coupled with a magical love that cannot be denied.

Dawn

Good Girls Book Six

Dawn Callahan's dream of freedom and a life of independence is shattered. After she realizes she somehow stepped through a portal into a different century all she has left to fight for is her sanity along with a way to return to the time of her birth. To do that she has to give up her autonomy. With no money to her name or a roof over her head, she needs Gordan Murray's help. In return she refuses to give him what he wants the most. Answers to his questions.

On first sight, Gordan means to take her into his home. Intends to give her everything she wants. When she refuses his sincere offers, he withdraws into himself searching for a means to convince her he has only good intentions toward her.

On that sunny day in July when Dawn tumbles from a whorehouse to land on her delectable little butt a woman was the last thing in the world he was looking for. He has a fine life. Finds willing women with a smile coupled with a nod.

Love has a way of changing the rules.

Maggie
Good Girls Book Seven

Sheltered, Maggie MacRae is shocked to learn her mother has agreed to a marriage proposal for her made to a man she detests. All her dreams are ripped away from her when she realizes escape is unlikely. For her, there is no viable way out of the engagement. Choices needed to be made. The man she is to become engaged to is ruthless, a dangerous power. Terrified of her future with this man, Maggie is left with few options.

Feeling as if her world has shattered, Maggie flees the night her engagement is announced. She puts her life in the hands of a man she doesn't know, a man who could be as cold-blooded and treacherous as the one who is now her fiancé...a man who awakens her to a world she never knew existed.

Jasper Kenworthy has spent his life with few cares and he has no intention of changing the patterns of his existence. When he finds that Maggie can offer him something he never thought would be his, it's all the excuse he needs to help her. Yet every breathless night spent tangled together in each other's arms has given Jasper a taste for Maggie. He discovers he would do anything, risk everything to keep Maggie safe and within the shelter of his embrace.

www.ingramcontent.com/pod-product-compliance
Lightning Source LLC
Chambersburg PA
CBHW070617260626
47161CB00007B/2473
9781624208706